PENGUIN CLASSICS

OROONOKO, THE ROVER AND OTHER WORKS

Little is known about Aphra Behn's early life, from what religious and social background she came or how she obtained her extraordinary education, which allowed her to translate from French with ease, to allude frequently to the classics and to take part in the philosophical, political and scientific debates of her time. She was probably born around 1640 in Kent and in the early 1660s claims to have visited the British colony of Surinam, which forms the setting of her best-known short story, *Oroonoko, or the History of the Royal Slave* (1688), an early discussion of slavery and innate nobility. In 1666 she was employed by Charles II's government as a spy in Antwerp during the Dutch wars; after she received no payment, she turned to literature for a living, writing poetry, political propaganda for the Tory party and numerous short stories, as well as adapting or composing at least nineteen stage plays, many of them extremely successful, such as the comic depiction of Cavalier exile, *The Rover* (1677), and an early farce, *The Emperor of the Moon* (1687). She had strong sympathy for Roman Catholicism but was also drawn to the sceptical and materialist philosophy of the libertines with whom she associated. Virginia Woolf acclaimed her as the first English woman to earn her living by writing, declaring, 'All women together ought to let flowers fall upon the tomb of Aphra Behn, for it was she who earned them the right to speak their minds.'

JANET TODD is Professor of English Literature at the University of East Anglia. She was formerly a Fellow of Sidney Sussex College, Cambridge, and a Professor at Rutgers University. Her publications include *Women's Friendship in Literature* (1980), *Feminist Literary History* (1988), *The Sign of Angellica: Women, Writing and Fiction* (1989) and, with Marilyn Butler, an edition of Mary Wollstonecraft's work. She is currently editing the complete works of Aphra Behn.

APHRA BEHN

OROONOKO, THE ROVER AND OTHER WORKS

EDITED BY JANET TODD

PENGUIN BOOKS

PENGUIN BOOKS

Published by the Penguin Group
Penguin Books Ltd, 27 Wrights Lane, London W8 5TZ, England
Penguin Books USA Inc., 375 Hudson Street, New York, New York, 10014, USA
Penguin Books Australia Ltd, Ringwood, Victoria, Australia
Penguin Books Canada Ltd, 10 Alcorn Avenue, Toronto, Ontario, Canada M4V 3B2
Penguin Books (NZ) Ltd, 182–190 Wairau Road, Auckland 10, New Zealand

Penguin Books Ltd, Registered Offices: Harmondsworth, Middlesex, England

This edition first published 1992
5 7 9 10 8 6 4

Printed in England by Clays Ltd, St Ives plc

CONTENTS

CONTENTS

ACKNOWLEDGEMENTS

I should like to thank most warmly Elizabeth Spearing and Virginia Crompton for their generous help in the preparation of this volume.

INTRODUCTION

> Let me with Sappho and Orinda be
> Oh ever sacred nymph, adorned by thee;
> And give my verses immortality.[1]

Aphra Behn addressed these lines to the laurel, giver of fame,
shortly before she died in 1689. She had some reason to expect
literary 'immortality': she was the first recognized professional
woman writer in English and she had long been praised as 'sole
Empress of the Land of Wit', famous for her androgynous perfec-
tions, her 'female sweetness' and her 'manly grace'.[2] After her
death and burial in Westminster Abbey – where the register
recorded her *nom de plume* 'Astrea' rather than her supposedly
given name 'Aphra' – her reputation seemed assured and her
praise continued. A 'young Lady of Quality' wrote:

> Of her own sex, not one is found
> Who dares her laurel wear
> Withheld by impotence or fear;
> With her it withers on the ground.[3]

Yet history was against Behn. She died when the ideal of
nobility, royalty and authenticity about which she had written so
fervently were vanishing with the last Stuart king's flight from his
kingdom, and when her principles of frankness in men and
women were giving way to a more gendered vision of feminine
modesty and masculine condescension. In her life she had been
attacked by the satirist Robert Gould as a vile 'punk and poetess'
and she had often defended herself against charges of conventional
bawdiness. But in the centuries that followed she was silenced less
by abuse than by a neglect deriving from disgust. The 'Modest
Muse' came to dominate the female pen in the eighteenth and
nineteenth centuries and Behn's frank, erotic verses were dropped
from anthologies of women writers. 'The Apotheosis of Milton'

I

in the *Gentleman's Magazine* of 1738 imagines a fiery-eyed and bare-breasted Aphra who has tried to join the male poets being told that 'none of her sex has any right to a seat there'. In the Victorian period she suffered from the general distaste for the rakish Restoration and by 1883 Eric Robertson, compiling his *English Poetesses*, could hardly bring himself to contemplate the horrific impurity of Aphra Behn. Her slow rehabilitation in this century owes much to Montague Summers's impressive but incomplete and flawed collection of her work in 1915 and the references to her in Virginia Woolf's *A Room of One's Own*: 'All women together ought to let flowers fall upon the tomb of Aphra Behn, for it was she who earned them the right to speak their minds.'[4] But it took a long time for women to avail themselves of the right to frank moral and erotic expression, and only recently has Behn's contribution to female writing begun to receive adequate appreciation.

For an author so famous or notorious surprisingly little is known of her life, which spreads in a shadowy way across the continents. Her association with the West Indies now seems documented, as does her short period of espionage in Antwerp, but it is also possible that she spent time in Virginia and Italy and lived some of her childhood in Flanders. The main clue to her early years comes from the anonymous 'Life and Memoirs' prefixed to a posthumous edition of her work in 1696. This announces that she was a 'gentlewoman' of good family from Canterbury and called Johnson. It immediately throws some doubt on the generally accepted date of birth, 1640, when it claims that Aphra Behn was too young to respond to amorous youths just before her journey to Surinam in 1663. When this is placed beside her pleading of her youth during her espionage in 1666, it might suggest a later birth date; in the Restoration world girls like Nell Gwyn began their amorous and professional careers in their early teens.

Speculation on Aphra Behn's status and childhood follows two main courses. The first is influenced by contemporary testimonies, one from the poet Ann Finch, Countess of Winchilsea, who claimed in a marginal note to one of her poems that Aphra Behn was the daughter of a barber, and the other from the rather eccentric Colonel Colepeper who reported in his huge manuscript books of scientific jottings, lineages and legal documents that Behn's mother had been his nurse 'and gave him suck for some time'. The two accounts can be reconciled if Aphra Behn is the Aphra Johnson born to a barber, Bartholomew Johnson, and the probably illiterate Elizabeth Denham in 1640; she would then be sister of Frances whose birth would be close enough to that of Colepeper's sister for the wet-nursing to have taken place. If this is indeed Aphra Behn, then she is of humbler birth than the 'Memoirs' suggest, although her mother's family had some claim to a gentlemanly status; it is possible that her extraordinary education and language skills came through contact with the orphaned Colepeper children and their aristocratic relatives – who included many of the later dedicatees of her works – and through association with Huguenot and Dutch immigrants in Canterbury. The other, perhaps more fanciful line of speculation has concentrated on Behn's literary sophistication, her seeming knowledge of political events on the Continent, her possible experience of Roman Catholicism, her easy association with courtiers when she first began writing in London, and her lifelong commitment to the aristocratic principle, to put forward a more glamorous background depending on distant relationships with the famous Sidney and Howard families and a possible sojourn in a Catholic establishment in Flanders. In this scenario Behn becomes aligned with two of the most famous literary women of the immediate past, the Countess of Pembroke and Lady Mary Wroth. In *The History of the Nun* (1689), the narrator claims to have been 'designed an humble votary in the house of devotion', though she chose to deny herself 'that content'; so far, none of the autobiographical claims made by the narrators of Behn's late fiction has been conclusively proved false or true.[5]

It is difficult to infer background from opinion. Behn's lifelong faith in the aristocratic principle might suggest some noble connection, but it might also indicate inclination and desire, and it could be argued that the principle manifested itself for her more in style and culture than in political doctrine and relationship. So also with religion, which often appears a matter of style as much as of content. Behn admired the baroque side of Catholicism and avoided much overt piety and concern with substance. Indeed in many works she puts forward a vigorous and sometimes sceptical rationalism and she rails against those who would unsettle the state with religious squabbling. Perhaps she was converted to Roman Catholicism late in life since her approving references to it tend to come from her later works, as do the dedications to notable Catholics, such as Lord Maitland for *Oroonoko* and Henry Nevil Payne for *The Fair Jilt*. But her burial in the Anglican Westminster Abbey suggests that, whatever her private opinions, she did not need to make a public profession of them.

In 1663 a royal grant gave the exploration of Surinam to Lord Willoughby. According to the 'Memoirs', shortly afterwards Aphra Behn travelled to Surinam where it was claimed that her father had been appointed 'Lieutenant-General' of many islands and 'the continent of Surinam' because of his relationship to Lord Willoughby. He apparently died on the passage out, leaving his family to await a ship back to England. Hints of Aphra Behn's stay in the colony come from *Oroonoko*, written decades later when Surinam had been lost to the Dutch. This story describes the family's stay in the most substantial house in the colony and their meeting with many characters who were historical personages, including the royalist but ignoble villain of the tale, William Byam, Lord Willoughby's deputy, as well as the good John Treffry, overseer of Willoughby's plantation, and George Marten, a planter in the colony; there is as yet no historical corroboration for the romantic figure of the noble prince Oroonoko but in the 1670s Behn probably heard of a betrayed 'African king' on display in Oxford. She declared that she began her play, *The Young King*, the 'first essay of my infant-poetry', in Surinam; based on French and Spanish sources and saturated with romantic conventions of feminine love and masculine heroics, it was published much later, in 1683.

Behn was not the only avid reader of romance in colonial Surinam. When Byam sent his reports to England he used names from the popular French fiction *L'Astrée* to refer to his subjects. Aphra Behn became the heroine 'Astrea', a name she was to use all her life, and a William Scot became her lover 'Celadon'.

Scot was the son of 'Cromwell's Intelligencer' (the phrase

comes from Pepys), a regicide later executed by Charles II. He was a lawyer much in demand by the authorities in England, from which he had fled; with his cavalier style and Puritan past – a feature of many of the men connected with the royalist Aphra Behn – Scot was watched by Byam as a possible troublemaker in the politically factious and volatile colony. But all Byam apparently saw was a flirtation with the young Aphra, after whom he believed 'Celadon' might have gone in pursuit when a passage home was finally arranged for the bereaved family.

On her lengthy way to or from England Aphra may have visited Virginia, to which ships frequently sailed carrying sugar from Surinam. This was the setting of her posthumously published work *The Widow Ranter*, the first English play to be set in the American colonies. Perhaps she wrote from memory of a short stay in North America or perhaps she travelled there later; alternatively the vulgar, litigious and misgoverned society described in the play may have been based on Surinam itself, which Willoughby in 1664 called 'that poor and sad colony' and whose government was described in *Oroonoko* as consisting of 'such notorious villains as Newgate never transported, and possibly originally were such, who understood neither the laws of God or man'.

Whatever her Atlantic route, Aphra eventually arrived back in England where she gave some butterflies to 'His Majesty's Antiquaries' and a set of Indian feathers to the King's Company of players under Thomas Killigrew; the feathers were mentioned in *Oroonoko*, to whose events they would later give tangible and historical validity, and they were probably used in a revival of *The Indian Queen* by Robert Howard and John Dryden. Perhaps they were also used after her death in her own *Widow Ranter*, which presents the Indians in heroic style.

The next years are unrecorded, but in them Aphra may have married a London merchant of Dutch or German extraction, perhaps a seaman met on the voyage from Surinam or in Surinam itself. Or perhaps he was a necessary invention to provide widowed respectability. The evidence of repetition in her plays and stories suggests that he might have been a good deal older than his wife since there are many detailed and repellent descriptions of old men forcing themselves on young girls – as in *Oroonoko* and

The Rover, although in the latter case the description is also present in the source she used. Possibly 'Mr Behn' died almost immediately or possibly the couple agreed to part, thus preventing Aphra from contemplating a second marriage. Certainly there seems no further question of matrimony in her life, and many of her works end with the unlikely and perhaps wish-fulfilling option of the unwanted elderly man bowing out of the union. However it turned out in reality, there is no further mention of Mr Behn and, by 1666, the independent woman 'A. Behn' had been born.

In that year she entered official records, this time with her own letters. The theatrical Killigrew was also groom of the royal bedchamber and he recommended her to Lord Arlington as of use to his intelligence network during a period of political difficulty with Holland, which included the second Anglo-Dutch War. 'Mrs Aphora' was recruited as a spy in Antwerp on a mission which she later described as 'unusual with my sex, or to my years'.[6]

Despite Byam's conjecture, William Scot had not followed his Astrea to England but had in fact gone to Holland. There he was involved with the dissident English and Scots, who were hoping to use the hostility of the Dutch and English governments to pursue their aim of undoing the royalist Restoration and regaining political power. Behn's assignment was to encourage Scot in his desire to become a double agent and to help him report on expatriate activities and on Dutch naval plans.

Her letters back to her control in London suggest that some mental and perhaps physical seduction was accomplished by the pair but it is unclear who was seducing and outwitting whom. Behn trusted Scot's intelligence relayed to England, but the recipients of her coded letters in London were less credulous. To keep Scot faithful she felt bound to give him money in the mistaken belief that she would be reimbursed. In time she would come to realize that 'his Majesty's friends here do all complain upon the slenderness of their rewards'; soon she had pawned her rings to keep herself and was writing desperately to Killigrew, who rather harshly complained of her 'ill management' and sent nothing. In fact there is evidence that Scot gave some true pieces of information: he provided an early warning that the Dutch were planning to sail up the Thames, as they duly did to the surprise of the unprepared English. But soon Scot himself was in a debtors' prison and Aphra Behn was appealing for money to return home. Nothing was paid, but she managed privately to raise a loan and so sailed for England.

Like the time in Surinam, the stay in Antwerp might have been short, but Aphra Behn was at an impressionable age and she seems to have kept 'journal-observations' of people and events. Much later in life she would call on these periods abroad to furnish material for her allegedly factual fictions such as *Oroonoko* and *The Fair Jilt*. For example, the *London Gazette* for 28–31 May 1666 describes an extraordinary event in The Hague:

The Prince Torquino being condemned at Antwerp to be beheaded, for endeavouring the death of his sister in law: Being on the scaffold, the executioner tied an handkerchief about his head and by great accident his blow lighted upon the knot, giving him only a slight wound. Upon which, the people being in a tumult, he was carried back to the town-house, and is in hopes both of his pardon and his recovery.

A version of this incident forms the climax of *The Fair Jilt*, published in 1688.

Back in London, Behn found herself powerless to pay off the debt incurred in the royal service and by 1668 she was appealing directly to the King 'after more than two years suffering'. Her urgent notes were ignored and soon she was facing prison: 'I have cried myself dead and could find in my heart to break through all and get to the king and never rise till he were pleased to pay this, but I am sick and weak and unfit for that or a prison.' But she concludes vigorously, 'I will not starve.'

It is not known who paid the money but certainly Aphra Behn left prison and lived through the next years. Perhaps she became a kept woman or a whore, but there is little evidence. Perhaps she acted, but this is also unlikely since actresses too were regarded as close to prostitutes and no Restoration woman is known to have combined the roles of actor and playwright, although the combination was common for men. Probably she was writing for part of the time as she arrived fully fledged on the literary scene in 1670, ready to provide commendatory poems and edit collections –

Covent Garden Drollery, a selection of theatrical pieces, appeared in 1672 and included some of her own works which had probably been in circulation for a time. She was also ready to write plays.

On his Restoration, Charles II had hurried to re-open the stage. He licensed two companies, the King's under Killigrew and the Duke's under Sir William Davenant, and he took the unprecedented step of encouraging women publicly to play female roles; indeed in 1662 a royal warrant decreed that they must do so in place of the boys used on the Renaissance stage. The arrival of actresses greatly affected the presentation of female characters, since the body of the woman on the stage was heavily sexualized. Several of the leading actresses were mistresses of important men – the King kept Nell Gwyn and Moll Davis, and the Earl of Rochester the celebrated Elizabeth Barry – and off-stage exploits were commented on in prologues and epilogues. Private notoriety became part of the theatrical image.

Women were also in the audience. Their effect on the drama, much commented on, is difficult to gauge since the evidence mainly comes from the complaints of playwrights. These assumed that women preferred sentimentalized pictures of their sex and objected to anything that seemed to degrade the female character. Prologues and epilogues often spoke of women's liking for romantic love-scenes and associated a female presence in the audience with the move from masculine heroics and bawdry to feminine pathos and sentiment. This view may, however, be playwrights' convention, and the increase in scenes of pathos and romance in the late Restoration may have had more to do with the skills of particular actresses in this star-dominated theatre than with the demands of a female audience. None the less, in her address to the reader before *Sir Patient Fancy* (1678) Behn noted the shifting taste and grumbled at the hypocritical complaints of women that her plays were bawdy; she insisted that she wrote conventionally as men did because she wrote 'for bread'. In her prologue and epilogue she also railed against men who abused her for being a *woman* writer and she declared that wit was ungendered.

Constantly Behn would raise the matter of her sex in her justifications of her practice and it was certainly surprising for a woman to be writing for the Restoration theatre. It was, however, not unknown: already the poet Katherine Philips ('Orinda'), the chaste wife and mother with whom the shady Behn would often be coupled and contrasted, had had her tragedies produced on the stage, as had Frances Boothby the year before Behn arrived, and Elizabeth Polwhele was writing in the early 1670s. But none of these women produced more than one or two plays and the advent of Aphra Behn, probably author of almost twenty plays, was something new. Despite (or perhaps because of) the earlier professional connection with Killigrew, she produced her first drama with the Duke's Company under his rival Davenant, a good choice since it had the best comediennes at the time. Davenant had died in 1668 and in 1670 the company was controlled by his widow Henrietta Maria, the only woman involved in theatre management in these early years. It is not certain that she encouraged women's plays or had much to do with the choosing of plays at all, but Behn might have been attracted to a company run by a woman and Lady Davenant did preside over the production of many works with spirited cross-dressing heroines who exposed the female predicament as well as the female legs.

Behn entered a conventional theatre with a patriarchal and aristocratic Court ethos, although the small playhouses were attended by all ranks, from servants, merchants, town misses and 'strumpets' to 'persons of quality'. Her early plays used the popular ballad motif of cross-dressing; although often returning the heroine to petticoats for marriage, they did allow discussion of gender roles and issues such as forced and arranged marriages. Only in her posthumous play *The Widow Ranter*, with its portrait of the drinking, smoking widow, did she present a fighting cross-dresser who took her man with her 'breeches on'.

Her first play, *The Forced Marriage*, a romantic tragicomedy, supported the central heroine by a lighter, more spirited one, the ancestor of her later frank and witty female lover. The supporting character resembled the one Nell Gwyn had made famous, but, by the time Behn perfected it, Nell had become the King's mistress and had left the stage. This first play came with a prologue that was at once audacious and anxious, declaring its author a 'poetess' able to play the sexual war-games and yet enter the theatre not as a conqueror but as a 'scout' for women of wit: 'Discourage but this first attempt, and then/They'll hardly dare to sally out again.' The play's theatrical success must have reassured the author because she published it in the following year with the traditional literary farewell, '*Va mon enfant, prends ta fortune.*'

Over the next years Behn wrote prolifically, with sometimes only months between plays. Occasionally she was discouraged, as she was after the shoddy staging and consequent poor reception of *The Dutch Lover* in 1673. In her vigorous preface to the printed version she accuses her critics of abusing her because of her sex; women were as capable as men at making plays since their composition was no great business, she argued, drama having nothing to do with morality or 'learning'. No acknowledged works immediately followed this outburst, although she may have written and published several anonymously. In time, she must have decided to follow the advice she had given a fellow dramatist in 1671 on the failure of his play on the stage:

> Write on! and let not after ages say,
> The whistle or rude hiss could lay
> Thy mighty spright of poetry . . .
> Silence will like submission show:
> And give advantage to the foe![7]

By 1676 she was back in good form with *Abdelazar*, a powerful tragedy of a woman's sexual obsession and its cruel results; it began with the song 'Love Armed', a popular work which she later included in her collected poems. A group of comic plays quickly followed, conforming to the increased taste for the farcical, bawdy and fast-paced. Many of these, like *The Roundheads* (1681), were overtly political, attacking the mercantile city party of the Whigs and what she saw as debased commercial values; all ridiculed Puritans and their assumed hypocrisy and dullness. Meanwhile prologues and epilogues commented on the political upheavals of the various real and invented plots and counter-plots such as the Popish Plot, the Rye-House Plot and the Meal-Tub Plot, as well as the twists and turns of the Exclusion Crisis concerning the barring of the Catholic James from the throne; invariably they declared for peace and loyalty to the Stuart brothers, her much-admired Charles and James.

Often the prologues and epilogues (a distinctive Restoration form relating author and specific audience) were spoken by a particular actor, or more usually actress, who would draw attention to her own private life as well as to political events. The actress with whom Behn was most associated, one whose private life was extremely public, was Elizabeth Barry, who joined the Duke's Company in the mid 1670s. She was the most famous actress of her day, said to have been coached in the stylized drama of the Restoration by the Earl of Rochester for a wager. She is probably the 'Mris B' described in Behn's poem about her friends, 'Our Cabal', and, after first appearing in *Abdelazar*, she took part in most of Behn's plays thereafter. Although she later played the passionate roles, initially she was cast as the pert heroines of the sort Nell Gwyn had made famous. These included Hellena in Behn's greatest hit of this period, *The Rover* (1677), a character considerably altered from the heroine of Killigrew's play *Thomaso* on which her work was based. *The Rover* proved extremely popular and was watched and approved by both the King and his brother James, to whom Behn dedicated a sequel in 1681.[8]

The later history of this play is amusing. It was frequently staged in the early eighteenth century but, on the evidence of a prompt book probably marked up during this period, some of its sentiments were already too baldly expressed for the times and many of the franker utterances of Willmore on his sexual needs, of Hellena on physically unappetizing men and of Blunt on castrating femininity were excised. By the late eighteenth century John Philip Kemble had rewritten the play as *Love in Many Masks*, thoroughly refining the earthy relationship of Hellena and Willmore and improving the demeanour of the drunken rake. Recently, however, John Barton's Royal Shakespeare Company revival pulled the play in the opposite direction of bawdiness, making a more liberated heroine than Behn's world would easily have accommodated.

In *The Rover* two spirited women battle for the cavalier hero, Willmore, follower of the 'Rover of Fortune', the exiled Charles II (the play is set in the Interregnum). One woman is the cross-dressing virgin Hellena, who proves that male dress allows a freedom to women otherwise available only to a whore like her rival, Angellica Bianca. Although the loser in the contest and in the end almost too passionate to be contained in the modern conception of a comedy, this latter figure is treated neither with the ferocity Renaissance drama reserved for the whore and passionate woman nor with the complexity of Killigrew's earlier play *Thomaso* where, shadowed by other whores, she becomes an investigation of prostitution itself within a morally corrupt society. In *The Rover* Angellica Bianca is wittily linked with the author both through her initials and through Behn's 'Postscript' in the printed version, which brings playwright and prostitute together as entertainers of men: '. . . I, vainly proud of my judgment, hang out the sign of Angellica . . . to give notice where a great part of the wit dwelt'.

The second part of *The Rover* is not as sparkling as the first and it relies more heavily on farce in the courtship of two monstrous rich women, a giant and a dwarf, and in the trickeries of a disguised mountebank, all taken from *Thomaso*, but in its different denouement it provides an interesting dialogue with the first. The second *Rover* retells the story of the cavalier Willmore, now a widower and faced once more with the choice of witty and rich virginal girl as bride or experienced and impecunious whore as companion. This time he chooses the whore – there is never any question of marriage for this character in Behn – and stays true to gallantry: 'Give me thy hand, no poverty shall part us,' Willmore says as he makes the bargain 'without the formal foppery of marriage'. The whore replies, 'She that will not take thy word as soon as the parson's of the parish, deserves not the blessing.' The virgin is left to lovelessness and a respectable appearance.

This change of direction and characterization may reflect Behn's darkening vision of sexual relations and social demands, her fear of the enslaving nature of any marriage, even one entered into by so knowing a heroine as Hellena. In its stress on the libertine world view and the passing of youth and beauty, it may also be responding to the death of the person many spectators regarded as the original of the cavalier rake Willmore: Wilmot, Earl of Rochester, also reputed to be the model for one of the most famous Restoration heroes, Dorimant in Etherege's *Man of Mode* (1676).

Rochester's reputed deathbed conversion to Christian piety after a life of cavalier libertinism may have dismayed Behn since she lays no stress on it (nor did she follow *Thomaso* in thoroughly reforming her hero, Willmore), preferring to emphasize the witty courtier who, in Dr Johnson's words, 'blazed out his youth and health in lavish voluptuousness'.⁹ Among the role-playing Rochester's many pranks had been his disguise, reminiscent of Willmore's in *The Rover*, Part II, as a mountebank pretending to restore their youthful attractions to ageing women.

Finally the change may also have had something to do with the skills of Elizabeth Barry, Rochester's one-time mistress, who played the whore in the second *Rover* as she had played the virgin in the first – she would go on to play Angellica rather than Hellena in revivals of Part I. She was good at portraying passionate women tormented by their desire to give up everything for love and their equal horror at being used as 'A man's convenience, his leisure hours, his bed of ease/... The slave, the hackney of his lawless lust!', as the character she played in Behn's sour comedy *The City Heiress* (1682) expressed it.

In many of these plays of the late 1670s and early 1680s the cavalier libertine figure is presented as irresistible to women, although he may simultaneously be ridiculous, a buffoon and a rake at once. Willmore of the two parts of *The Rover* is very much the object of clever women's desire, and he spends a good deal of his time drunk or so blinded by lust that he cannot tell one female from another or resist falling on the nearest petticoat. Yet he does represent something of an ideal when set against men and women who couple out of lust for power and money; the free love he offers is, however, never quite free for women, as Hellena wittily points out.

Perhaps this rakish figure, with his libertine and cavalier associations, had in addition some autobiographical resonance. Throughout the 1670s and early 1680s Aphra Behn had been writing occasional verses addressing her friends under conventional pastoral names. Many of these were collected in her volume of 1684, *Poems on Several Occasions*; together they investigate the relations between men and women and describe sexual arousal and fulfilment often in a kind of classical pastoral golden-age setting, where no constraining social context need surround the amorous play. In other poems, however, Behn humorously portrays the manoeuvres of men and women as they struggle both for sexual gratification and for social power. On the evidence of these works it seems that for a considerable time she was uneasily in love with yet another lawyer with cavalier style but Puritan background, described in 'Our Cabal' before the affair started as a haughty, inconstant man, dangerously attractive to both sexes; he was also a thorough libertine in philosophy and action: 'A wit uncommon, and facetious,/A great admirer of Lucretius'. This figure, probably John Hoyle, portrayed after his murder in a quarrel in 1692 as 'an atheist, a sodomite professed, a corrupter of youth and a blasphemer of Christ', seems to have inspired the series of letters, *Love-Letters to a Gentleman*, printed after Behn died. While having an autobiographical ring since they portray Behn as 'of a generous and open temper, something passionate', to use the words of the 'Memoirs', these also conform to the literary model of the desiring and complaining woman recently made popular by the translation of the French *Letters of a Portuguese Nun*. As with the Portuguese Nun, the amorous pain of the lady in *Love-Letters* seems to be subtly assuaged by the written expression of it and by the dramatizing of a writing self.

It is possible that many of her most famous poems, as well as *Love-Letters* and some of her dramatic characters, were inspired by the affair with Hoyle. 'The Disappointment', distantly based, like Rochester's 'The Imperfect Enjoyment', on Ovid's *Amores* but deriving more directly from a recent French poem, records a sexual experience of premature ejaculation. But unlike the male-authored poems it is told from the female point of view, so that conventional male seduction tactics and sexual habits can both be mocked; where Rochester's poem ends with the woman more or less forgotten and the man railing against his limp penis, Behn's hero is left blaming fate and the lady whose resentment is quite understood by the presumably female narrator. Unlike the French original which allows the man to compensate for his initial failure with a later more piquant success, Behn's lover is left with his embarrassment. The disappointing experience recurs in the first part of Behn's novel of the 1680s, *Love-Letters between a Nobleman and his Sister*.

In the late 1670s and early 1680s London, much addicted to scheming throughout Charles II's reign, faced the major catastrophe of the Popish Plot brought on by Titus Oates's allegations of Roman Catholic designs on the kingdom. The impetus was the problematic succession to the throne, for Charles, though he had numerous illegitimate offspring including the popular and Protestant Duke of Monmouth, had no legitimate ones and his successor was therefore his brother, James, Duke of York, a declared Catholic and anathema to the Whigs, many of whom supported Monmouth. To Aphra Behn, who was devoted to James as both duke and future king, it seemed that the Civil War of the 1640s was about to be fought all over again.

The unrest had more than political consequences. The 'cursed plotting age' emptied the theatres, she complained in the prologue to *The Feigned Courtesans* (1679). This fact did not, however, prevent her from subjecting the remaining audience to a partisan view of courtly Tory virtue and Whig and city corruption, and in several plays she wittily turned Whig and Puritan politics into bedroom farce. No doubt too she maintained the 'royal cause' outside the theatre by writing Tory 'doggerel', mentioned in the 'Letter to Mr Creech at Oxford' and in the prologue to *The False Count* (1681), although, as with her espionage, it appears that she was not paid by His Majesty for her efforts. Despite all the outspoken loyalty to 'the King and his Royal Brother' she managed to offend the former in the summer of 1682 in an epilogue to an anonymous play in which, beyond her usual berating of the Whigs, she castigated the Duke of Monmouth for his sin of 'rebelling 'gainst a king and father'. This was displeasing to Charles and she was briefly arrested.

In the same year the theatres were in financial as well as political trouble. The King's Company collapsed and the two companies were merged. The need for new plays was drastically curtailed and this, together with some political anxiety, may have silenced Behn for a time. In a letter probably of 1683, printed in the *Gentleman's Magazine* of 1836, she wrote to her publisher Jacob Tonson, 'I have been without getting so long that I am just on the point of breaking, especially since a body has no credit at the playhouse for money as we used to have . . .', although she did go on to produce more plays, the successful and darkly cynical *The Lucky Chance* and the popular farce *The Emperor of the Moon*. Never a frugal person, she gave generously to others, was famous for her 'milk punch' and evidently delighted in eating and drinking in pleasant company. In addition, as the 1680s progressed, she was increasingly in ill-health and needed money for doctors – presumably the fall on to the icy road described in the 'Letter to Mr Creech at Oxford' could not have helped her condition. In the letter quoted above she ended by asking an extra £5 for some work from her publisher and admitting, 'I want extremely'; in 1685 she borrowed £6, offering her publisher as security.

Clearly she had to find other literary means for support to augment her play-writing. Given her knowledge of French it was probably inevitable that she should choose translation. Although she turned many French scientific and poetic works into English, she also based some of her poems on Latin originals while claiming in her verses to the young classical translator Thomas Creech to know nothing of the language. She also began at this time to produce her own short stories and novels, a few based on or inspired by French originals; they turned out to be some of the most innovative prose works of the seventeenth century.

The 1680s, a troubled political period which, like the Civil War decade of the 1640s, seems to have inspired more women than usual into print, saw some of Behn's most erotic and complex writing. Probably she fell in love again at this time or perhaps her troubled relationship with Hoyle took a different turn, and her writings seem more anxious about female sexuality and its social context than her earlier ones. 'On Desire', which describes the 'welcome plague', and the voyeuristic first part of *Love-Letters between a Nobleman and his Sister* probably date from these perplexed years. The last work shows, beyond the joy of sexual fulfilment, the misery of lost reputation and of the need for caution, that 'debaucher of the generous heart', when every impulse demands spontaneity. Other works reveal the absurdity as well as the pleasure of desire. Nothing about sexuality within culture is simple, as the baroque 'To the fair Clarinda, who made Love to me, imagined more than Woman' suggests, with its dualistic play on sex and gender.

In 1685 she was probably in her early forties (she had called the Duke of Monmouth's mistress old at thirty) and satirists were mocking her faded charms, although the denigration was as conventional as praise for beauty. The political instability was intensifying; after Charles's death, James became king and harshly suppressed the rising of his nephew Monmouth, whose sorry fate is charted in the novel *Love-Letters* with its rakish anti-hero based on a close and possibly false friend of Monmouth. In the political ferment Aphra Behn seems to have held on to her lifelong fantasy of a golden age of social and sexual frankness, which she somehow managed to associate with the far from frank royal brothers but which was more easily embodied in the society of the unsophisticated Indians in *Oroonoko*; in her golden-age vision there was no conventional shame and no libertine selfishness, and people lived without kings, hierarchy, religion, money, power and manipulative sex.

Holding to such a vision, Behn had no sympathy with a Whiggish view of political or economic progress and, as *The Widow Ranter* shows, no belief in the political abilities and rights of the common people, who in her view needed enlightened aristocrats to prevent their degenerating into a mob. She seems to have had no more sympathy with the Christian vision of redemption and afterlife; even her effort at paraphrasing the Lord's Prayer manages to concentrate on earthly love more than divine, as the satirist Tom Brown later noted in his *The Late Converts Exposed* in 1690, in which he described her 'strange fits of piety' interrupted by Cupid. In several works she expressed rationalist scientific beliefs and she frequently came down on the side of philosophical freedom and scepticism. The two versions of the commendatory poem on Creech's translation of Lucretius, the Greek philosopher often blamed with Epicurus for Restoration cynicism and libertinism, may suggest her views and the difficulty she encountered in holding publicly to them; the earlier published version used by Creech to preface his second edition of his translation in 1683 may have been tampered with by the anxious author, as seems to be suggested by a letter she wrote to the publisher Jacob Tonson: 'As for Mr Creech, I would not have you afflict him with a thing can not now be helped, so never let him know my resentment.' In her own printed version, Lucretian philosophy which, although not preaching atheism, did deny the afterlife and urge happiness as a goal of living, is equated with reason which here compels the mind beyond the dull oracles of 'poor feeble faith', called 'the last shift of routed argument'; in Creech's version, however, this reason only *equals* faith, which becomes 'resistless' instead of 'dull' and is termed 'the secure retreat of routed argument'.

Despite the Indians of *Oroonoko*, there is not much of the pleasure-filled golden age in the fiction Aphra Behn wrote during these years, the spare short stories and the novel *Love-Letters*. These relate private and public lives and show an artificial self being constructed from narratives, representations and partial interpretations. Both the novel and *The Fair Jilt*, based on real events, chart the moral disintegration of women of 'false but snowy arms' who give in to what is originally an authentic sexual passion but which is soon superseded by passion for power and money pursued through sexual manipulation. In both these stories the moral disintegration is linked with a political one: in *Love-Letters* it becomes clear that the person who can betray a king will betray anyone, while in *The Fair Jilt* the noble, gullible Prince Tarquin is brought down by a wicked woman as, in many versions, was the royal martyr himself, Charles I, whose end on the scaffold was frequently blamed on the influence of his French queen, Henrietta Maria. Unlike Prince Tarquin, however, Charles I was not saved from the law by the people. Like the foolish Duke of Monmouth with his false royal credentials, rather than the truly royal Charles, the dubious 'prince' Tarquin also suffered a painful, bungled execution.

Both *The Fair Jilt* and *Oroonoko* were published in the revolutionary year of 1688 when James, at last the father of a legitimate son, was overthrown by the Whigs and Parliament. Both deal with kingship and aristocracy and both present essentially good men fooled and subdued by lesser people. Behind the cruelly killed black Oroonoko, with his European features, his courtly ways and anxiety over his unborn child, is again inevitably the figure of the martyred Charles I and more urgently of his son, the soon-to-be-betrayed James II, one of the 'black' (i.e. dark haired and complexioned) Stuarts, like Oroonoko called 'Caesar' in her poem on his coronation and like the slave anxious about the fate of his long-awaited son. Resembling Bacon in *The Widow Ranter*, Oroonoko is a rebel only in a debased world of law rather than honour, of communal expediency rather than personal integrity.

Much is rightly made of Oroonoko's blackness and slave status, although he himself is a slave-owner, but, beyond the issue of colonialism and race, which were to become important themes in the eighteenth century, is the seventeenth-century theme of aristocracy. For Aphra Behn neither race nor gender creates the category of the Other, as both would come to do in the next age, and neither is as important as class, breeding and inherent nobility, which alone oppose the shoddy commercialization and commodification of values and feelings she saw around her in London. Fittingly, the Surinam of *Oroonoko* will, as her first readers must have realized, fall to the base and mercenary Dutch shortly after the story must have occurred; in the same way the Stuart kingdom of England, deprived of loyalty and nobility with the exit of the last legitimate ruler and his legitimate son, will fall to the Dutchman William of Orange. It was left to the playwright Thomas Southerne, who used both *Oroonoko* and *The Widow Ranter* to form his tragicomic play *Oroonoko* in 1695, to remove the specific historical reference and instead discuss slavery and its relation to the oppression of women, only a faint theme in Behn's work.

The later parts of the novel *Love-Letters* and the short stories use the device of a narrator, a woman who is sometimes detached and sometimes involved, sometimes pitiless in her presentation and at others emotionally overwhelmed; occasionally she is even implicated, as in *Oroonoko*, where she blames herself for being silent about the plot to hold the hero, caught by her conflicting roles of sympathetic and powerless female and of politically influential European. Usually, however, the narrator is a watcher and a listener, a recipient of gossip and news, commonsensical in her comments, but not omniscient and not able to deliver poetic justice in place of real-life happening or to provide a simple and single version of people and events. Miranda, the fair jilt, seems attractive and vivacious on the one hand and on the other lewd, criminal and grasping; she avoids moral justice and lives to be happy after her appalling crimes. The good Oroonoko dies to the stench of the rotting corpse of his once-beautiful bride Imoinda. Like the earlier black Othello whom he occasionally resembles, he lives in the mode of heroic drama but, like Tarquin, he cannot achieve the heroic death, suffering instead the grotesque realism of mutilation. In the next century women would come to write almost entirely in the sentimental mode, presenting themselves as feeling and morally impeccable ladies; the apparent amorality of Behn as well as her physicality, whether displayed in erotic verse or in descriptions of bodily mutilation, would become deeply shocking to readers and impossible for women writers to imitate.

The closest analogy to Behn's narrator is the spectator at the theatre and indeed there is much that is theatrical in her fiction. The characters themselves seem to know the dramatic conventions they should follow; the fair jilt Miranda plays to her advantage the conventional stage role of victimized woman when she is in fact the sexual aggressor; even Oroonoko is aware when to make the heroic speech, echoing Bacon, the hero of *The Widow Ranter*, who speaks in a poetic style in a world of prose. Both men who resign empire for love in the manner of heroic drama of the early Restoration appear to be characters out of an older dramatic mode, adrift in rather sordid comedies of later debased social manners. Baroque writers frequently saw the world as theatre and Behn is true to this vision when her narrators present love, religion and law in terms of drama. The law court, the altar and the scaffold all become places of spectacle and show.

While never declaring for atheism, Behn seems to have shared the libertine belief in the aesthetic or unified moment. Royalism and Catholicism were frequently presented as style in her works and she experienced to the full the public ritual moments of church and state. Love too seemed best when it shut out the sense of time and consequence and was accompanied by art, music and wine. Not for her an existence in which 'life but dully lingers on'.

Perhaps the intense moments were little shards from the golden age scattered in the dreary years of party politics and money-grubbing. If so, there were fewer of them as she entered her final year. As the new leaden age of William and Mary dawned it found Behn at a low ebb, poor, ill and disillusioned. The last poem she saw through publication in March 1689 expressed the predicament of a woman who openly declared she wrote for money and who should therefore have gone on trimming with the times, but who found in the end that her muse was surprisingly 'stubborn'. Her 'Pindaric Poem to the Reverend Doctor Burnet', a man fiercely opposed to Stuart pretensions, the reputed converter of the dying Rochester and one-time denigrator of Aphra Behn herself as a woman 'abominably vile', was a reply to a request from Burnet for a poem in support of the new king, William of Orange. The eulogy could not be delivered and the ambiguous 'Pindaric', at once satirical and sincere, conventional and personal, gives the reason why not. Behn died a few days after Burnet preached the sermon at William's coronation.

In 1678 in her address to the reader of *Sir Patient Fancy*, Aphra Behn had insisted that she was bawdy because other playwrights were so, that plays were frequently trivial and that she wrote them only for bread. By the end of her life she had clearly come to a juster appreciation of her own art and achievement. In the prologue to *The Lucky Chance*, printed nearly a decade later, when she again defended herself against the charge of bawdiness, she did not repeat the point about the triviality of her business or again claim lack of interest in fame. Indeed she now regarded herself as an author of some talent who did not write only for money on the third day (the receipts for the third theatrical performance traditionally went to the playwright). She wished to remain known for this talent, despite the conventional contempt for her sex:

... had the plays I have writ come forth under any man's name, and never known to have been mine; I appeal to all unbiased judges of sense, if they had not said that person had made as many good comedies, as any one man that has writ in our age; but a devil on't the woman damns the poet ... All I ask, is the privilege for my masculine part, the poet in me (if any such you will allow me), to tread in those successful paths my predecessors have so long thrived in ... If I must not, because of my sex, have this freedom, but that you will usurp all to yourselves; I lay down my quill, and you shall hear no more of me, no, not so much as to make comparisons, because I will be kinder to my brothers of the pen than they have been to a defenceless woman; for I am not content to write for a third day only. I value fame as much as if I had been born a hero; and if you rob me of that, I can retire from the ungrateful world, and scorn its fickle favours.

She did not retire and her muse, as the 'Pindaric Poem to the Reverend Doctor Burnet' reveals, was stubborn and demanding to the end.

JANET TODD

SELECTED BIBLIOGRAPHY OF
SECONDARY WORKS

Brown, Laura, 'The Romance of Empire: *Oroonoko* and the Trade in Slaves', in *The New Eighteenth Century*, ed. Felicity Nussbaum and Laura Brown (New York: Methuen, 1987).

Cameron, William J., *New Light on Aphra Behn* (Auckland: University of Auckland Press, 1961, reprinted 1978).

Cotton, Nancy, *Women Playwrights in England c. 1363–1750* (Lewisburg: Bucknell University Press, 1980).

Duffy, Maureen, *The Passionate Shepherdess: Aphra Behn 1640–89* (London: Cape, 1977).

Gallagher, Catherine, 'Who was that masked woman? The prostitute and the playwright in the comedies of Aphra Behn', in *Last Laughs*, ed. Regina Barreca (New York: Gordon & Breach, 1988), pp. 23–42.

Goreau, Angeline, *Reconstructing Aphra: A Social Biography of Aphra Behn* (New York: Dial, 1980).

Greer, Germaine, Introduction to *The Uncollected Verse of Aphra Behn* (Stump Cross: Stump Cross Books, 1989).

Guffey, George, 'Aphra Behn's *Oroonoko*: Occasion and Accomplishment', in *Two English Novelists* (Los Angeles: Clark Library, 1975).

Hume, Robert D., 'Diversity and Development in Restoration Comedy, 1660–1679', *Eighteenth-Century Studies*, 5, 1972, pp. 365–97.

McKeon, Michael, *The Origins of the English Novel, 1600–1740* (Baltimore: The Johns Hopkins University Press, 1987).

Mendelson, Sara Heller, *The Mental World of Stuart Women: Three Studies* (Brighton: Harvester, 1987).

O'Donnell, Mary Ann, *Aphra Behn: An Annotated Bibliography of Primary and Secondary Sources* (New York: Garland Publishing, 1986).

Pearson, Jacqueline, *The Prostituted Muse: Images of Women and Women Dramatists 1642–1737* (London: Harvester, 1988).

Spencer, Jane, *The Rise of the Woman Novelist: From Aphra Behn to Jane Austen* (Oxford: Blackwell, 1986).

Todd, Janet, *The Sign of Angellica: Women, Writing and Fiction 1660–1800* (London: Virago, 1989).

Woodcock, George, *The Incomparable Aphra* (London: Boardman, 1948).

NOTE ON THE TEXT

Except in the case of *Love-Letters to a Gentleman* which is taken from an edition of 1700, I have used as the basis for this volume the first printed version of Aphra Behn's plays and prose works. Her poems are mainly printed from *Poems on Several Occasions* (1684), a volume over which she appears to have had some control. In the case of a few poems, this collection represents the second printing: 'The Disappointment' first appeared in 1680 in the Earl of Rochester's *Poems on Several Occasions*; 'To Mr Creech ... on his Excellent Translation of Lucretius' was first printed in 1683 in Thomas Creech's work; 'Love Armed' was included in *Abdelazar* in 1677. In these three cases I have noted substantive changes between versions in the end notes.

It was common seventeenth-century practice to vary type for effect and emphasis, with proper names and important passages in italics and occasionally in variously sized capitals and in gothic script; in addition, nouns and other parts of speech were frequently capitalized. Spelling often differs from modern spelling and is inconsistent within the works and across works, and punctuation occasionally obscures meaning for a modern reader. Since this is a collection for the general reader I have regularized spelling and modernized punctuation, but only where this seems necessary. I have in addition avoided capitalization, italics and typographical extravagancies. I have not, however, altered words in the original except when the sense demanded it; these occasions have been recorded in the end notes. It is possible that Aphra Behn had the opportunity to correct works published in her lifetime; posthumously produced, *The Widow Ranter*, which may have been printed from manuscript or possibly from actors' copies, is by far the most carelessly presented of her plays and it requires considerably more emendation and addition than the other works included in this anthology.

Information about the source and publishing history of individual plays, poems and prose works collected in this volume is provided in the initial end note to each work.

THE FAIR JILT [1]

OR

THE HISTORY OF PRINCE TARQUIN AND MIRANDA

AS love is the most noble and divine passion of the soul, so is it that to which we may justly attribute all the real satisfactions of life, and without it, man is unfinished, and unhappy.

There are a thousand things to be said of the advantages this generous passion brings to those, whose hearts are capable of receiving its soft impressions; for 'tis not every one that can be sensible of its tender touches. How many examples, from history and observation could I give of its wondrous power, nay, even to a degree of transmigration? How many idiots has it made wise? How many fools, eloquent? How many home-bred squires, accomplished? How many cowards, brave? And there is no sort of species of mankind on whom it cannot work some change and miracle, if it be a noble, well-grounded passion, except on the fop in fashion, the hardened, incorrigible fop so often wounded, but never reclaimed. For still, by a dire mistake, conducted by vast opinionatreism,[2] and a greater portion of self-love, than the rest of the race of man, he believes that affectation in his mien and dress, that mathematical movement, that formality in every action, that face managed with care, and softened into ridicule, the languishing turn, the toss, and the back shake of the periwig, is the direct way to the heart of the fine person he adores; and instead of curing love in his soul, serves only to advance his folly; and the more he is enamoured, the more industriously he assumes (every hour) the coxcomb. These are love's playthings, a sort of animals with whom he sports, and whom he never wounds, but when he is in good humour, and always shoots laughing. 'Tis the diversion of the little god, to see what a fluttering and bustle one of these sparks, new-wounded, makes, to what fantastic fooleries he has recourse: the glass is every moment called to counsel, the valet consulted and plagued for new invention of dress, the footman and scrutore[3] perpetually employed; *billets-doux*[4] and madrigals take up all his mornings, till play-time in dressing, till night in gazing; still, like a sun-flower, turned towards the beams of the fair eyes of his Celia, adjusting himself in the most amorous posture he can assume, his hat under his arm, while the other hand is put carelessly into his bosom, as if laid upon his panting heart, his head a little bent to one side, supported with a world of cravat-string, which he takes mighty care not to put into disorder, as one may guess by a never-failing, and horrid stiffness in his neck; and if he have an occasion to look aside, his whole body turns at the same time, for fear the motion of the head alone should incommode the cravat or periwig. And sometimes the glove is well managed, and the white hand displayed. Thus, with a thousand other little motions and formalities, all in the common place or road of foppery, he takes infinite pains to show himself to the pit and boxes,[5] a most accomplished ass. This is he, of all human kind, on whom love can do no miracles; and who can no where, and upon no occasion, quit one grain of his refined foppery, unless in a duel, or a battle, if ever his stars should be so severe and ill-mannered to reduce him to the necessity of either. Fear then would ruffle that fine form he had so long preserved in nicest order, with grief considering that an unlucky, chance wound in his face, if such a dire misfortune should befall him, would spoil the sale of it for ever.

Perhaps it will be urged, that since no metamorphosis can be made in a fop by love, you must consider him one of those that only talks of love, and thinks himself that happy thing, a lover; and wanting fine sense enough for the real passion, believes what he feels to be it. There are in the quiver of the god a great many different darts; some that wound for a day, and others for a year; they are all fine, painted, glittering darts, and show as well as those made of the noblest metal; but the wounds they make, reach the desire only, and are cured by possessing, while the short-lived passion betrays the cheats. But 'tis that refined and illustrious passion of the soul, whose aim is virtue, and whose end is honour, that has the power of changing nature, and is capable of performing all those heroic things, of which history is full.

How far distant passions may be from one another, I shall be able to make appear in these following rules. I'll prove to you the strong effects of love in some unguarded and ungoverned hearts; where it rages beyond the inspirations of a god all soft and gentle, and reigns more like a Fury from Hell.

I do not pretend here to entertain you with a feigned story, or anything pieced together with romantic accidents; but every circumstance, to a tittle, is truth. To a great part of the main, I myself was an eye-witness;[6] and what I did not see, I was confirmed of

by actors in the intrigue, holy men, of the Order of St Francis.[7]
But for the sake of some of her relations, I shall give my fair
jilt a feigned name, that of Miranda; but my hero must retain his
own, it being too illustrious to be concealed.

You are to understand, that in all the Catholic countries where
Holy Orders are established, there are abundance of differing
kinds of religious, both of men and women. Amongst the women
there are those we call nuns, that make solemn vows of perpetual
chastity; there are others who make but a simple vow, as, for five
or ten years, or more or less; and that time expired, they may
contract anew for longer time, or marry, or dispose of themselves
as they shall see good; and these are ordinarily called Galloping
Nuns.[8] Of these there are several Orders; as, Chanonesses,[9]
Beguines,[10] Quests,[11] Swart-sisters,[12] and Jesuitesses,[13] with sev-
eral others I have forgot. Of those of the Beguines was our fair
votress.

These Orders are taken up by the best persons of the town,
young maids of fortune, who live together, not enclosed, but in
palaces that will hold about fifteen hundred or two thousand of
these *filles dévotes,*[14] where they have a regulated government,
under a sort of abbess, or prioress; or rather, a governante.[15]
They are obliged to a method of devotion, and are under a sort of
obedience. They wear a habit much like our widows of quality in
England, only without a bando;[16] and their veil is of a thicker
crape than what we have here, through which one cannot see the
face; for when they go abroad, they cover themselves all over with
it, but they put them up in the churches, and lay them by in the
houses. Every one of these have a confessor, who is to them a
sort of steward: for, you must know, they that go into these
places, have the management of their own fortunes, and what
their parents design them. Without the advice of this confessor,
they act nothing, nor admit of a lover that he shall not approve
of; at least, this method ought to be taken, and is by almost all of
them, though Miranda thought her wit above it, as her spirit was.

But as these women are, as I said, of the best quality, and live
with the reputation of being retired from the world a little more
than ordinary, and because there is a sort of difficulty to approach
them, they are the people the most courted, and liable to the

greatest temptations; for as difficult as it seems to be, they receive visits from all the men of the best quality, especially strangers. All the men of wit and conversation meet at the apartments of these fair *filles dévotes*, where all manner of gallantries are performed, while all the study of these maids is to accomplish themselves for these noble conversations. They receive presents, balls, serenades and billets; all the news, wit, verses, songs, novels, music, gaming, and all fine diversion, is in their apartments, they themselves being of the best quality and fortune. So that to manage these gallantries, there is no sort of female arts they are not practised in, no intrigues they are ignorant of, and no management of which they are not capable.

Of this happy number was the fair Miranda, whose parents being dead, and a vast estate divided between herself, and a young sister (who lived with an unmarried old uncle, whose estate afterwards was all divided between them) put herself into this unenclosed religious house; but her beauty, which had all the charms that ever Nature gave, became the envy of the whole sisterhood. She was tall, and admirably shaped; she had a bright hair, and hazel eyes, all full of love and sweetness. No art could make a face so fair as hers by Nature, which every feature adorned with a grace that imagination cannot reach: every look, every motion charmed, and her black dress showed the lustre of her face and neck. She had an air, though gay as so much youth could inspire, yet so modest, so nobly reserved, without formality, or stiffness, that one who looked on her would have imagined her soul the twin-angel of her body; and both together, made her appear something divine. To this she had a great deal of wit, read much, and retained all that served her purpose. She sang delicately, and danced well, and played on the lute to a miracle. She spoke several languages naturally; for being co-heiress to so great a fortune, she was bred with nicest care, in all the finest manners of education; and was now arrived to her eighteenth year.

'Twere needless to tell you how great a noise the fame of this young beauty, with so considerable a fortune, made in the world; I may say, the world, rather than confine her fame to the scanty limits of a town; it reached to many others; and there was not a man of any quality that came to Antwerp, or passed through the

city, but made it his business to see the lovely Miranda, who was
universally adored. Her youth and beauty, her shape and majesty
of mien, and air of greatness, charmed all her beholders; and
thousands of people were dying by her eyes, while she was vain
enough to glory in her conquest, and make it her business to
wound. She loved nothing so much as to behold sighing slaves at
her feet, of the greatest quality; and treated them all with an
affability that gave them hope. Continual music as soon as it was
dark, and songs of dying lovers, were sung under her windows;
and she might well have made herself a great fortune (if she had
not been so already) by the rich presents that were hourly made
her; and everybody daily expected when she would make someone
happy, by suffering herself to be conquered by love and honour,
by the assiduities and vows of some one of her adorers. But
Miranda accepted their presents, heard their vows with pleasure,
and willingly admitted all their soft addresses; but would not yield
her heart, or give away that lovely person to the possession of
one, who could please itself with so many. She was naturally
amorous, but extremely inconstant: she loved one for his wit,
another for his face, a third for his mien; but above all, she
admired quality. Quality alone had the power to attack her
entirely; yet not to one man, but that virtue was still admired by
her in all; wherever she found that, she loved, or at least acted the
lover with such art, that (deceiving well) she failed not to complete
her conquest; and yet she never durst trust her fickle humour with
marriage. She knew the strength of her own heart, and that it
could not suffer itself to be confined to one man, and wisely
avoided those inquietudes, and that uneasiness of life she was sure
to find in that married life, which would, against her nature,
oblige her to the embraces of one, whose humour was to love all
the young and the gay. But Love, who had hitherto but played
with her heart, and given it naught but pleasing, wanton wounds,
such as afforded only soft joys, and not pains, resolved, either out
of revenge to those numbers she had abandoned and who had
sighed so long in vain, or to try what power he had upon so fickle
a heart, sent an arrow dipped in the most tormenting flames that
rage in hearts most sensible![17] He struck it home and deep, with
all the malice of an angry god.

There was a church belonging to the Cordeliers,[18] whither Miranda often repaired to her devotion; and being there one day, accompanied with a young sister of the order, after the mass was ended, as 'tis the custom, some one of the fathers goes about the church with a box, for contribution, or charity-money; it happened that day, that a young father, newly initiated, carried the box about, which, in his turn, he brought to Miranda. She had no sooner cast her eyes on this young friar, but her face was overspread with blushes of surprise: she beheld him steadfastly, and saw in his face all the charms of youth, wit and beauty; he wanted no one grace that could form him for love, he appeared all that is adorable to the fair sex, nor could the misshapen habit hide from her the lovely shape it endeavoured to cover, nor those delicate hands that approached her too near with the box. Besides the beauty of his face and shape, he had an air altogether great; in spite of his professed poverty, it betrayed the man of quality; and that thought weighed greatly with Miranda. But Love who did not design she should now feel any sort of those easy flames with which she had heretofore burnt, made her soon lay all those considerations aside which used to invite her to love, and now loved she knew not why.

She gazed upon him while he bowed before her, and waited for her charity, till she perceived the lovely friar to blush, and cast his eyes to the ground. This awakened her shame, and she put her hand into her pocket, and was a good while in searching for her purse, as if she thought of nothing less than what she was about; at last she drew it out, and gave him a pistole;[19] but that with so much deliberation and leisure, as easily betrayed the satisfaction she took in looking on him; while the good man, having received her bounty, after a very low obeisance, proceeded to the rest; and Miranda casting after him a look all languishing, as long as he remained in the church, departed with a sigh as soon as she saw him go out, and returned to her apartment, without speaking one word all the way to the young *fille dévote* who attended her, so absolutely was her soul employed with this young holy man. Cornelia (so was this maid called who was with her) perceiving she was so silent, who used to be all wit and good humour, and observing her little disorder at the sight of the young father, though she was far from imagining it to be love, took an occasion, when she was come home, to speak of him. 'Madam,' said she, 'did you not observe that fine young Cordelier, who brought the box?' At a question that named that object of her thoughts, Miranda blushed; and the finding she did so, redoubled her confusion, and she had scarce courage enough to say, 'Yes, I did observe him.' And then, forcing herself to smile a little, continued, 'And I wondered to see so jolly a young friar of an order so severe, and mortified.' 'Madam,' replied Cornelia, 'when you know his story, you will not wonder.' Miranda, who was impatient to know all that concerned her new conqueror, obliged her to tell his story; and Cornelia obeyed, and proceeded.

THE STORY OF PRINCE HENRICK

'You must know, madam, that this young holy man is a prince of Germany, of the house of — whose fate it was, to fall most passionately in love with a fair young lady, who loved him with an ardour equal to what he vowed her. Sure of her heart, and wanting only the approbation of her parents, and his own, which her quality did not suffer him to despair of, he boasted of his happiness to a young prince, his elder brother, a youth amorous and fierce, impatient of joys, and sensible of beauty, taking fire with all fair eyes. He was his father's darling, and delight of his fond mother; and by an ascendant over both their hearts, ruled their wills.

'This young prince no sooner saw, but loved the fair mistress of his brother, and with an authority of a sovereign, rather than the advice of a friend, warned his brother Henrick (this now young friar) to approach no more this lady, whom he had seen; and seeing, loved.

'In vain the poor surprised prince pleads his right of love, his exchange of vows, and assurance of a heart that could never be but for himself. In vain he urges his nearness of blood, his friendship, his passion, or his life, which so entirely depended on the possession of the charming maid. All his pleading served but to blow his brother's flame; and the more he implores, the more the other burns; and while Henrick follows him on his knees, with humble submissions, the other flies from him in rages of trans-ported love; nor could his tears, that pursued his brother's steps, move him to pity: hot-headed, vain-conceited of his beauty, and greater quality, as elder brother, he doubts not his success, and resolved to sacrifice all to the violence of his new-born passion.

'In short, he speaks of his design to his mother, who promised him her assistance; and accordingly, proposing it first to the prince, her husband, urging the languishment of her son, she soon wrought so on him, that a match being concluded between the parents of this young beauty, and Henrick's brother, the hour was appointed before she knew of the sacrifice she was to be made. And while this was in agitation, Henrick was sent on some great affairs, up into Germany, far out of the way; not but his boding heart, with perpetual sighs and throbs, eternally foretold him his fate.

'All the letters he writ were intercepted, as well as those she writ to him. She finds herself every day perplexed with the addresses of the prince she hated; he was ever sighing at her feet. In vain were all her reproaches, and all her coldness, he was on the surer side; for what he found love would not do, force of parents would.

'She complains in her heart on young Henrick, from whom she could never receive one letter; and at last, could not forbear bursting into tears, in spite of all her force, and feigned courage; when on a day the prince told her, that Henrick was withdrawn, to give him time to court her, to whom, he said, he confessed he had made some vows, but did repent of them, knowing himself too young to make them good; that it was for that reason he brought him first to see her; and for that reason that after that, he never saw her more, nor so much as took leave of her (when, indeed, his death lay upon the next visit, his brother having sworn to murder him; and to that end, put a guard upon him, till he was sent into Germany).

'All this he uttered with so many passionate asseverations, vows and seeming pity for her being so inhumanely abandoned, that she almost gave credit to all he had said, and had much ado to keep herself within the bounds of moderation, and silent grief. Her heart was breaking, her eyes languished, and her cheeks grew pale, and she had like to have fallen dead into the treacherous arms of him that had reduced her to this discovery; but she did what she could to assume her courage, and to show as little resentment as possible for a heart, like hers, oppressed with love, and now abandoned by the dear subject of its joys and pains.

'But, madam, not to tire you with this adventure, the day arrived wherein our still weeping fair unfortunate was to be sacrificed to the capriciousness of love; and she was carried to court by her parents, without knowing to what end, where she was almost compelled to marry the prince.

'Henrick, who, all this while, knew no more of his unhappiness, than what his fears suggested, returns, and passes even to the presence of his father, before he knew anything of his fortune; where he beheld his mistress and his brother, with his father, in such a familiarity, as he no longer doubted his destiny. 'Tis hard to judge whether the lady or himself was most surprised; she was all pale and unmoveable in her chair, and Henrick fixed like a statue; at last grief and rage took place of amazement, and he could not forbear crying out, "Ah, traitor! Is it thus you have treated a friend, and brother? And you, O perjured charmer! Is it thus you have rewarded all my vows?" He could say no more; but reeling against the door, had fallen in a swoon upon the floor, had not his page caught him in his arms, who was entering with him. The good old prince, the father, who knew not what all this meant, was soon informed by the young, weeping princess; who, in relating the story of her amour with Henrick, told her tale in so moving a manner, as brought tears to the old man's eyes, and rage to those of her husband; he immediately grew jealous to the last degree. He finds himself in possession ('tis true) of the beauty he adored, but the beauty adoring another; a prince, young, and charming as the light, soft, witty, and raging with an equal passion. He finds this dreaded rival in the same house with him, with an authority equal to his own; and fancies, where two hearts are so entirely agreed, and have so good an understanding, it would not be impossible to find opportunities to satisfy and ease that mutual flame that burnt so equally in both; he therefore resolved to send him out of the world, and to establish his own repose by a deed, wicked, cruel and unnatural, to have him assassinated the first opportunity he could find. This resolution set him a little at ease, and he strove to dissemble kindness to Henrick, with all the art he was capable of, suffering him to come often to the apartment of the princess, and to entertain her oftentimes with discourse, when he was not near enough to hear what he spoke; but still watching their eyes, he found those of Henrick full of tears, ready to flow, but restrained, looking all dying, and yet reproaching, while those of the princess were ever bent to the earth, and she, as much as possible, shunning his conversation. Yet this did not satisfy the jealous husband; 'twas not her complaisance that could appease him; he found her heart was panting within whenever Henrick approached her, and every visit more and more confirmed his death.

'The father often found the disorders of the sons; the softness and address of the one gave him as much fear, as the angry blushings, the fierce looks, and broken replies of the other, when-ever he beheld Henrick approach his wife. So that the father fearing some ill consequence of this, besought Henrick to with-draw to some other country, or travel into Italy, he being now of an age that required a view of the world. He told his father, that he would obey his commands, though he was certain, that moment he was to be separated from the sight of the fair princess, his sister, would be the last of his life; and, in fine, made so pitiful a story of his suffering love, as almost moved the old prince to compassionate him so far, as to permit him to stay; but he saw inevitable danger in that, and therefore bid him prepare for his journey.

'That which passed between the father and Henrick being a secret, none talked of his departing from court; so that the design the brother had, went on; and making an hunting-match one day, where most young people of quality were, he ordered some whom he had hired to follow his brother, so as if he chanced to go out of the way, to dispatch him; and accordingly, fortune gave them an opportunity; for he lagged behind the company, and turned aside into a pleasant thicket of hazels, where alighting, he walked on foot in the most pleasant part of it, full of thought how to divide his soul between love and obedience. He was sensible that he ought not to stay, that he was but an affliction to the young princess, whose honour could never permit her to ease any part of his flame; nor was he so vicious, to entertain a thought that should stain her virtue. He beheld her now as his brother's wife, and that secured his flame from all loose desires, if her native modesty had not been sufficient of itself to have done it, and that profound respect he paid her. And he considered, in obeying his father, he left her at ease, and his brother freed of a thousand fears; he went to seek a cure, which if he could not find, at last he could but die; and so he must, even at her feet; however, that 'twas more noble to seek a remedy for his disease, than expect a certain death by staying. After a thousand reflections on his hard fate, and bemoaning himself, and blaming his cruel stars, that had doomed him to die so young; after an infinity of sighs and tears, resolvings and unresolvings, he on the sudden was interrupted by the trampling of some horses he heard, and their rushing through the boughs, and saw four men make towards him; he had not time to mount, being walked some paces from his horse. One of the men advanced, and cried, "Prince, you must die." "I do believe thee," replied Henrick, "but not by a hand so base as thine," and at the same time, drawing his sword, ran him into the groin. When the fellow found himself so wounded, he wheeled off, and cried, "Thou art a prophet, and hast rewarded my treachery with death." The rest came up, and one shot at the prince, and shot him into the shoulder; the other two hastily laying hold (but too late) on the hand of the murderer, cried, "Hold, traitor; we relent, and he shall not die." He replied, "'Tis too late, he is shot; and see, he lies dead. Let us provide for ourselves, and tell the prince, we have done the work; for you are as guilty as I am." At that they all fled, and left the prince lying under a tree, weltering in his blood.

'About the evening, the forester going his walks, saw the horse richly caparisoned, without a rider, at the entrance of the wood; and going farther, to see if he could find its owner, found there the prince almost dead. He immediately mounts him on the horse, and himself behind, bore him up, and carried him to the lodge; where he had only one old man, his father, well skilled in surgery, and a boy. They put him to bed, and the old forester, with what art he had, dressed his wound, and in the morning sent for an abler surgeon, to whom the prince enjoined secrecy, because he knew him. The man was faithful, and the prince, in time, was recovered of his wounds; and as soon as he was well, he came for Flanders, in the habit of a pilgrim, and after some time, took the Order of St Francis, none knowing what became of him, till he was professed; and then he writ his own story to the prince his father, to his mistress, and his ungrateful brother. The young princess did not long survive his loss, she languished from the moment of his departure; and he had this to confirm his devout life, to know she died for him.

'My brother, madam, was an officer under the prince, his father, and knew his story perfectly well; from whose mouth I had it.'

'What!' replied Miranda then, 'is Father Henrick a man of quality?' 'Yes, madam,' said Cornelia, 'and has changed his name to Francisco.' But Miranda, fearing to betray the sentiments of her heart, by asking any more questions about him, turned the discourse; and some persons of quality came in to visit her (for her apartment was, about six o'clock, like the presence-chamber of a queen, always filled with the greatest people). There meet all the *beaux esprits*,[20] and all the beauties. But it was visible Miranda was not so gay as she used to be; but pensive, and answering *mal à propos*[21] to all that was said to her. She was a thousand times going to speak, against her will, something of the charming friar, who was never from her thoughts; and she imagined, if he could inspire love in a coarse, grey, ill-made habit, a shorn crown, a hair-cord about his waist, bare legged, in sandals instead of shoes, what must he do, when looking back on time, she beholds him in a prospect of glory, with all that youth and illustrious beauty set off by the advantage of dress and equipage. She frames an idea of him all gay and splendid, and looks on his present habit as some disguise proper for the stealths of love; some feigned put-on shape, with the more security to approach a mistress, and make himself happy; and that, the robe laid by, she has the lover in his proper beauty, the same he would have been if any other habit (though never so rich) were put off: in the bed, the silent, gloomy night, and the soft embraces of her arms, he loses all the friar, and assumes all the prince; and that awful reverence, due alone to his holy habit, he exchanges for a thousand dalliances for which his youth was made; for love, for tender embraces, and all the happiness of life. Some moments she fancies him a lover, and that the fair object that takes up all his heart has left no room for her there; but that was a thought that did not long perplex her, and which, almost as soon as born, she turned to her advantage. She beholds him a lover, and therefore finds he has a heart sensible and tender; he had youth to be fired, as well as to inspire; he was far from the loved object, and totally without hope; and she reasonably considered, that flame would of itself soon die, that had only despair to feed on. She beheld her own charms; and experience, as well as her glass, told her, they never failed of conquest, especially, where they designed it; and she believed Henrick would be glad, at least, to quench that flame in himself, by an amour with her, which was kindled by the young princess of — his sister.

These, and a thousand other self-flatteries, all vain and indiscreet, took up her waking nights, and now more retired days; while love, to make her truly wretched, suffered her to soothe herself with fond imaginations, not so much as permitting her reason to plead one moment, to save her from undoing. She would not suffer it to tell her, he had taken holy orders, made sacred and solemn vows of everlasting chastity, that 'twas impossible he could marry her, or lay before her any argument that might prevent her ruin; but love, mad, malicious love was always called to counsel, and, like easy monarchs, she had no ears, but for flatterers.

Well then, she is resolved to love, without considering to what end, and what must be the consequence of such an amour. She now missed no day of being at that little church, where she had the happiness, or rather, the misfortune (so Love ordained) to see this ravisher of her heart and soul; and every day she took new fire from his lovely eyes. Unawares, unknown and unwillingly he gave her wounds, and the difficulty of her cure made her rage the more: she burnt, she languished, and died for the young innocent, who knew not he was the author of so much mischief.

Now she revolves a thousand ways in her tortured mind, to let him know her anguish, and at last pitched upon that of writing to him soft billets, which she had learnt the art of doing; or if she had not, she had now fire enough to inspire her with all that could charm and move. These she delivered to a young wench who waited on her, and whom she had entirely subdued to her interest, to give to a certain lay-brother of the order, who was a very simple, harmless wretch, and who served in the kitchen in the nature of a cook in the monastery of Cordeliers; she gave him gold to secure his faith and service; and not knowing from whence they came (with so good credentials) he undertook to deliver the letters to Father Francisco, which letters were all afterwards, as you shall hear, produced in open court. These letters failed not to come every day; and the sense of the first was, to tell him that a very beautiful young lady, of a great fortune, was in love with him, without naming her; but it came as from a third person, to let him know the secret, that she desired he would let her know whether she might hope any return from him; assuring him, he needed but only see the fair languisher, to confess himself her slave.

This letter, being delivered him, he read by himself, and was surprised to receive words of this nature, being so great a stranger in that place; and could not imagine, or would not give himself the trouble of guessing who this should be, because he never designed to make returns.

The next day Miranda, finding no advantage from her messenger of love, in the evening sends another (impatient of delay) confessing that she who suffered the shame of writing and imploring, was the person herself who adored him. 'Twas there her raging love made her say all things that discovered the nature of its flame, and propose to flee with him to any part of the world, if he would quit the convent; that she had a fortune considerable enough to make him happy, and that his youth and quality were not given him to so unprofitable an end as to lose themselves in a convent, where poverty and ease was all their business. In fine, she leaves nothing unurged that might debauch and invite him,

not forgetting to send him her own character of beauty, and left
him to judge of her wit and spirit by her writing, and her love by
the extremity of passion she professed. To all which the lovely
friar made no return, as believing a gentle capitulation or exhorta-
tion to her would but inflame her the more, and give new
occasions for her continuing to write. All her reasonings, false and
vicious, he despised, pities the error of her love, and was proof
against all she could plead. Yet notwithstanding his silence, which
left her in doubt, and more tormented her, she ceased not to
pursue him with her letters, varying her style; sometimes all
wanton, loose and raving; sometimes feigning a virgin-modesty all
over, accusing herself, blaming her conduct, and sighing her
destiny, as one compelled to the shameful discovery by the auster-
ity of his vow and habit, asking his pity and forgiveness; urging
him in charity to use his fatherly care to persuade and reason with
her wild desires, and by his counsel drive the god from her heart,
whose tyranny was worse than that of a fiend; and he did not
know what his pious advice might do. But still she writes in vain,
in vain she varies her style, by a cunning, peculiar to a maid
possessed with such a sort of passion.

This cold neglect was still oil to the burning lamp, and she tries
yet more arts, which, for want of right thinking, were as fruitless.
She has recourse to presents; her letters came loaded with rings of
great price, and jewels, which fops of quality had given her. Many
of this sort he received, before he knew where to return them, or
how; and on this occasion alone he sent her a letter, and restored
her trifles, as he called them; but his habit having not made him
forget his quality and education, he writ to her with all the
profound respect imaginable, believing by her presents, and the
liberality with which she parted with them, that she was of
quality. But the whole letter, as he told me afterwards, was to
persuade her from the honour she did him, by loving him; urging
a thousand reasons, solid and pious, and assuring her, he had
wholly devoted the rest of his days to Heaven, and had no need of
those gay trifles she had sent him, which were only fit to adorn
ladies so fair as herself, and who had business with this glittering
world, which he disdained, and had for ever abandoned. He sent
her a thousand blessings, and told her, she should be ever in his

prayers, though not in his heart, as she desired; and abundance of goodness more he expressed, and counsel he gave her, which had the same effect with his silence; it made her love but the more, and the more impatient she grew. She now had a new occasion to write, she now is charmed with his wit; this was the new subject. She rallies his resolution, and endeavours to recall him to the world, by all the arguments that human invention is capable of.

But when she had above four months languished thus in vain, not missing one day, wherein she went not to see him, without discovering herself to him; she resolved, as her last effort, to show her person, and see what that, assisted by her tears, and soft words from her mouth, could do, to prevail upon him.

It happened to be on the eve of that day when she was to receive the sacrament, that she, covering herself with her veil, came to Vespers, purposing to make choice of the conquering friar for her confessor.

She approached him; and as she did so, she trembled with love; at last she cried, 'Father, my confessor is gone for some time from the town, and I am obliged tomorrow to receive, and beg you will be pleased to take my confession.'

He could not refuse her; and led her into the sacristy,[22] where there is a confession-chair, in which he seated himself; and on one side of him she kneeled down, over against a little altar, where the priests' robes lie, on which was placed some lighted wax candles, that made the little place very light and splendid, which shone full upon Miranda.

After the little preparation usual in Confession, she turned up her veil, and discovered to his view the most wondrous object of beauty he had ever seen, dressed in all the glory of a young bride; her hair and stomacher[23] full of diamonds, that gave a lustre all dazzling to her brighter face and eyes. He was surprised at her amazing beauty, and questioned whether he saw a woman or an angel at his feet. Her hands, which were elevated, as if in prayer, seemed to be formed of polished alabaster; and he confessed, he had never seen anything in nature so perfect, and so admirable.

He had some pain to compose himself to hear her confession, and was obliged to turn away his eyes, that his mind might not be perplexed with an object so diverting; when Miranda, opening the finest mouth in the world, and discovering new charms, began her confession.

'Holy father,' said she, 'amongst the number of my vile offences, that which afflicts me to the greatest degree is, that I am in love. Not,' continued she, 'that I believe simple and virtuous love a sin when 'tis placed on an object proper and suitable; but, my dear father,' said she, and wept, 'I love with a violence which cannot be contained within the bounds of reason, moderation, or virtue. I love a man whom I cannot possess without a crime, and a man who cannot make me happy without becoming perjured.' 'Is he married?' replied the father. 'No,' answered Miranda. 'Are you so?' continued he. 'Neither,' said she. 'Is he too near allied to you?' said Francisco, 'a brother, or relation?' 'Neither of these,' said she, 'he is unenjoyed, unpromised; and so am I. Nothing opposes our happiness, or makes my love a vice, but you – 'tis you deny me life! 'Tis you that forbids my flame! 'Tis you will have me die, and seek my remedy in my grave, when I complain of tortures, wounds and flames. O cruel charmer, 'tis for you I languish; and here, at your feet, implore that pity which all my addresses have failed of procuring me.'

With that, perceiving he was about to rise from his seat, she held him by his habit, and vowed she would in that posture follow him, wherever he flew from her. She elevated her voice so loud, he was afraid she might be heard, and therefore suffered her to force him into his chair again; where being seated, he began, in the most passionate terms imaginable, to dissuade her; but finding she but the more persisted in eagerness of passion, he used all the tender assurance that he could force from himself, that he would have for her all the respect, esteem and friendship that he was capable of paying; that he had a real compassion for her; and at last, she prevailed so far with him by her sighs and tears, as to own he had a tenderness for her, and that he could not behold so many charms, without being sensibly touched by them, and finding all those effects that a maid so young and fair causes in the souls of men of youth and sense. [24] But that, as he was assured he could never be so happy to marry her, and as certain he could not grant anything but honourable passion, he humbly besought her not to expect more from him than such; and then began to tell her how

short life was, and transitory its joys; how soon she would grow
weary of vice, and how often change to find real repose in it, but
never arrive to it. He made an end by new assurance of his eternal
friendship, but utterly forbade her to hope.

Behold her now denied, refused and defeated, with all her
pleading youth, beauty, tears and knees, imploring, as she lay,
holding fast his scapular,[25] and embracing his feet. What shall she
do? She swells with pride, love, indignation and desire; her burning
heart is bursting with despair, her eyes grow fierce, and from
grief, she rises to a storm; and in her agony of passion, which
looks all disdainful, haughty, and full of rage, she began to revile
him, as the poorest of animals: tells him, his soul was dwindled to
the meanness of his habit, and his vows of poverty were suited to
his degenerate mind. 'And,' said she, 'since all my nobler ways
have failed me; and that, for a little hypocritical devotion, you
resolve to lose the greatest blessings of life, and to sacrifice me to
your religious pride and vanity, I will either force you to abandon
that dull dissimulation; or you shall die, to prove your sanctity
real. Therefore answer me immediately, answer my flame, my
raging fire, which your eyes have kindled; or here, in this very
moment, I will ruin thee; and make no scruple of revenging the
pains I suffer, by that which shall take away your life and
honour.'

The trembling young man, who, all this while, with extreme
anguish of mind, and fear of the dire result, had listened to her
ravings, full of dread, demanded what she would have him do.
When she replied, 'Do that which thy youth and beauty were
ordained to do! – this place is private, a sacred silence reigns here,
and no one dares to pry into the secrets of this holy place. We are
as secure from fears of interruption, as in deserts uninhabited, or
caves forsaken by wild beasts. The tapers too shall veil their
lights, and only that glimmering lamp shall be witness of our dear
stealths of love. – Come to my arms, my trembling, longing arms;
and curse the folly of thy bigotry that has made thee so long lose a
blessing, for which so many princes sigh in vain.'

At these words she rose from his feet, and snatching him in her
arms, he could not defend himself from receiving a thousand
kisses from the lovely mouth of the charming wanton; after

which, she ran herself, and in an instant put out the candles. But he cried to her, 'In vain, O too indiscreet fair one; in vain you put out the light; for Heaven still has eyes, and will look down upon my broken vows. I own your power, I own I have all the sense in the world of your charming touches; I am frail flesh and blood, but yet – yet – yet I can resist; and I prefer my vows to all your powerful temptations. – I will be deaf and blind, and guard my heart with walls of ice, and make you know, that when the flames of true devotion are kindled in a heart, it puts out all other fires; which are as ineffectual, as candles lighted in the face of the sun. – Go, vain wanton, and repent, and mortify that blood which has so shamefully betrayed thee, and which will one day ruin both thy soul and body.'

At these words Miranda, more enraged, the nearer she imagined herself to happiness, made no reply; but throwing herself, in that instant, into the confessing-chair, and violently pulling the young friar into her lap, she elevated her voice to such a degree, in crying out, 'Help, help! A rape! Help, help,' that she was heard all over the church, which was full of people at the evening's devotion; who flocked about the door of the sacristy, which was shut with a spring-lock on the inside, but they durst not open the door.

'Tis easily to be imagined, in what condition our young friar was, at this last devilish stratagem of his wicked mistress. He strove to break from those arms that held him so fast; and his bustling to get away, and hers to retain him, disordered her hair and her habit to such a degree, as gave the more credit to her false accusation.

The fathers had a door on the other side, by which they usually entered, to dress in this little room; and at the report that was in an instant made them, they hasted thither, and found Miranda and the good father very indecently struggling; which they misinterpreted, as Miranda desired; who, all in tears, immediately threw herself at the feet of the provincial,[26] who was one of those that entered; and cried, 'O holy father, revenge an innocent maid, undone and lost to fame and honour, by that vile monster, born of goats, nursed by tigers, and bred up on savage mountains, where humanity and religion are strangers. For, O holy father, could it have entered into the heart of man, to have done so barbarous and horrid a deed, as to attempt the virgin-honour of an unspotted maid, and one of my degree, even in the moment of my confession, in that holy time, when I was prostrate before him and Heaven, confessing those sins that pressed my tender conscience; even then to load my soul with the blackest of infamies, to add to my number a weight that must sink me to Hell? Alas, under the security of his innocent looks, his holy habit, and his awful function, I was led into this room, to make my confession; where, he locking the door, I had no sooner begun, but he gazing on me, took fire at my fatal beauty; and starting up, put out the candles, and caught me in his arms; and raising me from the pavement, set me in the confession-chair; and then – Oh, spare me the rest.'

With that a shower of tears burst from her fair dissembling eyes, and sobs so naturally acted, and so well managed, as left no doubt upon the good men, but all she had spoken was truth.

'At first,' proceeded she, 'I was unwilling to bring so great a scandal on his order, as to cry out; but struggled as long as I had breath, pleaded the heinousness of the crime; urging my quality, and the danger of the attempt. But he, deaf as the winds, and ruffling as a storm, pursued his wild design with so much force and insolence, as I at last, unable to resist, was wholly vanquished, robbed of my native purity. With what life and breath I had, I called for assistance, both from men and Heaven; but Oh, alas! your succours come too late. – You find me here a wretched, undone and ravished maid. Revenge me, fathers; revenge me on the perfidious hypocrite, or else give me a death that may secure your cruelty and injustice from ever being proclaimed o'er the world; or my tongue will be eternally reproaching you, and cursing the wicked author of my infamy.'

She ended as she began, with a thousand sighs and tears; and received from the provincial all assurances of revenge.

The innocent betrayed victim, all this while she was speaking, heard her with an astonishment that may easily be imagined; yet showed no extravagant signs of it, as those would do, who feign it to be thought innocent; but being really so, he bore, with an humble, modest, and blushing countenance, all her accusations: which silent shame they mistook for evident signs of his guilt.

When the provincial demanded, with an unwonted severity in his eyes and voice, what he could answer for himself, calling him profaner of his sacred vows, and infamy to the holy order, the injured, but the innocently accused, only replied, 'May Heaven forgive that bad woman, and bring her to repentance. For his part, he was not so much in love with life, as to use many arguments to justify his innocence; unless it were to free that order from a scandal, of which he had the honour to be professed. But as for himself, life or death were things indifferent to him, who heartily despised the world.'

He said no more, and suffered himself to be led before the magistrate; who committed him to prison, upon the accusation of this implacable beauty; who, with so much feigned sorrow, prosecuted the matter, even to his trial and condemnation; where he refused to make any great defence for himself. But being daily visited by all the religious, both of his own, and other orders, they obliged him (some of them knowing the austerity of his life, others his cause of griefs that first brought him into orders, and others pretending a nearer knowledge even of his soul itself) to stand upon his justification, and discover what he knew of that wicked woman; whose life had not been so exemplary for virtue, not to have given the world a thousand suspicions of her lewdness and prostitution.

The daily importunities of these fathers made him produce her letters. But as he had all the gown-men[27] on his side, she had all the hats and feathers on hers; all the men of quality taking her part, and all the church-men his. They heard his daily protestations and vows, but not a word of what passed at confession was yet discovered. He held that as a secret sacred on his part; and what was said in nature of a confession, was not to be revealed, though his life depended on the discovery. But as to the letters, they were forced from him, and exposed; however, matters were carried with so high a hand against him, that they served for no proof at all of his innocence, and he was at last condemned to be burned at the market-place.

After his sentence was passed, the whole body of priests made their addresses to Marquis Casteil Roderigo,[28] the then governor of Flanders, for a reprieve; which, after much ado, was granted him for some weeks, but with an absolute denial of pardon; so prevailing were the young cavaliers of his court, who were all adorers of this fair jilt.

About this time, while the poor, innocent young Henrick was thus languishing in prison, in a dark and dismal dungeon; and Miranda, cured of her love, was triumphing in her revenge, expecting, and daily gaining new conquests; and who, by this time, had re-assumed all her wonted gaiety, there was a great noise about the town, that a prince of mighty name, and famed for all the excellencies of his sex, was arrived; a prince young, and gloriously attended, called Prince Tarquin.

We had often heard of this great man, and that he was making his travels in France and Germany; and we had also heard, that some years before, he being about eighteen years of age, in the time when our King Charles of blessed memory was in Brussels,[29] in the last year of his banishment, that all on a sudden this young man rose up upon them like the sun, all-glorious and dazzling, demanding place of all the princes in that court. And when his pretence was demanded, he owned himself Prince Tarquin, of the race of the last kings of Rome,[30] made good his title, and took his place accordingly. After that, he travelled for about six years up and down the world, and then arrived at Antwerp, about the time of my being sent thither by His Late Majesty.

Perhaps there could be nothing seen so magnificent as this prince: he was, as I said, extremely handsome, from head to foot exactly formed, and he wanted nothing that might adorn that native beauty to the best advantage. His parts were suitable to the rest: he had an accomplishment fit for a prince, an air haughty, but a carriage affable, easy in conversation, and very entertaining, liberal and good-natured, brave and inoffensive. I have seen him[31] pass the streets with twelve footmen, and four pages; the pages all in green velvet coats, laced with gold,[32] and white velvet trunks; the men in cloth, richly laced with gold; his coaches, and all other officers, suitable to a great man.

He was all the discourse of the town; some laughing at his title, others reverencing it. Some cried, that he was an imposture; others, that he had made his title as plain, as if Tarquin had reigned but a year ago. Some made friendships with him, others would have nothing to say to him; but all wondered where this revenue was that supported this grandeur; and believed, though he could make his descent from the Roman kings very well out, that he could not lay so good a claim to the Roman land. Thus everybody meddled with what they had nothing to do; and, as in other places, thought themselves on the surer side, if, in these doubtful cases, they imagined the worst.

But the men might be of what opinion they pleased concerning him, the ladies were all agreed that he was a prince, and a young, handsome prince, and a prince not to be resisted. He had all their wishes, all their eyes, and all their hearts. They now dressed only for him; and what church he graced, was sure, that day, to have the beauties, and all that thought themselves so.

You may believe, our amorous Miranda was not the last conquest he made. She no sooner heard of him, which was as soon as he arrived, but she fell in love with his very name. Jesu! – A young King of Rome! Oh, 'twas so novel, that she doted on the title; and had not cared whether the rest had been man or monkey almost. She was resolved to be the Lucretia,[33] that this young Tarquin should ravish.

To this end, she was no sooner up the next day, but she sent him a *billet-doux*, assuring him how much she admired his fame; and that being a stranger in the town, she begged the honour of introducing him to all the belle-conversations, etc. Which he took for the invitation of some coquet, who had interest in fair ladies; and civilly returned her an answer, that he would wait on her. She had him that day watched to church; and impatient to see what she heard so many people flock to see, she went also to the same church; those sanctified abodes being too often profaned by such devotees, whose business is to ogle and ensnare.

But what a noise and humming was heard all over the church when Tarquin entered; his grace, his mien, his fashion, his beauty, his dress, and his equipage surprised all that were present; and by the good management and care of Miranda, she got to kneel at the side of the altar, just over against the Prince; so that, if he would, he could not avoid looking full upon her. She had turned up her veil, and all her face and shape appeared such, and so enchanting as I have described; and her beauty heightened with blushes, and her eyes full of spirit and fire, with joy to find the young Roman monarch so charming, she appeared like something more than mortal, and compelled his eyes to a fixed gazing on her face. She never glanced that way, but she met them; and then would feign so modest a shame, and cast her eyes downward with such inviting art, that he was wholly ravished and charmed, and she overjoyed to find he was so.

The ceremony being ended, he sent a page to follow that lady home, himself pursuing her to the door of the church; where he took some holy water, and threw upon her, and made her a profound reverence. She forced an innocent look, and a modest gratitude in her face, and bowed, and passed forward, half assured of her conquest; leaving him to go home to his lodging, and impatiently wait the return of his page. And all the ladies who saw this first beginning between the prince and Miranda, began to curse and envy her charms, who had deprived them of half their hopes.

After this, I need not tell you, he made Miranda a visit; and from that day, never left her apartment, but when he went home at nights, or unless he had business; so entirely was he conquered by this fair one. But the bishop, and several men of quality in orders, that professed friendship to him, advised him from her company; and spoke several things to him, that might (if love had not made him blind) have reclaimed him from the pursuit of his ruin. But whatever they trusted him with, she had the art to wind herself about his heart, and make him unravel all his secrets; and then knew as well, by feigned sighs and tears, to make him disbelieve all. So that he had no faith, but for her; and was wholly enchanted and bewitched by her, at last, in spite of all that would have opposed it, he married this famous woman, possessed by so many great men and strangers before, while all the world was pitying his shame and misfortunes.

Being married, they took a great house; and as she was indeed a great fortune, and now a great princess, there was nothing wanting that was agreeable to their quality; all was splendid and magnificent. But all this would not acquire them the world's esteem; they had an abhorrence for her former life, despised her, and for his espousing a woman so infamous, they despised him. So that though they admired, and gazed upon their equipage, and glorious dress, they foresaw the ruin that attended it; and paid her quality very little respect.

She was no sooner married, but her uncle died; and dividing his fortune between Miranda and her sister, leaves the young heiress, and all her fortune, entirely in the hands of the princess.

We will call this sister Alcidiana; she was about fourteen years of age, and now had chosen her brother, the prince, for her guardian.

If Alcidiana were not altogether so great a beauty as her sister, she had charms sufficient to procure her a great many lovers, though her fortune had not been so considerable as it was; but with that addition, you may believe, she wanted no courtships from those of the best quality; though everybody deplored her being under the tutorage of a lady so expert in all the vices of her sex, and so cunning a manager of sin, as was the princess; who, on her part, failed not, by all the caresses, and obliging endearments, to engage the mind of this young maid, and to subdue her wholly to her government. All her senses were eternally regaled with the most bewitching pleasures they were capable of: she saw nothing but glory and magnificence, heard nothing but music of the sweetest sounds; the richest perfumes employed her smelling, and all she ate and touched was delicate and inviting; and being too young to consider how this state and grandeur was to be continued, little imagined her vast fortune was every day diminishing, towards its needless support.

When the princess went to church, she had her gentleman bare [34] before her, carrying a great velvet cushion, with great golden tassels, for her to kneel on, and her train borne up a most prodigious length; led by a gentleman-usher, bare; followed by innumerable footmen, pages and women. And in this state she would walk in the streets, as in those countries 'tis the fashion for the great ladies to do, who are well; and in her train, two or three coaches, and perhaps a rich velvet chair embroidered, would follow in state.

'Twas thus for some time they lived, and the princess was daily pressed by young sighing lovers, for her consent to marry Alcidiana; but she had still one art or other to put them off, and so continually broke all the great matches that were proposed to her, notwithstanding their kindred, and other friends, had industriously endeavoured to make several great matches for her; but the princess was still positive in her denial, and one way or other broke all. At last it happened, there was one proposed yet more advantageous; a young count, with whom the young maid grew passionately in love, and besought her sister to consent that she might have him, and got the prince to speak in her behalf; but he had no sooner heard the secret reasons Miranda gave him, but (entirely her slave) he changed his mind, and suited it to hers, and she, as before, broke off that amour; which so extremely incensed Alcidiana, that she, taking an opportunity, got from her guard, and ran away, putting herself into the hands of a wealthy merchant, her kinsman, and one who bore the greatest authority in the city; him she chooses for her guardian, resolving to be no longer a slave to the tyranny of her sister. And so well she ordered matters, that she writ to this young cavalier, her last lover, and retrieved him; who came back to Antwerp again, to renew his courtship.

Both parties being agreed, it was no hard matter to persuade all but the princess; but though she opposed it, it was resolved on, and the day appointed for marriage, and the portion demanded; demanded only, but never to be paid, the best part of it being spent. However, she put them off from day to day, by a thousand frivolous delays. And when she saw they would have recourse to force, and that all her magnificence would be at an end, if the law should prevail against her; and that, without this sister's fortune, she could not long support her grandeur, she bethought herself of a means to make it all her own, by getting her sister made away; but she being out of her tuition,[35] she was not able to accomplish so great a deed of darkness. But since 'twas resolved it must be done, she revolves on a thousand stratagems; and at last, pitches upon an effectual one.

She had a page, called Van Brune, a youth of great address and wit, and one she had long managed for her purpose. This youth was about seventeen years of age, and extremely beautiful; and in the time when Alcidiana lived with the princess, she was a little in love with this handsome boy; but 'twas checked in its infancy, and never grew up to a flame. Nevertheless, Alcidiana retained still a sort of tenderness for him, while he burned in good earnest with love for the princess.

The princess one day ordering this page to wait on her in her closet, she shut the door; and after a thousand questions of what he would undertake to serve her, the amorous boy, finding himself alone, and caressed by the fair person he adored, with joyful blushes, that beautified his face, told her, there was nothing upon earth, he would not do, to obey her least commands. She grew more familiar with him, to oblige him; and seeing love dance in his eyes, of which she was so good a judge, she treated him more like a lover, than a servant; till at last the ravished youth, wholly transported out of himself, fell at her feet, and impatiently implored to receive her commands quickly, that he might fly to execute them; for he was not able to bear her charming words, looks and touches, and retain his duty. At this she smiled, and told him, the work was of such a nature, as would mortify all flames about him; and he would have more need of rage, envy and malice, than the aids of a passion so soft as what she now found him capable of. He assured her, he would stick at nothing, though even against his nature, to recompense for the boldness he now, through indiscretion, had discovered. She smiling, told him, he had committed no fault; and that possibly, the pay he should receive for the service she required at his hands, should be – what he most wished for in the world. To this he bowed to the earth; and kissing her feet, bade her command. And then she boldly told him, 'twas to kill her sister Alcidiana. The youth, without so much as starting, or pausing upon the matter, told her, it should be done; and bowing low, immediately went out of the closet. She called him back, and would have given him some instruction; but he refused it, and said, the action, and the contrivance should be all his own. And offering to go again, she – again recalled him; putting into his hand a purse of a hundred pistoles, which he took; and with a low bow, departed.

He no sooner left her presence, but he goes directly and buys a dose of poison, and went immediately to the house where Alcidiana lived; where, desiring to be brought to her presence, he fell a-weeping; and told her, his lady had fallen out with him, and dismissed him her service; and since, from a child, he had been brought up in the family, he humbly besought Alcidiana to receive him into hers, she being in a few days to be married. There needed not much entreaty to a thing that pleased her so well, and she immediately received him to pension.[36] And he waited some days on her, before he could get an opportunity to administer his devilish potion. But one night, when she drank wine with roasted apples, which was usual with her; instead of sugar, or with the sugar, the baneful drug was mixed, and she drank it down.

About this time there was a great talk of this page's coming from one sister, to go to the other. And Prince Tarquin, who was ignorant of the design, from the beginning to the end, hearing some men of quality at his table speaking of Van Brune's change of place (the princess then keeping her chamber upon some trifling indisposition) he answered, that surely they were mistaken, that he was not dismissed from the princess's service. And calling some of his servants, he asked for Van Brune; and whether anything had happened between Her Highness and him, that had occasioned his being turned off. They all seemed ignorant of this matter; and those who had spoke of it, began to fancy there was some juggle[37] in the case, which time would bring to light.

The ensuing day 'twas all about the town, that Alcidiana was poisoned; and though not dead, yet very near it; and that the doctors said, she had taken mercury. So that there was never so formidable a sight as this fair young creature; her head and body swollen, her eyes starting out, her face black, and all deformed; so that diligent search was made, who it should be that did this; who gave her drink and meat. The cook and butler were examined, the footmen called to an account; but all concluded, she received nothing, but from the hand of her new page, since he came into her service. He was examined, and showed a thousand guilty looks. And the apothecary, then attending among the doctors, proved he had bought mercury of him three or four days before; which he could not deny; and making excuses for his buying it, betrayed him the more; so ill he chanced to dissemble. He was immediately sent to be examined by the Margrave[38] or Justice, who made his mittimus,[39] and sent him to prison.

'Tis easy to imagine in what fears and confusion the princess was at this news. She took her chamber upon it, more to hide her guilty face, than for any indisposition. And the doctors applied such remedies to Alcidiana, such antidotes against the poison, that in a short time she recovered; but lost the finest hair in the world, and the complexion of her face ever after.

It was not long before the trials for criminals came on; and the day being arrived, Van Brune was tried the first of all; everybody having already read his destiny, according as they wished it; and none would believe, but just indeed as it was; so that for the revenge they hoped to see fall upon the princess, everyone wished he might find no mercy, that she might share of his shame and misery.

The sessions-house was filled that day with all the ladies, and chief of the town, to hear the result of his trial; and the sad youth was brought loaded with chains, and pale as death; where every circumstance being sufficiently proved against him, and he making but a weak defence for himself, he was convicted, and sent back to prison, to receive his sentence of death on the morrow; where he owned all, and who set him on to do it. He owned 'twas not reward of gain he did it for, but hope he should command at his pleasure, the possession of his mistress, the princess; who should deny him nothing, after having entrusted him with so great a secret; and that besides, she had elevated him with the promise of that glorious reward, and had dazzled his young heart with so charming a prospect, that blind and mad with joy, he rushed forward, to gain the desired prize; and thought on nothing but his coming happiness; that he saw too late the follies of his presumptuous flame, and cursed the deluding flatteries of the fair hypocrite, who had soothed him to his undoing; that he was a miserable victim to her wickedness, and hoped he should warn all young men, by his fall, to avoid the dissimulation of the deceiving fair; that he hoped they would have pity on his youth, and attribute his crime to the subtle persuasions alone of his mistress, the princess: and that since Alcidiana was not dead, they would grant him mercy, and permit him to live to repent of his grievous crime, in some part of the world, whither they might banish him.

He ended with tears, that fell in abundance from his eyes; and immediately the princess was apprehended, and brought to prison, to the same prison where yet the poor young Father Francisco was languishing, he having been from week to week reprieved, by the intercession of the fathers; and possibly, she there had time to make some reflections.

You may imagine Tarquin left no means unessayed, to prevent the imprisonment of the princess, and the public shame and infamy she was likely to undergo in this affair. But the whole city being overjoyed that she should be punished, as an author of all this mischief, were so generally bent against her, both priests, magistrates and people; the whole force of the stream running that way, she found no more favour than the meanest criminal. The prince therefore, when he saw 'twas impossible to rescue her from the hands of justice, suffered with grief unspeakable what he could not prevent; and led her himself to the prison, followed by all his people, in as much state, as if he had been going to his marriage; where, when she came, she was as well attended and served as before, he never stirring one moment from her.

The next day she was tried in open and common court; where she appeared in glory, led by Tarquin, and attended according to her quality. And she could not deny all the page had alleged against her, who was brought thither also in chains; and after a great many circumstances, she was found guilty, and both received sentence; the page to be hanged, till he was dead, on a gibbet in the market-place; and the princess to stand under the gibbet, with a rope about her neck, the other end of which was to be fastened to the gibbet where the page was hanging; and to have an inscription in large characters upon her back and breast, of the cause why; where she was to stand from ten in the morning, to twelve.

This sentence, the people, with one accord, believed too favourable for so ill a woman, whose crimes deserved death, equal to that of Van Brune. Nevertheless, there were some who said, it was infinitely more severe than the death itself.

The following Friday was the day of execution, and one need not tell of the abundance of people, who were flocked together in the market-place. All the windows were taken down, and filled with spectators, and the tops of houses, when, at the hour appointed, the fatal beauty appeared. She was dressed in a black velvet gown, with a rich row of diamonds all down the fore-part of the breast, and a great knot of diamonds at the peak behind; and a petticoat of flowered gold, very rich, and laced;[40] with all things else suitable. A gentleman carried her great velvet cushion before her, on which her prayer-book, embroidered, was laid; her train was borne up by a page, and the prince led her, bare;[41] followed by his footmen, pages, and other officers of his house.

When they arrived to the place of execution, the cushion was laid on the ground, upon a Portugal-mat,[42] spread there for that purpose; and the princess stood on the cushion, with her prayer-book in her hand, and a priest by her side; and was accordingly tied up to the gibbet.

She had not stood there ten minutes, but she had the mortification (at least, one would think it so to her) to see her sad page Van Brune approach; fair as an angel, but languishing and pale. That sight moved all the beholders with as much pity, as that of the princess did disdain and pleasure.

He was dressed all in mourning, and very fine linen; bare-headed, with his own hair, the fairest that could be seen, hanging all in curls on his back and shoulders, very long. He had a prayer-book of black velvet in his hand, and behaved himself with much penitence and devotion.

When he was brought under the gibbet, he seeing his mistress in that condition, showed an infinite concern, and his fair face was covered over with blushes; and falling at her feet, he humbly asked her pardon for having been the occasion of so great an infamy to her, by a weak confession, which the fears of youth, and hopes of life, had obliged him to make, so greatly to her dishonour; for, indeed, he had wanted that manly strength, to bear the efforts of dying as he ought, in silence, rather than of committing so great a crime against his duty, and honour itself; and that he could not die in peace, unless she would forgive him. The princess only nodded her head, and cried, 'I do.'

And after having spoken a little to his father confessor, who was with him, he cheerfully mounted the ladder; and in the sight of the princess, he was turned off, while a loud cry was heard through all the market-place, especially from the fair sex; he hanging there till the time the princess was to depart. And when she was put into a rich embroidered chair, and carried away; Tarquin going into his; for he had all that time stood supporting the princess under the gallows, and was very weary, she was sent back, till her releasement came; which was that night, about seven of the clock; and then she was conducted to her own house in great state, with a dozen white wax flambeaux about her chair.

If the affairs of Alcidiana and her friends before were impatient of having the portion out of the hands of these extravagants, 'tis not to be imagined, but they were now much more so; and the next day they sent an officer, according to law, to demand it; or to summon the prince to give reasons, why he would not. And the officer received for answer, that the money should be called in, and paid in such a time; setting a certain time, which I have not been so curious as to retain, or put in my journal observations; but I am sure it was not long, as may be easily imagined; for they every moment suspected the prince would pack up, and be gone some time or other on the sudden; and for that reason they would not trust him without bail, or two officers to remain in his house, to watch that nothing should be removed or touched. As for bail, or security, he could give none; everyone slunk their heads out of the collar when it came to that; so that he was obliged, at his own expense, to maintain officers in his house.

The princess finding herself reduced to the last extremity, and that she must either produce the value of a hundred thousand crowns, or see the prince, her husband, lodged for ever in a prison, and all their glory vanish; and that it was impossible to fly, since guarded; she had recourse to an extremity, worse than the affair of Van Brune. And in order to this, she first puts on a world of sorrow and concern, for what she feared might arrive to the prince; and indeed, if ever she shed tears which she did not dissemble, it was upon this occasion. But here she almost over-acted: she stirred not from her bed, and refused to eat, or sleep, or see the light; so that the day being shut out of her chamber, she lived by wax-lights, and refused all comfort and consolation.

The prince, all raving with love, tender compassion and grief, never stirred from her bedside, nor ceased to implore, that she would suffer herself to live. But she, who was not now so passionately in love with Tarquin, as she was with the prince; not so fond of the man, as his titles, and of glory, foresaw the total ruin of the last, if not prevented, by avoiding the payment of this great sum; which could no otherwise be, than by the death of Alcidiana. And therefore, without ceasing, she wept, and cried out, she could not live, unless Alcidiana died. 'This Alcidiana,' continued she, 'who has been the author of my shame; who has exposed me under a gibbet, in the public market-place. – Oh! – I am deaf to all reason, blind to natural affection. I renounce her. I hate her as my mortal foe, my stop to glory, and the finisher of my days, e'er half my race of life be run.'

Then throwing her false, but snowy, charming arms about the neck of her heart-breaking lord, and lover, who lay sighing and listening by her side, he was charmed and bewitched into saying all things that appeased her. And lastly, told her, Alcidiana should be no longer an obstacle to her repose; but that, if she would look up, and cast her eyes of sweetness and love upon him, as heretofore; forget her sorrows, and redeem her lost health, he would take what measures she should propose, to dispatch this fatal stop to her happiness out of the way.

These words failed not to make her caress him in the most endearing manner that love and flattery could invent; and she kissed him to an oath, a solemn oath, to perform what he had promised; and he vowed liberally. And she assumed in an instant her good humour, and suffered a supper to be prepared, and did eat; which in many days before she had not done; so obstinate and powerful was she in dissembling well.

The next thing to be considered was, which way this deed was to be done; for they doubted not, but when 'twas done, all the world would lay it upon the princess, as done by her command. But she urged, suspicion was no proof; and that they never put to death anyone, but when they had great and certain evidences, who were the offenders. She was sure of her own constancy, that racks and tortures should never get the secret from her breast; and if he were as confident on his part, there was no danger. Yet this preparation she made, towards the laying the fact on others, that she caused several letters to be written from Germany, as from the relations of Van Brune, who threatened Alcidiana with death, for depriving their kinsman (who was a gentleman) of his life, though he had not taken away hers. And it was the report of the town, how this young maid was threatened. And indeed, the death of the page had so afflicted a great many, that Alcidiana had procured herself abundance of enemies upon that account, because she might have saved him if she had pleased; but on the contrary, she was a spectator, and in full health and vigour, at his execution. And people were not so much concerned for her at this report, as they would have been.

The Prince, who now had, by reasoning the matter soberly with Miranda, found it absolutely necessary to dispatch Alcidiana; he resolved himself, and with his own hand, to execute it; not daring to trust to any of his most favourite servants, though he had many who, possibly, would have obeyed him; for they loved him, as he deserved; and so would all the world, had he not been so poorly deluded by this fair enchantress. He therefore, as I said, resolved to keep this great secret to himself; and taking a pistol, charged well with two bullets, he watched an opportunity to shoot her as she should go out, or into her house or coach some evening.

To this end he waited several nights, near her lodgings; but still, either she went not out; or when she returned, she was so guarded with friends, or her lover, and flambeaux, that he could not aim at her, without endangering the life of some other. But one night, above the rest, upon a Sunday, when he knew she would be at the theatre; for she never missed that day, seeing the play; he waited at the corner of the state-house,[43] near the theatre, with his cloak cast over his face, and a black periwig, all alone, with his pistol ready cocked; and remained not very long, but he saw her kinsman's coach come along. 'Twas almost dark; day was just shutting up her beauties, and left such a light to govern the world, as served only just to distinguish one object from another, and a convenient help to mischief. He saw alight out of the coach, only one young lady, the lover, and then the destined victim; which he (drawing near) knew rather by her tongue, than shape. The lady ran into the playhouse, and left Alcidiana to be conducted by her lover into it; who led her to the door, and went to give some order to the coachman; so that the lover was about twenty yards from Alcidiana, when she stood the fairest mark in the world, on the threshold of the entrance of the theatre; there being many coaches about the door, so that hers could not come so near. Tarquin was resolved not to lose so fair an opportunity; and advanced, but went behind the coaches; and when he came over against the door, through a great booted, velvet coach,[44] that stood between him and her, he shot; and she having her train of her gown and petticoat on her arm, in great quantity, he missed her body, and shot through her clothes, between her arm, and her body. She, frightened to find something hit her, and to see the smoke, and hear the report of the pistol, running in, cried, 'I am shot, I am dead.'

This noise quickly alarmed her lover; and all the coachmen and footmen immediately ran, some one way, and some another. One of them seeing a man haste away in a cloak, he being a lusty, bold German, stopped him; and drawing upon him, bade him stand, and deliver his pistol, or he would run him through.

Tarquin being surprised at the boldness of this fellow to demand his pistol, as if he positively knew him to be the murderer (for so he thought himself, since he believed Alcidiana dead), had so much presence of mind, as to consider, if he suffered himself to be taken, he should poorly die a public death; and therefore resolved upon one mischief more, to secure himself from the first. And in the moment that the German bade him deliver his pistol, he cried, 'Though I have no pistol to deliver, I have a sword to chastise thy insolence.' And throwing off his cloak, and flinging his pistol from him, he drew, and wounded and disarmed the fellow.

This noise of swords brought everybody to the place; and immediately the bruit[45] ran, The murderer was taken, the murderer was taken; though none knew which was he, nor the cause of the quarrel between the two fighting men, which none yet knew, for it now was darker than before. But at the noise of the murderer being taken, the lover of Alcidiana, who by this time found his lady unhurt, all but the trains of her gown and petticoat, came running to the place, just as Tarquin had disarmed the German, and was ready to have killed him; when laying hold of his arm, they arrested the stroke, and redeemed the footman.

They then demanded who this stranger was, at whose mercy the fellow lay; but the prince, who now found himself venturing for his last stake, made no reply; but with two swords in his hands, went to fight his way through the rabble. And though there were above a hundred persons, some with swords, others with long whips (as coachmen), so invincible was the courage of this poor, unfortunate gentleman at that time, that all these were not able to seize him; but he made his way through the ring that encompassed him, and ran away; but was however so closely pursued, the company still gathering as they ran, that toiled with fighting, oppressed with guilt, and fear of being taken, he grew fainter and fainter, and suffered himself, at last, to yield to his pursuers, who soon found him to be Prince Tarquin in disguise. And they carried him directly to prison, being Sunday, to wait the coming day, to go before a magistrate.

In an hour's time the whole fatal adventure was carried all over the city, and everyone knew that Prince Tarquin was the intended murderer of Alcidiana; and not one but had a real sorrow and compassion for him. They heard how bravely he had defended himself, how many he had wounded before he could be taken, and what numbers he had fought through; and even those that saw his valour and bravery, and who had assisted at his being seized, now repented from the bottom of their hearts, their having any hand in the ruin of so gallant a man; especially, since they knew the lady was not hurt. A thousand addresses were made to her, not to prosecute him; but her lover, a hot-headed fellow, more fierce than brave, would by no means be pacified; but vowed to pursue him to the scaffold.

The Monday came, and the prince being examined, confessed the matter of fact, since there was no harm done; believing a generous confession the best of his game; but he was sent back to closer imprisonment, loaded with irons, to expect the next sessions. All his household goods were seized, and all they could find, for the use of Alcidiana. And the princess, all in rage, tearing her hair, was carried to the same prison, to behold the cruel effects of her hellish designs.

One need not tell here how sad and horrid this meeting appeared between her lord and she; let it suffice it was the most melancholy and mortifying object that ever eyes beheld. On Miranda's part, 'twas sometimes all rage and fire, and sometimes all tears and groans; but still 'twas sad love, and mournful tenderness on his.

Nor could all his sufferings, and the prospect of death itself, drive from his soul one spark of that fire the obstinate god had fatally kindled there. And in the midst of all his sighs, he would recall himself, and cry, 'I have Miranda still.'

He was eternally visited by his friends and acquaintance; and this last action of bravery had got him more, than all his former conduct had lost. The fathers were perpetually with him; and all joined with one common voice in this, that he ought to abandon a woman so wicked as the princess; and that however Fate dealt with him, he could not show himself a true penitent, while he laid the author of so much evil in his bosom; that Heaven would never bless him, till he had renounced her. And on such conditions, he would find those that would employ their utmost interest to save his life, who else would not stir in his affair. But he was so deaf to all, that he could not so much as dissemble a repentance for having married her.

He lay a long time in prison, and all that time the poor Father Francisco remained there also; and the good fathers, who daily visited these two amorous prisoners, the prince and princess, and who found, by the management of matters, it would go very hard with Tarquin, entertained them often with holy matters relating to the life to come; from which, before his trial, he gathered what his stars had appointed, and that he was destined to die.

This gave an unspeakable torment to the now-repenting beauty, who had reduced him to it; and she began to appear with a more solid grief. Which being perceived by the good fathers, they resolved to attack her on the yielding side; and after some discourse upon the judgment for sin, they came to reflect on the business of Father Francisco; and told her, she had never thrived since her accusing of that father, and laid it very home to her conscience; assuring her, that they would do their utmost in her service, if she would confess that secret sin to all the world; so that she might atone for the crime, by the saving that good man. At first she seemed inclined to yield; but shame of being her own detector in so vile a matter, recalled her goodness, and she faintly persisted in it.

At the end of six months, Prince Tarquin was called to his trial; where I will pass over the circumstances, which are only what is usual in such criminal cases, and tell you, that he, being found guilty of the intent of killing Alcidiana, was condemned to lose his head in the market-place, and the princess to be banished her country.

After sentence pronounced, to the real grief of all the spectators, he was carried back to prison. And now the fathers attack her anew; and the whole griefs daily increased, with a languishment that brought her very near her grave, at last confessed all her life, all the lewdness of her practices with several princes and great men, besides her lusts with people that served her, and others in mean capacity; and lastly, the whole truth of the young friar; and how she had drawn the page, and the prince, her husband, to this designed murder of her sister. This she signed with her hand, in the presence of the prince, her husband, and several holy men who were present. Which being signified to the magistrates, the friar was immediately delivered from his irons (where he had languished more than two whole years) in great triumph, and with much honour, and lives a most exemplary pious life, and as he did before; for he is yet living in Antwerp.

After the condemnation of these two unfortunate persons, who begot such different sentiments in the minds of the people (the prince, all the compassion and pity imaginable; and the princess, all the contempt and despite); they languished almost six months longer in prison; so great an interest there was made, in order to the saving his life, by all the men of the robe. On the other side, the princes, and great men of all nations, who were at the court of Brussels, who bore a secret revenge in their hearts against a man who had, as they pretended, set up a false title, only to take place of them; who, indeed, was but a merchant's son of Holland, as they said, so incensed them against him, that they were too hard at court for the churchmen. However, this dispute gave the prince his life some months longer than was expected; which gave him also some hope, that a reprieve for ninety years would have been granted, as was desired. Nay, Father Francisco so interested himself in this concern, that he writ to his father, and several princes of Germany, with whom Marquis Casteil de Roderigo was well acquainted, to intercede with him for the saving of Tarquin; since 'twas more by his persuasions, than those of all who attacked her, that made Miranda confess the truth of her affair with him. But at the end of six months, when all applications were found fruitless and vain, the prince received news, that in two days he was to die, as his sentence had been before pronounced; and for which he prepared himself with all cheerfulness.

On the following Friday, as soon as it was light, all people of any condition came to take their leaves of him, and none departed with dry eyes, or hearts unconcerned to the last degree. For Tarquin, when he found his fate inevitable, bore it with a fortitude that showed no signs of regret; but addressed himself to all about him with the same cheerful, modest and great air, he was wont to do in his most flourishing fortune. His valet was dressing him all the morning, so many interruptions they had by visitors; and he was all in mourning, and so were all his followers; for even to the last, he kept up his grandeur, to the amazement of all people. And indeed, he was so passionately beloved by them, that those he had dismissed served him voluntarily, and would not be persuaded to abandon him while he lived.

The princess was also dressed in mourning, and her two women; and notwithstanding the unheard-of lewdness and villainies she had confessed of herself, the prince still adored her, for she had still those charms that made him first do so; nor, to his last moment, could be brought to wish that he had never seen her. But on the contrary, as a man yet vainly proud of his fetters, he said, all the satisfaction this short moment of life could afford him was, that he died in endeavouring to serve Miranda, his adorable princess.

After he had taken leave of all who thought it necessary to leave him to himself for some time, he retired with his confessor, where they were about an hour in prayer, all the ceremonies of devotions that were fit to be done being already past. At last the bell tolled, and he was to take leave of the princess, as his last work of life, and the most hard he had to accomplish. He threw himself at her feet; and gazing on her, as she sat more dead than alive, o'erwhelmed with silent grief, they both remained some moments speechless; and then, as if one rising tide of tears had supplied both their eyes, it burst out in streams at the same instant; and when his sighs gave way, he uttered a thousand farewells, so soft, so passionate and moving, that all who were by were extremely touched with it, and said, that nothing could be seen more deplorable and melancholy. A thousand times they bade farewell, and still some tender look or word would prevent his going; then embrace, and bid farewell again. A thousand times she asked his pardon for being the occasion of that fatal separation; a thousand times assuring him, she would follow him, for she could not live without him. And Heaven knows when their soft and sad caresses would have ended, had not the officers assured him, 'twas time to mount the scaffold. At which words the princess fell fainting in the arms of her women, and they led Tarquin out of the prison.

When he came to the market-place, whither he walked on foot, followed by his own domestics and some bearing a black velvet coffin, with silver hinges; the headsman before him, with his fatal scimitar drawn; his confessor by his side, and many gentlemen and churchmen, with Father Francisco, attending him; the people showering millions of blessings on him, and beholding with weeping eyes, he mounted the scaffold, which was strewed with some sawdust about the place where he was to kneel, to receive the blood. For they behead people kneeling, and with the back-stroke of a scimitar; and not lying on a block, and with an axe, as we in England. The scaffold had a low rail about it, that everybody might more conveniently see; this was hung with black, and all that state that such a death could have, was here in most decent order.

He did not say much upon the scaffold. The sum of what he said to his friends was, to be kind, and take care of the poor penitent, his wife; to others, recommending his honest and generous servants, whose fidelity was so well known and commended, that they were soon promised all preferment. He was some time in prayer, and a very short time speaking to his confessor; then he turned to the headsman, and desired him to do his office well, and gave him twenty *Louis d'or*;[46] and undressing himself with the help of his valet and page, he pulled off his coat, and had underneath a white satin waistcoat. He took off his periwig, and put on a white satin cap, with a holland one, done with point,[47] under it, which he pulled a little over his eyes; then took a

cheerful leave of all, and kneeled down, and said, when he lifted
up his hands the third time, the headsman should do his office.
Which accordingly was done, and the headsman gave him his last
stroke, and the prince fell on the scaffold. The people, with one
common voice, as if it had been but one entire one, prayed for his
soul, and murmurs of sighs were heard from the whole multitude,
who scrambled for some of the bloody sawdust, to keep for his
memory.

The headsman going to take up the head, as the manner is, to
show to the people, he found he had not struck it off, and that the
body stirred. With that he stepped to an engine which they always
carry with them, to force those who may be refractory, thinking,
as he said, to have twisted the head from the shoulders, conceiving
it to hang but by a small matter of flesh. Though 'twas an odd
shift of the fellow's, yet 'twas done, and the best shift he could
suddenly propose. The Margrave and another officer, old men,
were on the scaffold, with some of the prince's friends and
servants; who seeing the headsman put the engine about the neck
of the prince, began to call out, and the people made a great
noise. The prince, who found himself yet alive; or rather, who
was past thinking, but had some sense of feeling left, when the
headsman took him up, and set his back against the rail, and
clapped the engine about his neck, got his two thumbs between
the rope and his neck, feeling himself pressed there; and struggling
between life and death, and bending himself over the rail back-
ward, while the headsman pulled forward, he threw himself quite
over the rail by chance, and not design, and fell upon the heads
and shoulders of the people, who were crying out with amazing
shouts of joy. The headsman leapt after him, but the rabble had
like to have pulled him to pieces. All the city was in an uproar,
but none knew what the matter was, but those who bore the body
of the prince, whom they found yet living; but how, or by what
strange miracle preserved, they knew not, nor did examine; but
with one accord, as if the whole crowd had been one body, and
had but one motion, they bore the prince on their heads, about a
hundred yards from the scaffold, where there is a monastery of
Jesuits; and there they secured him. All this was done, his behead-
ing, his falling, and his being secured, almost in a moment's time;

the people rejoicing, as at some extraordinary victory won. One of the officers being, as I said, an old, timorous man, was so frightened at the accident, the bustle, the noise, and the confusion, of which he was wholly ignorant, that he died with amazement and fear; and the other was fain to be let blood.[48]

The officers of justice went to demand the prisoner, but they demanded in vain; they had now a right to protect him, and would do so. All his overjoyed friends went to see in what condition he was, and all of quality found admittance. They saw him in bed, going to be dressed by the most skilful surgeons, who yet could not assure him of life. They desired nobody should speak to him, or ask him any questions. They found that the headsman had struck him too low, and had cut him into the shoulder-bone. A very great wound, you may be sure; for the sword, in such executions, carries an extreme force. However, so good care was taken on all sides, and so greatly the fathers were concerned for him, that they found an amendment, and hopes of a good effect of their incomparable charity and goodness.

At last, when he was permitted to speak, the first news he asked was after the princess. And his friends were very much afflicted to find that all his loss of blood had not quenched that flame, nor let out that which made him still love that bad woman. He was solicited daily to think no more of her; and all her crimes were laid so open to him, and so shamefully represented, and on the other side, his virtues so admired; and which, they said, would have been eternally celebrated, but for his folly with this infamous creature; that at last, by assuring him of all their assistance if he abandoned her, and to renounce him, and deliver him up, if he did not, they wrought so far upon him, as to promise he would suffer her to go alone into banishment, and would not follow her, or live with her any more. But, alas! this was but his gratitude that compelled this complaisance, for in his heart he resolved never to abandon her; nor was he able to live, and think of doing it. However, his reason assured him, he could not do a deed more justifiable, and one that would regain his fame sooner.

His friends asked him some questions concerning his escape; and that since he was not beheaded, but only wounded, why he did not immediately rise up. But he replied, he was so absolutely prepossessed, that at the third lifting up his hands, he should receive the stroke of death, that at the same instant the sword touched him, he had no sense, nay, not even of pain, so absolutely dead he was with imagination; and knew not that he stirred, as the headsman found he did; nor did he remember anything, from the lifting up of his hands, to his fall; and then awakened, as out of a dream, or rather a moment's sleep, without dream, he found he lived; and wondered what was arrived to him, or how he came to live, having not, as yet, any sense of his wound, though so terrible a one.

After this, Alcidiana, who was extremely afflicted for having been the prosecutor of this great man; who, bating[49] his last design against her, which she knew was the instigation of her sister, had obliged her with all the civility imaginable; now sought all means possible of getting his pardon, and that of her sister; though of a hundred thousand crowns which she should have paid her she could get but ten thousand; which was from the sale of her rich beds, and some other furniture. So that the young count, who before should have married her, now went off for want of fortune; and a young merchant (perhaps the best of the two) was the man to whom she was destined.

At last, by great intercession, both their pardons were obtained; and the prince, who would be no more seen in a place that had proved every way so fatal to him, left Flanders, promising never to live with the fair hypocrite more; but e'er he departed, he writ her a letter, wherein he ordered her, in a little time, to follow him into Holland; and left a bill of exchange with one of his trusty servants, whom he had left to wait upon her, for money for her accommodations, so that she was now reduced to one woman, one page, and this gentleman. The prince, in this time of his imprisonment, had several bills of great sums from his father, who was exceeding rich, and this all the children he had in the world, and whom he tenderly loved.

As soon as Miranda was come into Holland, she was welcomed with all imaginable respect and endearment by the old father; who was imposed upon so, as that he knew not she was the fatal occasion of all these disasters to his son, but rather looked on her as a woman who had brought him a hundred and fifty thousand

crowns, which his misfortunes had consumed. But, above all, she
was received by Tarquin with a joy unspeakable; who, after some
time, to redeem his credit, and gain himself a new fame, put
himself into the French army, where he did wonders; and after
three campaigns,[50] his father dying, he returned home, and retired
to a country house, where, with his princess, he lives as a private
gentleman, in all the tranquillity of a man of a good fortune. They
say Miranda has been very penitent for her life past, and gives
Heaven the glory for having given her these afflictions, that have
reclaimed her, and brought her to as perfect a state of happiness
as this troublesome world can afford.

Since I began this relation, I heard that Prince Tarquin died
about three quarters of a year ago.

OROONOKO [1]

OR

THE ROYAL SLAVE

A TRUE HISTORY

I DO not pretend, in giving you the history of this royal slave, to entertain my reader with the adventures of a feigned hero, whose life and fortunes fancy may manage at the poet's pleasure; nor in relating the truth, design to adorn it with any accidents, but such as arrived in earnest to him. And it shall come simply into the world, recommended by its own proper merits, and natural intrigues; there being enough of reality to support it, and to render it diverting, without the addition of invention.

I was myself an eye-witness, to a great part, of what you will find here set down; and what I could not be witness of, I received from the mouth of the chief actor in this history, the hero himself, who gave us the whole transactions of his youth; and though I shall omit, for brevity's sake, a thousand little accidents of his life, which, however pleasant to us, where history was scarce, and adventures very rare; yet might prove tedious and heavy to my reader, in a world where he finds diversions for every minute, new and strange. But we who were perfectly charmed with the character of this great man, were curious to gather every circumstance of his life.[2]

The scene of the last part of his adventures lies in a colony in America, called Surinam,[3] in the West Indies.

But before I give you the story of this gallant slave, 'tis fit I tell you the manner of bringing them to these new colonies; for those they make use of there, are not natives of the place;[4] for those we live with in perfect amity, without daring to command them; but on the contrary, caress them with all the brotherly and friendly affection in the world; trading with them for their fish, venison, buffaloes, skins, and little rarities; as marmosets, a sort of monkey as big as a rat or weasel, but of a marvellous and delicate shape, and has face and hands like an human creature; and cousheries,[5] a little beast in the form and fashion of a lion, as big as a kitten; but so exactly made in all parts like that noble beast, that it is it in miniature. Then for little parakeets, great parrots, macaws, and a thousand other birds and beasts of wonderful and surprising forms, shapes, and colours. For skins of prodigious snakes, of which there are some threescore yards in length; as is the skin of one that may be seen at His Majesty's Antiquaries, where are also some rare flies,[6] of amazing forms and colours, presented to them

75

by myself, some as big as my fist, some less; and all of various excellencies, such as art cannot imitate. Then we trade for feathers, which they order into all shapes, make themselves little short habits of them, and glorious wreaths for their heads, necks, arms and legs, whose tinctures are inconceivable. I had a set of these presented to me, and I gave them to the King's Theatre, and it was the dress of the *Indian Queen*,[7] infinitely admired by persons of quality, and were inimitable. Besides these, a thousand little knacks, and rarities in Nature, and some of art; as their baskets, weapons, aprons, etc. We dealt with them with beads of all colours, knives, axes, pins and needles; which they used only as tools to drill holes with in their ears, noses and lips, where they hang a great many little things; as long beads, bits of tin, brass, or silver, beat thin; and any shining trinket. The beads they weave into aprons about a quarter of an ell[8] long, and of the same breadth; working them very prettily in flowers of several colours of beads; which apron they wear just before them, as Adam and Eve did the fig leaves; the men wearing a long strip of linen, which they deal with us for. They thread these beads also on long cotton threads, and make girdles to tie their aprons to, which come twenty times, or more, about the waist; and then cross, like a shoulder-belt, both ways, and round their necks, arms and legs. This adornment, with their long black hair, and the face painted in little specks or flowers here and there, makes them a wonderful figure to behold. Some of the beauties which indeed are finely shaped, as almost all are, and who have pretty features, are very charming and novel; for they have all that is called beauty, except the colour, which is a reddish yellow; or after a new oiling, which they often use to themselves, they are of the colour of a new brick, but smooth, soft and sleek. They are extreme modest and bashful, very shy, and nice[9] of being touched. And though they are all thus naked, if one lives for ever among them, there is not to be seen an indecent action, or glance; and being continually used to see one another so unadorned, so like our first parents before the Fall, it seems as if they had no wishes; there being nothing to heighten curiosity, but all you can see, you see at once, and every moment see; and where there is no novelty, there can be no curiosity.[10] Not but I have seen a handsome young Indian, dying for love of a very beautiful young Indian maid; but all his courtship was, to fold his arms, pursue her with his eyes, and sighs were all his language; while she, as if no such lover were present, or rather, as if she desired none such, carefully guarded her eyes from beholding him; and never approached him, but she looked down with all the blushing modesty I have seen in the most severe and cautious of our world. And these people represented to me an absolute idea of the first state of innocence, before man knew how to sin; and 'tis most evident and plain, that simple Nature is the most harmless, inoffensive and virtuous mistress. 'Tis she alone, if she were permitted, that better instructs the world than all the inventions of man; religion would here but destroy that tranquillity they possess by ignorance, and laws would but teach them to know offence, of which now they have no notion. They once made mourning and fasting for the death of the English governor, who had given his hand to come on such a day to them, and neither came, nor sent; believing, when once a man's word was past, nothing but death could or should prevent his keeping it. And when they saw he was not dead, they asked him, what name they had for a man who promised a thing he did not do? The governor told them, such a man was a liar, which was a word of infamy to a gentleman. Then one of them replied, 'Governor, you are a liar, and guilty of that infamy.' They have a native justice, which knows no fraud; and they understand no vice, or cunning, but when they are taught by the white men. They have plurality of wives, which, when they grow old, they serve those that succeed them, who are young; but with a servitude easy and respected; and unless they take slaves in war, they have no other attendants.

Those on that continent where I was, had no king; but the oldest war captain was obeyed with great resignation.

A war captain is a man who has led them on to battle with conduct, and success; of whom I shall have occasion to speak more hereafter, and of some other of their customs and manners, as they fall in my way.

With these people, as I said, we live in perfect tranquillity, and good understanding, as it behoves us to do; they knowing all the places where to seek the best food of the country, and the means of getting it; and for very small and invaluable trifles, supply us with what 'tis impossible for us to get; for they do not only in the wood, and over the savannahs,[11] in hunting, supply the parts of hounds, by swiftly scouring through those almost impassable places, and by the mere activity of their feet, run down the nimblest deer, and other eatable beasts; but in the water, one would think they were gods of the rivers, or fellow-citizens of the deep, so rare an art they have in swimming, diving, and almost living in water, by which they command the less swift inhabitants of the floods. And then for shooting; what they cannot take, or reach with their hands, they do with arrows, and have so admirable an aim, that they will split almost a hair; and at any distance that an arrow can reach, they will shoot down oranges, and other fruit, and only touch the stalk with the darts' points, that they may not hurt the fruit. So that they being, on all occasions, very useful to us, we find it absolutely necessary to caress them as friends, and not to treat them as slaves; nor dare we do other, their numbers so far surpassing ours in that continent.

Those then whom we make use of to work in our plantations of sugar are negroes, black slaves altogether, which are transported thither in this manner.

Those who want slaves, make a bargain with a master, or captain of a ship, and contract to pay him so much apiece, a matter of twenty pound a head for as many as he agrees for, and to pay for them when they shall be delivered on such a plantation. So that when there arrives a ship laden with slaves, they who have so contracted, go aboard, and receive their number by lot; and perhaps in one lot that may be for ten, there may happen to be three or four men; the rest, women and children; or be there more or less of either sex, you are obliged to be contented with your lot.

Coramantien,[12] a country of blacks so called, was one of those places in which they found the most advantageous trading for these slaves; and thither most of our great traders in that merchandise trafficked; for that nation is very warlike and brave, and having a continual campaign, being always in hostility with one neighbouring prince or other, they had the fortune to take a great many captives; for all they took in battle, were sold as slaves, at least, those common men who could not ransom themselves. Of these slaves so taken, the general only has all the profit; and of these generals, our captains and masters of ships buy all their freights.

The king of Coramantien was himself a man of a hundred and odd years old, and had no son, though he had many beautiful black wives; for most certainly, there are beauties that can charm of that colour. In his younger years he had had many gallant men to his sons, thirteen of which died in battle, conquering when they fell; and he had only left him for his successor, one grandchild, son to one of these dead victors; who, as soon as he could bear a bow in his hand, and a quiver at his back, was sent into the field, to be trained up by one of the oldest generals, to war; where, from his natural inclination to arms, and the occasions given him, with the good conduct of the old general, he became, at the age of seventeen, one of the most expert captains, and bravest soldiers, that ever saw the field of Mars; so that he was adored as the wonder of all that world, and the darling of the soldiers. Besides, he was adorned with a native beauty so transcending all those of his gloomy race, that he struck an awe and reverence, even in those that knew not his quality; as he did in me, who beheld him with surprise and wonder, when afterwards he arrived in our world.

He had scarce arrived at his seventeenth year, when fighting by his side, the general was killed with an arrow in his eye, which the Prince Oroonoko [13] (for so was this gallant Moor called) very narrowly avoided; nor had he, if the general, who saw the arrow shot, and perceiving it aimed at the prince, had not bowed his head between, on purpose to receive it in his own body rather than it should touch that of the prince, and so saved him.

'Twas then, afflicted as Oroonoko was, that he was proclaimed general in the old man's place; and then it was, at the finishing of that war, which had continued for two years, that the prince came to court; where he had hardly been a month together, from the time of his fifth year to that of seventeen; and 'twas amazing to imagine where it was he learned so much humanity; or, to give his accomplishments a juster name, where 'twas he got that real greatness of soul, those refined notions of true honour, that absolute generosity, and that softness that was capable of the highest passions of love and gallantry, whose objects were almost continually fighting men, or those mangled, or dead; who heard no sounds, but those of war and groans. Some part of it we may attribute to the care of a Frenchman of wit and learning, who finding it turn to very good account to be a sort of royal tutor to this young Black, and perceiving him very ready, apt, and quick of apprehension, took a great pleasure to teach him morals, language and science, and was for it extremely beloved and valued by him. Another reason was, he loved, when he came from war, to see all the English gentlemen that traded thither; and did not only learn their language, but that of the Spaniards also, with whom he traded afterwards for slaves.

I have often seen and conversed with this great man, and been a witness to many of his mighty actions; and do assure my reader, the most illustrious courts could not have produced a braver man, both for greatness of courage and mind, a judgment more solid, a wit more quick, and a conversation more sweet and diverting. He knew almost as much as if he had read much: he had heard of, and admired the Romans; he had heard of the late Civil Wars in England, and the deplorable death of our great monarch,[14] and would discourse of it with all the sense, and abhorrence of the injustice imaginable. He had an extreme good and graceful mien, and all the civility of a well-bred great man. He had nothing of barbarity in his nature, but in all points addressed himself as if his education had been in some European court.

This great and just character of Oroonoko gave me an extreme curiosity to see him, especially when I knew he spoke French and English, and that I could talk with him. But though I had heard so much of him, I was as greatly surprised when I saw him as if I had heard nothing of him, so beyond all report I found him. He came into the room, and addressed himself to me, and some other women, with the best grace in the world. He was pretty tall, but of a shape the most exact that can be fancied; the most famous statuary[15] could not form the figure of a man more admirably turned from head to foot. His face was not of that brown, rusty black which most of that nation are, but a perfect ebony, or polished jet. His eyes were the most awful that could be seen, and very piercing; the white of them being like snow, as were his teeth. His nose was rising and Roman, instead of African and flat. His mouth, the finest shaped that could be seen; far from those great turned lips, which are so natural to the rest of the Negroes. The whole proportion and air of his face was so noble, and exactly formed, that, bating[16] his colour, there could be nothing in nature more beautiful, agreeable and handsome. There was no one grace wanting, that bears the standard of true beauty. His hair came down to his shoulders, by the aids of art; which was, by pulling it out with a quill, and keeping it combed, of which he took particular care. Nor did the perfections of his mind come short of those of his person; for his discourse was admirable upon almost any subject; and whoever had heard him speak, would have been convinced of their errors, that all fine wit is confined to the white men, especially to those of Christendom; and would have confessed that Oroonoko was as capable even of reigning well, and of governing as wisely, had as great a soul, as politic[17] maxims, and was as sensible of power as any prince civilized in the most refined schools of humanity and learning, or the most illustrious courts.

This prince, such as I have described him, whose soul and body were so admirably adorned, was (while yet he was in the court of his grandfather) as I said, as capable of love, as 'twas possible for a brave and gallant man to be; and in saying that, I have named the highest degree of love; for sure, great souls are most capable of that passion.

I have already said the old general was killed by the shot of an arrow, by the side of this prince, in battle; and that Oroonoko was made general. This old dead hero had one only daughter left of his race; a beauty that, to describe her truly, one need say only, she was female to the noble male; the beautiful black Venus, to our young Mars; as charming in her person as he, and of delicate virtues. I have seen an hundred white men sighing after her, and making a thousand vows at her feet, all vain, and unsuccessful; and she was, indeed, too great for any, but a prince of her own nation to adore.

Oroonoko coming from the wars (which were now ended)

after he had made his court to his grandfather, he thought in honour he ought to make a visit to Imoinda, the daughter of his foster-father, the dead general; and to make some excuses to her, because his preservation was the occasion of her father's death; and to present her with those slaves that had been taken in this last battle, as the trophies of her father's victories. When he came, attended by all the young soldiers of any merit, he was infinitely surprised at the beauty of this fair Queen of Night, whose face and person was so exceeding all he had ever beheld; that lovely modesty with which she received him, that softness in her look, and sighs, upon the melancholy occasion of this honour that was done by so great a man as Oroonoko, and a prince of whom she had heard such admirable things; the awfulness wherewith she received him, and the sweetness of her words and behaviour while he stayed, gained a perfect conquest over his fierce heart, and made him feel the victor could be subdued. So that having made his first compliments, and presented her a hundred and fifty slaves in fetters, he told her with his eyes that he was not insensible of her charms; while Imoinda, who wished for nothing more than so glorious a conquest, was pleased to believe she understood that silent language of new-born love; and from that moment, put on all her additions to beauty.

The prince returned to court with quite another humour than before; and though he did not speak much of the fair Imoinda, he had the pleasure to hear all his followers speak of nothing but the charms of that maid; insomuch that, even in the presence of the old king, they were extolling her, and heightening, if possible, the beauties they had found in her; so that nothing else was talked of, no other sound was heard in every corner where there were whisperers, but 'Imoinda! Imoinda!'

'Twill be imagined Oroonoko stayed not long before he made his second visit; nor, considering his quality, not much longer before he told her, he adored her. I have often heard him say, that he admired by what strange inspiration he came to talk things so soft, and so passionate, who never knew love, nor was used to the conversation of women; but (to use his own words) he said, most happily, some new, and till then unknown power instructed his heart and tongue in the language of love, and at the same time, in favour of him, inspired Imoinda with a sense of his passion. She was touched with what he said, and returned it all in such answers as went to his very heart, with a pleasure unknown before. Nor did he use those obligations ill that love had done him; but turned all his happy moments to the best advantage; and as he knew no vice, his flame aimed at nothing but honour, if such a distinction may be made in love; and especially in that country, where men take to themselves as many as they can maintain; and where the only crime and sin with woman is to turn her off, to abandon her to want, shame and misery. Such ill morals are only practised in Christian countries, where they prefer the bare name of religion; and, without virtue or morality, think that's sufficient. But Oroonoko was none of those professors; but as he had right notions of honour, so he made her such propositions as were not only and barely such; but, contrary to the custom of his country, he made her vows she should be the only woman he would possess while he lived; that no age or wrinkles should incline him to change, for her soul would be always fine, and always young; and he should have an eternal idea in his mind of the charms she now bore, and should look into his heart for that idea, when he could find it no longer in her face.

After a thousand assurances of his lasting flame, and her eternal empire over him, she condescended to receive him for her husband; or rather, received him, as the greatest honour the gods could do her.

There· is a certain ceremony in these cases to be observed, which I forgot to ask him how performed; but 'twas concluded on both sides that, in obedience to him, the grandfather was to be first made acquainted with the design; for they pay a most absolute resignation to the monarch, especially when he is a parent also.

On the other side, the old king, who had many wives, and many concubines, wanted not court flatterers to insinuate in his heart a thousand tender thoughts for this young beauty; and who represented her to his fancy as the most charming he had ever possessed in all the long race of his numerous years. At this character his old heart, like an extinguished brand, most apt to take fire, felt new sparks of love, and began to kindle; and now grown to his second childhood, longed with impatience to behold this gay thing, with whom, alas, he could but innocently play. But how he should be confirmed she was this wonder, before he used his power to call her to court (where maidens never came, unless for the king's private use) he was next to consider; and while he was so doing, he had intelligence brought him, that Imoinda was most certainly mistress to the Prince Oroonoko. This gave him some chagrin; however, it gave him also an opportunity, one day, when the prince was a-hunting, to wait on a man of quality, as his slave and attendant, who should go and make a present to Imoinda, as from the prince; he should then, unknown, see this fair maid, and have an opportunity to hear what message she would return the prince for his present; and from thence gather the state of her heart, and degree of her inclination. This was put in execution, and the old monarch saw, and burnt; he found her all he had heard, and would not delay his happiness, but found he should have some obstacle to overcome her heart; for she expressed her sense of the present the prince had sent her, in terms so sweet, so soft and pretty, with an air of love and joy that could not be dissembled, insomuch that 'twas past doubt whether she loved Oroonoko entirely. This gave the old king some affliction, but he salved it with this, that the obedience the people pay their king, was not at all inferior to what they paid their gods, and what love would not oblige Imoinda to do, duty would compel her to.

He was therefore no sooner got to his apartment, but he sent the royal veil to Imoinda, that is, the ceremony of invitation; he sends the lady, he has a mind to honour with his bed, a veil, with which she is covered and secured for the king's use; and 'tis death to disobey; besides, held a most impious disobedience.

'Tis not to be imagined the surprise and grief that seized this lovely maid at this news and sight. However, as delays in these cases are dangerous, and pleading worse than treason, trembling, and almost fainting, she was obliged to suffer herself to be covered and led away.

They brought her thus to court; and the king, who had caused a very rich bath to be prepared, was led into it, where he sat under a canopy in state, to receive this longed for virgin; whom he having commanded should be brought to him, they (after disrobing her) led her to the bath, and making fast the doors, left her to descend. The king, without more courtship, bade her throw off her mantle and come to his arms. But Imoinda, all in tears, threw herself on the marble on the brink of the bath, and besought him to hear her. She told him, as she was a maid, how proud of the divine glory she should have been of having it in her power to oblige her king; but as by the laws he could not, and from his royal goodness would not take from any man his wedded wife, so she believed she should be the occasion of making him commit a great sin, if she did not reveal her state and condition, and tell him she was another's, and could not be so happy to be his.

The king, enraged at this delay, hastily demanded the name of the bold man that had married a woman of her degree without his consent. Imoinda, seeing his eyes fierce, and his hands tremble, whether with age or anger, I know not, but she fancied the last, almost repented she had said so much, for now she feared the storm would fall on the prince; she therefore said a thousand things to appease the raging of his flame, and to prepare him to hear who it was with calmness; but before she spoke, he imagined who she meant, but would not seem to do so, but commanded her to lay aside her mantle and suffer herself to receive his caresses; or, by his gods, he swore, that happy man whom she was going to name should die, though it were even Oroonoko himself. 'Therefore,' said he, 'deny this marriage, and swear thyself a maid.' 'That,' replied Imoinda, 'by all our powers I do, for I am not yet known to my husband.' ''Tis enough,' said the king, ''tis enough to satisfy both my conscience, and my heart.' And rising from his seat, he went and led her into the bath, it being in vain for her to resist.

In this time the prince, who was returned from hunting, went to visit his Imoinda, but found her gone; and not only so, but heard she had received the royal veil. This raised him to a storm, and in his madness they had much ado to save him from laying violent hands on himself. Force first prevailed, and then reason. They urged all to him that might oppose his rage; but nothing weighed so greatly with him as the king's old age, incapable of injuring him with Imoinda. He would give way to that hope, because it pleased him most, and flattered best his heart. Yet this served not altogether to make him cease his different passions, which sometimes raged within him, and sometimes softened into showers. 'Twas not enough to appease him, to tell him, his grandfather was old, and could not that way injure him, while he retained that aweful duty which the young men are used there to pay to their grave relations. He could not be convinced he had no cause to sigh and mourn for the loss of a mistress he could not with all his strength and courage retrieve. And he would often cry, 'O my friends! Were she in walled cities, or confined from me in fortifications of the greatest strength; did enchantments or monsters detain her from me, I would venture through any hazard to free her. But here, in the arms of a feeble old man, my youth, my violent love, my trade in arms, and all my vast desire of glory avail me nothing. Imoinda is as irrecoverably lost to me, as if she were snatched by the cold arms of death. Oh! she is never to be retrieved. If I would wait tedious years, till fate should bow the old king to his grave, even that would not leave me Imoinda free; but still that custom that makes it so vile a crime for a son to marry his father's wives or mistress would hinder my happiness; unless I would either ignobly set an ill precedent to my successors, or abandon my country, and fly with her to some unknown world, who never heard our story.'

But it was objected to him, that his case was not the same; for Imoinda being his lawful wife, by solemn contract, 'twas he was the injured man, and might, if he so pleased, take Imoinda back, the breach of the law being on his grandfather's side; and that if he could circumvent him, and redeem her from the otan,[18] which is the palace of the king's women, a sort of seraglio, it was both just and lawful for him so to do.

This reasoning had some force upon him, and he should have been entirely comforted, but for the thought that she was possessed by his grandfather. However, he loved so well that he was resolved to believe what most favoured his hope, and to endeavour to learn from Imoinda's own mouth, what only she could satisfy him in: whether she was robbed of that blessing, which was only due to his faith and love. But as it was very hard to get a sight of the women, for no men ever entered into the otan, but when the king went to entertain himself with some one of his wives or mistresses, and 'twas death at any other time for any other to go in, so he knew not how to contrive to get a sight of her.

While Oroonoko felt all the agonies of love, and suffered under a torment the most painful in the world, the old king was not exempted from his share of affliction. He was troubled for having been forced by an irresistible passion to rob his son of a treasure he knew could not but be extremely dear to him, since she was the most beautiful that ever had been seen; and had besides, all the sweetness and innocence of youth and modesty, with a charm of wit surpassing all. He found that, however she was forced to expose her lovely person to his withered arms, she could only sigh and weep there, and think of Oroonoko; and oftentimes could not forbear speaking of him, though her life were, by custom, forfeited by owning her passion. But she spoke not of a lover only, but of a prince dear to him to whom she spoke; and of the praises of a man, who, till now, filled the old man's soul with joy at every recital of his bravery, or even his name. And 'twas this dotage on our young hero that gave Imoinda a thousand privileges to speak of him without offending; and this condescension in the old king that made her take the satisfaction of speaking of him so very often.

Besides, he many times enquired how the prince bore himself; and those of whom he asked, being entirely slaves to the merits and virtues of the prince, still answered what they thought conduced best to his service; which was, to make the old king fancy that the prince had no more interest in Imoinda, and had resigned her willingly to the pleasure of the king; that he diverted himself with his mathematicians, his fortifications, his officers, and his hunting.

This pleased the old lover, who failed not to report these things again to Imoinda, that she might, by the example of her young lover, withdraw her heart and rest better contented in his arms. But however she was forced to receive this unwelcome news, in all appearance, with unconcern, and content, her heart was bursting within, and she was only happy when she could get alone, to vent her griefs and moans with sighs and tears.

What reports of the prince's conduct were made to the king, he thought good to justify as far as possibly he could by his actions; and when he appeared in the presence of the king, he showed a face not at all betraying his heart; so that in a little time the old man, being entirely convinced that he was no longer a lover of Imoinda, he carried him with him, in his train to the otan, often to banquet with his mistress. But as soon as he entered, one day, into the apartment of Imoinda, with the king, at the first glance from her eyes, notwithstanding all his determined resolution, he was ready to sink in the place where he stood; and had certainly done so, but for the support of Aboan, a young man, who was next to him; which, with his change of countenance, had betrayed him, had the king chanced to look that way. And I have observed, 'tis a very great error in those who laugh when one says, a Negro can change colour; for I have seen them as frequently blush, and look pale, and that as visibly as ever I saw in the most beautiful white. And 'tis certain that both these changes were evident, this day, in both these lovers. And Imoinda, who saw with some joy the change in the prince's face, and found it in her own, strove to divert the king from beholding either, by a forced caress, with which she met him, which was a new wound in the heart of the poor dying prince. But as soon as the king was busied in looking on some fine thing of Imoinda's making, she had time to tell the prince with her angry, but love-darting eyes, that she resented his coldness, and bemoaned her own miserable captivity. Nor were his eyes silent, but answered hers again, as much as eyes could do, instructed by the most tender, and most passionate heart that ever loved. And they spoke so well, and so effectually, as Imoinda no longer doubted, but she was the only delight, and the darling of that soul she found pleading in them its right of love, which none was more willing to resign than she. And 'twas this powerful language alone that in an instant conveyed all the thoughts of their souls to each other, that they both found there wanted but opportunity to make them both entirely happy. But when he saw another door opened by Onahal, a former old wife of the king's who now had charge of Imoinda, and saw the prospect of a bed of state made ready with sweets and flowers for the dalliance of the king, who immediately led the trembling victim from his sight, into that prepared repose. What rage! What wild frenzies seized his heart! Which forcing to keep within bounds, and to suffer without noise, it became the more insupportable and rent his soul with ten thousand pains. He was forced to retire to vent his groans, where he fell down on a carpet, and lay struggling a long time, and only breathing now and then, 'O Imoinda!' When Onahal had finished her necessary affair within, shutting the door, she came forth to wait, till the king called; and hearing some one sighing in the other room, she passed on, and found the prince in that deplorable condition which she thought needed her aid. She gave him cordials, but all in vain; till finding the nature of his disease, by his sighs, and naming Imoinda. She told him he had not so much cause as he imagined to afflict himself; for if he knew the king so well as she did, he would not lose a moment in jealousy, and that she was confident that Imoinda bore, at this minute, part in his affliction. Aboan was of the same opinion; and both together, persuaded him to reassume his courage; and all sitting down on the carpet, the prince said so many obliging things to Onahal, that he half persuaded her to be of his party. And she promised him she would thus far comply with his just desires, that she would let Imoinda know how faithful he was, what he suffered, and what he said.

This discourse lasted till the king called, which gave Oroonoko a certain satisfaction; and with the hope Onahal had made him conceive, he assumed a look as gay as 'twas possible a man in his circumstances could do; and presently after, he was called in with the rest who waited without. The king commanded music to be brought, and several of his young wives and mistresses came all together by his command, to dance before him; where Imoinda performed her part with an air and grace so passing all the rest, as her beauty was above them, and received the present, ordained as a prize. The prince was every moment more charmed with the new beauties and graces he beheld in this fair one; and while he gazed and she danced, Onahal was retired to a window with Aboan.

This Onahal, as I said, was one of the cast mistresses of the old king; and 'twas these (now past their beauty) that were made guardians, or governants [19] to the new, and the young ones; and whose business it was, to teach them all those wanton arts of love with which they prevailed and charmed heretofore in their turn; and who now treated the triumphing happy ones with all the severity, as to liberty and freedom, that was possible, in revenge of those honours they rob them of; envying them those satisfactions, those gallantries and presents, that were once made to themselves, while youth and beauty lasted, and which they now saw pass regardless by, and paid only to the bloomings. And certainly, nothing is more afflicting to a decayed beauty than to behold in itself declining charms, that were once adored, and to find those caresses paid to new beauties to which once she laid a claim; to hear them whisper as she passes by, 'That once was a delicate woman.' These abandoned ladies therefore endeavour to revenge all the despites and decays of time on these flourishing happy ones. And 'twas this severity that gave Oroonoko a thousand fears he should never prevail with Onahal to see Imoinda. But, as I said, she was now retired to a window with Aboan.

This young man was not only one of the best quality, but a man extremely well made, and beautiful; and coming often to attend the king to the otan, he had subdued the heart of the antiquated Onahal, which had not forgot how pleasant it was to be in love. And though she had some decays in her face, she had none in her sense and wit; she was there agreeable still, even to Aboan's youth, so that he took pleasure in entertaining her with discourses of love. He knew also, that to make his court to these she-favourites was the way to be great; these being the persons that do all affairs and business at court. He had also observed that she had given him glances more tender and inviting than she had done to others of his quality. And now, when he saw that her favour could so absolutely oblige the prince, he failed not to sigh in her ear, and to look with eyes all soft upon her, and give her hope that she had made some impressions on his heart. He found her pleased at this, and making a thousand advances to him; but the ceremony ending, and the king departing, broke up the company for that day, and his conversation.

Aboan failed not that night to tell the prince of his success, and how advantageous the service of Onahal might be to his amour with Imoinda. The prince was overjoyed with this good news, and besought him, if it were possible, to caress her, so as to engage her entirely; which he could not fail to do, if he complied with her desires. 'For then,' said the prince, 'her life lying at your mercy, she must grant you the request you make in my behalf.' Aboan understood him, and assured him he would make love so effectually, that he would defy the most expert mistress of the art, to find out whether he dissembled it or had it really. And 'twas with impatience they waited the next opportunity of going to the otan.

The wars came on, the time of taking the field approached, and 'twas impossible for the prince to delay his going at the head of his army to encounter the enemy; so that every day seemed a tedious year, till he saw his Imoinda, for he believed he could not live, if he were forced away without being so happy. 'Twas with impatience therefore, that he expected the next visit the king would make; and, according to his wish, it was not long.

The parley of the eyes of these two lovers had not passed so secretly, but an old jealous lover could spy it; or rather, he wanted not flatterers who told him they observed it. So that the prince was hastened to the camp, and this was the last visit he found he should make to the otan; he therefore urged Aboan to make the best of this last effort, and to explain himself so to Onahal, that she, deferring her enjoyment of her young lover no longer, might make way for the prince to speak to Imoinda.

The whole affair being agreed on between the prince and Aboan, they attended the king, as the custom was, to the otan; where, while the whole company was taken up in beholding the dancing and antic[20] postures the women royal made, to divert the king, Onahal singled out Aboan, whom she found most pliable to her wish. When she had him where she believed she could not be heard, she sighed to him, and softly cried, 'Ah, Aboan! When will you be sensible of my passion? I confess it with my mouth, because I would not give my eyes the lie; and you have but too much already perceived they have confessed my flame. Nor would I have you believe that because I am the abandoned mistress of a king I esteem myself altogether divested of charms. No, Aboan; I have still a rest of beauty enough engaging, and have learned to please too well, not to be desirable. I can have lovers still, but will have none but Aboan.' 'Madam,' replied the half-feigning youth, 'you have already, by my eyes, found you can

91

still conquer; and I believe 'tis in pity of me, you condescend to this kind confession. But, Madam, words are used to be so small a part of our country courtship, that 'tis rare one can get so happy an opportunity as to tell one's heart; and those few minutes we have are forced to be snatched for more certain proofs of love than speaking and sighing; and such I languish for.'

He spoke this with such a tone, that she hoped it true, and could not forbear believing it; and being wholly transported with joy, for having subdued the finest of all the king's subjects to her desires, she took from her ears two large pearls and commanded him to wear them in his. He would have refused them, crying, 'Madam, these are not the proofs of your love that I expect; 'tis opportunity, 'tis a lone hour only, that can make me happy.' But forcing the pearls into his hand, she whispered softly to him, 'Oh! Do not fear a woman's invention, when love sets her a-thinking.' And pressing his hand, she cried, 'This night you shall be happy. Come to the gate of the orange groves, behind the otan, and I will be ready, about midnight, to receive you.' 'Twas thus agreed, and she left him, that no notice might be taken of their speaking together.

The ladies were still dancing, and the king, laid on a carpet, with a great deal of pleasure, was beholding them, especially Imoinda, who that day appeared more lovely than ever, being enlivened with the good tidings Onahal had brought her of the constant passion the prince had for her. The prince was laid on another carpet, at the other end of the room, with his eyes fixed on the object of his soul; and as she turned, or moved, so did they; and she alone gave his eyes and soul their motions. Nor did Imoinda employ her eyes to any other use, than in beholding with infinite pleasure the joy she produced in those of the prince. But while she was more regarding him than the steps she took, she chanced to fall, and so near him as that leaping with extreme force from the carpet, he caught her in his arms as she fell; and 'twas visible to the whole presence, the joy wherewith he received her. He clasped her close to his bosom, and quite forgot that reverence that was due to the mistress of a king, and that punishment that is the reward of a boldness of this nature; and had not the presence of mind of Imoinda (fonder of his safety, than her own) befriended him in making her spring from his arms and fall into her dance again, he had, at that instant, met his death; for the old king, jealous to the last degree, rose up in rage, broke all the diversion, and led Imoinda to her apartment, and sent out word to the prince to go immediately to the camp; and that if he were found another night in court, he should suffer the death ordained for disobedient offenders.

You may imagine how welcome this news was to Oroonoko, whose unseasonable transport and caress of Imoinda was blamed by all men that loved him; and now he perceived his fault, yet cried, that for such another moment, he would be content to die.

All the otan was in disorder about this accident; and Onahal was particularly concerned, because on the prince's stay depended her happiness, for she could no longer expect that of Aboan. So that, e'er they departed, they contrived it so that the prince and he should come both that night to the grove of the otan, which was all of oranges and citrons, and that there they should wait her orders.

They parted thus, with grief enough, till night; leaving the king in possession of the lovely maid. But nothing could appease the jealousy of the old lover. He would not be imposed on, but would have it that Imoinda made a false step on purpose to fall into Oroonoko's bosom, and that all things looked like a design on both sides, and 'twas in vain she protested her innocence. He was old and obstinate, and left her more than half assured that his fear was true.

The king going to his apartment, sent to know where the prince was, and if he intended to obey his command. The messenger returned, and told him he found the prince pensive, and altogether unpreparing for the campaign; that he lay negligently on the ground, and answered very little. This confirmed the jealousy of the king, and he commanded that they should very narrowly and privately watch his motions; and that he should not stir from his apartment, but one spy or other should be employed to watch him. So that the hour approaching, wherein he was to go to the citron grove, and taking only Aboan along with him, he leaves his apartment, and was watched to the very gate of the otan, where he was seen to enter, and where they left him, to carry back the tidings to the king.

Oroonoko and Aboan were no sooner entered but Onahal led
the prince to the apartment of Imoinda, who, not knowing any-
thing of her happiness, was laid in bed. But Onahal only left him
in her chamber to make the best of his opportunity, and took her
dear Aboan to her own, where he showed the height of complai-
sance²¹ for his prince, when, to give him an opportunity, he
suffered himself to be caressed in bed by Onahal.

The prince softly wakened Imoinda, who was not a little
surprised with joy to find him there, and yet she trembled with a
thousand fears. I believe he omitted saying nothing to this young
maid, that might persuade her to suffer him to seize his own, and
take the rights of love; and I believe she was not long resisting
those arms where she so longed to be; and having opportunity,
night and silence, youth, love and desire, he soon prevailed; and
ravished in a moment what his old grandfather had been endeav-
ouring for so many months.

'Tis not to be imagined the satisfaction of these two young
lovers; nor the vows she made him, that she remained a spotless
maid till that night; and that what she did with his grandfather had
robbed him of no part of her virgin honour, the gods in mercy and
justice having reserved that for her plighted lord, to whom of right
it belonged. And 'tis impossible to express the transports he
suffered, while he listened to a discourse so charming from her
loved lips, and clasped that body in his arms, for whom he had so
long languished; and nothing now afflicted him, but his sudden
departure from her; for he told her the necessity and his commands;
but should depart satisfied in this, that since the old king had
hitherto not been able to deprive him of those enjoyments which
only belonged to him, he believed for the future he would be less
able to injure him. So that, abating the scandal of the veil, which
was no otherwise so, than that she was wife to another, he believed
her safe, even in the arms of the king, and innocent; yet would he
have ventured at the conquest of the world, and have given it all, to
have had her avoided that honour of receiving the royal veil. 'Twas
thus, between a thousand caresses, that both bemoaned the hard
fate of youth and beauty, so liable to that cruel promotion; 'twas a
glory that could well have been spared here, though desired, and
aimed at by all the young females of that kingdom.

But while they were thus fondly employed, forgetting how time ran on, and that the dawn must conduct him far away from his only happiness, they heard a great noise in the otan, and unusual voices of men; at which the prince, starting from the arms of the frighted Imoinda, ran to a little battle-axe he used to wear by his side; and having not so much leisure as to put on his habit, he opposed himself against some who were already opening the door; which they did with so much violence, that Oroonoko was not able to defend it, but was forced to cry out with a commanding voice, 'Whoever ye are that have the boldness to attempt to approach this apartment thus rudely, know that I, the Prince Oroonoko, will revenge it with the certain death of him that first enters. Therefore stand back, and know this place is sacred to love, and me this night; tomorrow 'tis the king's.'

This he spoke with a voice so resolved and assured, that they soon retired from the door, but cried, ' 'Tis by the king's command we are come; and being satisfied by thy voice, O Prince, as much as if we had entered, we can report to the king the truth of all his fears, and leave thee to provide for thy own safety, as thou art advised by thy friends.'

At these words they departed, and left the prince to take a short and sad leave of his Imoinda; who trusting in the strength of her charms, believed she should appease the fury of a jealous king by saying she was surprised, and that it was by force of arms he got into her apartment. All her concern now was for his life, and therefore she hastened him to the camp, and with much ado, prevailed on him to go. Nor was it she alone that prevailed, Aboan and Onahal both pleaded, and both assured him of a lie that should be well enough contrived to secure Imoinda. So that, at last, with a heart sad as death, dying eyes, and sighing soul, Oroonoko departed, and took his way to the camp.

It was not long after the king in person came to the otan, where beholding Imoinda with rage in his eyes, he upbraided her wickedness and perfidy, and threatening her royal lover, she fell on her face at his feet, bedewing the floor with her tears and imploring his pardon for a fault which she had not with her will committed, as Onahal, who was also prostrate with her, could testify that, unknown to her, he had broke into her apartment, and ravished her. She spoke this much against her conscience; but to save her own life, 'twas absolutely necessary she should feign this falsity. She knew it could not injure the prince, he being fled to an army that would stand by him against any injuries that should assault him. However, this last thought of Imoinda's being ravished changed the measures of his revenge, and whereas before he designed to be himself her executioner, he now resolved she should not die. But as it is the greatest crime in nature amongst them to touch a woman, after having been possessed by a son, a father, or a brother, so now he looked on Imoinda as a polluted thing, wholly unfit for his embrace; nor would he resign her to his grandson, because she had received the royal veil. He therefore removes her from the otan, with Onahal; whom he put into safe hands, with order they should be both sold off, as slaves, to another country, either Christian, or heathen; 'twas no matter where.

This cruel sentence, worse than death, they implored might be reversed; but their prayers were vain, and it was put in execution accordingly, and that with so much secrecy, that none, either without or within the otan, knew anything of their absence, or their destiny.

The old king, nevertheless, executed this with a great deal of reluctance; but he believed he had made a very great conquest over himself when he had once resolved, and had performed what he resolved. He believed now, that his love had been unjust, and that he could not expect the gods, or Captain of the Clouds (as they call the unknown power) should suffer a better consequence from so ill a cause. He now begins to hold Oroonoko excused; and to say, he had reason for what he did; and now everybody could assure the king, how passionately Imoinda was beloved by the prince; even those confessed it now who said the contrary before his flame was abated. So that the king being old and not able to defend himself in war, and having no sons of all his race remaining alive, but only this, to maintain him on the throne; and looking on this as a man disobliged, first by the rape of his mistress, or rather, wife; and now by depriving him wholly of her, he feared, might make him desperate, and do some cruel thing, either to himself, or his old grandfather, the offender; he began to repent him extremely of the contempt he had, in his rage, put on Imoinda. Besides, he considered he ought in honour to have killed her for this offence, if it had been one. He ought to have had so much value and consideration for a maid of her quality, as to have nobly put her to death, and not to have sold her like a common slave, the greatest revenge, and the most disgraceful of any, and to which they a thousand times prefer death, and implore it as Imoinda did, but could not obtain that honour. Seeing therefore it was certain that Oroonoko would highly resent this affront, he thought good to make some excuse for his rashness to him, and to that end he sent a messenger to the camp with orders to treat with him about the matter, to gain his pardon, and to endeavour to mitigate his grief; but that by no means he should tell him she was sold, but secretly put to death; for he knew he should never obtain his pardon for the other.

When the messenger came, he found the prince upon the point of engaging with the enemy, but as soon as he heard of the arrival of the messenger he commanded him to his tent, where he embraced him, and received him with joy; which was soon abated, by the downcast looks of the messenger, who was instantly demanded the cause by Oroonoko, who, impatient of delay, asked a thousand questions in a breath; and all concerning Imoinda. But there needed little return, for he could almost answer himself of all he demanded from his sighs and eyes. At last, the messenger casting himself at the prince's feet and kissing them with all the submission of a man that had something to implore which he dreaded to utter, he besought him to hear with calmness what he had to deliver to him, and to call up all his noble and heroic courage to encounter with his words, and defend himself against the ungrateful things he must relate. Oroonoko replied, with a deep sigh, and a languishing voice, 'I am armed against their worst efforts – for I know they will tell me, Imoinda is no more – and after that, you may spare the rest.' Then, commanding him to rise, he laid himself on a carpet under a rich pavilion, and remained a good while silent, and was hardly heard to sigh. When he was come a little to himself, the messenger asked him leave to deliver that part of his embassy which the prince had not yet divined, and the prince cried, 'I permit thee'. Then he told him the affliction the old king was in for the rashness he had committed in his cruelty to Imoinda; and how he deigned to ask pardon for his offence, and to implore the prince would not suffer that loss to touch his heart too sensibly which now all the gods could not restore him, but might recompense him in glory which he begged he would pursue; and that death, that common revenger of all injuries, would soon even the account between him and a feeble old man.

Oroonoko bade him return his duty to his lord and master, and to assure him there was no account of revenge to be adjusted between them; if there were, 'twas he was the aggressor, and that death would be just, and, maugre²² his age, would see him righted; and he was contented to leave his share of glory to youths more fortunate, and worthy of that favour from the gods. That henceforth he would never lift a weapon, or draw a bow, but abandon the small remains of his life to sighs and tears, and the continual thoughts of what his lord and grandfather had thought good to send out of the world, with all that youth, that innocence, and beauty.

After having spoken this, whatever his greatest officers, and men of the best rank could do, they could not raise him from the carpet, or persuade him to action and resolutions of life; but commanding all to retire, he shut himself into his pavilion all that day, while the enemy was ready to engage; and wondering at the delay, the whole body of the chief of the army then addressed themselves to him, and to whom they had much ado to get admittance. They fell on their faces at the foot of his carpet, where they lay, and besought him with earnest prayers and tears, to lead them forth to battle, and not let the enemy take advantages of them; and implored him to have regard to his glory, and to the world that depended on his courage and conduct. But he made no other reply to all their supplications but this, that he had now no more business for glory; and for the world, it was a trifle not worth his care. 'Go,' continued he, sighing, 'and divide it amongst you; and reap with joy what you so vainly prize, and leave me to my more welcome destiny.'

They then demanded what they should do, and whom he would constitute in his room, that the confusion of ambitious youth and power might not ruin their order, and make them a prey to the enemy. He replied, he would not give himself the trouble; but wished them to choose the bravest man amongst them, let his quality or birth be what it would, 'For, O my friends!' said he, 'it is not titles make men brave, or good; or birth that bestows courage and generosity, or makes the owner happy. Believe this, when you behold Oroonoko, the most wretched, and abandoned by fortune of all the creation of the gods.' So turning himself about, he would make no more reply to all they could urge or implore.

The army beholding their officers return unsuccessful, with sad faces, and ominous looks, that presaged no good luck, suffered a thousand fears to take possession of their hearts, and the enemy to come even upon them, before they would provide for their safety by any defence; and though they were assured by some, who had a mind to animate them, that they should be immediately headed by the prince, and that in the meantime Aboan had orders to command as general, yet they were so dismayed for want of that great example of bravery that they could make but a very feeble resistance; and at last, downright, fled before the enemy, who pursued them to the very tents, killing them. Nor could all Aboan's courage, which that day gained him immortal glory, shame them into a manly defence of themselves. The guards that were left behind, about the prince's tent, seeing the soldiers flee before the enemy, and scatter themselves all over the plain, in great disorder, made such outcries as roused the prince from his amorous slumber, in which he had remained buried for two days, without permitting any sustenance to approach him. But, in spite of all his resolutions, he had not the constancy of grief to that degree as to make him insensible of the danger of his army; and in that instant he leapt from his couch, and cried, 'Come, if we must die, let us meet death the noblest way; and 'twill be more like Oroonoko to encounter him at an army's head, opposing the torrent of a conquering foe, than lazily, on a couch, to wait his lingering pleasure, and die every moment by a thousand wrecking thought[s]; or be tamely taken by an enemy and led a whining, love-sick slave, to adorn the triumphs of Jamoan, that young victor, who already is entered beyond the limits I had prescribed him.'

While he was speaking, he suffered his people to dress him for the field; and sallying out of his pavilion, with more life and vigour in his countenance than ever he showed, he appeared like some divine power descended to save his country from destruction; and his people had purposely put him on all things that might make him shine with most splendour, to strike a reverend awe into the beholders. He flew into the thickest of those that were pursuing his men, and being animated with despair, he fought as if he came on purpose to die, and did such things as will not be believed that human strength could perform, and such as soon inspired all the rest with new courage and new order. And now it was that they began to fight indeed, and so, as if they would not be outdone even by their adored hero, who turning the tide of the victory, changing absolutely the fate of the day, gained an entire conquest; and Oroonoko having the good fortune to single out Jamoan, he took him prisoner with his own hand, having wounded him almost to death.

This Jamoan afterwards became very dear to him, being a man very gallant and of excellent graces, and fine parts, so that he never put him amongst the rank of captives, as they used to do, without distinction, for the common sale or market, but kept him in his own court, where he retained nothing of the prisoner but the name, and returned no more into his own country, so great an affection he took for Oroonoko; and by a thousand tales and adventures of love and gallantry, flattered his disease of melancholy and languishment, which I have often heard him say had certainly killed him, but for the conversation of this prince and Aboan, [and] the French governor he had from his childhood, of whom I have spoken before, and who was a man of admirable wit, great ingenuity and learning, all which he had infused into his young pupil. This Frenchman was banished out of his own country for some heretical notions he held; and though he was a man of very little religion, he had admirable morals, and a brave soul.

After the total defeat of Jamoan's army, which all fled, or were left dead upon the place, they spent some time in the camp; Oroonoko choosing rather to remain a while there in his tents, than enter into a p[a]lace, or live in a court where he had so

lately suffered so great a loss. The officers therefore, who saw and
knew his cause of discontent, invented all sorts of diversions and
sports to entertain their prince: so that what with those amuse-
ments abroad, and others at home, that is, within their tents, with
the persuasions, arguments and care of his friends and servants
that he more peculiarly prized, he wore off in time a great part of
that chagrin and torture of despair which the first effects[23] of
Imoinda's death had given him; insomuch as having received a
thousand kind embassies from the king, and invitations to return
to court, he obeyed, though with no little reluctance; and when
he did so, there was a visible change in him, and for a long time he
was much more melancholy than before. But time lessens all
extremes, and reduces them to mediums and unconcern; but no
motives or beauties, though all endeavoured it, could engage him
in any sort of amour, though he had all the invitations to it, both
from his own youth and others' ambitions and designs.

Oroonoko was no sooner returned from this last conquest, and
received at court with all the joy and magnificence that could be
expressed to a young victor, who was not only returned trium-
phant, but beloved like a deity, when there arrived in the port an
English ship.

This person had often before been in these countries, and was
very well known to Oroonoko, with whom he had trafficked for
slaves, and had used to do the same with his predecessors.

This commander was a man of a finer sort of address and
conversation, better bred, and more engaging than most of that
sort of men are; so that he seemed rather never to have been bred
out of a court, than almost all his life at sea. This captain
therefore was always better received at court, than most of the
traders to those countries were; and especially by Oroonoko, who
was more civilized, according to the European mode, than any
other had been, and took more delight in the white nations, and,
above all, men of parts and wit. To this captain he sold abundance
of his slaves, and for the favour and esteem he had for him, made
him many presents, and obliged him to stay at court as long as
possibly he could. Which the captain seemed to take as a very
great honour done him, entertaining the prince every day with
globes and maps, and mathematical discourses and instruments;

eating, drinking, hunting and living with him with so much familiarity, that it was not to be doubted, but he had gained very greatly upon the heart of this gallant young man. And the captain, in return of all these mighty favours, besought the prince to honour his vessel with his presence, some day or other, to dinner, before he should set sail; which he condescended to accept, and appointed his day. The captain, on his part, failed not to have all things in a readiness, in the most magnificent order he could possibly. And the day being come, the captain, in his boat, richly adorned with carpets and velvet cushions, rowed to the shore to receive the prince; with another long-boat, where was placed all his music and trumpets, with which Oroonoko was extremely delighted; who met him on the shore, attended by his French governor, Jamoan, Aboan, and about an hundred of the noblest of the youths of the court. And after they had first carried the prince on board, the boats fetched the rest off; where they found a very splendid treat, with all sorts of fine wines, and were as well entertained, as 'twas possible in such a place to be.

The prince having drunk hard of punch, and several sorts of wine, as did all the rest (for great care was taken, they should want nothing of that part of the entertainment) was very merry, and in great admiration of the ship, for he had never been in one before; so that he was curious of beholding every place, where he decently might descend. The rest, no less curious, who were not quite overcome with drinking, rambled at their pleasure fore and aft, as their fancies guided them: so that the captain, who had well laid his design before, gave the word and seized on all his guests; they clapping great irons suddenly on the prince when he was leaped down in the hold to view that part of the vessel, and locking him fast down, secured him. The same treachery was used to all the rest; and all in one instant, in several places of the ship, were lashed fast in irons and betrayed to slavery. That great design over, they set all hands to work to hoist sail; and with as treacherous and fair a wind they made from the shore with this innocent and glorious prize, who thought of nothing less than such an entertainment.

Some have commended this act, as brave in the captain; but I will spare my sense of it, and leave it to my reader to judge as he pleases.

It may be easily guessed in what manner the prince resented this indignity, who may be best resembled to a lion taken in a toil; so he raged, so he struggled for liberty, but all in vain; and they had so wisely managed his fetters, that he could not use a hand in his defence, to quit himself of a life that would by no means endure slavery; nor could he move from the place where he was tied to any solid part of the ship against which he might have beat his head, and have finished his disgrace that way; so that being deprived of all other means, he resolved to perish for want of food. And pleased at last with that thought, and toiled and tired by rage and indignation, he laid himself down, and sullenly resolved upon dying, and refused all things that were brought him.

This did not a little vex the captain, and the more so because he found almost all of them of the same humour; so that the loss of so many brave slaves, so tall and goodly to behold, would have been very considerable. He therefore ordered one to go from him (for he would not be seen himself) to Oroonoko, and to assure him he was afflicted for having rashly done so inhospitable a deed, and which could not be now remedied, since they were far from shore; but since he resented it in so high a nature, he assured him he would revoke his resolution, and set both him and his friends ashore on the next land they should touch at; and of this the messenger gave him his oath, provided he would resolve to live. And Oroonoko, whose honour was such as he never had violated a word in his life himself, much less a solemn asseveration, believed in an instant what this man said, but replied he expected for a confirmation of this to have his shameful fetters dismissed. This demand was carried to the captain, who returned him answer that the offence had been so great which he had put upon the prince, that he durst not trust him with liberty while he remained in the ship, for fear lest by a valour natural to him, and a revenge that would animate that valour, he might commit some outrage fatal to himself and the king his master, to whom his vessel did belong. To this Oroonoko replied, he would engage his honour to behave himself in all friendly order and manner, and obey the command of the captain, as he was lord of the king's vessel, and general of those men under his command.

This was delivered to the still doubting captain, who could not resolve to trust a heathen he said, upon his parole,[24] a man that had no sense or notion of the God that he worshipped. Oroonoko then replied he was very sorry to hear that the captain pretended to the knowledge and worship of any gods who had taught him no better principles, than not to credit as he would be credited; but they told him the difference of their faith occasioned that distrust: for the captain had protested to him upon the word of a Christian, and sworn in the name of a great God, which if he should violate, he would expect eternal torment in the world to come. 'Is that all the obligation he has to be just to his oath?' replied Oroonoko. 'Let him know I swear by my honour, which to violate, would not only render me contemptible and despised by all brave and honest men, and so give myself perpetual pain, but it would be eternally offending and diseasing all mankind, harming, betraying, circumventing and outraging all men; but punishments hereafter are suffered by oneself; and the world takes no cognizances whether this god have revenged them, or not, 'tis done so secretly, and deferred so long; while the man of no honour suffers every moment the scorn and contempt of the honester world, and dies every day ignominiously in his fame, which is more valuable than life. I speak not this to move belief, but to show you how you mistake, when you imagine that he who will violate his honour, will keep his word with his gods.' So turning from him with a disdainful smile, he refused to answer him when he urged him to know what answer he should carry back to his captain; so that he departed without saying any more.

The captain pondering and consulting what to do, it was concluded that nothing but Oroonoko's liberty would encourage any of the rest to eat, except the Frenchman, whom the captain could not pretend to keep prisoner, but only told him he was secured because he might act something in favour of the prince, but that he should be freed as soon as they came to land. So that they concluded it wholly necessary to free the prince from his irons that he might show himself to the rest, that they might have an eye upon him, and that they could not fear a single man.

This being resolved, to make the obligation the greater, the captain himself went to Oroonoko; where, after many compliments, and assurances of what he had already promised, he receiving from the prince his parole, and his hand, for his good behaviour, dismissed his irons, and brought him to his own cabin; where, after having treated and reposed him a while, for he had neither eaten nor slept in four days before, he besought him to visit those obstinate people in chains, who refused all manner of sustenance; and entreated him to oblige them to eat, and assure them of their liberty the first opportunity.

Oroonoko, who was too generous[25] not to give credit to his words, showed himself to his people, who were transported with excess of joy at the sight of their darling prince; falling at his feet, and kissing and embracing them, believing, as some divine oracle, all he assured them. But he besought them to bear their chains with that bravery that became those whom he had seen act so nobly in arms; and that they could not give him greater proofs of their love and friendship, since 'twas all the security the captain (his friend) could have against the revenge, he said, they might possibly justly take, for the injuries sustained by him. And they all, with one accord, assured him they could not suffer enough when it was for his repose and safety.

After this they no longer refused to eat, but took what was brought them and were pleased with their captivity, since by it they hoped to redeem the prince, who, all the rest of the voyage, was treated with all the respect due to his birth, though nothing could divert his melancholy; and he would often sigh for Imoinda, and think this a punishment due to his misfortune, in having left that noble maid behind him that fatal night in the otan, when he fled to the camp.

Possessed with a thousand thoughts of past joys with this fair young person, and a thousand griefs for her eternal loss, he endured a tedious voyage, and at last arrived at the mouth of the river of Surinam, a colony belonging to the King of England, and where they 'were to deliver some part of their slaves. There the merchants and gentlemen of the country going on board to demand those lots of slaves they had already agreed on, and amongst those the overseers of those plantations where I then chanced to be, the captain, who had given the word, ordered his men to bring up those noble slaves in fetters, whom I have spoken of; and having put them, some in one, and some in other lots, with women and children (which they call pickaninnies[26]), they sold them off as slaves to several merchants and gentlemen; not putting any two in one lot, because they would separate them far from each other; not daring to trust them together, lest rage and courage should put them upon contriving some great action, to the ruin of the colony.

Oroonoko was first seized on and sold to our overseer, who had the first lot, with seventeen more of all sorts and sizes, but not one of quality with him. When he saw this, he found what they meant; for, as I said, he understood English pretty well; and being wholly unarmed and defenceless, so as it was in vain to make any resistance, he only beheld the captain with a look all fierce and disdainful, upbraiding him with eyes, that forced blushes on his guilty cheeks, he only cried in passing over the side of the ship, 'Farewell, Sir! 'Tis worth my suffering to gain so true a knowledge both of you and of your gods by whom you swear.' And desiring those that held him to forbear their pains, and telling them he would make no resistance, he cried, 'Come, my fellow-slaves, let us descend, and see if we can meet with more honour and honesty in the next world we shall touch upon.' So he nimbly leapt into the boat, and showing no more concern, suffered himself to be rowed up the river with his seventeen companions.

The gentleman that bought him was a young Cornish gentleman, whose name was Trefry;[27] a man of great wit, and fine learning, and was carried into those parts by the Lord — Governor, to manage all his affairs. He reflecting on the last words of Oroonoko to the captain, and beholding the richness of his vest, no sooner came into the boat, but he fixed his eyes on him; and finding something so extraordinary in his face, his shape and mien, a greatness of look, and haughtiness in his air, and finding he spoke English, had a great mind to be enquiring into his quality and fortune; which, though Oroonoko endeavoured to hide by only confessing he was above the rank of common slaves, Trefry soon found he was yet something greater than he confessed; and from that moment began to conceive so vast an esteem for him, that he ever after loved him as his dearest brother, and showed him all the civilities due to so great a man.

Trefry was a very good mathematician, and a linguist; could speak French and Spanish; and in the three days they remained in the boat (for so long were they going from the ship to the plantation) he entertained Oroonoko so agreeably with his art and discourse, that he was no less pleased with Trefry, than he was with the prince; and he thought himself, at least, fortunate in this, that since he was a slave, as long as he would suffer himself to remain so, he had a man of so excellent wit and parts for a master. So that before they had finished their voyage up the river, he made no scruple of declaring to Trefry all his fortunes and most part of what I have here related, and put himself wholly into the hands of his new friend, whom he found resenting all the injuries were done him, and was charmed with all the greatnesses of his actions, which were recited with that modesty and delicate sense, as wholly vanquished him, and subdued him to his interest. And he promised him on his word and honour, he would find the means to reconduct him to his own country again; assuring him, he had a perfect abhorrence of so dishonourable an action; and that he would sooner have died, than have been the author of such a perfidy. He found the prince was very much concerned to know what became of his friends, and how they took their slavery; and Trefry promised to take care about the enquiring after their condition, and that he should have an account of them.

Though, as Oroonoko afterwards said, he had little reason to credit the words of a backearary,[28] yet he knew not why, but he saw a kind of sincerity and awful truth in the face of Trefry; he saw an honesty in his eyes, and he found him wise and witty enough to understand honour; for it was one of his maxims, 'A man of wit could not be a knave or villain.'

In their passage up the river they put in at several houses for refreshment, and ever when they landed numbers of people would flock to behold this man; not but their eyes were daily entertained with the sight of slaves, but the fame of Oroonoko was gone before him, and all people were in admiration of his beauty. Besides, he had a rich habit on, in which he was taken, so different from the rest, and which the captain could not strip him of because he was forced to surprise his person in the minute he sold him. When he found his habit made him liable, as he thought, to be gazed at the more, he begged Trefry to give him something more befitting a slave; which he did, and took off his robes. Nevertheless, he shone through all and his osenbrigs (a sort of brown holland[29] suit he had on) could not conceal the graces of his looks and mien; and he had no less admirers than when he had his dazzling habit on. The royal youth appeared in spite of the slave, and people could not help treating him after a different manner without designing it; as soon as they approached him they venerated and esteemed him; his eyes insensibly commanded respect, and his behaviour insinuated it into every soul. So that there was nothing talked of but this young and gallant slave, even by those who yet knew not that he was a prince.

I ought to tell you, that the Christians never buy any slaves but they give them some name of their own, their native ones being likely very barbarous, and hard to pronounce; so that Mr Trefry gave Oroonoko that of Caesar, which name will live in that country as long as that (scarce more) glorious one of the great Roman, for 'tis most evident, he wanted no part of the personal courage of that Caesar,[30] and acted things as memorable, had they been done in some part of the world replenished with people and historians that might have given him his due. But his misfortune was to fall in an obscure world, that afforded only a female pen to celebrate his fame, though I doubt not but it had lived from others' endeavours, if the Dutch, who, immediately after his time, took that country, had not killed, banished, and dispersed all those that were capable of giving the world this great man's life, much better than I have done. And Mr Trefry, who designed it, died before he began it, and bemoaned himself for not having undertook it in time.[31]

For the future therefore, I must call Oroonoko, Caesar, since by that name only he was known in our western world, and by that name he was received on shore at Parham-House,[32] where he was destined a slave. But if the king himself (God bless him) had come ashore, there could not have been greater expectations by all the whole plantation, and those neighbouring ones, than was on ours at that time; and he was received more like a governor than a slave. Notwithstanding, as the custom was, they assigned him his portion of land, his house, and his business, up in the plantation.

But as it was more for form than any design to put him to his task, he endured no more of the slave but the name, and remained some days in the house, receiving all visits that were made him, without stirring towards that part of the plantation where the Negroes were.

At last, he would needs go view his land, his house, and the business assigned him. But he no sooner came to the houses of the slaves, which are like a little town by itself, the Negroes all having left work, but they all came forth to behold him, and found he was that prince who had, at several times, sold most of them to these parts; and, from a veneration they pay to great men, especially if they know them, and from the surprise and awe they had at the sight of him, they all cast themselves at his feet, crying out, in their language, 'Live, O King! Long live, O King!' And kissing his feet, paid him even divine homage.

Several English gentlemen were with him; and what Mr Trefry had told them, was here confirmed of which he himself before had no other witness than Caesar himself. But he was infinitely glad to find his grandeur confirmed by the adoration of all the slaves.

Caesar, troubled with their over-joy, and over-ceremony, besought them to rise, and to receive him as their fellow-slave, assuring them, he was no better. At which they set up with one accord a most terrible and hideous mourning and condoling, which he and the English had much ado to appease. But at last they prevailed with them, and they prepared all their barbarous music, and everyone killed and dressed something of his own stock (for every family has their land apart, on which, at their leisure-times, they breed all eatable things) and clubbing it together, made a most magnificent supper, inviting their grandee captain, their prince, to honour it with his presence, which he did, and several English with him, where they all waited on him, some playing, others dancing before him all the time, according to the manners of their several nations, and with unwearied industry, endeavouring to please and delight him.

While they sat at meat Mr Trefry told Caesar, that most of these young slaves were undone in love, with a fine she slave, whom they had had about six months on their land. The prince, who never heard the name of love without a sigh, nor any

mention of it without the curiosity of examining further into that
tale, which of all discourses was most agreeable to him, asked,
how they came to be so unhappy, as to be all undone for one fair
slave? Trefry, who was naturally amorous, and loved to talk of
love as well as anybody, proceeded to tell him, they had the most
charming black that ever was beheld on their plantation, about
fifteen or sixteen years old, as he guessed; that, for his part, he
had done nothing but sigh for her ever since she came; and that all
the white beauties he had seen, never charmed him so absolutely
as this fine creature had done; and that no man, of any nation,
ever beheld her, that did not fall in love with her; and that she
had all the slaves perpetually at her feet; and the whole country
resounded with the fame of Clemene, for so, said he, we have
christened her. But she denies us all with such a noble disdain,
that 'tis a miracle to see that she, who can give such eternal
desires, should herself be all ice, and all unconcern. She is adorned
with the most graceful modesty that ever beautified youth; the
softest sigher – that, if she were capable of love, one would swear
she languished for some absent happy man; and so retired, as if
she feared a rape even from the God of Day, or that the breezes
would steal kisses from her delicate mouth. Her task of work
some sighing lover every day makes it his petition to perform for
her, which she accepts blushing, and with reluctance, for fear he
will ask her a look for a recompense, which he dares not presume
to hope, so great an awe she strikes into the hearts of her
admirers. 'I do not wonder', replied the prince, 'that Clemene
should refuse slaves, being as you say so beautiful, but wonder
how she escapes those who can entertain her as you can do. Or
why, being your slave, you do not oblige her to yield.' 'I confess,'
said Trefry, 'when I have, against her will, entertained her with
love so long, as to be transported with my passion, even above
decency, I have been ready to make use of those advantages of
strength and force Nature has given me. But oh! she disarms me,
with that modesty and weeping so tender and so moving, that I
retire, and thank my stars she overcame me.' The company
laughed at his civility to a slave, and Caesar only applauded the
nobleness of his passion and nature, since that slave might be
noble, or, what was better, have true notions of honour and virtue

in her. Thus passed they this night, after having received, from the slaves, all imaginable respect and obedience.

The next day Trefry asked Caesar to walk, when the heat was allayed, and designedly carried him by the cottage of the fair slave, and told him, she whom he spoke of last night lived there retired. 'But,' says he, 'I would not wish you to approach, for, I am sure, you will be in love as soon as you behold her.' Caesar assured him, he was proof against all the charms of that sex, and that if he imagined his heart could be so perfidious to love again, after Imoinda, he believed he should tear it from his bosom. They had no sooner spoke, but a little shock dog, [33] that Clemene had presented her, which she took great delight in, ran out, and she, not knowing anybody was there, ran to get it in again, and bolted out on those who were just speaking of her. When seeing them, she would have run in again, but Trefry caught her by the hand, and cried, 'Clemene, however you fly a lover, you ought to pay some respect to this stranger' (pointing to Caesar). But she, as if she had resolved never to raise her eyes to the face of a man again, bent them the more to the earth, when he spoke, and gave the prince the leisure to look the more at her. There needed no long gazing, or consideration, to examine who this fair creature was. He soon saw Imoinda all over her; in a minute he saw her face, her shape, her air, her modesty, and all that called forth his soul with joy at his eyes, and left his body destitute of almost life. It stood without motion, and, for a minute, knew not that it had a being. And, I believe, he had never come to himself, so oppressed he was with over-joy, if he had not met with this allay, [34] that he perceived Imoinda fall dead in the hands of Trefry. This awakened him, and he ran to her aid, and caught her in his arms, where, by degrees, she came to herself; and 'tis needless to tell with what transports, what ecstasies of joy, they both a while beheld each other, without speaking, then snatched each other to their arms, then gaze again, as if they still doubted whether they possessed the blessing they grasped. But when they recovered their speech, 'tis not to be imagined what tender things they expressed to each other, wondering what strange fate had brought them again together. They soon informed each other of their fortunes, and equally bewailed their fate; but, at the same time, they mutually protested, that even fetters and slavery were soft and easy, and would be supported with joy and pleasure, while they could be so happy to possess each other, and to be able to make good their vows. Caesar swore he disdained the empire of the world, while he could behold his Imoinda, and she despised grandeur and pomp, those vanities of her sex, when she could gaze on Oroonoko. He adored the very cottage where she resided, and said, that little inch of the world would give him more happiness than all the universe could do, and she vowed, it was a palace, while adorned with the presence of Oroonoko.

Trefry was infinitely pleased with this novel,[35] and found this Clemene was the fair mistress of whom Caesar had before spoke; and was not a little satisfied, that Heaven was so kind to the prince, as to sweeten his misfortunes by so lucky an accident, and leaving the lovers to themselves, was impatient to come down to Parham-House (which was on the same plantation) to give me an account of what had happened. I was as impatient to make these lovers a visit, having already made a friendship with Caesar, and from his own mouth learned what I have related, which was confirmed by his Frenchman, who was set on shore to seek his fortunes, and of whom they could not make a slave, because a Christian, and he came daily to Parham Hill to see and pay his respects to his pupil prince. So that concerning and interesting myself in all that related to Caesar, whom I had assured of liberty as soon as the governor arrived, I hasted presently to the place where the lovers were, and was infinitely glad to find this beautiful young slave (who had already gained all our esteems, for her modesty and her extraordinary prettiness) to be the same I had heard Caesar speak so much of. One may imagine then, we paid her a treble respect; and though from her being carved in fine flowers and birds all over her body, we took her to be of quality before, yet, when we knew Clemene was Imoinda, we could not enough admire her.

I had forgot to tell you, that those who are nobly born of that country are so delicately cut and raced[36] all over the fore part of the trunk of their bodies, that it looks as if it were japanned;[37] the works being raised like high point[38] round the edges of the flowers. Some are only carved with a little flower, or bird, at the sides of the temples, as was Caesar; and those who are so carved over the body, resemble our ancient Picts, that are figured in the chronicles,[39] but these carvings are more delicate.

From that happy day Caesar took Clemene for his wife, to the general joy of all people, and there was as much magnificence as the country would afford at the celebration of this wedding. And in a very short time after she conceived with child; which made Caesar even adore her, knowing he was the last of his great race. This new accident made him more impatient of liberty, and he was every day treating with Trefry for his and Clemene's liberty; and offered either gold, or a vast quantity of slaves, which should be paid before they let him go, provided he could have any security that he should go when his ransom was paid. They fed him from day to day with promises, and delayed him, till the Lord Governor should come, so that he began to suspect them of falsehood, and that they would delay him till the time of his wife's delivery, and make a slave of that too, for all the breed is theirs to whom the parents belong. This thought made him very uneasy, and his sullenness gave them some jealousies of him, so that I was obliged, by some persons, who feared a mutiny (which is very fatal sometimes in those colonies that abound so with slaves that they exceed the whites in vast numbers),[40] to discourse with Caesar, and to give him all the satisfaction I possibly could. They knew he and Clemene were scarce an hour in a day from my lodgings, that they ate with me, and that I obliged them in all things I was capable of: I entertained him with the lives of the Romans, and great men, which charmed him to my company, and her, with teaching her all the pretty works that I was mistress of, and telling her stories of nuns,[41] and endeavouring to bring her to the knowledge of the true God. But of all discourses Caesar liked that the worst, and would never be reconciled to our notions of the Trinity, of which he ever made a jest; it was a riddle, he said, would turn his brain to conceive, and one could not make him understand what faith was. However, these conversations failed not altogether so well to divert him, that he liked the company of us women much above the men, for he could not drink, and he is but an ill companion in that country that cannot. So that obliging him to love us very well, we had all the liberty of speech with him, especially myself, whom he called his Great Mistress; and indeed my word would go a great way with him. For these reasons, I had opportunity to take notice to him, that he was not well pleased of late, as he used to be, was more retired and thoughtful, and told him, I took it ill he should suspect we would break our words with him, and not permit both him and Clemene to return to his own kingdom, which was not so long away, but when he was once on his voyage he would quickly arrive there. He made me some answers that showed a doubt in him, which made me ask him, what advantage it would be to doubt? It would but give us a fear of him, and possibly compel us to treat him so as I should be very loth to behold: that is, it might occasion his confinement. Perhaps this was not so luckily spoke of me, for I perceived he resented that word, which I strove to soften again in vain. However, he assured me, that whatsoever resolutions he should take, he would act nothing upon the white people. And as for myself, and those upon that plantation where he was, he would sooner forfeit his eternal liberty, and life itself, than lift his hand against his greatest enemy on that place. He besought me to suffer no fears upon his account, for he could do nothing that honour should not dictate, but he accused himself for having suffered slavery so long; yet he charged that weakness on love alone, who was capable of making him neglect even glory itself, and, for which, now he reproaches himself every moment of the day. Much more to this effect he spoke, with an air impatient enough to make me know he would not be long in bondage, and though he suffered only the name of a slave, and had nothing of the toil and labour of one, yet that was sufficient to render him uneasy, and he had been too long idle, who used to be always in action, and in arms. He had a spirit all rough and fierce, and that could not be tamed to lazy rest, and though all endeavours were used to exercise himself in such actions and sports as this world afforded, as running, wrestling, pitching the bar,[42] hunting and fishing, chasing and killing tigers of a monstrous size, which this continent affords in abundance; and wonderful snakes, such as Alexander is reported to have encountered at the river of Amazons, and which Caesar took great delight to overcome; yet these were not actions great enough for his large soul, which was still panting after more renowned action.

personal trust ignoring material circumstances

Before I parted that day with him, I got, with much ado, a promise from him to rest yet a little longer with patience, and wait the coming of the Lord Governor, who was every day expected on our shore. He assured me he would, and this promise he desired me to know was given perfectly in complaisance to me, in whom he had an entire confidence.

After this, I neither thought it convenient to trust him much out of our view, nor did the country who feared him; but with one accord it was advised to treat him fairly, and oblige him to remain within such a compass, and that he should be permitted, as seldom as could be, to go up to the plantations of the Negroes; or, if he did, to be accompanied by some that should be rather in appearance attendants than spies. This care was for some time taken, and Caesar looked upon it as a mark of extraordinary respect, and was glad his discontent had obliged them to be more observant to him. He received new assurance from the overseer, which was confirmed to him by the opinion of all the gentlemen of the country, who made their court to him. During this time that we had his company more frequently than hitherto we had had, it may not be unpleasant to relate to you the diversions we entertained him with, or rather he us.

faceless herd

My stay was to be short in that country, because my father died at sea, and never arrived to possess the honour was designed him (which was lieutenant-general of six and thirty islands, besides the continent of Surinam), nor the advantages he hoped to reap by them, so that though we were obliged to continue on our voyage, we did not intend to stay upon the place. Though, in a word, I must say thus much of it, that certainly had his late Majesty, of sacred memory, but seen and known what a vast and charming world he had been master of in that continent, he would never have parted so easily with it to the Dutch.[43] 'Tis a continent whose vast extent was never yet known, and may contain more noble earth than all the universe besides; for, they say, it reaches from east to west, one way as far as China, and another to Peru. It affords all things both for beauty and use; 'tis there eternal Spring, always the very months of April, May and June. The shades are perpetual, the trees, bearing at once all degrees of leaves and fruit, from blooming buds to ripe Autumn,[44]

groves of oranges, lemons, citrons, figs, nutmegs, and noble aro-
matics, continually bearing their fragrancies. The trees appearing
all like nosegays adorned with flowers of different kind; some
are all white, some purple, some scarlet, some blue, some yellow;
bearing, at the same time, ripe fruit and blooming young, or
producing every day new. The very wood of all these trees have
an intrinsic value above common timber, for they are, when cut,
of different colours, glorious to behold, and bear a price consider-
able, to inlay withal. Besides this, they yield rich balm, and gums,
so that we make our candles of such an aromatic substance, as
does not only give a sufficient light, but, as they burn, they cast
their perfumes all about. Cedar is the common firing, and all the
houses are built with it. The very meat we eat, when set on the
table, if it be native, I mean of the country, perfumes the whole
room, especially a little beast called an armadillo, a thing which I
can liken to nothing so well as a rhinoceros. 'Tis all in white
armour so jointed, that it moves as well in it, as if it had nothing
on. This beast is about the bigness of a pig of six weeks old. But it
were endless to give an account of all the divers wonderful and
strange things that country affords, and which we took a very
great delight to go in search of, though those adventures are
oftentimes fatal and at least dangerous. But while we had Caesar
in our company on these designs we feared no harm, nor suffered
any.

As soon as I came into the country, the best house in it was
presented me, called St John's Hill.[45] It stood on a vast rock of
white marble, at the foot of which the river ran a vast depth
down, and not to be descended on that side. The little waves still
dashing and washing the foot of this rock, made the softest
murmurs and purlings in the world, and the opposite bank was
adorned with such vast quantities of different flowers eternally
blowing, and every day and hour new, fenced behind them with
lofty trees of a thousand rare forms and colours, that the prospect
was the most rav[ish]ing[46] that sands can create. On the edge of
this white rock, towards the river, was a walk or grove of orange
and lemon trees, about half the length of the Mall[47] here, whose
flowery and fruity branches[48] meet at the top, and hindered the
sun, whose rays are very fierce there, from entering a beam into

the grove, and the cool air that came from the river made it not only fit to entertain people in, at all the hottest hours of the day, but refreshed the sweet blossoms, and made it always sweet and charming, and sure the whole globe of the world cannot show so delightful a place as this grove was. Not all the gardens of boasted Italy can produce a shade to out-vie this, which Nature had joined with Art to render so exceeding fine. And 'tis a marvel to see how such vast trees, as big as English oaks, could take footing on so solid a rock, and in so little earth, as covered that rock, but all things by Nature there are rare, delightful and wonderful. But to our sports.

Sometimes we would go surprising, and in search of young tigers in their dens, watching when the old ones went forth to forage for prey, and oftentimes we have been in great danger, and have fled apace for our lives, when surprised by the dams. But once, above all other times, we went on this design, and Caesar was with us, who had no sooner stolen a young tiger from her nest, but going off, we encountered the dam, bearing a buttock of a cow, which he[49] had torn off with his mighty paw, and going with it towards his den. We had only four women, Caesar, and an English gentleman, brother to Harry Martin, the great Oliverian.[50] We found there was no escaping this enraged and ravenous beast. However, we women fled as fast as we could from it, but our heels had not saved our lives, if Caesar had not laid down his cub, when he found the tiger quit her prey to make the more speed towards him, and taking Mr Martin's sword desired him to stand aside, or follow the ladies. He obeyed him, and Caesar met this monstrous beast of might, size, and vast limbs, who came with open jaws upon him, and fixing his awful stern eyes full upon those of the beast, and putting himself into a very steady and good aiming posture of defence, ran his sword quite through his breast down to his very heart, home to the hilt of the sword. The dying beast stretched forth her paw, and going to grasp his thigh, surprised with death in that very moment, did him no other harm than fixing her long nails in his flesh very deep, feebly wounded him, but could not grasp the flesh to tear off any. When he had done this, he hollowed to us to return, which, after some assurance of his victory, we did, and found him lugging out the sword from the bosom of the tiger, who was laid in her blood on the ground. He took up the cub, and with an unconcern, that had nothing of the joy or gladness of a victory, he came and laid the whelp at my feet. We all extremely wondered at his daring, and at the bigness of the beast, which was about the height of an heifer, but of mighty, great, and strong limbs.

Another time, being in the woods, he killed a tiger, which had long infested that part, and borne away abundance of sheep and oxen, and other things, that were for the support of those to whom they belonged. Abundance of people assailed this beast, some affirming they had shot her with several bullets quite through the body, at several times, and some swearing they shot her through the very heart, and they believed she was a devil rather than a mortal thing. Caesar had often said, he had a mind to encounter this monster, and spoke with several gentlemen who had attempted her, one crying, I shot her with so many poisoned arrows, another with his gun in this part of her, and another in that. So that he remarking all these places where she was shot, fancied still he should overcome her, by giving her another sort of a wound than any had yet done, and one day said (at the table) 'What trophies and garlands Ladies will you make me, if I bring you home the heart of this ravenous beast, that eats up all your lambs and pigs?' We all promised he should be rewarded at all our hands. So taking a bow, which he chose out of a great many, he went up in the wood, with two gentlemen, where he imagined this devourer to be. They had not passed very far in it, but they heard her voice, growling and grumbling, as if she were pleased with something she was doing. When they came in view, they found her muzzling in the belly of a new ravished sheep, which she had torn open, and seeing herself approached, she took fast hold of her prey, with her fore paws, and set a very fierce raging look on Caesar, without offering to approach him, for fear, at the same time, of losing what she had in possession. So that Caesar remained a good while, only taking aim, and getting an opportunity to shoot her where he designed. 'Twas some time before he could accomplish it, and to wound her, and not kill her, would but have enraged her more, and endangered him. He had a quiver of arrows at his side, so that if one failed he could be supplied. At last, retiring a little, he gave her opportunity to eat, for he found she was ravenous, and fell to as soon as she saw him retire, being more eager of her prey than of doing new mischiefs. When he going softly to one side of her, and hiding his person behind certain herbage that grew high and thick, he took so good aim, that, as he intended, he shot her just into the eye, and the arrow was sent with so good a will, and so sure a hand, that it stuck in her brain, and made her caper, and become mad for a moment or two, but being seconded by another arrow, he fell dead upon the prey. Caesar cut him open with a knife, to see where those wounds were that had been reported to him, and why he did not die of them. But I shall now relate a thing that possibly will find no credit among men, because 'tis a notion commonly received with us, that nothing can receive a wound in the heart and live; but when the heart of this courageous animal was taken out, there were seven bullets of lead in it, and the wounds seamed up with great scars, and she lived with the bullets a great while, for it was long since they were shot. This heart the conqueror brought up to us, and 'twas a very great curiosity, which all the country came to see; and which gave Caesar occasion of many fine discourses, of accidents in war, and strange escapes.

At other times he would go a-fishing, and discoursing on that diversion, he found we had in that country a very strange fish, called, a numb eel[51] (an eel of which I have eaten) that while it is alive, it has a quality so cold, that those who are angling, though with a line of never so great a length, with a rod at the end of it, it shall, in the same minute the bait is touched by this eel, seize him or her that holds the rod with benumbedness, that shall deprive them of sense, for a while. And some have fallen into the water, and others dropped as dead on the banks of the rivers where they stood, as soon as this fish touches the bait. Caesar used to laugh at this, and believed it impossible a man could lose his force at the touch of a fish; and could not understand that philosophy, that a cold quality should be of that nature. However, he had a great curiosity to try whether it would have the same effect on him it had on others, and often tried, but in vain. At last, the sought for fish came to the bait, as he stood angling on the bank; and instead of throwing away the rod, or giving it a sudden twitch out of the water, whereby he might have caught both the eel, and have dismissed the rod, before it could have too much power over him for experiment sake, he grasped it but the harder, and fainting fell into the river. And being still possessed of the rod, the tide carried him senseless as he was a great way, till an Indian boat took him up, and perceived, when they touched him, a numbness seize them, and by that knew the rod was in his hand, which, with a paddle (that is, a short oar) they struck away, and snatched it into the boat, eel and all. If Caesar were almost dead, with the effect of this fish, he was more so with that of the water, where he had remained the space of going a league, and they found they had much ado to bring him back to life. But, at last, they did, and brought him home, where he was in a few hours well recovered and refreshed; and not a little ashamed to find he should be overcome by an eel, and that all the people, who heard his defiance, would laugh at him. But we cheered him up, and he, being convinced, we had the eel at supper; which was a quarter of an ell about, and most delicate meat; and was of the more value, since it cost so dear as almost the life of so gallant a man.

About this time we were in many mortal fears, about some disputes the English had with the Indians, so that we could scarce trust ourselves, without great numbers, to go to any Indian towns, or place, where they abode, for fear they should fall upon us, as they did immediately after my coming away, and that it was in the possession of the Dutch, who used them not so civilly as the English, so that they cut in pieces all they could take, getting into houses, and hanging up the mother, and all her children about her, and cut a footman, I left behind me, all in joints, and nailed him to trees.

This feud began while I was there, so that I lost half the satisfaction I proposed, in not seeing and visiting the Indian towns. But one day, bemoaning of our misfortunes upon this account, Caesar told us, we need not fear, for if we had a mind to go, he would undertake to be our guard. Some would, but most would not venture. About eighteen of us resolved, and took barge, and, after eight days, arrived near an Indian town. But approaching it, the hearts of some of our company failed, and they would not venture on shore, so we polled who would, and who would not. For my part, I said, if Caesar would, I would go. He resolved, so did my brother, and my woman, a maid of good courage. Now none of us speaking the language of the people, and imagining we should have a half diversion in gazing only and not knowing what they said, we took a fisherman that lived at the mouth of the river, who had been a long inhabitant there, and obliged him to go with us. But because he was known to the Indians, as trading among them, and being, by long living there, become a perfect Indian in colour, we, who resolved to surprise them, by making them see something they never had seen (that is, white people) resolved only myself, my brother, and woman should go. So Caesar, the fisherman, and the rest, hiding behind some thick reeds and flowers, that grew on the banks, let us pass on towards the town, which was on the bank of the river all along. A little distant from the houses, or huts, we saw some dancing, others busied in fetching and carrying of water from the river. They had no sooner spied us, but they set up a loud cry, that frighted us at first. We thought it had been for those that should kill us, but it seems it was of wonder and amazement. They were all naked, and we were dressed, so as is most commode for the hot countries, very glittering and rich, so that we appeared extremely fine. My own hair was cut short, and I had a taffeta cap, with black feathers, on my head. My brother was in a stuff suit, with silver loops and buttons, and abundance of green ribbon. This was all infinitely surprising to them, and because we saw them stand still, till we approached them, we took heart and advanced, came up to them, and offered them our hands, which they took, and looked on us round about, calling still for more company; who came swarming out, all wondering, and crying out *tepeeme*,[52] taking their hair up in their hands, and spreading it wide to those they called out to, as if they would say (as indeed it signified) 'numberless wonders', or not to be recounted, no more than to number the hair of their heads.[53] By degrees they grew more bold, and from gazing upon us round, they touched us, laying their hands upon all the features of our faces, feeling our breasts and arms, taking up one petticoat, then wondering to see another, admiring our shoes and stockings, but more our garters, which we gave them, and they tied about their legs, being laced with silver lace at the ends, for they much esteem any shining things. In fine, we suffered them to survey us as they pleased, and we thought they would never have done admiring us. When Caesar, and the rest, saw we were received with such wonder, they came up to us, and finding the Indian trader whom they knew (for 'tis by these fishermen, called Indian traders, we hold a commerce with them; for they love not to go far from home, and we never go to them), when they saw him therefore they set up a new joy, and cried, in their language, 'Oh! here's our *tiguamy*, and we shall now know whether those things can speak.' So advancing to him, some of them gave him their hands, and cried, '*Amora tiguamy*',[54] which is as much as, 'How do you', or 'Welcome friend', and all, with one din, began to gabble to him, and asked, If we had sense, and wit? If we could talk of affairs of life, and war, as they could do? If we could hunt, swim, and do a thousand things they use? He answered them, we could. Then they invited us into their houses, and dressed venison and buffalo for us; and, going out, gathered a leaf of a tree, called a sarumbo leaf, of six yards long, and spread it on the ground for a table-cloth,[55] and cutting another in pieces instead of plates, setting us on little bow Indian stools, which they cut out of one entire piece of wood, and paint, in a sort of japan work. They serve everyone their mess on these pieces of leaves, and it was very good, but too high seasoned with pepper. When we had eaten, my brother and I took out our flutes, and played to them, which gave them new wonder, and I soon perceived, by an admiration that is natural to these people, and by the extreme ignorance and simplicity of them, it were not difficult to establish any unknown or extravagant religion among them, and to impose any notions or fictions upon them. For seeing a kinsman of mine set some paper a-fire, with a burning-glass, a trick they had never before seen, they were like to have adored him for a god, and begged he would give them the characters or figures of his name, that they might oppose it against winds and storms, which he did, and they held it up in those seasons, and fancied it had a charm to conquer them, and kept it like a holy relic. They are very superstitious, and called him the great *peeie*, that is, prophet.[56] They showed us their Indian *peeie*, a youth of about sixteen years old, as handsome as Nature could make a man. They consecrate a beautiful youth from his infancy, and all arts are used to complete him in the finest manner, both in beauty and shape. He is bred to all the little arts and cunning they are capable of, to all the legerdemain tricks, and sleight of hand, whereby he imposes upon the rabble, and is both a doctor in physic and divinity. And by these tricks makes the sick believe he sometimes eases their pains, by drawing from the afflicted part little serpents, or odd flies, or worms, or any strange thing; and though they have besides undoubted good remedies, for almost all their diseases, they cure the patient more by fancy than by medicines, and make themselves feared, loved, and reverenced. This young *peeie* had a very young wife, who seeing my brother kiss her, came running and kissed me; after this, they kissed one another, and made it a very great jest, it being so novel, and new admiration and laughing went round the multitude, that they never will forget that ceremony, never before used or known. Caesar had a mind to see and talk with their war captains, and we were conducted to one of their houses, where we beheld several of the great captains, who had been at council. But so frightful a vision it was to see them no fancy can create; no such dreams can represent so dreadful a spectacle. For my part I took them for hobgoblins, or fiends, rather than men. But however their shapes appeared, their souls were very humane and noble, but some wanted their noses, some their lips, some both noses and lips, some their ears, and others cut through each cheek, with long slashes, through which their teeth appeared; they had several other [57] formidable wounds and scars, or rather dismemberings. They had *comitias*, [58] or little aprons before them, and girdles of cotton, with their knives naked, stuck in it, a bow at their backs, and a quiver of arrows on their thighs, and most had feathers on their heads of diverse colours. They cried '*Amora tigame*' to us at our entrance, and were pleased we said as much to them. They feted us, and gave us drink of the best sort, and wondered, as much as the others had done before, to see us. Caesar was marvelling as much at their faces, wondering how they should all be so wounded in war; he was impatient to know how they all came by those frightful marks of rage or malice, rather than wounds got in noble battle. They told us, by our interpreter, that when any war was waging, two men chosen out by some old captain, whose fighting was past, and who could only teach the theory of war, these two men were to stand in competition for the generalship, or Great War Captain, and being brought before the old judges, now past labour, they are asked, what they dare do to show they are worthy to lead an army? When he, who is first asked, making no reply, cuts off his nose, and throws it contempt-ibly on the ground, and the other does something to himself that he thinks surpasses him, and perhaps deprives himself of lips and an eye. So they slash on till one gives out, and many have died in this debate. And 'tis by a passive valour they show and prove their activity, a sort of courage too brutal to be applauded by our black hero; nevertheless he expressed his esteem of them.

In this voyage Caesar begot so good an understanding between the Indians and the English, that there were no more fears, or heartburnings during our stay, but we had a perfect, open, and free trade with them. Many things remarkable, and worthy recit-ing, we met with in this short voyage, because Caesar made it his business to search out and provide for our entertainment, especi-ally to please his dearly adored Imoinda, who was a sharer in all our adventures; we being resolved to make her chains as easy as we could, and to compliment the prince in that manner that most obliged him.

As we were coming up again, we met with some Indians of strange aspects, that is, of a larger size, and other sort of features, than those of our country. Our Indian slaves, that rowed us, asked them some questions, but they could not understand us, but showed us a long cotton string, with several knots on it, and told us, they had been coming from the mountains so many moons as there were knots. They were habited in skins of a strange beast, and brought along with them bags of gold dust, which, as well as they could give us to understand, came streaming in little small channels down the high mountains, when the rains fell, and offered to be the convoy to anybody, or persons, that would go to the mountains. We carried these men up to Parham, where they were kept till the Lord Governor came. And because all the country was mad to be going on this golden adventure, the governor, by his letters, commanded (for they sent some of the gold to him) that a guard should be set at the mouth of the river of Amazons (a river so called, almost as broad as the river of Thames), and prohibited all people from going up that river, it conducting to those mountains of gold. But we going off for England before the project was further prosecuted, and the governor being drowned in a hurricane, either the design died, or the Dutch have the advantage of it. And 'tis to be bemoaned what His Majesty lost by losing that part of America.[59]

Though this digression is a little from my story, however since it contains some proofs of the curiosity and daring of this great man, I was content to omit nothing of his character.

It was thus, for some time we diverted him. But now Imoinda began to show she was with child, and did nothing but sigh and weep for the captivity of her lord, herself, and the infant yet unborn, and believed, if it were so hard to gain the liberty of two, 'twould be more difficult to get that for three. Her griefs were so many darts in the great heart of Caesar, and taking his opportunity one Sunday, when all the whites were overtaken in drink, as there were abundance of several trades, and slaves for four years, that inhabited among the Negro houses, and Sunday was their day of debauch (otherwise they were a sort of spies upon Caesar), he went pretending out of goodness to them, to feast amongst them, and sent all his music, and ordered a great treat for the whole gang, about three hundred Negroes. And about a hundred and fifty were able to bear arms, such as they had, which were sufficient to do execution with spirits accordingly. For the English had none but rusty swords, that no strength could draw from a scabbard, except the people of particular quality, who took care to oil them and keep them in good order. The guns also, unless here and there one, or those newly carried from England, would do no good or harm, for 'tis the nature of that county to rust and eat up iron, or any metals, but gold and silver. And they are very inexpert at the bow, which the Negroes and Indians are perfect masters of.

Caesar, having singled out these men from the women and children, made a harangue to them of the miseries, and ignominies of slavery; counting up all their toils and sufferings, under such loads, burdens, and drudgeries, as were fitter for beasts than men;

senseless brutes, than human souls. He told them it was not for days, months, or years, but for eternity; there was no end to be of their misfortunes. They suffered not like men who might find a glory, and fortitude in oppression, but like dogs that loved the whip and bell,[60] and fawned the more they were beaten. That they had lost the divine quality of men, and were become insensible asses, fit only to bear. Nay worse, an ass, or dog, or horse having done his duty, could lie down in retreat, and rise to work again, and while he did his duty endured no stripes, but men, villainous, senseless men, such as they, toiled on all the tedious week till black Friday, and then, whether they worked or not, whether they were faulty or meriting, they promiscuously, the innocent with the guilty, suffered the infamous whip, the sordid stripes, from their fellow slaves till their blood trickled from all parts of their body, blood whose every drop ought to be revenged with a life of some of those tyrants that impose it. 'And why,' said he, 'my dear friends and fellow sufferers, should we be slaves to an unknown people? Have they vanquished us nobly in fight? Have they won us in honourable battle? And are we, by the chance of war, become their slaves? This would not anger a noble heart, this would not animate a soldier's soul. No, but we are bought and sold like apes, or monkeys, to be the sport of women, fools and cowards, and the support of rogues, runagades,[61] that have abandoned their own countries, for raping, murders, thefts and villainies. Do you not hear every day how they upbraid each other with infamy of life, below the wildest salvages,[62] and shall we render obedience to such a degenerate race, who have no one human virtue left, to distinguish them from the vilest creatures? Will you, I say, suffer the lash from such hands?'[63] They all replied, with one accord, 'No, no, no; Caesar has spoke like a great captain, like a great king.'

After this he would have proceeded, but was interrupted by a tall Negro of some more quality than the rest. His name was Tuscan, who bowing at the feet of Caesar, cried, 'My lord, we have listened with joy and attention to what you have said, and, were we only men, would follow so great a leader through the world. But oh! consider, we are husbands and parents too, and have things more dear to us than life: our wives and children unfit for travel, in these impassable woods, mountains and bogs. We have not only difficult lands to overcome, but rivers to wade, and monsters to encounter, ravenous beasts of prey –' To this, Caesar replied, that honour was the first principle in Nature that was to be obeyed; but as no man would pretend to that, without all the acts of virtue, compassion, charity, love, justice and reason, he found it not inconsistent with that, to take an equal care of their wives and children, as they would of themselves, and that he did not design, when he led them to freedom, and glorious liberty, that they should leave that better part of themselves to perish by the hand of the tyrant's whip. But if there were a woman among them so degenerate from love and virtue to choose slavery before the pursuit of her husband, and with the hazard of her life, to share with him in his fortunes, that such an one ought to be abandoned, and left as a prey to the common enemy.

To which they all agreed – and bowed. After this, he spoke of the impassable woods and rivers, and convinced them, the more danger, the more glory. He told them that he had heard of one Hannibal a great captain, had cut his way through mountains of solid rocks,[64] and should a few shrubs oppose them, which they could fire before them? No, 'twas a trifling excuse to men resolved to die, or overcome. As for bogs, they are with a little labour filled and hardened, and the rivers could be no obstacle, since they swam by nature, at least by custom, from their first hour of their birth. That when the children were weary they must carry them by turns, and the woods and their own industry would afford them food. To this they all assented with joy.

Tuscan then demanded, what he would do? He said, they would travel towards the sea; plant a new colony, and defend it by their valour; and when they could find a ship, either driven by stress of weather, or guided by providence that way, they would seize it, and make it a prize, till it had transported them to their own countries. At least, they should be made free in his kingdom, and be esteemed as his fellow sufferers, and men that had the courage, and the bravery to attempt, at least, for liberty. And if they died in the attempt it would be more brave, than to live in perpetual slavery.

They bowed and kissed his feet at this resolution, and with one accord vowed to follow him to death. And that night was appointed to begin their march; they made it known to their wives, and directed them to tie their hamaca[65] about their shoulder, and under their arm like a scarf; and to lead their children that could go, and carry those that could not. The wives who pay an entire obedience to their husbands obeyed, and stayed for them, where they were appointed. The men stayed but to furnish themselves with what defensive arms they could get, and all met at the rendezvous, where Caesar made a new encouraging speech to them, and led them out.

But, as they could not march far that night, on Monday early, when the overseers went to call them all together, to go to work, they were extremely surprised to find not one upon the place, but all fled with what baggage they had. You may imagine this news was not only suddenly spread all over the plantation, but soon reached the neighbouring ones, and we had by noon about six hundred men, they call the militia of the county, that came to assist us in the pursuit of the fugitives. But never did one see so comical an army march forth to war. The men, of any fashion, would not concern themselves, though it were almost the common cause, for such revoltings are very ill examples, and have very fatal consequences oftentimes in many colonies. But they had a respect for Caesar, and all hands were against the Parhamites, as they called those of Parham Plantation,[66] because they did not, in the first place, love the Lord Governor, and secondly, they would have it, that Caesar was ill used, and baffled with.[67] And 'tis not impossible but some of the best in the country was of his counsel in this flight, and depriving us of all the slaves, so that they of the better sort would not meddle in the matter. The deputy governor, of whom I have had no great occasion to speak, and who was the most fawning fair-tongued fellow in the world, and one that pretended the most friendship to Caesar, was now the only violent man against him, and though he had nothing, and so need fear nothing, yet talked and looked bigger than any man. He was a fellow, whose character is not fit to be mentioned with the worst of the slaves. This fellow would lead his army forth to meet Caesar, or rather to pursue him. Most of their arms were of those sort of cruel whips they call cat with nine tails;[68] some had rusty useless guns for show; others old basket-hilts, whose blades had never seen the light in this age, and others had long staffs, and clubs. Mr Trefry went along, rather to be a mediator than a conqueror, in such a battle; for he foresaw, and knew, if by fighting they put the Negroes into despair, they were a sort of sullen fellows, that would drown, or kill themselves, before they would yield, and he advised that fair means was best. But Byam[69] was one that abounded in his own wit, and would take his own measures.

It was not hard to find these fugitives, for as they fled they were forced to fire and cut the woods before them, so that night or day they pursued them by the light they made, and by the path they had cleared. But as soon as Caesar found he was pursued, he put himself in a posture of defence, placing all the women and children in the rear, and himself, with Tuscan by his side, or next to him, all promising to die or conquer. Encouraged thus, they never stood to parley, but fell on pell-mell upon the English, and killed some, and wounded a good many, they having recourse to their whips, as the best of their weapons. And as they observed no order, they perplexed the enemy so sorely, with lashing them in the eyes. And the women and children, seeing their husbands so treated, being of fearful cowardly dispositions, and hearing the English cry out, 'Yield and live, yield and be pardoned', they all ran in amongst their husbands and fathers, and hung about them, crying out, 'Yield, yield, and leave Caesar to their revenge', that by degrees the slaves abandoned Caesar, and left him only Tuscan and his heroic Imoinda, who, grown big as she was, did nevertheless press near her lord, having a bow, and a quiver full of poisoned arrows, which she managed with such dexterity, that she wounded several, and shot the governor into the shoulder, of which wound he had like to have died, but that an Indian woman, his mistress, sucked the wound, and cleansed it from the venom. But however, he stirred not from the place till he had parlied with Caesar, who he found was resolved to die fighting, and would not be taken; no more would Tuscan, or Imoinda. But he, more thirsting after revenge of another sort, than that of depriving him of life, now made use of all his art of talking, and dissembling, and besought Caesar to yield himself upon terms, which he himself should propose, and should be sacredly assented to and kept by him. He told him, it was not that he any longer feared him, or could believe the force of two men, and a young heroine, could overcome all them, with all the slaves now on their side also, but it was the vast esteem he had for his person, the desire he had to serve so gallant a man, and to hinder himself from the reproach hereafter, of having been the occasion of the death of a prince, whose valour and magnanimity deserved the empire of the world. He protested to him, he looked upon this action, as gallant and brave, however tending to the prejudice of his lord and master, who would by it have lost so considerable a number of slaves, that this flight of his should be looked on as a heat of youth, and rashness of a too forward courage, and an unconsidered impatience of liberty, and no more; and that he laboured in vain to accomplish that which they would effectually perform, as soon as any ship arrived that would touch on his coast. 'So that if you will be pleased,' continued he, 'to surrender yourself, all imaginable respect shall be paid you; and yourself, your wife, and child, if it be here born, shall depart free out of our land.' But Caesar would hear of no composition, though Byam urged, if he pursued, and went on in his design, he would inevitably perish, either by great snakes, wild beasts, or hunger, and he ought to have regard to his wife, whose condition required ease, and not the fatigues of tedious travel, where she could not be secured from being devoured. But Caesar told him, there was no faith in the white men, or the gods they adored, who instructed them in principles so false, that honest men could not live amongst them; though no people professed so much, none performed so little; that he knew what he had to do, when he dealt with men of honour, but with them a man ought to be eternally on his guard, and never to eat and drink with Christians without his weapon of defence in his hand, and, for his own security, never to credit one word they spoke. As for the rashness and inconsiderateness of his action he would confess the governor is in the right, and that he was ashamed of what he had done, in endeavouring to make those free, who were by nature slaves, poor wretched rogues, fit to be used as Christians' tools; dogs, treacherous and cowardly, fit for such masters, and they wanted only but to be whipped into the knowledge of the Christian gods to be the vilest of all creeping things, to learn to worship such deities as had not power to make them just, brave, or honest. In fine, after a thousand things of this nature, not fit here to be recited, he told Byam, he had rather die than live upon the same earth with such dogs. But Trefry and Byam pleaded and protested together so much, that Trefry believing the governor to mean what he said, and speaking very cordially himself, generously put himself into Caesar's hands, and took him aside, and persuaded him, even with tears, to live, by surrendering himself, and to name his conditions. Caesar was overcome by his wit and reasons, and in consideration of Imoinda, and demanding what he desired, and that it should be ratified by their hands in writing, because he had perceived that was the common way of contract between man and man, amongst the whites. All this was performed, and Tuscan's pardon was put in, and they surrender to the governor, who walked peaceably down into the plantation with them, after giving order to bury their dead. Caesar was very much toiled with the bustle of the day, for he had fought like a Fury, and what mischief was done he and Tuscan performed alone, and gave their enemies a fatal proof that they durst do anything, and feared no mortal force.

But they were no sooner arrived at the place, where all the slaves receive their punishments of whipping, but they laid hands on Caesar and Tuscan, faint with heat and toil; and, surprising them, bound them to two several stakes, and whipped them in a most deplorable and inhumane manner, rending the very flesh from their bones; especially Caesar, who was not perceived to make any moan, or to alter his face, only to roll his eyes on the faithless governor, and those he believed guilty, with fierceness and indignation. And, to complete his rage, he saw every one of those slaves, who, but a few days before, adored him as something more than mortal, now had a whip to give him some lashes, while he strove not to break his fetters, though, if he had, it were impossible. But he pronounced a woe and revenge from his eyes, that darted fire, that 'twas at once both awful and terrible to behold.[70]

When they thought they were sufficiently revenged on him, they untied him, almost fainting, with loss of blood, from a thousand wounds all over his body, from which they had rent his clothes, and led him bleeding and naked as he was, and loaded him all over with irons, and then rubbed his wounds, to complete their cruelty, with Indian pepper, which had like to have made him raving mad, and, in this condition, made him so fast to the ground that he could not stir, if his pains and wounds would have given him leave. They spared Imoinda, and did not let her see this barbarity committed towards her lord, but carried her down to Parham, and shut her up, which was not in kindness to her, but for fear she should die with the sight, or miscarry, and then they should lose a young slave, and perhaps the mother.

You must know, that when the news was brought on Monday morning, that Caesar had betaken himself to the woods, and carried with him all the Negroes, we were possessed with extreme fear, which no persuasions could dissipate, that he would secure himself till night, and then, that he would come down and cut all our throats. This apprehension made all the females of us fly down the river, to be secured, and while we were away, they acted this cruelty. For I suppose I had authority and interest enough there, had I suspected any such thing, to have prevented it, but we had not gone many leagues, but the news overtook us that Caesar was taken, and whipped like a common slave. We met on the river with Colonel Martin, a man of great gallantry, wit, and goodness, and, whom I have celebrated in a character of my new comedy, by his own name, in memory of so brave a man.[71] He was wise and eloquent, and, from the fineness of his parts, bore a great sway over the hearts of all the colony. He was a friend to Caesar, and resented this false dealing with him very much. We carried him back to Parham, thinking to have made an accommodation; when we came, the first news we heard was, that the governor was dead of a wound Imoinda had given him, but it was not so well. But it seems he would have the pleasure of beholding the revenge he took on Caesar, and before the cruel ceremony was finished, he dropped down, and then they perceived the wound he had on his shoulder was by a venomed arrow, which, as I said, his Indian mistress healed, by sucking the wound.

We were no sooner arrived, but we went up to the plantation to see Caesar, whom we found in a very miserable and inexpressible condition, and I have a thousand times admired how he lived, in so much tormenting pain. We said all things to him, that trouble, pity, and good nature could suggest, protesting our innocence of the fact, and our abhorrence of such cruelties; making a thousand professions of services to him, and begging as many pardons for the offenders, till we said so much, that he believed we had no hand in his ill treatment, but told us, he could never pardon Byam. As for Trefry, he confessed he saw his grief and sorrow, for his suffering, which he could not hinder, but was like to have been beaten down by the very slaves, for speaking in his defence. But for Byam, who was their leader, their head – and should, by his justice, and honour, have been an example to them – for him, he wished to live, to take a dire revenge of him, and said, 'It had been well for him, if he had sacrificed me, instead of giving me the contemptible whip.' He refused to talk much, but begging us to give him our hands, he took them, and protested never to lift up his, to do us any harm. He had a great respect for Colonel Martin, and always took his counsel, like that of a parent, and assured him, he would obey him in anything, but his revenge on Byam. 'Therefore,' said he, 'for his own safety, let him speedily dispatch me, for if I could dispatch myself, I would not, till that justice were done to my injured person, and the contempt of a soldier. No, I would not kill myself, even after a whipping, but will be content to live with that infamy, and be pointed at by every grinning slave, till I have completed my revenge; and then you shall see that Oroonoko scorns to live with the indignity that was put on Caesar.' All we could do could get no more words from him, and we took care to have him put immediately into a healing bath, to rid him of his pepper, and ordered a chirurgeon[72] to anoint him with healing balm, which he suffered, and in some time he began to be able to walk and eat. We failed not to visit him every day, and, to that end, had him brought to an apartment at Parham.

The governor was no sooner recovered, and had heard of the menaces of Caesar, but he called his council, who (not to disgrace them, or burlesque the government there) consisted of such notorious villains as Newgate[73] never transported, and possibly originally were such, who understood neither the laws of God or man, and had no sort of principles to make them worthy the name of men. But, at the very council table, would contradict and fight with one another, and swear so bloodily that 'twas terrible to hear, and see them. (Some of them were afterwards hanged, when the Dutch took possession of the place; others sent off in chains.) But calling these special rulers of the nation together, and requiring their counsel in this weighty affair, they all concluded, that (damn them) it might be their own cases, and that Caesar ought to be made an example to all the Negroes, to fright them from daring to threaten their betters, their lords and masters, and, at this rate, no man was safe from his own slaves, and concluded, *nemine contradicente*,[74] that Caesar should be hanged.

Trefry then thought it time to use his authority, and told Byam his command did not extend to his lord's plantation, and that Parham was as much exempt from the law as Whitehall; and that they ought no more to touch the servants of the lord — (who there represented the king's person) than they could those about the king himself; and that Parham was a sanctuary, and though his lord were absent in person, his power was still in being there, which he had entrusted with him, as far as the dominions of his particular plantations reached, and all that belonged to it; the rest of the country, as Byam was lieutenant to his lord, he might exercise his tyranny upon. Trefry had others as powerful, or more, that interested themselves in Caesar's life, and absolutely said, he should be defended. So turning the governor, and his wise council, out of doors (for they sat at Parham-House) we[75] set a guard upon our landing place, and would admit none but those we called friends to us and Caesar.

The governor having remained wounded at Parham, till his recovery was completed, Caesar did not know but he was still there, and indeed, for the most part, his time was spent there, for he was one that loved to live at other people's expense, and if he were a day absent, he was ten present there, and used to play, and walk, and hunt, and fish, with Caesar. So that Caesar did not at all doubt, if he once recovered strength, but he should find an opportunity of being revenged on him. Though, after such a revenge, he could not hope to live, for if he escaped the fury of the English mobile,[76] who perhaps would have been glad of the occasion to have killed him, he was resolved not to survive his whipping, yet he had, some tender hours, a repenting softness, which he called his fits of coward, wherein he struggled with love for the victory of his heart, which took part with his charming Imoinda there, but, for the most part, his time was passed in melancholy thought, and black designs. He considered, if he should do this deed, and die either in the attempt, or after it, he left his lovely Imoinda a prey, or at best a slave, to the enraged multitude; his great heart could not endure that thought. 'Perhaps,' said he, 'she may be first ravished by every brute, exposed first to their nasty lusts, and then a shameful death.' No, he could not live a moment under that apprehension, too insupportable to be borne. These were his thoughts, and his silent arguments with his heart, as he told us afterwards, so that now resolving not only to kill Byam, but all those he thought had enraged him, pleasing his great heart with the fancied slaughter he should make over the whole face of the plantation. He first resolved on a deed, that (however horrid it at first appeared to us all) when we had heard his reasons, we thought it brave and just. Being able to walk, and, as he believed, fit for the execution of his great design, he begged Trefry to trust him into the air, believing a walk would do him good, which was granted him, and taking Imoinda with him, as he used to do in his more happy and calmer days, he led her up into a wood, where, after (with a thousand sighs, and long gazing silently on her face, while tears gushed, in spite of him, from his eyes), he told her his design first of killing her, and then his enemies, and next himself, and the impossibility of escaping, and therefore he told her the necessity of dying. He found the heroic wife faster pleading for death than he was to propose it, when she found his fixed resolution, and, on her knees, besought him, not to leave her a prey to his enemies. He (grieved to death) yet pleased at her noble resolution, took her up, and embracing her, with all the passion and languishment of a dying lover, drew his knife to kill this treasure of his soul, this pleasure of his eyes. While tears trickled down his cheeks, hers were smiling with joy she should die by so noble a hand, and be sent in her own country (for that's their notion of the next world) by him she so tenderly loved, and so truly adored in this, for wives have a respect for their husbands equal to what any other people pay a deity, and when a man finds any occasion to quit his wife, if he love her, she dies by his hand, if not, he sells her, or suffers some other to kill her. It being thus, you may believe the deed was soon resolved on, and 'tis not to be doubted, but the parting, the eternal leave-taking of two such lovers, so greatly born, so sensible, so beautiful, so young, and so fond, must be very moving, as the relation of it was to me afterwards.

All that love could say in such cases, being ended, and all the intermitting irresolutions being adjusted, the lovely, young, and adored victim lays herself down, before the sacrificer, while he, with a hand resolved, and a heart breaking within, gave the fatal stroke,[77] first, cutting her throat, and then severing her, yet smiling, face from that delicate body, pregnant as it was with fruits of tenderest love. As soon as he had done, he laid the body decently on leaves and flowers, of which he made a bed, and concealed it under the same coverlid of Nature, only her face he left yet bare to look on. But when he found she was dead, and past all retrieve, never more to bless him with her eyes, and soft language, his grief swelled up to rage; he tore, he raved, he roared, like some monster of the wood, calling on the loved name of Imoinda. A thousand times he turned the fatal knife that did the deed, toward his own heart, with a resolution to go immediately after her, but dire revenge, which now was a thousand times more fierce in his soul than before, prevents him, and he would cry out, 'No, since I have sacrificed Imoinda to my revenge, shall I lose that glory which I have purchased so dear, as at the price of the fairest, dearest, softest creature that ever Nature made? No, no!' Then, at her name, grief would get the ascendant of rage, and he would lie down by her side, and water her face with showers of tears, which never were wont to fall from those eyes. And however bent he was on his intended slaughter, he had not power to stir from the sight of this dear object, now more beloved, and more adored than ever.

He remained in this deploring condition for two days, and never rose from the ground where he had made his sad sacrifice. At last, rousing from her side, and accusing himself with living too long, now Imoinda was dead, and that the deaths of those barbarous enemies were deferred too long, he resolved now to finish the great work; but offering to rise, he found his strength so decayed, that he reeled to and fro, like boughs assailed by contrary winds, so that he was forced to lie down again, and try to summon all his courage to his aid. He found his brains turn round, and his eyes were dizzy, and objects appeared not the same to him [as] they were wont to do; his breath was short, and all his limbs surprised with a faintness he had never felt before. He had not eaten in two days, which was one occasion of this feebleness, but excess of grief was the greatest; yet still he hoped he should recover vigour to act his design, and lay expecting it yet six days longer, still mourning over the dead idol of his heart, and striving every day to rise, but could not.

In all this time you may believe we were in no little affliction for Caesar, and his wife. Some were of opinion he was escaped never to return; others thought some accident had happened to him. But however, we failed not to send out a hundred people several ways to search for him. A party, of about forty, went that way he took, among whom was Tuscan, who was perfectly reconciled to Byam. They had not gone very far into the wood, but they smelt an unusual smell, as of a dead body, for stinks must be very noisome that can be distinguished among such a quantity of natural sweets, as every inch of that land produces. So that they concluded they should find him dead, or somebody that was so. They passed on towards it, as loathsome as it was, and made such a rustling among the leaves that lie thick on the ground, by continual falling, that Caesar heard he was approached, and though he had, during the space of these eight days, endeavoured to rise, but found he wanted strength, yet looking up, and seeing his pursuers, he rose, and reeled to a neighbouring tree, against which he fixed his back. And being within a dozen yards of those that advanced, and saw him, he called out to them, and bid them approach no nearer, if they would be safe, so that they stood still, and hardly believing their eyes, that would persuade them that it was Caesar that spoke to them, so much was he altered. They asked him, what he had done with his wife? for they smelt a stink that almost struck them dead. He, pointing to the dead body, sighing, cried, 'Behold her there.'

They put off the flowers that covered her with their sticks, and found she was killed, and cried out, 'Oh monster! that hast murdered thy wife.' Then asking him, why he did so cruel a deed. He replied, he had no leisure to answer impertinent questions. 'You may go back,' continued he, 'and tell the faithless governor, he may thank Fortune that I am breathing my last, and that my arm is too feeble to obey my heart, in what it had designed him.' But his tongue faltering, and trembling, he could scarce end what he was saying. The English taking advantage by his weakness, cried, 'Let us take him alive by all means.' He heard them; and, as if he had revived from a fainting, or a dream, he cried out, 'No, gentlemen, you are deceived, you will find no more Caesars to be whipped, no more find a faith in me. Feeble as you think me, I have strength yet left to secure me from a second indignity.' They swore all anew, and he only shook his head, and beheld them with scorn. Then they cried out, 'Who will venture on this single man? Will nobody?' They stood all silent while Caesar replied, 'Fatal will be the attempt to the first adventurer, let him assure himself', and, at that word, held up his knife in a menacing posture, 'Look ye, ye faithless crew,' said he, ''tis not life I seek, nor am I afraid of dying', and, at that word, cut a piece of flesh from his own throat, and threw it at them, 'yet still I would live if I could, till I had perfected my revenge. But oh! it cannot be. I feel life gliding from my eyes and heart, and, if I make not haste, I shall yet fall a victim to the shameful whip.' At that, he ripped up his own belly, and took his bowels and pulled them out, with what strength he could, while some, on their knees imploring, besought him to hold his hand. But when they saw him tottering, they cried out, 'Will none venture on him?' A bold English cried, 'Yes, if he were the Devil' (taking courage when he saw him almost dead) and swearing a horrid oath for his farewell to the world he rushed on[.] Caesar with his armed hand met him so fairly, as stuck him to the heart, and he fell dead at his feet. Tuscan seeing that, cried out, 'I love thee, oh Caesar, and therefore will not let thee die, if possible.' And, running to him, took him in his arms, but, at the same time, warding a blow that Caesar made at his bosom, he received it quite through his arm, and Caesar having not the strength to pluck the knife forth, though he attempted it, Tuscan neither pulled it out himself, nor suffered it to be pulled out, but came down with it sticking in his arm, and the reason he gave for it was, because the air should not get into the wound. They put their hands across, and carried Caesar between six of them, fainted as he was, and they thought dead, or just dying, and they brought him to Parham, and laid him on a couch, and had the chirurgeon immediately to him, who dressed his wounds, and sewed up his belly, and used means to bring him to life, which they effected. We ran all to see him; and, if before we thought him so beautiful a sight, he was now so altered, that his face was like a death's head blacked over, nothing but teeth, and eye-holes. For some days we suffered nobody to speak to him, but caused cordials to be poured down his throat, which sustained his life, and in six or seven days he recovered his senses. For, you must know, that wounds are almost to a miracle cured in the Indies, unless wounds in the legs, which rarely ever cure.

When he was well enough to speak, we talked to him, and asked him some questions about his wife, and the reasons why he killed her. And he then told us what I have related of that resolution, and of his parting, and he besought us, we would let him die, and was extremely afflicted to think it was possible he might live. He assured us, if we did not despatch him, he would prove very fatal to a great many. We said all we could to make him live, and gave him new assurances, but he begged we would not think so poorly of him, or of his love to Imoinda, to imagine we could flatter him to life again; but the chirurgeon assured him, he could not live, and therefore he need not fear. We were all (but Caesar) afflicted at this news; and the sight was gashly.[78] His discourse was sad; and the earthly smell about him so strong, that I was persuaded to leave the place for some time (being myself but sickly, and very apt to fall into fits of dangerous illness upon any extraordinary melancholy). The servants, and Trefry, and the chirurgeons, promised all to take what possible care they could of the life of Caesar, and I, taking boat, went with other company to Colonel Martin's, about three days' journey down the river, but I was no sooner gone, but the governor taking Trefry, about some pretended earnest business, a day's journey up the river, having communicated his design to one Banister,[79] a wild Irishman, and one of the council, a fellow of absolute barbarity, and fit to execute any villainy, but was rich. He came up to Parham, and forcibly took Caesar, and had him carried to the same post where he was whipped, and causing him to be tied to it, and a great fire made before him, he told him, he should die like a dog, as he was. Caesar replied, this was the first piece of bravery that ever Banister did, and he never spoke sense till he pronounced that word, and, if he would keep it, he would declare, in the other world, that he was the only man, of all the whites, that ever he heard speak truth. And turning to the men that bound him, he said, 'My friends, am I to die, or to be whipped?' And they cried, 'Whipped! no; you shall not escape so well.' And then he replied, smiling, 'A blessing on thee', and assured them, they need not tie him, for he would stand fixed, like a rock, and endure death so as should encourage them to die. 'But if you whip me,' said he, 'be sure you tie me fast.'

He had learned to take tobacco, and when he was assured he should die, he desired they would give him a pipe in his mouth, ready lighted, which they did,[80] and the executioner came, and first cut off his members, and threw them into the fire. After that, with an ill-favoured knife, they cut his ears, and his nose, and burned them; he still smoked on, as if nothing had touched him. Then they hacked off one of his arms, and still he bore up, and held his pipe. But at the cutting off the other arm, his head sunk, and his pipe dropped, and he gave up the ghost, without a groan, or a reproach. My mother and sister were by him all the while, but not suffered to save him, so rude and wild were the rabble, and so inhuman were the justices, who stood by to see the execution, who after paid dearly enough for their insolence. They cut Caesar in quarters, and sent them to several of the chief plantations. One quarter was sent to Colonel Martin, who refused it, and swore, he had rather see the quarters of Banister, and the governor himself, than those of Caesar, on his plantations, and that he could govern his Negroes without terrifying and grieving them with frightful spectacles of a mangled king.

Thus died this great man, worthy of a better fate, and a more sublime wit than mine to write his praise. Yet, I hope, the reputation of my pen is considerable enough to make his glorious name to survive to all ages, with that of the brave, the beautiful, and the constant Imoinda.

LOVE-LETTERS TO
A GENTLEMAN [1]

LETTER I

YOU bid me write, and I wish it were only the effects of complaisance² that makes me obey you: I should be very angry with myself and you, if I thought it were any other motive: I hope it is not, and will not have you believe otherwise. I cannot help however, wishing you no mirth, nor any content in your dancing design; and this unwonted malice in me I do not like, and would have concealed it if I could, lest you should take it for something which I am not, nor will believe myself guilty of. May your women be all ugly, ill-natured, ill-dressed, ill-fashioned, and unconversable;³ and, for your greater disappointment may every moment of your time there be taken up with thoughts of me (a sufficient curse), and yet you will be better entertained than me, who possibly am, and shall be, uneasy with thoughts not so good. Perhaps you had eased me of some trouble, if you had let me see you, or known you had been well: but there are favours for better friends; and I'll endeavour not to resent the loss, or rather the miss of them. It may be, since I have so easily granted this desire of yours, in writing to you, you will fear you have pulled a trouble on —. But do not: I do, by this send for you – you know what you gave your hand upon; the date of banishment is already out, and I could have wished you had been so good-natured as to have disobeyed me. Pray take notice therefore I am better natured than you: I am profoundly melancholy since I saw you; I know not why; and should be glad to see you when your occasions will permit you to visit.

Astrea.

LETTER II

YOU may tell me a thousand years, my dear Lycidas, of your unbounded friendship; but after so unkind a departure as that last night, give me leave (when serious) to doubt it; nay, 'tis past doubt: I know you rather hate me. What else could hurry you from me, when you saw me surrounded with all the necessary impossibilities of speaking to you? I made as broad signs as one could do, who durst not speak, both for your sake and my own: I acted even imprudently, to make my soul be understood, that was then (if I may say so) in real agonies for your departure. 'Tis a wonder a woman so violent in all her passions as I, did not (forgetting all prudence, all considerations) fly out into absolute commands, or at least entreaties, that you would give me a moment's time longer. I burst to speak with you, to know a thousand things; but particularly, how you came to be so barbarous, as to carry away all that could make my satisfaction. You carried away my letter, and you carried away Lycidas; I will not call him mine, because he has so unkindly taken himself back. 'Twas with that design you came; for I saw all night with what reluctance you spoke, how coldly you entertained me, and with what pain and uneasiness you gave me the only conversation I value in the world. I am ashamed to tell you this: I know your peevish virtue will misinterpret me. But take it how you will, think of it as you please; I am undone, and will be free; I will tell you, you did not use me well: I am ruined, and will rail at you. – Come then, I conjure you, this evening, that after it I may shut those eyes that have been too long waking. I have committed a thousand madnesses in this, but you must pardon the faults you have created. Come and do so; for I must see you tonight, and that in a better humour than you were last night. No more; obey me as you have that friendship for me you profess; and assure yourself to find a very welcome reception from (Lycidas)

Your Astrea.

LETTER III

WHEN shall we understand one another? For I thought, dear Lycidas, you had been a man of your parole.[4] I will as soon believe you will forget me, as that you have not remembered the promise you made me. Confess you are the teasingest creature in the world, rather than suffer me to think you neglect me, or would put a flight upon me, that have chosen you from all the whole creation, to give my entire esteem to. This I had assured you yesterday, but that I dreaded the effects of your censure today; and though I scorn to guard my tongue, as hoping 'twill never offend willingly; yet I can, with much ado, hold it, when I have a great mind to say a thousand things I know will be taken in an ill sense. Possibly you will wonder what compels me to write, what moves me to send where I find so little welcome; nay, where I meet with such returns, it may be I wonder too. You say I am changed: I had rather almost justify an ill, than repent; maintain false arguments, than yield I am in the wrong. In fine, charming friend Lycidas, whatever I was since you knew me, believe I am still the same in soul and thought; but that is, what shall never hurt you, what shall never be but to serve you; why then did you say you would not sit near me? Was that, my friend, was that the esteem you profess? Who grows cold first? Who is changed? and who the aggressor? 'Tis I was first in friendship, and shall be last in constancy. You, by inclination, and not for want of friends, have I placed highest in my esteem; and for that reason your conversation is the most acceptable and agreeable of any in the world – and for this reason you shun mine. Take your course; be a friend like a foe, and continue to impose upon me, that you esteem me when you fly me. Renounce your false friendship, or let me see you give it entire to

Astrea.

LETTER IV

I HAD rather, dear Lycidas, set myself to write to any man on earth than you; for I fear your severe prudence and discretion, so nice, may make an ill judgment of what I say. Yet you bid me not dissemble; and you need not have cautioned me, who so naturally hate those little arts of my sex, that I often run on freedoms that may well enough bear a censure from people so scrupulous as Lycidas. Nor dare I follow all my inclinations neither, nor tell all the little secrets of my soul. Why I write them,

I can give no account; 'tis but fooling myself, perhaps, into an undoing. I do but (by this soft entertainment) look in my heart, like a young gamester, to make it venture its last stake. This, I say, may be the danger; I may come off unhurt, but cannot be a winner: why then should I throw an uncertain cast,[5] where I hazard all, and you nothing? Your staunch prudence is proof against love, and all the bank's on my side. You are so unreasonable, you would have me pay, where I have contracted no debt; you would have me give, and you, like a miser, would distribute nothing. Greedy Lycidas! Unconscionable and ungenerous! You would not be in love, for all the world, yet wish I were so, Uncharitable! – Would my fever cure you? or a curse on me, make you blessed? Say, Lycidas, will it? I have heard, when two souls kindly meet, 'tis a vast pleasure, as vast as the curse must be, when kindness is not equal; and why should you believe that necessary for me, that will be so very incommode for you? Will you, dear Lycidas, allow then, that you have less good-nature than I? Pray be just, till you can give such proofs of the contrary, as I shall be judge of; or give me a reason for your ill-nature. So much for loving.

Now, as you are my friend, I conjure you to consider what resolution I took up, when I saw you last (which methinks is a long time), of seeing no man till I saw your face again; and when you remember that, you will possibly be so kind, as to make what haste you can to see me again. Till then, have thoughts as much in favour of me as you can, for when you know me better, you will believe I merit all. May you be impatient and uneasy till you see me again; and bating that, may all the blessings of Heaven and Earth light on you, is the continued prayers of (dear Lycidas)

Your true Astrea.

LETTER V

THOUGH it be very late, I cannot go to bed, but I must tell thee I have been very good ever since I saw thee, and have been a writing, and have seen no face of man, or other body, save my own people. I am mightily pleased with your kindness to me tonight; and 'twas, I hope and believe, very innocent and undisturbing on both sides. My Lycidas says, he can be soft and dear when he please to put off his haughty pride, which is only assumed to see how far I dare love him ununited. Since then my soul's delight you are, and may ever be assured I am and ever will be yours, befall me what will, and that all the devils of Hell shall not prevail against thee. Show then, I say, my dearest love, thy native sweet temper. Show me all the love thou hast undissembled; then, and never till then, shall I believe you love; and deserve my heart, for God's sake, to keep me well; and if thou hast love (as I shall never doubt, if thou art always as tonight) show that love, I beseech thee; there being nothing so grateful to God, and mankind, as plain-dealing. 'Tis too late to conjure thee farther: I will be purchased with softness, and dear words, and kind expressions, sweet eyes, and a low voice.

Farewell; I love thee dearly, passionately and tenderly, and am resolved to be eternally (my only dear delight, and joy of my life)

Thy Astrea.

LETTER VI

SINCE you, my dearest Lycidas, have prescribed me laws and rules, how I shall behave myself to please and gain you; and that one of these is not lying or dissembling; and that I had tonight promised you should never have a tedious letter from me more, I will begin to keep my word, and stint my heart and hand. I promised though to write; and though I have no great matter to say more, than the assurance of my eternal love to you, yet to obey you, and not only so, but to oblige my own impatient heart, I must, late as 'tis, say something to thee.

I stayed after thee tonight, till I had read a whole act of my new play;[6] and then he led me over all the way, saying, 'Gad you were the man.' And beginning some rallying love discourse after supper, which he fancied was not so well received as it ought, he said you were not handsome, and called Philly[7] to own it; but he did not, but was of my side, and said you were handsome. So he went on a while, and all ended that concerned you. And this, upon my word, is all.

Your articles I have read over, and do not like them; you have broke one, even before you have sworn or sealed them; that is, they are writ with reserve. I must have a better account of your heart tomorrow, when you come. I grow desperate fond of you, and would fain be used well; if not, I will march off. But I will believe you mean to keep your word, as I will for ever do mine. Pray make haste to see me tomorrow; and if I am not at home when you come, send for me over the way,[8] where I have engaged to dine, there being an entertainment on purpose tomorrow for me.

For God's sake make no more niceties and scruples than need, in your way of living with me; that is, do not make me believe this distance is to ease you, when indeed 'tis meant to ease us both of love; and, for God's sake, do not misinterpret my excess of fondness; and if I forget myself, let the check you give be sufficient to make me desist. Believe me, dear creature, 'tis more out of humour and jest, than any inclination on my side; for I could sit eternally with you, without that part of disturbance. Fear me not, for you are (from that) as safe as in Heaven itself. Believe me, dear Lycidas, this truth, and trust me. 'Tis late, farewell; and come, for God's sake, betimes tomorrow, and put off your foolish fear and niceties, and do not shame me with your perpetual ill opinion; my nature is proud and insolent, and cannot bear it: I will be used something better, in spite of all your apprehensions falsely grounded. Adieu, keep me as I am ever yours,

Astrea.

By this letter, one would think I were the nicest thing on earth; yet I know a dear friend goes far beyond me in that unnecessary fault.

LETTER VII

My charming unkind,

I WOULD have engaged my life you could not have left me so coldly, so unconcerned as you did; but you are resolved to give me proofs of your no love. Your counsel, which was given you tonight, has wrought the effects which it usually does in hearts like yours. Tell me no more you love me; for 'twill be hard to make me think it, though it be the only blessing I ask on earth. But if love can merit a heart, I know who ought to claim yours. My soul is ready to burst with pride and indignation; and at the same time, love, with all his softness assails me, and will make me write: so that between one and the other, I can express neither as I ought. What shall I do to make you know I do not use to condescend to so much submission, nor to tell my heart so freely? Though you think it use, methinks, I find my heart swell with disdain at this minute, for my being ready to make asseverations of the contrary, and to assure you I do not, nor never did love, or talk at the rate I do to you, since I was born. I say, I would swear this, but something rolls up my bosom, and checks my very thought as it rises. You ought, oh faithless, and infinitely adorable Lycidas! to know and guess my tenderness; you ought to see it grow, and daily increase upon your hands. If it be troublesome, 'tis because I fancy you lessen, whilst I increase, in passion; or rather, that by your ill judgment of mine, you never had any in your soul for me. Oh unlucky, oh vexatious thought! Either let me never see that charming face, or ease my soul of so tormenting an agony, as the cruel thought of not being beloved. Why, my lovely dear, should I flatter you? or, why make more words of my tenderness, than another woman, that loves as well, would do, as once you said? No, you ought rather to believe that I say more, because I have more than any woman can be capable of. My soul is formed of no other material than love; and all that soul of love was formed for my dear, faithless Lycidas – methinks I have a fancy, that something will prevent my going tomorrow morning. However, I conjure thee, if possible, to come tomorrow about seven or eight at night, that I may tell you in what a deplorable condition you left me tonight. I cannot describe it; but I feel it, and with you the same pain, for going so inhumanely. But oh! you went to joys, and left me to torments! You went to love alone, and left me love and rage, fevers and calentures,⁹ even madness itself! Indeed, indeed, my soul! I know not to what degree I love you; let it suffice I do most passionately, and can have no thoughts of any other man, whilst I have life. No! Reproach me, defame me, lampoon me, curse me, and kill me, when I do, and let Heaven do so too.

Farewell – I love you more and more every moment of my life. Know it, and goodnight. Come tomorrow, being Wednesday, to, my adorable Lycidas, your

Astrea.

LETTER VIII

WHY, my dearest charmer, do you disturb that repose I had resolved to pursue, by taking it unkindly that I did not write? I cannot disobey you, because indeed I would not, though 'twere better much for both I had been for ever silent: I prophesy so, but at the same time cannot help my fate, and know not what force or credit there is in the virtue we both profess; but I am sure 'tis not good to tempt it: I think I am sure, and I think my Lycidas just. But, oh! to what purpose is all this fooling? You have often wisely considered it; but I never stayed to think 'til 'twas too late; and whatever resolutions I make in the absence of my lovely friend, one single sight turns me all woman, and all his. Take notice then, my Lycidas, I will henceforth never be wise more; never make any vows against my inclinations, or the little winged deity. I own I have neither the coldness of Lycidas, nor the prudence; I cannot either not love, or have a thousand arts of hiding it; I have nobody to fear, and therefore may have somebody to love. But if you are destined to be he, the Lord have mercy on me; for I'm sure you'll have none. I expect a reprimand for this plain confession; but I must justify it, and I will, because I cannot help it: I was born to ill luck; and this loss of my heart, is, possibly, not the least part on't. Do not let me see you disapprove it, I may one day grow ashamed of it, and reclaim, but never, whilst you blow the flame, though perhaps against your will. I expect now a very wise answer; and, I believe, with abundance of discretion, you will caution me to avoid this danger that threatens. Do so, if you have a mind to make me launch farther into the main Sea of Love: rather deal with me as with a right woman; make me believe myself infinitely beloved. I may chance from the natural inconstancy of my sex, to be as false as you would wish, and leave you in quiet. For as I am satisfied I love in vain, and without return, I'm satisfied that nothing, but the thing that hates me, could treat me as Lycidas does; and 'tis only the vanity of being beloved by me can make you countenance a softness so displeasing to you. How could anything, but the man that hates me, entertain me so unkindly? Witness your excellent opinion of me, of loving others; witness your passing by the end of the street where I live, and squandering away your time at any coffee-house, rather than allow me what you know in your soul is the greatest blessing of my life, your dear dull melancholy company; I call it dull, because you can never be gay or merry where Astrea is. How could this indifference possess you, when your malicious soul knew I was languishing for you? I died, I fainted, and pained for an hour of what you lavished out, regardless of me, and without so much as thinking on me! What can you say, that judgment may not pass? that you may not be condemned for the worst-natured, incorrigible thing in the world? Yield, and at least say, my honest friend Astrea, I neither do love thee, nor can, nor ever will; at least let me say, you were generous and told me plain blunt truth: I know it; nay worse, you impudently (but truly) told me your business would permit you to come every night, but your inclinations would not. At least this was honest, but very unkind, and not over civil. Do not you, my amiable Lycidas, know I would purchase your sight at any rate; why this neglect then? Why keeping distance? But as much as to say, 'Astrea, truly you will make me love you, you will make me be fond of you, you will please and delight me with your conversation, and I am a fellow that do not desire to be pleased, therefore be not so civil to me; for I do not desire civil company, nor company that diverts me.' A pretty speech this; and yet if I do obey, desist being civil, and behave myself very rudely, as I have done, you say, these two or three days – then, Oh, Astrea! where is your profession? Where your love so boasted? Your good nature, etc.? Why truly, my dear Lycidas, where it was, and ever will be, so long as you have invincible charms, and show your eyes, and look so dearly;

though you may, by your prudent counsel, and your wise conduct of absence, and marching by my door without calling in, oblige me to stay my hand, and hold my tongue. I can conceal my kindness, though not dissemble one; I can make you think I am wise, if I list; but when I tell you I have friendship, love and esteem for you, you may pawn your soul upon't. Believe 'tis true, and satisfy yourself you have, my dear Lycidas, in your Astrea all she professes. I should be glad to see you as soon as possible (you say Thursday) you can: I beg you will, and shall, with impatience expect you betimes. Fail me not, as you would have me think you have any value for

Astrea.

I beg you will not fail to let me hear from you, today being Wednesday, and see you at night if you can.

THE ROVER [1]

OR

THE BANISHED CAVALIERS [2]

THE ACTORS' NAMES

Don Antonio, the Viceroy's son.
Don Pedro, a noble Spaniard, his friend.
Belvile, an English Colonel in love with Florinda.
Willmore, the Rover.
Frederick, an English gentleman, and friend to Belvile and Blunt.
Blunt, an English country gentleman.
Stephano, servant to Don Pedro.
Philippo, Lucetta's gallant.
Sancho, pimp to Lucetta.
Biskey
and   } Two bravoes to Angellica.
Sebastian,
Officers and Soldiers
[*Diego,*] *Page* to Don Antonio.

WOMEN

Florinda, sister to Don Pedro.
Hellena, a gay young woman designed for a nun, and sister to Florinda.
Valeria, a kinswoman to Florinda.
Angellica Bianca, a famous courtesan.
Moretta, her woman.
Callis, governess to Florinda and Hellena.
Lucetta, a jilting wench.
Servants, other masqueraders, men and women.

The scene: NAPLES, in Carnival time.³

PROLOGUE

WITS, like physicians never can agree,
  When of a different society.
And Rabel's Drops[4] were never more cried down
By all the learned doctors of the town,
Than a new play whose author is unknown.
Nor can those doctors with more malice sue
(And powerful purses) the dissenting few,
Than those with an insulting pride, do rail
At all who are not of their own cabal.[5]

  If a young poet hit your humour right,
You judge him then out of revenge and spite.
So amongst men there are ridiculous elves,[6]
Who monkeys hate for being too like themselves.
So that the reason of the grand debate,
Why wit so oft is damned, when good plays take,
Is, that you censure as you love, or hate.

  Thus like a learned conclave poets sit,
Catholic judges both of sense and wit,
And damn or save, as they themselves think fit.
Yet those who to others' faults are so severe,
Are not so perfect but themselves may err.
Some write correct indeed, but then the whole
(Bating[7] their own dull stuff i' th' play) is stole:
As bees do suck from flowers their honeydew,
So they rob others, striving to please you.

  Some write their characters genteel and fine,
But then they do so toil for every line,
That what to you does easy seem, and plain,
Is the hard issue of their labouring brain.
And some th' effects of all their pains we see,
Is but to mimic good extempore.
Others by long converse about the town,
Have wit enough to write a lewd lampoon,[8]
But their chief skill lies in a bawdy song.
In short, the only wit that's now in fashion,

157

Is but the gleanings of good conversation.
As for the author of this coming play,
I asked him what he thought fit I should say
In thanks for your good company today:
He called me fool, and said it was well known,
You came not here for our sakes, but your own.[9]
New plays are stuffed with wits, and with debauches,[10]
That crowd and sweat like cits,[11] in May-Day coaches.[12]

Written by a Person of Quality.

ACT I

SCENE I. *A chamber.*

Enter Florinda *and* Hellena.

FLORINDA What an impertinent thing is a young girl bred in a nunnery! How full of questions! Prithee no more Hellena, I have told thee more than thou understand'st already.

HELLENA The more's my grief, I would fain know as much as you, which makes me so inquisitive; nor is't enough I know you're a lover, unless you tell me too, who 'tis you sigh for.

FLORINDA When you're a lover, I'll think you fit for a secret of that nature.

HELLENA 'Tis true, I never was a lover yet – but I begin to have a shrewd guess what 'tis to be so, and fancy it very pretty to sigh, and sing, and blush, and wish, and dream and wish, and long and wish to see the man; and when I do look pale and tremble; just as you did when my brother brought home the fine English Colonel to see you – what do you call him, Don Belvile.

FLORINDA Fie, Hellena.

HELLENA That blush betrays you. – I am sure 'tis so – or is it Don Antonio the viceroy's son?[13] – or perhaps the rich old Don Vincentio, whom my father designs you for a husband? – why do you blush again?

FLORINDA With indignation, and how near soever my father thinks I am to marrying that hated object, I shall let him see, I understand better what's due to my beauty, birth and fortune, and more to my soul, than to obey those unjust commands.

HELLENA Now hang me, if I don't love thee for that dear disobedience. I love mischief strangely, as most of our sex do, who are come to love nothing else – but tell me dear Florinda, don't you love that fine *Anglese*? – for I vow, next to loving him myself, 'twill please me most that you do so, for he is so gay and so handsome.

FLORINDA Hellena, a maid designed for a nun, ought not to be so curious in a discourse of love.

HELLENA And dost thou think that ever I'll be a nun? or at least till I'm so old, I'm fit for nothing else – faith no, sister; and that which makes me long to know whether you love Belvile, is because I hope he has some mad companion or other, that will spoil my devotion, nay I'm resolved to provide myself this carnival, if there be e'er a handsome proper fellow of my humour above ground, though I ask first.

FLORINDA Prithee be not so wild.

HELLENA Now you have provided yourself of a man, you take no care for poor me – prithee tell me, what dost thou see about me that is unfit for love – have I not a world of youth? a humour gay? a beauty passable? a vigour desirable? well shaped? clean limbed? sweet breathed? and sense enough to know how all these ought to be employed to the best advantage; yes I do and will, therefore lay aside your hopes of my fortune by my being a devote,[14] and tell me how you came acquainted with this Belvile? for I perceive you knew him before he came to Naples.

FLORINDA Yes, I knew him at the Siege of Pamplona,[15] he was then a colonel of French horse, who when the town was ransacked, nobly treated my brother and myself, preserving us from all insolences; and I must own (besides great obligations) I have I know not what, that pleads kindly for him about my heart, and will suffer no other to enter. – But see my brother.

Enter Don Pedro, Stephano *with a masquing habit, and* Callis.

PEDRO Good morrow, sister. – Pray when saw you your lover Don Vincentio?

FLORINDA I know not, sir – Callis, when was he here? for I consider it so little, I know not when it was.

PEDRO I have a command from my father here to tell you, you ought not to despise him, a man of so vast a fortune, and such a passion for you – Stephano, my things.

[*Puts on his masquing habit.*

FLORINDA A passion for me, 'tis more than e'er I saw, or he had a desire should be known – I hate Vincentio, Sir, and I would not have a man so dear to me as my brother, follow the ill customs of our country, and make a slave of his sister – and sir, my father's will I'm sure you may divert.

PEDRO I know not how dear I am to you, but I wish only to be ranked in your esteem equal with the English Colonel Belvile – why do you frown and blush? is there any guilt belongs to the name of that cavalier?

FLORINDA I'll not deny I value Belvile, when I was exposed to such dangers as the licensed lust of common soldiers threatened, when rage and conquest flew through the city – then Belvile, this criminal, for my sake, threw himself into all dangers to save my honour, and will you not allow him my esteem?

PEDRO Yes, pay him what you will in honour – but you must consider Don Vincentio's fortune, and the jointure[16] he'll make you.

FLORINDA Let him consider my youth, beauty and fortune; which ought not to be thrown away on his age and jointure.

PEDRO 'Tis true, he's not so young and fine a gentleman as that Belvile, – but what jewels will that cavalier present you with? those of his eyes and heart?

HELLENA And are not those better than any Don Vincentio has brought from the Indies?

PEDRO Why how now! has your nunnery breeding taught you to understand the value of hearts and eyes?

HELLENA Better than to believe Vincentio's deserve value from any woman – he may perhaps increase her bags,[17] but not her family.

PEDRO This is fine – go – up to your devotion, you are not designed for the conversation of lovers.

HELLENA Nor saints, yet awhile I hope.   [Aside.
Is't not enough you make a nun of me, but you must cast my sister away too? exposing her to a worse confinement than a religious life. Loveless marriage or passionless marriage?

PEDRO The girl's mad – it is a confinement to be carried into the country, to an ancient villa belonging to the family of the Vincentios these five hundred years, and have no other prospect than that pleasing one of feeling all her own that meets her eyes – a fine air, large fields and gardens, where she may walk and gather flowers.

HELLENA When, by moonlight? For I am sure she dares not encounter with the heat of the sun, that were a task only for Don Vincentio and his Indian breeding,[18] who loves it in the dog days.[19] – And if these be her daily divertisements, what are those of the night, to lie in a wide moth-eaten bedchamber, with furniture in fashion in the reign of King Sancho the First;[20] the bed, that which his forefathers lived and died in.

PEDRO Very well.

HELLENA This apartment (new furbished and fitted out for the young wife) he (out of freedom) makes his dressing room, and being a frugal and a jealous coxcomb, instead of a valet to uncase his feeble carcass, he desires you to do that office – signs of favour I'll assure you, and such as you must not hope for, unless your woman be out of the way.

PEDRO Have you done yet?

HELLENA That honour being past, the giant stretches itself; yawns and sighs a belch or two, loud as a musket, throws himself into bed, and expects you in his foul sheets, and e'er you can get yourself undressed, calls you with a snore or two[21] – and are not these fine blessings to a young lady?

PEDRO Have you done yet?

HELLENA And this man you must kiss, nay you must kiss none but him too – and nuzzle through his beard to find his lips.[22] – And this you must submit to for threescore years, and all for a jointure.

PEDRO For all your character of Don Vincentio, she is as like to marry him, as she was before.

HELLENA Marry Don Vincentio! Hand me, such a wedlock would be worse than adultery with another man. I had rather see her in the Hostel de Dieu,[23] to waste her youth there in vows, and be a hand-maid to lazars[24] and cripples, than to lose it in such a marriage.[25]

PEDRO You have considered, sister, that Belvile has no fortune to bring to you; banished his country, despised at home, and pitied abroad.

HELLENA What then? the Viceroy's son is better than that old Sir Fifty, Don Vincentio! Don Indian! He thinks he's trading to Gambo[26] still, and would barter himself (that bell and bauble) for your youth and fortune.

PEDRO Callis, take her hence, and lock her up all this carnival, and at Lent she shall begin her everlasting penance in a monastery.

HELLENA I care not, I had rather be a nun, than be obliged to marry as you would have me, if I were designed for it.

PEDRO Do not fear the blessing of that choice – you shall be a nun.

HELLENA Shall I so? you may chance to be mistaken in my way of devotion: – a nun! yes, I am like to make a fine nun! I have an excellent humour for a grate;²⁷ no, I'll have a saint of my own to pray to shortly, if I like any that dares venture on me.²⁸

PEDRO [aside] Callis, make it your business to watch this wild cat. As for you, Florinda, I've only tried you all this while and urged my father's will; but mine is, that you would love Antonio, he is brave and young, and all that can complete the happiness of a gallant maid – this absence of my father will give us opportunity to free you from Vincentio by marrying here, which you must do tomorrow.

FLORINDA Tomorrow!

PEDRO Tomorrow, or 'twill be too late – 'tis not my friendship to Antonio which makes me urge this, but love to thee, and hatred to Vincentio – therefore resolve upon tomorrow.

FLORINDA Sir, I shall strive to do, as shall become your sister.

PEDRO I'll both believe and trust you – adieu.

[Exeunt Pedro and Stephano.

HELLENA As becomes his sister! – that is to be as resolved your way, as he is his –   [Hellena goes to Callis.

FLORINDA I ne'er till now perceived my ruin near,
I've no defence against Antonio's love,
For he has all the advantages of Nature,
The moving arguments of youth and fortune.

HELLENA But hark you Callis, you will not be so cruel to lock me up indeed, will you?

CALLIS I must obey the commands I have – besides, do you consider what a life you are going to lead?

HELLENA Yes, Callis, that of a nun: and till then I'll be indebted a world of prayers to you, if you'll let me now see, what I never did, the divertisements of a carnival.

CALLIS What, go in masquerade? 'twill be a fine farewell to the world I take it – pray what would you do there?

HELLENA That which all the world does, as I am told, be as mad as the rest, and take all innocent freedoms – sister, you'll go too, will you not? come prithee, be not sad. – We'll outwit twenty brothers, if you'll be ruled by me – come, put off this dull humour with your clothes, and assume one as gay, and as fantastic, as the dress my cousin Valeria and I have provided, and let's ramble.

FLORINDA Callis, will you give us leave to go?

CALLIS I have a youthful itch of going myself.   [*Aside.*
– madam, if I thought your brother might not know it, and I might wait on you; for by my troth I'll not trust young girls alone.

FLORINDA Thou see'st my brother's gone already, and thou shalt attend, and watch us.

Enter Stephano.

STEPHANO Madam, the habits are come, and your cousin Valeria is dressed, and stays for you.

FLORINDA 'Tis well. – I'll write a note, and if I chance to see Belvile, and want an opportunity to speak to him, that shall let him know what I've resolved in favour of him.

HELLENA Come, let's in and dress us.   [*Exeunt.*

SCENE II. *A long street.*

Enter Belvile *melancholy,* Blunt *and* Frederick.

FREDERICK Why,[29] what the devil ails the colonel? In a time when all the world is gay, to look like mere Lent thus? Hadst thou been long enough in Naples to have been in love, I should have sworn some such judgment had befallen thee.

BELVILE No, I have made no new amours since I came to Naples.

FREDERICK You have left none behind you in Paris?

BELVILE Neither.

FREDERICK I cannot divine the cause then, unless the old cause, the want of money.

BLUNT And another old cause, the want of a wench – Would not that revive you?

BELVILE You are mistaken, Ned.

BLUNT Nay, 'sheartlikins, then thou'rt past cure.

FREDERICK I have found it out; thou hast renewed thy acquaintance with the lady that cost thee so many sighs at the Siege of Pamplona – pox on't, what d'you call her – her brother's a noble Spaniard – nephew to the dead general – Florinda – aye, Florinda – and will nothing serve thy turn but that damned virtuous woman? whom on my conscience thou lovest in spite too, because thou seest little or no possibility of gaining her.

BELVILE Thou art mistaken, I have interest enough in that lovely virgin's heart, to make me proud and vain, were it not abated by the severity of a brother, who perceiving my happiness –

FREDERICK Has civilly forbid thee the house?

BELVILE 'Tis so, to make way for a powerful rival, the viceroy's son, who has the advantage of me, in being a man of fortune, a Spaniard, and her brother's friend, which gives him liberty to make his court, whilst I have recourse only to letters, and distant looks from her window, which are as soft and kind –
As those which Heaven sends down on penitents.

BLUNT Heyday! 'Sheartlikins, simile! by this light the man is quite spoiled. – Fred, what the devil are we made of, that we cannot be thus concerned for a wench – 'sheartlikins, our Cupids are like the cooks of the camp, they can roast or boil a woman, but they have none of the fine tricks to set 'em off, no hogoes[30] to make the sauce pleasant and the stomach sharp.

FREDERICK I dare swear I have had a hundred as young, kind and handsome as this Florinda; and dogs eat me, if they were not as troublesome to me i'th morning, as they were welcome o'er night.

BLUNT And yet I warrant, he would not touch another woman, if he might have her for nothing.

BELVILE That's thy joy, a cheap whore.

BLUNT Why, 'sheartlikins, I love a frank soul – when did you ever hear of an honest woman that took a man's money? I warrant 'em good ones – but gentlemen, you may be free, you have been kept so poor with Parliaments and Protectors, that the little stock you have is not worth preserving – but I thank my stars, I had more grace than to forfeit my estate by cavaliering.

BELVILE Methinks only following the court[31] should be sufficient to entitle 'em to that.

BLUNT 'Sheartlikins, they know I follow it to do it no good, unless they pick a hole in my coat for lending you money now and then, which is a greater crime to my conscience, gentlemen, than to the Commonwealth.

Enter Willmore.

WILLMORE Ha! dear Belvile! noble colonel!

BELVILE Willmore! welcome ashore, my dear rover! – what happy wind blew us this good fortune?

WILLMORE Let me salute my dear Fred and then command me. – How is't, honest lad?

FREDERICK Faith, sir, the old compliment, infinitely the better to see my dear mad Willmore again. – Prithee why camest thou ashore? and where's the prince?[32]

WILLMORE He's well, and reigns still lord of the watery element. – I must aboard again within a day or two, and my business ashore was only to enjoy myself a little this carnival.

BELVILE Pray know our new friend, sir, he's but bashful, a raw traveller, but honest, stout, and one of us.   [*Embraces* Blunt.

WILLMORE That you esteem him, gives him an interest here.

BLUNT Your servant, sir.

WILLMORE But well, – faith I'm glad to meet you again in a warm climate, where the kind sun has its god-like power still over the wine and women – love and mirth are my business in Naples, and if I mistake not the place, here's an excellent market for chapmen[33] of my humour.

BELVILE See, here be those kind merchants of love you look for.

Enter several men in masquing habits,[34] some playing on music, others dancing after, women dressed like courtesans, with papers pinned on their breasts, and baskets of flowers in their hands.

BLUNT 'Sheartlikins, what have we here?

FREDERICK Now the game begins.

WILLMORE Fine pretty creatures! may a stranger have leave to look and love? – What's here – 'Roses for every month'?

[*Reads the papers.*

BLUNT 'Roses for every month'? what means that?

BELVILE They are, or would have you think they're courtesans, who here in Naples are to be hired by the month.

WILLMORE Kind, and obliging to inform us – Pray where do these roses grow? I would fain plant some of 'em in a bed of mine.

WOMAN Beware such roses, sir.

WILLMORE A pox of fear: I'll be baked with thee between a pair of sheets, and that's thy proper still; so I might but strew such roses over me, and under me – fair one, would you would give me leave to gather at your bush this idle month; I would go near to make somebody smell of it all the year after.

BELVILE And thou hast need of such a remedy, for thou stinkest of tar and ropes ends, like a dock or pest-house.

   [*The woman puts herself into the hands of a man, and exeunt.*]

WILLMORE Nay, nay, you shall not leave me so.

BELVILE By all means use no violence here.

WILLMORE Death! Just as I was going to be damnably in love, to have her led off! I could pluck that rose out of his hand, and even kiss the bed the bush grew in.

FREDERICK No friend to love like a long voyage at sea.

BLUNT Except a nunnery, Fred.

WILLMORE Death! But will they not be kind? quickly be kind? Thou know'st I'm no tame sigher, but a rampant lion of the forest.

   Advances from the farther end of the scenes, two men dressed all over with horns [35] *of several sorts, making grimaces at one another, with papers pinned on their backs.*

BELVILE Oh the fantastical rogues, how they're dressed. 'Tis a satire against the whole sex.

WILLMORE Is this a fruit that grows in this warm country?

BELVILE Yes. 'Tis pretty to see these Italians start, swell and stab, at the word cuckold, and yet stumble at horns on every threshold.

WILLMORE See what's on their back – 'Flowers of every night'. [*Reads*] – Ah rogue! and more sweet than roses of every month! This is a gardener of Adam's own breeding.

                                                            [*They dance.*

BELVILE What think you of those grave people?
– is a wake in Essex half so mad or extravagant?

WILLMORE I like their sober grave way, 'tis a kind of legal authorized fornication, where the men are not chid for't, nor the women despised,[36] as amongst our dull English, even the monsieurs want that part of good manners.

BELVILE But here in Italy, Monsieur is the humblest, best-bred gentleman – duels are so bafled by bravoes,[37] that an age shows not one but between a Frenchman, and a hangman, who is as much too hard for him on the piazza as they are for a Dutchman on the New Bridge[38] – but see, another crew.

Enter Florinda, Hellena *and* Valeria, *dressed like gipsies;* Callis *and* Stephano, Lucetta, Philippo *and* Sancho *in masquerade.*

HELLENA Sister, there's your Englishman, and with him a handsome proper fellow – I'll to him, and instead of telling him his fortune, try my own.

WILLMORE Gipsies on my life – sure these will prattle if a man cross their hands.[39]   [*Goes to* Hellena.
– Dear, pretty (and I hope) young devil, will you tell an amorous stranger, what luck he's like to have?

HELLENA Have a care how you venture with me, sir, lest I pick your pocket, which will more vex your English humour, than an Italian fortune will please you.

WILLMORE How the devil camst thou to know my country and humour?

HELLENA The first I guess by a certain forward impudence, which does not displease me at this time, and the loss of your money will vex you, because I hope you have but very little to lose.

WILLMORE Egad, child, thou'rt i'th'right, it is so little, I dare not offer it thee for a kindness – but cannot you divine what other things of more value I have about me, that I would more willingly part with?

HELLENA Indeed no, that's the business of a witch, and I am but a gipsy yet. – Yet without looking in your hand, I have a parlous[40] guess, 'tis some foolish heart you mean, an inconstant English heart, as little worth stealing as your purse.

WILLMORE Nay, then thou dost deal with the devil, that's certain. – Thou hast guessed as right, as if thou hadst been one of that number it has languished for. – I find you'll be better acquainted with it, nor can you take it in a better time; for I am come from sea, child, and Venus not being propitious to me in her own element: I have a world of love in store – would you would be good-natured and take some on't off my hands.

HELLENA Why, I could be inclined that way – but for a foolish vow I am going to make – to die a maid.

WILLMORE Then thou art damned without redemption, and as I am a good Christian, I ought in charity to divert so wicked a design – therefore prithee, dear creature, let me know quickly when and where I shall begin to set a helping hand to so good a work.

HELLENA If you should prevail with my tender heart (as I begin to fear you will, for you have horrible loving eyes) there will be difficulty in't that you'll hardly undergo for my sake.

WILLMORE Faith, child, I have been bred in dangers, and wear a sword, that has been employed in a worse cause than for a handsome kind woman – name the danger – let it be anything but a long siege – and I'll undertake it.

HELLENA Can you storm?

WILLMORE Oh most furiously.

HELLENA What think you of a nunnery wall? for he that wins me, must gain that first.

WILLMORE A nun! Oh how I love thee for't! There's no sinner like a young saint – nay now there's no denying me, the old law had no curse (to a woman) like dying a maid; witness Jephtha's daughter.[41]

HELLENA A very good text this, if well handled, and I perceive, father captain, you would impose no severe penance on her who were inclined to console herself before she took orders.[42]

WILLMORE If she be young and handsome.

HELLENA Aye, there's it – but if she be not –

WILLMORE By this hand, child, I have an implicit faith, and dare venture on thee with all faults – besides, 'tis more meritorious to leave the world, when thou hast tasted and proved the pleasure on't. Then 'twill be a virtue in thee, which now will be pure ignorance.

HELLENA I perceive, good father captain, you design only to make me fit for Heaven – but if on the contrary, you should quite divert me from it, and bring me back to the world again, I should have a new man to seek I find; and what a grief that will be – for when I begin, I fancy I shall love like anything, I never tried yet.

WILLMORE Egad and that's kind – prithee, dear creature, give me credit for a heart, for faith I'm a very honest fellow – Oh, I long to come first to the banquet of love! and such swinging appetite I bring – Oh I'm impatient. – Thy lodging, sweetheart, thy lodging! or I'm a dead man!

HELLENA Why must we be either guilty of fornication or murder if we converse with you men – and is there no difference between leave to love me, and leave to lie with me?

WILLMORE Faith child, they were made to go together.

LUCETTA Are you sure this is the man?   [Pointing to Blunt.

SANCHO When did I mistake your game?

LUCETTA This is a stranger, I know by his gazing; if he be brisk he'll venture to follow me; and then if I understand my trade, he's mine; he's English too, and they say that's a sort of good-natured loving people, and have generally so kind an opinion of themselves, that a woman with any wit may flatter 'em into any sort of fool she pleases.

[She often passes by Blunt, and gazes on him, he struts and cocks, and walks and gazes on her.

BLUNT 'Tis so – she is taken – I have beauties which my false glass at home did not discover.

FLORINDA This woman watches me so, I shall get no opportunity to discover myself to him, and so miss the intent of my coming – but as I was saying, sir, – by this line you should be a lover.

[Looking in his hand.

BELVILE I thought how right you guessed, all men are in love, or pretend to be so – come let me go, I'm weary of this fooling.

FLORINDA I will not, till you have confessed whether the passion that you have vowed Florinda be true or false?

[She holds him, he strives to get from her. Walks away.

BELVILE Florinda!   [*Turns quick towards her.*

FLORINDA Softly.

BELVILE Thou hast named one will fix me here for ever.

FLORINDA She'll be disappointed then, who expects you this night at the garden gate, and if you fail not – as let me see the other hand – you will go near to do – she vows to die or make you happy.   [*Looks on* Callis, *who observes them.*

BELVILE What canst thou mean?

FLORINDA That which I say – farewell.   [*Offers to go.*

BELVILE Oh charming sybil, stay, complete that joy which as it is will turn into distraction! – where must I be? at the garden gate? I know it – at night, you say? – I'll sooner forfeit Heaven than disobey.

Enter Don Pedro *and other masquers, and pass over the stage.*

CALLIS Madam, your brother's here.

FLORINDA Take this to instruct you farther.

                 [*Gives him a letter, and goes off.*

FREDERICK Have a care, sir, what you promise; this may be a trap laid by her brother to ruin you.

BELVILE Do not disturb my happiness with doubts.

                 [*Opens the letter.*

WILLMORE My dear pretty creature, a thousand blessings on thee! still in this habit, you say? – and after dinner at this place.

HELLENA Yes, if you will swear to keep your heart, and not bestow it between this and that.

WILLMORE By all the little gods of love I swear, I'll leave it with you, and if you run away with it, those deities of justice will revenge me.   [*Exeunt all the women except* Lucetta.

FREDERICK Do you know the hand?

BELVILE 'Tis Florinda's. All blessings fall upon the virtuous maid.

FREDERICK Nay, no idolatry, a sober sacrifice I'll allow you.

BELVILE Oh friends, the welcomest news! the softest letter! – nay, you shall all see it! And could you now be serious, I might be made the happiest man the sun shines on!

WILLMORE The reason of this mighty joy?

BELVILE See how kindly she invites me to deliver her from the threatened violence of her brother – will you not assist me?

WILLMORE I know not what thou meanst, but I'll make one at any mischief where a woman's concerned – but she'll be grateful to us for the favour, will she not?

BELVILE How mean you?

WILLMORE How should I mean? thou knowst there's but one way for a woman to oblige me.

BELVILE Do not profane – the maid is nicely virtuous.

WILLMORE Who pox, then she's fit for nothing but a husband, let her e'en go, colonel.

FREDERICK Peace, she's the colonel's mistress, sir.

WILLMORE Let her be the devil, if she be thy mistress, I'll serve her – name the way.

BELVILE Read here this postscript. [*Gives him a letter.*

WILLMORE [*Reads*] 'At ten at night – at the garden gate – of which, if I cannot get the key, I will contrive a way over the wall – come attended with a friend or two.' – Kind heart, if we three cannot weave a string to let her down a garden wall, 'twere pity but the hangman wove one for us all.

FREDERICK Let her alone for that.[43] Your woman's wit, your fair kind woman, will out-trick a broker or a Jew, and contrive like a Jesuit in chains – but see, Ned Blunt is stolen out after the lure of a damsel. [*Exeunt* Blunt *and* Lucetta.

BELVILE So, he'll scarce find his way home again, unless we get him cried by the bellman[43] in the market-place, and 'twould sound prettily – a lost English boy of thirty.

FREDERICK I hope 'tis some common crafty sinner, one that will fit him; it may be she'll sell him for Peru, the rogue's sturdy, and would work well in a mine; at least I hope she'll dress him for our mirth, cheat him of all, then have him well-favouredly banged, and turned out naked at midnight.

WILLMORE Prithee what humour is he of, that you wish him so well?

BELVILE Why, of an English elder brother's humour, educated in a nursery, with a maid to tend him till fifteen, and lies with his grandmother till he's of age: one that knows no pleasure beyond riding to the next fair, or going up to London with his right worshipful father in Parliament-time; wearing gay clothes, or making honourable love to his lady mother's laundry-maid, gets drunk at a hunting-match, and ten to one then gives some proofs of his prowess. – A pox upon him, he's our banker, and has all our cash about him, and if he fail, we are all broke.

FREDERICK Oh, let him alone for that matter, he's of a damned stingy quality, that will secure our stock; [45] I know not in what danger it were indeed if the jilt should pretend she's in love with him, for 'tis a kind believing coxcomb; otherwise if he part with more than a piece of eight [46] – geld him: for which offer he may chance to be beaten, if she be a whore of the first rank.

BELVILE Nay, the rogue will not be easily beaten, he's stout enough; perhaps if they talk beyond his capacity, he may chance to exercise his courage upon some of them, else I'm sure they'll find it as difficult to beat as to please him.

WILLMORE 'Tis a lucky devil to light upon so kind a wench!

FREDERICK Thou hadst a great deal of talk with thy little gipsy, couldst thou do no good upon her? for mine was hard-hearted.

WILLMORE Hang her, she was some damned honest [47] person of quality I'm sure, she was so very free and witty. If her face be but answerable to her wit, and humour, I would be bound to constancy this month to gain her – in the meantime, have you made no kind acquaintance since you came to town? – you do not use to be honest so long, gentlemen.

FREDERICK Faith, love has kept us honest, we have been all fired with a beauty newly come to town, the famous Paduana [48] Angellica Bianca.

WILLMORE What, the mistress of the dead Spanish general?

BELVILE Yes, she's now the only adored beauty of all the youth in Naples, who put on all their charms to appear lovely in her sight, their coaches, liveries, and themselves, all gay, as on a monarch's birthday, to attract the eyes of this fair charmer, while she has the pleasure to behold all languish for her that see her.

FREDERICK 'Tis pretty to see with how much love the men regard her, and how much envy the women.

WILLMORE What gallant has she?

BELVILE None, she's exposed to sale, and four days in the week she's yours – for so much a month.

WILLMORE The very thought of it quenches all manner of fire in me – yet prithee, let's see her.

BELVILE Let's first to dinner, and after that we'll pass the day as you please – but at night ye must all be at my devotion.

WILLMORE I will not fail you. [Exeunt.

ACT II

SCENE I. *The long street.*

Enter Belvile *and* Frederick *in masquing habits, and* Willmore *in his own clothes, with a vizard* [49] *in his hand.*

WILLMORE But why thus disguised and muzzled?

BELVILE Because whatever extravagances we commit in these faces, our own may not be obliged to answer 'em.

WILLMORE I should have changed my eternal buff [50] too; but no matter, my little gipsy would not have found me out then; for if she should change hers, it is impossible I should know her, unless I should hear her prattle. – A pox on't, I cannot get her out of my head; pray Heaven, if ever I do see her again, she prove damnably ugly, that I may fortify myself against her tongue.

BELVILE Have a care of love; for o' my conscience she was not of a quality to give thee any hopes.

WILLMORE Pox on 'em, why do they draw a man in then? She has played with my heart so, that 'twill never lie still, till I have met with some kind wench that will play the game out with me – Oh, for my arms full of soft, white, kind – woman! such as I fancy Angellica.

BELVILE This is her house, if you were but in stock to get admittance; they have not dined yet, I perceive the picture is not out.

Enter Blunt.

WILLMORE I long to see the shadow of the fair substance; a man may gaze on that for nothing.

BLUNT Colonel. Thy hand – and thine, Fred. I have been an ass, a deluded fool, a very coxcomb from my birth till this hour, and heartily repent my little faith.

BELVILE What the devil's the matter with thee, Ned?

BLUNT – Oh such a mistress, Fred! such a girl!

WILLMORE Ha! where!

FREDERICK Aye! where!

BLUNT So fond, so amorous, so toying and so fine! and all for sheer love, ye rogue! Oh how she looked and kissed! and soothed my heart from my bosom – I cannot think I was awake, and yet methinks I see and feel her charms still – Fred, try if she have not left the taste of her balmy kisses upon my lips –[51]

[*Kisses him.*

BELVILE Ha! Ha! Ha!

WILLMORE Death, man, where is she?

BLUNT What a dog was I to stay in dull England so long – how have I laughed at the colonel when he sighed for love! but now the little archer has revenged him! and by this one dart, I can guess at all his joys, which then I took for fancies, mere dreams and fables. – Well, I'm resolved to sell all in Essex, and plant here for ever.

BELVILE What a blessing 'tis, thou hast a mistress thou darst boast of; for I know thy humour is rather to have a proclaimed clap,[52] than a secret amour.

WILLMORE Dost know her name?

BLUNT Her name? No, 'sheartlikins, what care I for names. – She's fair! young! brisk and kind! even to ravishment! and what a pox care I for knowing her by any other title.

WILLMORE Didst give her anything?

BLUNT Give her! – Ha, ha, ha! why, she's a person of quality; – that's a good one, give her! 'sheartlikins, dost think such creatures are to be bought? Or are we provided for such a purchase? give her, quoth ye? Why, she presented me with this bracelet, for the toy of a diamond I used to wear. No, gentlemen, Ned Blunt is not everybody – she expects me again tonight.

WILLMORE Egad, that's well; we'll all go.

BLUNT Not a soul: no, gentlemen, you are wits; I am a dull country rogue, I.

FREDERICK Well, Sir, for all your person of quality, I shall be very glad to understand your purse be secure; 'tis our whole estate at present, which we are loth to hazard in one bottom;[53] come, sir, unload.

BLUNT Take the necessary trifle useless now to me, that am beloved by such a gentlewoman – 'sheartlikins, money! Here, take mine too.

FREDERICK No, keep that to be cozened,[54] that we may laugh.

WILLMORE Cozened! – Death! would I could meet with one that would cozen me of all the love I could spare tonight.

FREDERICK Pox, 'tis some common whore upon my life.

BLUNT A whore! – yes, with such clothes! such jewels! such a house! such furniture, and so attended! a whore!

BELVILE Why yes, Sir, they are whores, though they'll neither entertain you with drinking, swearing, or bawdry; are whores in all those gay clothes, and right jewels, are whores with those great houses richly furnished with velvet beds, store of plate, handsome attendance, and fine coaches, are whores and errant[55] ones.

WILLMORE Pox on't, where do these fine whores live?

BELVILE Where no rogues in office ycleped[56] constables dare give 'em laws, nor the wine inspired bullies[57] of the town break their windows; yet they are whores though this Essex calf[58] believe 'em persons of quality.

BLUNT 'Sheartlikins, y'are all fools, there are things about this Essex calf, that shall take with the ladies, beyond all your wit and parts – this shape and size gentlemen are not to be despised – my waist too tolerably long, with other inviting signs, that shall be nameless.

WILLMORE Egad, I believe he may have met with some person of quality that may be kind to him.

BELVILE Dost thou perceive any such tempting things about him, that should make a fine woman, and of quality, pick him out from all mankind, to throw away her youth and beauty upon, nay and her dear heart too! – no, no, Angellica has raised the price too high.

WILLMORE May she languish for mankind till she die, and be damned for that one sin alone.

Enter two Bravoes, *and hang up a great picture of Angellica's against the balcony, and two little ones at each side of the door.*

BELVILE See there the fair sign to the inn where a man may lodge that's fool enough to give her price.

[Willmore *gazes on the picture.*

BLUNT 'Sheartlikins, gentlemen, what's this!

BELVILE A famous courtesan, that's to be sold.

BLUNT How? to be sold! nay, then I have nothing to say to her – sold! what impudence is practised in this country? – with what order and decency whoring's established here by virtue of the Inquisition – come, let's be gone, I'm sure we're no chapmen for this commodity.

FREDERICK Thou art none I'm sure, unless thou could'st have her in thy bed at a price of a coach in the street.

WILLMORE How wondrous fair she is – a thousand crowns a month [59] – by Heaven as many kingdoms were too little, a plague of this poverty – of which I ne'er complain, but when it hinders my approach to beauty, which virtue ne'er could purchase. [*Turns from the picture.*

BLUNT What's this? – [*Reads.*] A thousand crowns a month! – 'Sheartlikins, here's a sum! sure 'tis a mistake. – [*To one of the bravoes.*] Hark you, friend, does she take or give so much by the month?

FREDERICK A thousand crowns! why, 'tis a portion for the Infanta. [60]

BLUNT Hark ye, friends, won't she trust?

BRAVO This is a trade, sir, that cannot live by credit.

Enter Don Pedro *in masquerade, followed by* Stephano.

BELVILE See, here's more company, let's walk off a while.

[*Exeunt English.* Pedro *reads.*

Enter Angellica *and* Moretta *in the balcony, and draw a silk curtain.*

PEDRO Fetch me a thousand crowns, I never wished to buy this beauty at an easier rate. [*Passes off.*

ANGELLICA Prithee, what said those fellows to thee?

BRAVO Madam, the first were admirers of beauty only, but no purchasers, they were merry with your price and picture, laughed at the sum, and so passed off.

ANGELLICA No matter, I'm not displeased with their rallying; their wonder feeds my vanity, and he that wishes but to buy gives me more pride, than he that gives my price can make my pleasure.

BRAVO Madam, the last I knew through all his disguises to be Don Pedro, nephew to the general, and who was with him in Pamplona.

ANGELLICA Don Pedro! my old gallant's nephew, when his uncle died he left him a vast sum of money; it is he who was so in love with me at Padua, and who used to make the general so jealous.

MORETTA Is this he that used to prance before our window, and take such care to show himself an amorous ass? If I am not mistaken he is the likeliest man to give your price.

ANGELLICA The man is brave and generous, but of a humour so uneasy and inconstant, that the victory over his heart is as soon lost as won; a slave that can add little to the triumph of the conqueror: but inconstancy's the sin of all mankind, therefore I'm resolved that nothing but gold shall charm my heart.

MORETTA I'm glad on't; 'tis only interest that women of our profession ought to consider: though I wonder what has kept you from that general disease of our sex so long, I mean that of being in love.

ANGELLICA A kind, but sullen star under which I had the happiness to be born; yet I have had no time for love; the bravest and noblest of mankind have purchased my favours at so dear a rate, as if no coin but gold were current with our trade — but here's Don Pedro again, fetch me my lute — for 'tis for him or Don Antonio the viceroy's son, that I have spread my nets.

Enter at one door Don Pedro, Stephano; Don Antonio *and* Diego *at the other door with people following him in masquer-*

ade, anticly attired,[61] *some with music: they both go up to the picture.*

ANTONIO A thousand crowns! had not the painter flattered her, I should not think it dear.

PEDRO Flattered her! by Heaven he cannot, I have seen the original, nor is there one charm here more than adorns her face and eyes; all this soft and sweet, with a certain languishing air, that no artist can represent.

ANTONIO What I heard of her beauty before had fired my soul, but this confirmation of it has blown it to a flame.

PEDRO Ha!

PAGE Sir, I have known you throw away a thousand crowns on a worse face, and though y'are near your marriage, you may venture a little love here; Florinda will not miss it.

PEDRO Ha! Florinda! – sure 'tis Antonio.   [*Aside.*

ANTONIO Florinda! name not those distant joys, there's not one thought of her will check my passion here.

PEDRO Florinda scorned! and all my hopes defeated, of the possession of Angellica.

        [*A noise of a lute above.* Antonio *gazes up.*

Her injuries, by Heaven, he shall not boast of.

        [*Song to a lute above.*

SONG

When Damon first began to love
He languished in a soft desire,
And knew not how the gods to move,
To lessen or increase his fire.
For Celia in her charming eyes
Wore all love's sweets, and all his cruelties.

II

But as beneath a shade he lay,
Weaving of flowers for Celia's hair,

She chanced to lead her flock that way,
And saw the amorous shepherd there.
She gazed around upon the place,
And saw the grove (resembling night)
To all the joys of love invite,
Whilst guilty smiles and blushes dressed her face.
At this the bashful youth all transport grew,
And with kind force he taught the virgin how
To yield what all his sighs could never do.

ANTONIO By Heaven, she's charming fair!

Angellica *throws open the curtains, and bows to* Antonio, *who pulls off his vizard and bows and blows up kisses.* Pedro *unseen looks in his face.*

PEDRO 'Tis he; the false Antonio!
ANTONIO Friend, where must I pay my offering of love?

[*To the* Bravo.

My thousand crowns I mean.
PEDRO That offering I have designed to make.
And yours will come too late.
ANTONIO Prithee begone, I shall grow angry else,
And then thou art not safe.
PEDRO My anger may be fatal, sir, as yours;
And he that enters here may prove this truth.
ANTONIO I know not who thou art, but I am sure thou'rt worth
my killing, for aiming at Angellica.   [*They draw and fight.*

Enter Willmore *and* Blunt, *who draw and part them.*

BLUNT 'Sheartlikins, here's fine doings.
WILLMORE Tilting for the wench I'm sure – nay gad, if that would
win her, I have as good a sword as the best of ye. – Put up, – put up,
and take another time and place, for this is designed for lovers only.

[*They all put up.*

PEDRO We are prevented; dare you meet me tomorrow on the
Molo?[62]
For I've a title to a better quarrel,
That of Florinda, in whose credulous heart

Thou'st made an interest, and destroyed my hopes.

ANTONIO Dare!

I'll meet thee there as early as the day.

PEDRO We will come thus disguised, that whosoever chance to get the better, he may escape unknown.

ANTONIO It shall be so.   [*Exeunt* Pedro *and* Stephano.

Who should this rival be? unless the English colonel, of whom I've often heard Don Pedro speak; it must be he, and time he were removed, who lays a claim to all my happiness.

Willmore *having gazed all this while on the picture, pulls down a little one.*

WILLMORE This posture's loose and negligent,

The sight on't would beget a warm desire,

In souls whom impotence and age had chilled.

– This must along with me.

BRAVO What means this rudeness, sir? – restore the picture.

ANTONIO Ha! Rudeness committed to the fair Angellica! – restore the picture, sir –

WILLMORE Indeed I will not, sir.

ANTONIO By Heaven but you shall.

WILLMORE Nay, do not show your sword, if you do, by this dear beauty – I will show mine too.

ANTONIO What right can you pretend to't?

WILLMORE That of possession which I will maintain – you perhaps have a thousand crowns to give for the original.

ANTONIO No matter, sir, you shall restore the picture.

ANGELLICA Oh Moretta! what's the matter?

       [Angellica *and* Moretta, *above.*

ANTONIO Or leave your life behind.

WILLMORE Death! you lie – I will do neither.

ANGELLICA Hold, I command you, if for me you fight.

They fight, the Spaniards join with Antonio, Blunt *laying on like mad. They leave off and bow.*

WILLMORE How heavenly fair she is! – ah, plague of her price.

ANGELLICA You, Sir, in buff, you that appear a soldier, that first began this insolence –

WILLMORE 'Tis true, I did so, if you call it insolence for a man to preserve himself; I saw your charming picture and was wounded; quite through my soul each pointed beauty ran; and wanting a thousand crowns to procure my remedy – I laid this little picture to my bosom – which if you cannot allow me, I'll resign.

ANGELLICA No, you may keep the trifle.

ANTONIO You shall first ask me leave, and this.

[*Fight again as before.*

Enter Belvile *and* Frederick, *who join with the English.*

ANGELLICA Hold! will you ruin me! – Biskey – Sebastian – part them. – [*The Spaniards are beaten off.*

MORETTA Oh Madam, we're undone, a pox upon that rude fellow, he's set on to ruin us: we shall never see good days, till all these fighting poor rogues are sent to the galleys.

Enter Belvile, Blunt, Frederick, *and* Willmore *with his shirt bloody.*

BLUNT 'Sheartlikins, beat me at this sport, and I'll ne'er wear sword more.

BELVILE The devil's in thee for a mad fellow, thou art always one, at an unlucky adventure – [*To* Willmore.] Come, let's be gone whilst we're safe, and remember these are Spaniards, a sort of people that know how to revenge an affront.

FREDERICK You bleed! I hope you are not wounded.

WILLMORE Not much: – a plague on your dons, if they fight no better they'll ne'er recover Flanders. – What the devil was't to them that I took down the picture?

BLUNT Took it! 'Sheartlikins, we'll have the great one too; 'tis ours by conquest. – Prithee help me up and I'll pull it down –

ANGELLICA Stay sir, and e'er you affront me farther, let me know how you durst commit this outrage – to you I speak sir, for you appear a gentleman.

WILLMORE To me, madam – gentlemen your servant.

[Belvile *stays him.*

BELVILE Is the devil in thee? Dost know the danger of entering the house of an incensed courtesan?

WILLMORE I thank you for your care – but there are other matters in hand, there are, though we have no great temptation – death! let me go.

FREDERICK Yes, to your lodging if you will, but not in here. – Damn these gay harlots – by this hand I'll have as sound and handsome a whore, for a patacoon[63] – death, man, she'll murder thee.

WILLMORE Oh! fear me not, shall I not venture where a beauty calls? a lovely charming beauty! for fear of danger! when by Heaven there's none so great as to long for her, whilst I want money to purchase her.

PEDRO Therefore 'tis loss of time unless you had the thousand crowns to pay.

WILLMORE It may be she may give a favour, at least I shall have the pleasure of saluting her when I enter, and when I depart.

BELVILE Pox, she'll as soon lie with thee as kiss thee, and sooner stab than do either – you shall not go.

ANGELLICA Fear not, sir, all I have to wound with is my eyes.

BLUNT Let him go, 'sheartlikins, I believe the gentlewoman means well.

BELVILE Well take thy fortune, we'll expect you in the next street – farewell fool – farewell –

WILLMORE 'Bye, colonel – [Goes in.

FREDERICK The rogue's stark mad for a wench. [Exeunt.

SCENE [II.][64] A fine chamber.

Enter Willmore, Angellica and Moretta.

ANGELLICA Insolent sir, how durst you pull down my picture?

WILLMORE Rather, how durst you set it up, to tempt poor amorous mortals with so much excellence? which I find you have but too well consulted by the unmerciful price you set upon't. – Is all this Heaven of Beauty shown to move despair in those that cannot buy? and can you think the effects of that despair should be less extravagant than I have shown?

ANGELLICA I sent for you to ask my pardon, sir, not to aggravate your crime – I thought I should have seen you at my feet imploring it.

WILLMORE You are deceived, I came to rail at you, and rail such truths, too, as shall let you see the vanity of that pride, which taught you how to set such price on sin. For such it is, whilst that which is love's due is meanly bartered for.

ANGELLICA Ha! ha! ha! alas good captain, what pity 'tis your edifying doctrine will do no good upon me – Moretta! fetch the gentleman a glass, and let him survey himself. To see what charms he has – and guess my business.   [*Aside, in a soft tone.*

MORETTA He knows himself of old, I believe those breeches and he have been acquainted ever since he was beaten at Worcester.[65]

ANGELLICA Nay, do not abuse the poor creature –

MORETTA Good weather-beaten corporal, will you march off? We have no need of your doctrine, though you have of our charity, but at present we have no scraps, we can afford no kindness for God's sake; in fine sirrah, the price is too high i'th'mouth for you, therefore troop, I say.

WILLMORE Here, good forewoman of the shop, serve me, and I'll be gone.

MORETTA Keep it to pay your laundress, your linen stinks of the gun room; for here's no selling by retail.

WILLMORE Thou hast sold plenty of thy stale ware at a cheap rate.

MORETTA Aye, the more silly kind heart I, but this is an age wherein beauty is at higher rates – in fine, you know the price of this.

WILLMORE I grant you 'tis here set down a thousand crowns a month – pray how much may come to my share for a pistole?[66] – Bawd, take your black lead and sum it up,[67] that I may have a pistole's worth of this vain gay thing, and I'll trouble you no more.

MORETTA Pox on him, he'll fret me to death: – abominable fellow, I tell thee, we only sell by the whole piece.[68]

WILLMORE 'Tis very hard, the whole cargo or nothing – faith, madam, my stock will not reach it, I cannot be your chapman – yet I have countrymen in town, merchants of love like me; I'll see if they'll put in for a share, we cannot lose much by it, and what we have no use for, we'll sell upon the Friday's mart⁶⁹ at – 'Who gives more?' I am studying, madam, how to purchase you, though at present I am unprovided of money.

ANGELLICA Sure this from any other man would anger me – nor shall he know the conquest he has made – poor angry man, how I despise this railing.

WILLMORE Yes, I am poor – but I'm a gentleman,
And one that scorns this baseness which you practise;
Poor as I am, I would not sell myself,
No, not to gain your charming high-prized person.
Though I admire you strangely for your beauty,
Yet I condemn your mind.
– And yet I would at any rate enjoy you,
At your own rate – but cannot – see here
The only sum I can command on earth;
I know not where to eat when this is gone.
Yet such a slave I am to love and beauty
This last reserve I'll sacrifice to enjoy you.
– Nay, do not frown, I know you're to be bought,
And would be bought by me, by me,
For a mean trifling sum if I could pay it down.
Which happy knowledge I will still repeat,
And lay it to my heart, it has a virtue in't,
And soon will cure those wounds your eyes have made.
– And yet – there's something so divinely powerful there –
Nay, I will gaze – to let you see my strength.
                    [Holds her, looks on her, and pauses and sighs.
– By Heaven, bright creature – I would not for the world
Thy fame were half so fair as is thy face.
                                        [Turns her away from him.

ANGELLICA His words go through me to the very soul.   [Aside.
– If you have nothing else to say to me –

WILLMORE Yes, you shall hear how infamous you are –
For which I do not hate thee –
But that secures my heart, and all the flames it feels
Are but so many lusts –

I know it by their sudden bold intrusion,
The fire's impatient and betrays, 'tis false –
For had it been the purer flame of love,
I should have pined and languished at your feet,
E'er found the impudence to have discovered it.
I now dare stand your scorn, and your denial.

MORETTA Sure she's bewitched that she can stand thus tamely and hear his saucy railing – sirrah, will you be gone?

ANGELLICA How dare you take this liberty? – withdraw. [*To* Moretta.] – Pray tell me, sir, are not you guilty of the same mercenary crime, when a lady is proposed to you for a wife, you never ask, how fair – discreet – or virtuous she is; but what's her fortune – which if but small, you cry – she will not do my business – and basely leave her, though she languish for you – say, is not this as poor?[70]

WILLMORE It is a barbarous custom, which I will scorn to defend in our sex, and do despise in yours.

ANGELLICA Thou'rt a brave fellow! put up thy gold, and know,
That were thy fortune large as is thy soul,
Thou shouldst not buy my love,
Couldst thou forget those mean effects of vanity
Which set me out to sale, and, as a lover, prize my yielding
    joys.
Canst thou believe they'll be entirely thine,
Without considering they were mercenary?

WILLMORE I cannot tell, I must bethink me first – ha – death, I'm going to believe her.   [*Aside.*

ANGELLICA Prithee confirm that faith – or if thou canst not – flatter me a little, 'twill please me from thy mouth.

WILLMORE Curse on thy charming tongue! dost thou return
My feigned contempt with so much subtlety?   [*Aside.*
Thou'st found the easiest way into my heart,
Though I yet know, that all thou sayest is false.
                                    [*Turning from her in rage.*

ANGELLICA By all that's good 'tis real,
I never loved before, though oft a mistress.
– Shall my first vows be slighted?

WILLMORE What can she mean?   [*Aside.*

186

ANGELLICA I find you cannot credit me. –   [*In an angry tone.*
WILLMORE I know you take me for an errant ass,
　　An ass that may be soothed into belief,
　　And then be used at pleasure;
　　– But, madam, I have been so often cheated
　　By perjured soft deluding hypocrites,
　　That I've no faith left for the cozening sex;
　　Especially for women of your trade.
ANGELLICA The low esteem you have of me, perhaps
　　May bring my heart again:
　　For I have pride, that yet surmounts my love.
　　　　　　　　　　　[*She turns with pride; he holds her.*
WILLMORE Throw off this pride, this enemy to bliss,
　　And show the power of love: 'tis with those arms
　　I can be only vanquished, made a slave.
ANGELLICA Is all my mighty expectation vanished?
　　– No, I will not hear thee talk – thou hast a charm
　　In every word that draws my heart away.
　　And all the thousand trophies I designed
　　Thou hast undone – why art thou soft?
　　Thy looks are bravely rough, and meant for war.
　　Couldst thou not storm on still?
　　I then perhaps had been as free as thou.
WILLMORE Death, how she throws her fire about my soul! [*Aside.*
　　– Take heed, fair creature, how you raise my hopes,
　　Which once assumed pretend to all dominion.
　　There's not a joy thou hast in store,
　　I shall not then command.
　　– For which I'll pay thee back my soul! my life!
　　– Come, let's begin the account this happy minute!
ANGELLICA And will you pay me then the price I ask?
WILLMORE Oh, why dost thou draw me from an awful worship,
　　By showing thou art no divinity.
　　Conceal the fiend, and show me all the angel!
　　Keep me but ignorant, and I'll be devout
　　And pay my vows for ever at this shrine.
　　　　　　　　　　　[*Kneels and kisses her hand.*
ANGELLICA The pay, I mean, is but thy love for mine.

– Can you give that?

WILLMORE Entirely – come, let's withdraw! where I'll renew my vows – and breathe 'em with such ardour thou shalt not doubt my zeal.

ANGELLICA Thou hast a power too strong to be resisted.

[*Exeunt* Willmore *and* Angellica.

MORETTA Now my curse go with you – is all our project fallen to this? to love the only enemy to our trade? nay, to love such a shameroon,[71] a very beggar, nay a pirate beggar, whose business is to rifle, and be gone, a no purchase, no pay tatterdemalion,[72] and English picaroon.[73] A rogue that fights for daily drink, and takes a pride in being loyally lousy – Oh, I could curse now, if I durst. – This is the fate of most whores.

> Trophies, which from believing fops we win,
> Are spoils to those who cozen us again.

ACT III

SCENE I. *A street.*

Enter Florinda, Valeria, Hellena, *in antic different dresses from what they were in before.* Callis *attending.*

FLORINDA I wonder what should make my brother in so ill a humour? I hope he has not found out our ramble this morning.

HELLENA No, if he had, we should have heard on't at both ears, and have been mewed up this afternoon; which I would not for the world should have happened – hey ho, I'm as sad as a lover's lute. –

VALERIA Well, methinks we have learnt this trade of gipsies as readily as if we had been bred upon the road to Loretto:[74] and yet I did so fumble, when I told the stranger his fortune, that I was afraid I should have told my own and yours by mistake – but, methinks Hellena has been very serious ever since.

FLORINDA I would give my garters she were in love, to be revenged upon her for abusing me – how is't, Hellena?

HELLENA Ah – would I had never seen my mad monsieur – and yet for all your laughing, I am not in love – and yet this small acquaintance o' my conscience will never out of my head.

VALERIA Ha, ha, ha – I laugh to think how thou art fitted with a lover, a fellow that I warrant loves every new face he sees.

HELLENA Hum – he has not kept his word with me here – and may be taken up – that thought is not very pleasant to me – what the deuce should this be now, that I feel?

VALERIA What is't like?

HELLENA Nay, the Lord knows – but if I should be hanged, I cannot choose but be angry and afraid, when I think that mad fellow should be in love with anybody but me – what to think of myself, I know not – would I could meet with some true damned gipsy, that I might know my fortune.

VALERIA Know it! why, there's nothing so easy, thou wilt love this wandering inconstant, till thou findest thyself hanged about his neck, and then be as mad to get free again.

FLORINDA Yes, Valeria, we shall see her bestride his baggage horse, and follow him to the campaign.

HELLENA So, so, now you are provided for, there's no care taken of poor me – but since you have set my heart a-wishing – I am resolved to know for what, I will not die of the pip,[75] so I will not.

FLORINDA Art thou mad to talk so? who will like thee well enough to have thee, that hears what a mad wench thou art?

HELLENA Like me! I don't intend every he that likes me shall have me, but he that I like; I should have stayed in the nunnery still, if I had liked my Lady Abbess as well as she liked me – no, I came thence not (as my wise brother imagines) to take an eternal farewell of the world, but to love, and to be beloved, and I will be beloved, or I'll get one of your men, so I will.

VALERIA Am I put into the number of lovers?

HELLENA You? why, coz, I know thou'rt too good-natured to leave us in any design: thou wouldn't venture a cast,[76] though thou comest off a loser, especially with such a gamester. – I observed your man, and your willing ear incline that way; and if you are not a lover, 'tis an art soon learnt – that I find. [Sighs.

FLORINDA I wonder how you learnt to love so easily, I had a

thousand charms to meet my eyes and ears, e'er I could yield, and 'twas the knowledge of Belvile's merit, not the surprising person took my soul – thou art too rash to give a heart at first sight.

HELLENA Hang your considering lover; I never thought beyond the fancy that 'twas a very pretty, idle, silly kind of pleasure to pass one's time with, to write little soft nonsensical billets, and with great difficulty and danger receive answers; in which I shall have my beauty praised, my wit admired (though little or none) and have the vanity and power to know I am desirable; then I have the more inclination that way, because I am to be a nun, and so shall not be suspected to have any such earthly thoughts about me – but when I walk thus – and sigh thus – they'll think my mind's upon my monastery, and cry, 'How happy 'tis she's so resolved.'

– But not word of man.

FLORINDA What a mad creature's this?

HELLENA I'll warrant, if my brother hears either of you sigh, he cries (gravely) – 'I fear you have the indiscretion to be in love, but take heed of the honour of our house, and your own unspotted fame', and so he conjures on till he has laid the soft-winged god in your hearts, or broke the bird's nest – but see, here comes your lover, but where's my inconstant? Let's step aside, and we may learn something.   [Go *aside*.

Enter Belvile, Frederick *and* Blunt.

BELVILE What means this! the picture's taken in.

BLUNT It may be the wench is good-natured, and will be kind gratis. Your friend's a proper handsome fellow.

BELVILE I rather think she has cut his throat and is fled. I am mad he should throw himself into dangers – pox on't, I shall want him too at night – let's knock and ask for him.

HELLENA My heart goes a pit, a pat, for fear 'tis my man they talk of.   [*Knock,* Moretta *above.*

MORETTA What would you have!

BELVILE Tell the stranger that entered here about two hours ago, that his friends stay here for him.

MORETTA A curse upon him for Moretta, would he were at the

devil – but he's coming to you.

HELLENA Aye, Aye, 'tis he! Oh, how this vexes me.

BELVILE And how and how dear lad, has fortune smiled? Are we to break her windows? Or raise up altars to her? Hah!

WILLMORE Does not my fortune sit triumphant on my brow? Dost not see the little wanton god there all gay and smiling? Have I not an air about my face and eyes, that distinguish me from the crowd of common lovers?[77] By Heaven, Cupid's quiver has not half so many darts as her eyes! – Oh, such a bona roba![78] to sleep in her arms is lying in fresco, all perfumed air about me.

HELLENA Here's fine encouragement for me to fool on. [Aside.

WILLMORE Hark ye, where didst thou purchase that rich canary[79] we drank today? Tell me that I may adore the spigot, and sacrifice to the butt! the juice was divine! into which I must dip my rosary, and then bless all things that I would have bold or fortunate.

BELVILE Well sir, let's go take a bottle, and hear the story of your success.

FREDERICK Would not French wine do better?

WILLMORE Damn the hungry balderdash,[80] cheerful sack has a generous virtue in't inspiring a successful confidence, gives eloquence to the tongue! and vigour to the soul! and has in a few hours completed all my hopes and wishes! There's nothing left to raise a new desire in me – come, let's be gay and wanton – and gentlemen study, study what you want, for here are friends, – that will supply gentlemen, – hark! what a charming sound they make – 'tis he and she gold whilst here, and shall beget new pleasures every moment.

BLUNT But hark'ee Sir, you are not married are you?

WILLMORE All the honey of matrimony, but none of the sting,[81] friend.

BLUNT 'Sheartlikins, thou'rt a fortunate rogue!

WILLMORE I am so Sir, let these – inform you! – ha how sweetly they chime! – pox of poverty, it makes a man a slave, makes wit and honour sneak,[82] my soul grew lean and rusty for want of credit.

BLUNT 'Sheartlikins, this I like well, it looks like my lucky bargain! Oh how I long for the approach of my squire, that is to conduct me to her house again: why – here's two provided for.

FREDERICK By this light y'are happy men.

BLUNT Fortune is pleased to smile on us gentlemen – to smile on us.

Enter Sancho *and pulls down* Blunt *by the sleeve.*

SANCHO Sir, my lady expects you – she has removed all that might oppose your will and pleasure – and is impatient till you come.   [*They go aside.*

BLUNT Sir, I'll attend you – oh the happiest rogue! I'll take no leave, lest they either dog me, or stay me.   [*Exit with* Sancho.

BELVILE But then the little gipsy is forgot?

WILLMORE A mischief on thee for putting her into my thoughts. I had quite forgot her else, and this night's debauch had drunk her quite down.

HELLENA Had it so, good captain!   [*Claps him on the back.*

WILLMORE Hah! I hope she did not hear me.   [*Aside.*

HELLENA What, afraid of such a champion?

WILLMORE Oh! you're a fine lady of your word, are you not? to make a man languish a whole day –

HELLENA In tedious search of me.

WILLMORE Egad, child, thou'rt in the right, hadst thou seen what a melancholy dog I have been ever since I was a lover, how I have walked the streets like a Capuchin [83] with my hands in my sleeves – faith, sweetheart, thou would'st pity me.

HELLENA Now if I should be hanged I can't be angry with him, he dissembles so heartily – alas, good captain, what pains you have taken – now were I ungrateful not to reward so true a servant.

WILLMORE Poor soul! that's kindly said, I see thou bearest a conscience – come then for a beginning show me thy dear face.

HELLENA I'm afraid, my small acquaintance, you have been staying that swinging stomach you boasted of this morning; I then remember my little collation would have gone down with you, without the sauce of a handsome face – is your stomach so   .

queasy now?

WILLMORE Faith, long fasting, child, spoils a man's appetite – yet if you durst treat, I could so lay about me still –

HELLENA And would you fall to, before a priest says grace?

WILLMORE Oh fie, fie, what an old out-of-fashioned thing hast thou named? Thou couldst not dash me more out of countenance shouldst thou show me an ugly face.

Whilst he is seemingly courting Hellena, *enter* Angellica, Moretta, Biskey *and* Sebastian, *all in masquerade;* Angellica *sees* Willmore *and stares.*

ANGELLICA Heavens, 'tis he! and passionately fond to see another woman.

MORETTA What could you less expect from such a swaggerer?

ANGELLICA Expect! as much as I paid him, a heart entire
Which I had pride enough to think when ere I gave,
It would have raised the man above the vulgar,
Made him all soul! and that all soft and constant.

HELLENA You see, captain, how willing I am to be friends, with you, till time and ill luck make us lovers, and ask you the question first, rather then put your modesty to the blush by asking me (for alas!) I know you captains are such strict men, and such severe observers of your vows to chastity, that 'twill be hard to prevail with your tender conscience to marry a young willing maid.

WILLMORE Do not abuse me, for fear I should take thee at thy word, and marry thee indeed, which I'm sure will be revenge sufficient.

HELLENA O' my conscience, that will be our destiny, because we are both of one humour; I am as inconstant as you, for I have considered, captain, that a handsome woman has a great deal to do whilst her face is good, for then is our harvest-time to gather friends; and should I in these days of my youth catch a fit of foolish constancy, I were undone; 'tis loitering by daylight in our great journey: therefore I declare, I'll allow but one year for love, one year for indifference, and one year for hate – and then – go hang yourself – for I profess myself the gay, the kind, and the inconstant [84] – the devil's in't if this won't please you.

WILLMORE Oh most damnably – I have a heart with a hole quite through it too, no prison mine to keep a mistress in.

ANGELICA Perjured man! how I believe thee now.   [*Aside.*

HELLENA Well, I see our business as well as humours are alike, yours to cozen as many maids as will trust you, and I as many men as have faith – see if I have not as desperate a lying look, as you can have for the heart of you.

[*Pulls off her vizard: he starts.*

– How do you like it, captain?

WILLMORE Like it! by Heaven, I never saw so much beauty! Oh the charms of those sprightly black eyes! that strangely fair face! full of smiles and dimples! those soft round melting cherry lips! and small even white teeth! not to be expressed but silently adored! – oh, one look more! and strike me dumb, or I shall repeat nothing else till I'm mad.

[*He seems to court her to pull off her vizard: she refuses.*

ANGELICA I can endure no more – nor is it fit to interrupt him, for if I do, my jealousy has so destroyed my reason, – I shall undo him – therefore I'll retire – and you, Sebastian [*To one of her Bravoes.*] follow that woman, and learn who 'tis; while you tell the fugitive I would speak to him instantly.

[*To the other* Bravo.
[*Exit.*

This while Florinda *is talking to* Belvile, *who stands sullenly.* Frederick *courting* Valeria.

VALERIA Prithee, dear stranger, be not so sullen, for though you have lost your love, you see my friend frankly offers you hers to play with in the meantime.   [*To Belvile.*

BELVILE Faith madam, I am sorry I can't play at her game.

FREDERICK Pray leave your intercession, and mind your own affair, they'll better agree apart; he's a modest sigher in company, but alone no woman 'scapes him.

FLORINDA Sure he does but rally – yet if it should be true – I'll tempt him farther [*Aside.*] – believe me, noble stranger, I'm no common mistress – and for a little proof on't – wear this jewel – nay, take it, sir, 'tis right, and bills of exchange may sometimes miscarry.

BELVILE Madam, why am I chose out of all mankind to be the object of your bounty?

VALERIA There's another civil question asked.

FREDERICK Pox of's modesty, it spoils his own markets and hinders mine.   [*Aside.*

FLORINDA Sir, from my window I have often seen you, and women of my quality have so few opportunities for love, that we ought to lose none.

FREDERICK Ay, this is something! here's a woman! – when shall I be blessed with so much kindness from your fair mouth? – take the jewel, fool.   [*Aside to* Belvile.

BELVILE You tempt me strangely, madam, every way –

FLORINDA So, if I find him false, my whole repose is gone. [*Aside.*

BELVILE And but for a vow I've made to a very fair lady, this goodness had subdued me.

FREDERICK Pox on't, be kind, in pity to me be kind, for I am to thrive here but as you treat her friend.   [*Aside to* Belvile.

HELLENA Tell me what you did in yonder house, and I'll unmask.

WILLMORE Yonder house – oh – I went to – a – to – why, there's a friend of mine lives there.

HELLENA What, a she, or a he friend?

WILLMORE A man upon honour! a man – a she friend – no, no, madam, you have done my business I thank you.

HELLENA And was't your man friend, that had more darts in's eyes, than Cupid carries in's whole budget[85] of arrows?

WILLMORE So –

HELLENA Ah such a bona roba! to be in her arms is lying in fresco, all perfumed air about me – was this your man friend too?

WILLMORE So –

HELLENA That gave you the he, and the she gold, that begets young pleasures?

WILLMORE Well, well madam, then you see there are ladies in the world, that will not be cruel – there are madam, there are –

HELLENA And there be men too, as fine, wild inconstant fellows as yourself, there be captain, there be, if you go to that now – therefore I'm resolved –

WILLMORE Oh! –

HELLENA To see your face no more –

WILLMORE Oh!

HELLENA Till tomorrow.

WILLMORE Egad, you frighted me.

HELLENA Nor then neither, unless you'll swear never to see that lady more.

WILLMORE See her! – why never to think of womankind again.

HELLENA Kneel, – and swear –   [Kneels, she gives him her hand.

WILLMORE I do never to think – to see – to love – nor lie – with any but thyself.

HELLENA Kiss the Book.

WILLMORE Oh most religiously.   [Kisses her hand.

HELLENA Now what a wicked creature am I, to damn a proper fellow.

CALLIS Madam, I'll stay no longer, 'tis e'en dark.   [To Florinda.

FLORINDA However sir, I'll leave this with you – that when I'm gone, you may repent the opportunity you have lost, by your modesty.

[Gives him the jewel which is her picture, and exits. He gazes after her.

WILLMORE 'Twill be an age till tomorrow, – and till then I will most impatiently expect you – Adieu my dear pretty angel.
                              [Exeunt all the women.

BELVILE Ha! Florinda's picture – 'twas she herself – what a dull dog was I? I would have given the world for one minute's discourse with her –

FREDERICK This comes of your modesty! – ah pox o' your vow, 'twas ten to one but we had lost the jewel by't.

BELVILE Willmore! the blessedest opportunity lost! Florinda! Friends! Florinda!

WILLMORE Ah rogue! such black eyes! such a face! such a mouth! such teeth – and so much wit! –

BELVILE All, all, and a thousand charms besides.

WILLMORE Why, dost thou know her?

BELVILE Know her! Aye, aye, and a pox take me with all my heart for being modest.

WILLMORE But hark ye, friend of mine, are you my rival? and have I been only beating the bush all this while?

BELVILE I understand thee not – I'm mad – see here –

[*Shows the picture.*

WILLMORE Ha! whose picture's this! – 'tis a fine wench!

FREDERICK The colonel's mistress, sir.

WILLMORE Oh, oh here – I thought it had been another prize – come, come, a bottle will set thee right again.

[*Gives the picture back.*

BELVILE I am content to try, and by that time 'twill be late enough for our design.

WILLMORE Agreed.

> Love does all day the soul's great empire keep,
> But wine at night lulls the soft god asleep.   [*Exeunt.*

SCENE II. *Lucetta's house.*

Enter Blunt *and* Lucetta *with a light.*

LUCETTA Now we are safe and free; no fears of the coming home of my old jealous husband, which made me a little thoughtful when you came in first – but now love is all the business of my soul.

BLUNT I am transported! – pox on't, that I had but some fine things to say to her, such as lovers use, – I was a fool not to learn of Fred a little by heart before I came – something I must say –   [*Aside.*
'Sheartlikins, sweet soul! I am not used to compliment, but I'm an honest gentleman, and thy humble servant.

LUCETTA I have nothing to pay for so great a favour, but such a love as cannot but be great, since at first sight of that sweet face and shape, it made me your absolute captive.

BLUNT Kind heart! how prettily she talks! Egad, I'll show her husband a Spanish trick; send him out of the world and marry her: she's damnably in love with me, and will ne'er mind settlements,[86] and so there's that saved.   [*Aside.*

LUCETTA Well Sir, I'll go and undress me, and be with you instantly.

BLUNT Make haste then, for adsheartlikins, dear soul, thou canst not guess at the pain of a longing lover, when his joys are drawn within the compass of a few minutes.

LUCETTA You speak my sense, and I'll make haste to prove it.   [*Exit.*

BLUNT 'Tis a rare girl! and this one night's enjoyment with her will be worth all the days I ever passed in Essex. – would she would go with me into England; though to say truth there's plenty of whores already. – But a pox on 'em, they are such mercenary – prodigal whores, that they want such a one as this, that's free and generous, to give 'em good examples – Why, what a house she has, how rich and fine!

SANCHO Sir, my lady has sent me to conduct you to her chamber.

[*Enter* Sancho.

BLUNT Sir, I shall be proud to follow – here's one of her servants too! 'Sheartlikins, by this garb and gravity, he might be a Justice of Peace in Essex, and is but a pimp here.   [*Exeunt.*

The scene changes to a chamber with an alcove bed in it, a table, etc. Lucetta *in bed. Enter* Sancho *and* Blunt, *who takes the candle of* Sancho *at the door.*

SANCHO Sir, my commission reaches no farther.   [*Exit* Sancho.

BLUNT Sir, I'll excuse your compliment – what, in bed, my sweet mistress?

LUCETTA You see, I still outdo you in kindness.

BLUNT And thou shalt see what haste I'll make to quit scores – oh the luckiest rogue!   [*He undresses himself.*

LUCETTA Should you be false or cruel now! –

BLUNT False! 'Sheartlikins, what dost thou take me for? A Jew? an insensible heathen – a pox of thy old jealous husband; and he were dead, egad, sweet soul, it should be none of my fault if I did not marry thee.

LUCETTA It never should be mine.

BLUNT Good soul! I'm the fortunatest dog!

LUCETTA Are you not undressed yet?

BLUNT As much as my impatience will permit.

[*Goes towards the bed in his shirt, drawers, etc.*

LUCETTA Hold, sir, put out the light, it may betray us else.

BLUNT Anything, I need no other light, but that of thine eyes! –
'Sheartlikins, there I think I had it. [*Puts out the candle, the bed
descends, he gropes about to find it.*] – Why – why – where am I
got? what, not yet? – where are you, sweetest? – ah, the rogue's
silent now – a pretty love-trick this – how she'll laugh at me
anon! – you need not, my dear rogue! you need not! – I'm all on
fire already – come, come, now call me in pity. – Sure I'm
enchanted! I have been round the chamber, and can find neither
woman, nor bed – I locked the door, I'm sure she cannot go
that way – or if she could, the bed could not. – Enough,
enough, my pretty wanton, do not carry the jest too far –
[*Lights on a trap, and is let down.*] Ha, betrayed! Dogs!
Rogues! Pimps! – help! help!

Enter Lucetta, Philippo, *and* Sancho *with a light.*

PHILIPPO Ha, ha, ha, he's dispatched finely.

LUCETTA Now, sir, had I been coy, we had missed of this
booty.

PHILIPPO Nay, when I saw 'twas a substantial fool, I was molli-
fied; but when you dote upon a serenading coxcomb, upon a
face, fine clothes, and a lute, it makes me rage.

LUCETTA You know I was never guilty of that folly, my dear
Philippo, but with yourself – but come, let's see what we have
got by this.

PHILIPPO A rich coat! – sword and hat – these breeches too – are
well lined! – see here, a gold watch! – a purse – ha! – gold! – at
least two hundred pistoles! – a bunch of diamond rings! and
one with the family arms! – a gold box! – with a medal of his king!
and his lady mother's picture! – these were sacred relics, believe
me! – see, the waistband of his breeches have a mine of gold! –
old Queen Bess's, we have a quarrel to her ever since eighty-
eight,[87] and may therefore justify the theft, the Inquisition
might have committed it.

LUCETTA – See, a bracelet of bowed gold! these his sisters tied
about his arm at parting – but well – for all this, I fear his being
a stranger, may make a noise and hinder our trade with them
hereafter.

PHILIPPO That's our security; he is not only a stranger to us, but to the country too – the common shore[88] into which he is descended, thou knowest conducts him into another street, which this light will hinder him from ever finding again – he knows neither your name, nor that of the street where your house is, nay, nor the way to his own lodgings.

LUCETTA And art not thou an unmerciful rogue! not to afford him one night for all this? – I should not have been such a Jew.

PHILIPPO Blame me not, Lucetta, to keep as much of thee as I can to myself – come, that thought makes me wanton! – let's to bed! – Sancho, lock up these.

This is the fleece which fools do bear,
Designed for witty men to shear.   [*Exeunt.*

The scene changes, and discovers Blunt, *creeping out of a common shore, his face, etc. all dirty.*

BLUNT Oh Lord!   [*Climbing up.*
I am got out at last, and (which is a miracle) without a clue – and now to damning and cursing! – but if that would ease me, where shall I begin? with my fortune, myself, or the quean[89] that cozened me? – what a dog was I to believe in woman! oh coxcomb! – ignorant conceited coxcomb! to fancy she could be enamoured with my person! at first sight enamoured! – oh, I'm a cursed puppy! 'tis plain, fool was writ upon my forehead! she perceived it! – saw the Essex calf there – for what allurements could there be in this countenance? which I can endure, because I'm acquainted with it – oh, dull silly dog! to be thus soothed into a cozening! had I been drunk, I might fondly have credited the young quean! – but as I was in my right wits, to be thus cheated, confirms it: I am a dull believing English country fop – but my comrades! death and the devil! there's the worst of all – then a ballad will be sung tomorrow on the Prado,[90] to a lousy tune of the enchanted 'squire, and the annihilated damsel – but Fred that rogue! and the colonel, will abuse me beyond all Christian patience – had she left me my clothes, I have a bill of exchange at home, would have saved my credit – but now all hope is taken from me – well, I'll home (if I can find the way) with this consolation, that I am not the first kind believing cox-

comb; but there are, gallants, many such good natures amongst ye.

> And tho you've better arts to hide your follies,
> Adsheartlikins, y'are all as errant cullies.[91]   [*Exit.*

SCENE [III.] *The garden in the night.*

Enter Florinda *in an undress, with a key and a little box.*

FLORINDA Well, thus far I'm in my way to happiness; I have got myself free from Callis; my brother too, I find by yonder light, is got into his cabinet, and thinks not of me; I have, by good fortune, got the key of the garden back door. – I'll open it to prevent Belvile's knocking – a little noise will now alarm my brother. Now am I as fearful as a young thief.

> [*Unlocks the door.*

– hark – what noise is that – oh, 'twas the wind that played amongst the boughs – Belvile stays long, methinks – it's time – stay – for fear of a surprise – I'll hide these jewels in yonder jessamine.   [*She goes to lay down the box.*

Enter Willmore, *drunk.*

WILLMORE What the devil is become of these fellows, Belvile and Frederick, they promised to stay at the next corner for me, but who the devil knows the corner of a full moon – now – whereabouts am I? – hah – what have we here? a garden! – a very convenient place to sleep in – hah – what has God sent us here! – a female! – by this light a woman! – I'm a dog if it be not a very wench! –

FLORINDA He's come! – hah – who's there?

WILLMORE Sweet soul! let me salute thy shoe-string.

FLORINDA 'Tis not my Belvile. – good heavens! I know him not – who are you, and from whence come you?

WILLMORE Prithee – prithee, child – not so many hard questions– let it suffice I am here, child – come, come kiss me.

FLORINDA Good gods! what luck is mine?

WILLMORE Only good luck, child, parlous good luck – come hither, – 'tis a delicate shining wench – by this hand she's perfumed, and smells like any nosegay – prithee dear soul, let's the fool, and lose time – precious time – for as Gad ʌve me, I'm as honest a fellow as breathes, though I'm a disguised [92] at present – come, I say – why, thou mayst be ᵉ with me, I'll be very secret. I'll not boast who 'twas obliged ᵉ, not I – for hang me if I know thy name.

FLORINDA Heavens! what a filthy beast is this?

WILLMORE I am so, and thou oughtst the sooner to lie with me for that reason – for look you child, there will be no sin in't, because 'twas neither designed nor premeditated. 'Tis pure accident on both sides – that's a certain thing now – indeed should I make love to you, and you vow fidelity – and swear and lie till you believed and yielded – that were to make it wilful fornication – the crying sin of the nation – thou art therefore (as thou art a good Christian) obliged in conscience to deny me nothing. Now – come, be kind without any more idle prating.

FLORINDA Oh I am ruined – wicked man, unhand me.

WILLMORE Wicked! – egad child, a judge were he young and vigorous, and saw those eyes of thine, would know 'twas they gave the first blow – the first provocation – come, prithee let's lose no time, I say – this is a fine convenient place.

FLORINDA Sir, let me go, I conjure you, or I'll call out.

WILLMORE Aye, aye, you were best to call witness to see how finely you treat me – do –

FLORINDA I'll cry Murder! Rape! or anything! if you do not instantly let me go.

WILLMORE A rape! Come, come, you lie, you baggage, you lie, what, I'll warrant you would fain have the world believe now that you are not so forward as I. No, not you – why at this time of night was your cobweb door set open dear spider [93] – but to catch flies? – Hah – come – or I shall be damnably angry. – Why, what a coil [94] is here –

FLORINDA Sir, can you think –

WILLMORE That you would do't for nothing – oh, oh I find what you would be at – look here, here's a pistole [95] for you – here's a work indeed – here – take it I say –

FLORINDA For heaven's sake, sir, as you're a gentleman –

WILLMORE So – now – now – she would be wheedling me for more – what, you will not take it then – you are resolved you will not – come – come take it, or I'll put it up again – for look ye, I never give more – why, how now mistress, are you so high i'th' mouth a pistole won't down with you – hah – why, what a work's here – in good time – come, no struggling to be gone – but an y'are good at a dumb wrestle I'm for ye – look ye – I'm for ye –
[*She struggles with him.*

Enter Belvile *and* Frederick.

BELVILE The door is open, a pox of this mad fellow, I'm angry that we've lost him, I durst have sworn he had followed us.

FREDERICK But you were so hasty, colonel, to be gone.

FLORINDA Help! help! – murder! – help – oh I am ruined.

BELVILE Ha! sure that's Florinda's voice.   [*Comes up to them.*
– A man! Villain, let go that lady.
          [*A noise.* Willmore *turns and draws,* Frederick *interposes.*

FLORINDA Belvile! Heavens! my brother too is coming, and 'twill be impossible to escape – Belvile, I conjure you to walk under my chamber window, from whence I'll give you some instructions what to do – this rude man has undone us.   [*Exit.*

WILLMORE Belvile!

Enter Pedro, Stephano, *and other servants with lights.*

PEDRO I'm betrayed! run, Stephano, and see if Florinda be safe.
          [*Exit* Stephano. *They fight, and* Pedro's *party beats them out.*
So, who e'er they be, all is not well, I'll to Florinda's chamber.
          [*Going out, meets* Stephano.

STEPHANO You need not, sir, the poor lady's fast asleep and thinks no harm. I would not awake her, Sir, for fear of frighting her with your danger.

PEDRO I'm glad she's there – rascals, how came the garden door open?

STEPHANO That question comes too late, sir; some of my fellow servants masquerading, I'll warrant.

PEDRO Masquerading! a lewd custom to debauch our youth, – there's something more in this than I imagine.   [*Exeunt.*

[SCENE IV.] *Scene changes to the street.*

Enter Belvile *in rage.* Frederick *holding him, and* Willmore *melancholy.*

WILLMORE Why, how the devil should I know Florinda?

BELVILE Ah, plague of your ignorance! If it had not been Florinda, must you be a beast? – a brute? a senseless swine?

WILLMORE Well, sir, you see I am endued with patience – I can bear – though egad y'are very free with me, methinks. – I was in good hopes the quarrel would have been on my side, for so uncivilly interrupting me.

BELVILE Peace, brute! whilst thou'rt safe – oh I'm distracted.

WILLMORE Nay, nay, I'm an unlucky dog, that's certain.

BELVILE Ah, curse upon the star that ruled my birth! or whatsoever other influence that makes me still so wretched.

WILLMORE Thou breakest my heart with these complaints; there is no star in fault, no influence, but sack, the cursed sack I drank.

FREDERICK Why, how the devil came you so drunk?

WILLMORE Why, how the devil came you so sober?

BELVILE A curse upon his thin skull, he was always beforehand that way.

FREDERICK Prithee, dear colonel, forgive him, he's sorry for his fault.

BELVILE He's always so after he has done a mischief – a plague on all such brutes.

WILLMORE By this light, I took her for an errant harlot.

BELVILE Damn your debauched opinion! tell me, sot, hadst thou so much sense and light about thee to distinguish her woman, and couldst not see something about her face and person, to strike an awful reverence into thy soul?

WILLMORE Faith no, I considered her as mere a woman as I could wish.

BELVILE 'Sdeath, I have no patience – draw, or I'll kill you.

WILLMORE Let that alone till tomorrow, and if I set not all right again, use your pleasure.

BELVILE Tomorrow! damn it!
The spiteful light will lead me to no happiness.
Tomorrow is Antonio's, and perhaps

Guides him to my undoing; – oh that I could meet
This rival! this powerful fortunate!

WILLMORE What then?

BELVILE Let thy own reason, or my rage instruct thee.

WILLMORE I shall be finely informed then, no doubt; hear me, colonel – hear me – show me the man and I'll do his business.

BELVILE I know him no more than thou, or if I did I should not need thy aid.

WILLMORE This you say is Angellica's house, I promised the kind baggage to lie with her tonight.   [*Offers to go in.*

Enter Antonio *and his page.* Antonio *knocks with the hilt of his sword.*

ANTONIO You paid the thousand crowns I directed?

PAGE To the lady's old woman, Sir, I did.

WILLMORE Who the devil have we here!

BELVILE I'll now plant myself under Florinda's window, and if I find no comfort there, I'll die.   [*Exeunt* Belvile *and* Frederick.

Enter Moretta.

MORETTA Page!

PAGE Here's my lord.

WILLMORE How is this! a picaroon going to board my frigate! Here's one chase-gun [96] for you.

[*Drawing his sword, jostles* Antonio *who turns and draws. They fight;* Antonio *falls.*

MORETTA Oh bless us! We're all undone!

[*Runs in and shuts the door.*

PAGE Help! Murder!   [Belvile *returns at the noise of fighting.*

BELVILE Ha! the mad rogue's engaged in some unlucky adventure again.

Enter two or three masqueraders.

MASQUERADER Ha! a man killed!

WILLMORE How! a man killed! then I'll go home to sleep.

[*Puts up and reels out. Exeunt masqueraders another way.*

BELVILE Who should it be! Pray Heaven the rogue is safe for all my quarrel to him.

[*As* Belvile *is groping about, enter an officer and six soldiers.*

SOLDIER Who's there?

OFFICER So, here's one dispatched – secure the murderer.

BELVILE Do not mistake my charity for murder!
I came to his assistance.   [*Soldiers seize on* Belvile.

OFFICER That shall be tried, sir – St Jago,[97] swords drawn in the carnival time!   [*Goes to* Antonio.

ANTONIO Thy hand, prithee.

OFFICER Ha! Don Antonio! look well to the villain there. – How is it, Sir?

ANTONIO I'm hurt.

BELVILE Has my humanity made me a criminal?

OFFICER Away with him.

BELVILE What a cursed chance is this?

[*Exeunt Soldiers with* Belvile.

ANTONIO This is the man, that has set upon me twice – carry him to my apartment, till you have farther orders from me.

[*To the Officer. Exit* Antonio, *led.*

ACT IV

SCENE I. *A fine room.*

Discovers Belvile *as by dark alone.*

BELVILE When shall I be weary of railing on Fortune, who is resolved never to turn with smiles upon me? – Two such defeats in one night – none but the devil and that mad rogue could have contrived to have plagued me with – I am here a prisoner – but where – Heaven knows – and if there be murder done, I can soon decide the fate of a stranger in a nation without mercy – yet this is nothing to the torture my soul bows with, when I think of losing my fair, my dear Florinda – hark – my door opens – a light – a man – and seems of quality – armed too! – now shall I die like a dog without defence.

Enter Antonio *in a nightgown, with a light; his arm in a scarf, and a sword under his arm; he sets the candle on the table.*

ANTONIO Sir, I come to know what injuries I have done you, that could provoke you to so mean an action, as to attack me basely, without allowing time for my defence?

BELVILE Sir, for a man in my circumstances to plead innocence, would look like fear – but view me well, and you will find no marks of coward on me; nor anything that betrays that brutality you accuse me with.

ANTONIO In vain, sir, you impose upon my sense.
You are not only he who drew on me last night,
But yesterday before the same house, that of Angellica.
Yet there is something in your face and mien
That makes me wish I were mistaken.

BELVILE I own I fought today in the defence of a friend of mine, with whom you (if you're the same) and your party were first engaged.
Perhaps you think this crime enough to kill me,
But if you do, I cannot fear you'll do it basely.

ANTONIO No, sir, I'll make you fit for a defence with this.
[*Gives him the sword.*

BELVILE This gallantry surprises me – nor know I how to use this present, sir, against a man so brave.

ANTONIO You shall not need;
For know, I come to snatch you from a danger
That is decreed against you:
Perhaps your life, or long imprisonment;
And 'twas with so much courage you offended,
I cannot see you punished.

BELVILE How shall I pay this generosity?

ANTONIO It had been safer to have killed another.
Than have attempted me:
To show your danger, sir, I'll let you know my quality;
And 'tis the viceroy's son, whom you have wounded.

BELVILE The viceroy's son!
Death and confusion! was this plague reserved   [*Aside.*
To complete all the rest – obliged by him!
The man of all the world I would destroy.

ANTONIO You seem disordered, sir.

BELVILE Yes, trust me, sir, I am, and 'tis with pain
That man receives such bounties,
Who wants the power to pay them back again.

ANTONIO To gallant spirits 'tis indeed uneasy;
– But you may quickly overpay me, sir.

BELVILE Then I am well – kind Heaven! but set us even,
  That I may fight with him and keep my honour safe.   [*Aside.*
  – Oh, I'm impatient, sir, to be discounting [98]
  The mighty debt I owe you, command me quickly –
ANTONIO I have a quarrel with a rival, sir,
  About the maid we love.
BELVILE Death, 'tis Florinda he means –
  That thought destroys my reason,
  And I shall kill him –   [*Aside.*
ANTONIO My rival, sir,
  Is one has all the virtues man can boast of –
BELVILE Death! who should this be?   [*Aside.*
[ANTONIO] He challenged me to meet him on the Molo,
  As soon as day appeared, but last night's quarrel,
  Has made my arm unfit to guide a sword.
BELVILE I apprehend you, sir, you'd have me kill the man
  That lays a claim to the maid you speak of.
  – I'll do't – I'll fly to do't!
ANTONIO Sir, do you know her?
BELVILE – No, sir, but 'tis enough she is admired by you.
ANTONIO Sir, I shall rob you of the glory on't,
  For you must fight under my name and dress.
BELVILE That opinion must be strangely obliging that makes
  You think I can personate the brave Antonio,
  Whom I can but strive to imitate.
ANTONIO You say too much to my advantage;
  – Come, sir, the day appears that calls you forth.
  – Within, sir, is the habit.   [*Exit* Antonio.
BELVILE Fantastic Fortune, thou deceitful light,
  That cheats the wearied traveller by night,
  Though on a precipice each step you tread,
  I am resolved to follow where you lead.   [*Exit.*

SCENE [II.] *The Molo.*

Enter Florinda *and* Callis *in masques, with* Stephano.

FLORINDA I'm dying with my fears, Belvile's not coming as I
  expected under my window,

Makes me believe that all those fears are true.　　　　[*Aside.*
　– Canst thou not tell with whom my brother fights?

STEPHANO No, madam, they were both in masquerade, I was by
　when they challenged one another, and they had decided the
　quarrel then, but were prevented by some cavaliers; which
　made 'em put it off till now – but I am sure 'tis about you they
　fight.

FLORINDA Nay, then 'tis with Belvile, for what other lover have I
　that dares fight for me, except Antonio? and he is too much in
　favour with my brother – if it be he, for whom shall I direct my
　prayers to Heaven?　　　　[*Aside.*

STEPHANO Madam, I must leave you, for if my master see me, I
　shall be hanged for being your conductor – I escaped narrowly
　for the excuse I made for you last night i'th' garden.

FLORINDA And I'll reward thee for't – prithee, no more.

　　　　　　　　　　　　　　　　　　　[*Exit* Stephano.

Enter Don Pedro *in his masquing habit.*

PEDRO Antonio's late today, the place will fill, and we may be pre-
　vented.　　　　　　　　　　[*Walks about.*

FLORINDA Antonio? Sure I heard amiss.　　　　[*Aside.*

PEDRO But who will not excuse a happy lover
　When soft fair arms confine the yielding neck;
　And the kind whisper languishingly breathes,
　'Must you begone so soon?'
　Sure I had dwelt for ever on her bosom.
　– But stay, he's here.

Enter Belvile *dressed in* Antonio's *clothes.*

FLORINDA 'Tis not Belvile; half my fears are vanished.　　[*Aside.*
PEDRO Antonio!
BELVILE This must be he.　　　　　　　　　　[*Aside.*
　You're early, sir, – I do not use to be outdone this way.
PEDRO The wretched, sir, are watchful, and 'tis enough
　You've the advantage of me in Angellica.
BELVILE Angellica! or I've mistook my man! or else Antonio
　– Can he forget his interest in Florinda,
　And fight for common prize?　　　　　[*Aside.*

PEDRO Come, sir, you know our terms –

BELVILE By Heaven, not I.   [*Aside.*

   – No talking, I am ready, sir.   [*Offers to fight;* Florinda *runs in.*

FLORINDA Oh, hold! who e'er you be, I do conjure you hold!

   If you strike here – I die –   [*To* Belvile.

PEDRO Florinda!

BELVILE Florinda imploring for my rival!

PEDRO Away, this kindness is unseasonable.

   [*Puts her by; they fight; she runs in just as* Belvile *disarms* Pedro.

FLORINDA Who are you, sir, that dares deny my prayers?

BELVILE Thy prayers destroy him, if thou wouldst preserve him,

   Do that thou'rt unacquainted with and curse him.

                                                              [*She holds him.*

FLORINDA By all you hold most dear, by her you love,

   I do conjure you, touch him not.

BELVILE By her I love!

   See – I obey – and at your feet resign

   The useless trophy of my victory.   [*Lays his sword at her feet.*

PEDRO Antonio, you've done enough to prove you love
   Florinda.

BELVILE Love Florinda! Does Heaven love adoration! prayer! or
   penitence! Love her! here, sir, – your sword again.

                                 [*Snatches up the sword and gives it him.*

   Upon this truth I'll fight my life away.

PEDRO No, you've redeemed my sister, and my friendship!

   [*He gives him* Florinda *and pulls off his vizard to show his
   face and puts it on again.*

BELVILE Don Pedro!

PEDRO Can you resign your claims to other women,

   And give your heart entirely to Florinda?

BELVILE Entire! as dying saints' confessions are!

   I can delay my happiness no longer.

   This minute let me make Florinda mine.

PEDRO This minute let it be – no time so proper,

   This night my father will arrive from Rome,

   And possibly may hinder what we purpose!

FLORINDA Oh Heavens! this minute!

                                 [*Enter masqueraders and pass over.*

THE ROVER

BELVILE Oh, do not ruin me!

PEDRO The place begins to fill, and that we may not be observed, do you walk off to St Peter's Church, where I will meet you, and conclude your happiness.

BELVILE I'll meet you there. – If there be no more saints' churches in Naples.   [*Aside.*

FLORINDA Oh stay, sir, and recall your hasty doom!
  Alas I have not yet prepared my heart
  To entertain so strange a guest.

PEDRO Away, this silly modesty is assumed too late.

BELVILE Heaven, madam! what do you do?

FLORINDA Do! despise the man that lays a tyrant's claim
  To what he ought to conquer by submission.

BELVILE You do not know me – move a little this way.
                                             [*Draws her aside.*

FLORINDA Yes, you may force me even to the altar,
  But not the holy man that offers there
  Shall force me to be thine.   [Pedro *talks to* Callis *this while.*

BELVILE Oh do not lose so blest an opportunity!
  – See – 'tis your Belvile – not Antonio,
  Whom your mistaken scorn and anger ruins.
                                          [*Pulls off his vizard.*

FLORINDA Belvile.
  Where was my soul it could not meet thy voice!
  And take this knowledge in.

As *they are talking, enter* Willmore *finely dressed, and* Frederick.

WILLMORE No intelligence! no news of Belvile yet – well, I am the most unlucky rascal in Nature – ha – am I deceived – or is it he – look Fred – 'tis he – my dear Belvile.
    [*Runs and embraces him.* Belvile's *vizard falls out of his hand.*

BELVILE Hell and confusion seize thee!

PEDRO Ha! Belvile! I beg your pardon, sir.
                                        [*Takes* Florinda *from him.*

BELVILE Nay, touch her not, she's mine by conquest, sir,
  I won her by my sword.

WILLMORE Didst thou so – and egad, child, we'll keep her by the sword.   [*Draws on* Pedro. Belvile *goes between.*

211

BELVILE Stand off.
  Thou'rt so profanely lewd, so cursed by Heaven,
  All quarrels thou espousest must be fatal.
WILLMORE Nay, an you be so hot, my valour's coy, and shall be
  courted when you want it next.   [*Puts up his sword.*
BELVILE You know I ought to claim a victor's right.   [*To Pedro.*
  But you're the brother to divine Florinda,
  To whom I'm such a slave – to purchase her,
  I durst not hurt the man she holds so dear.
PEDRO 'Twas by Antonio's, not by Belvile's sword
  This question should have been decided, sir;
  I must confess much to your bravery's due,
  Both now, and when I met you last in arms.
  But I am nicely punctual[99] in my word,
  As men of honour ought, and beg your pardon.
  – For this mistake another time shall clear.
  – This was some plot between you and Belvile.
  But I'll prevent you.   [*Aside to* Florinda *as they are going out.*

Belvile *looks after her and begins to walk up and down in rage.*

WILLMORE Do not be modest now and lose the woman, but if we
  shall fetch her back so –
BELVILE Do not speak to me –
WILLMORE Not speak to you – egad, I'll speak to you, and will
  be answered too.
BELVILE Will you sir –
WILLMORE I know I've done some mischief, but I'm so dull a
  puppy that I'm the son of a whore, if I know how, or where –
  prithee inform my understanding –
BELVILE Leave me I say, and leave me instantly.
WILLMORE I will not leave you in this humour, nor till I know
  my crime.
BELVILE Death, I'll tell you sir –   [*Draws and runs at* Willmore;
          he runs out, Belvile *after him;* Frederick *interposes.*

          Enter Angellica, Moretta *and* Sebastian.

ANGELLICA Ha – Sebastian –
  Is not that Willmore? – haste – haste and bring him back.
          [*Exit* Sebastian.

FREDERICK The colonel's mad – I never saw him thus before, I'll
after 'em lest he do some mischief, for I am sure Willmore will
not draw on him. [*Exit.*

ANGELLICA I am all rage! my first desires defeated!
For one for ought he knows that has no
Other merit than her quality
– Her being Don Pedro's sister – he loves her!
I know 'tis so – dull, dull, insensible –
He will not see me now though oft invited;
And broke his word last night – false perjured man!
– He that but yesterday fought for my favours,
And would have made his life a sacrifice
To've gained one night with me,
Must now be hired and courted to my arms.

MORETTA I told you what would come on't, but Moretta's
an old doting fool – why did you give him five hundred
crowns, but to set himself out for other lovers! you should have
kept him poor, if you had meant to have had any good from
him.

ANGELLICA Oh, name not such mean trifles; – had I given him all
My youth has earned from sin,
I had not lost a thought nor sigh upon't.
But I have given him my eternal rest,
My whole repose, my future joys, my heart!
My virgin heart, Moretta! Oh 'tis gone!

MORETTA Curse on him, here he comes;
How fine she has made him too.

Enter Willmore *and* Sebastian; Angellica *turns and walks away.*

WILLMORE How now, turned shadow!
Fly when I pursue! and follow when I fly!

      Stay gentle shadow of my dove   [*Sings.*
        And tell me e'er I go,
      Whether the substance may not prove
        A fleeting thing like you.

There's a soft kind look remaining yet.
      [*As she turns she looks on him.*

ANGELLICA Well sir, you may be gay, all happiness, all joys
pursue you still, Fortune's your slave, and gives you every hour
choice of new hearts and beauties, till you are cloyed with the
repeated bliss, which others vainly languish for. –
But know false man, that I shall be revenged.

[*Turns away in rage.*

WILLMORE So, gad, there are of those faint-hearted lovers, whom
such a sharp lesson next their hearts would make as impotent
as fourscore – pox o' this whining. – My business is to laugh
and love – a pox on't, I hate your sullen lover, a man shall lose
as much time to put you in humour now, as would serve to
gain a new woman.

ANGELLICA I scorn to cool that fire I cannot raise,
Or do the drudgery of your virtuous mistress.

WILLMORE A virtuous mistress! death, what a thing thou hast
found out for me! Why, what the devil should I do with a
virtuous woman? – a sort of ill-natured creatures, that take a
pride to torment a lover, virtue is but an infirmity in woman; a
disease that renders even the handsome ungrateful; whilst the
ill-favoured, for want of solicitations and address, only fancy
themselves so. – I have lain with a woman of quality, who has
all the while been railing at whores.

ANGELLICA I will not answer for your mistress's virtue,
Though she be young enough to know no guilt;
And I could wish you would persuade my heart
'Twas the two hundred thousand crowns you courted.

WILLMORE Two hundred thousand crowns! What story's this? –
what trick? – what woman? – ha!

ANGELLICA How strange you make it, have you forgot the
creature you entertained on the piazza last night?

WILLMORE Ha! my gipsy worth two hundred thousand crowns! –
oh, how I long to be with her – pox, I knew she was of quality.

[*Aside.*

ANGELLICA False man! I see my ruin in thy face.
How many vows you breathed upon my bosom,
Never to be unjust – have you forgot so soon?

WILLMORE Faith no, I was just coming to repeat 'em – but here's
a humour indeed – would make a man a saint – would she

would be angry enough to leave me, and command me not to
wait on her.   [*Aside.*

Enter Hellena *dressed in man's clothes.*

HELLENA This must be Angellica! I know it by her mumping[100]
matron here – Aye, aye, 'tis she! my mad captain's with her
too, for all his swearing – how this unconstant humour makes
me love him! – Pray, good grave gentlewoman, is not this
Angellica?

MORETTA My too young sir, it is – I hope 'tis one from Don
Antonio.   [*Goes to* Angellica.

HELLENA Well, something I'll do to vex him for this.   [*Aside.*

ANGELLICA I will not speak with him; am I in humour to receive
a lover?

WILLMORE Not speak with him! why, I'll be gone – and wait
your idler minutes – can I show less obedience to the thing I
love so fondly?   [*Offers to go.*

ANGELLICA A fine excuse, this! – stay –

WILLMORE And hinder your advantage! Should I repay your
bounties so ungratefully?

ANGELLICA Come hither, boy – that I may let you see
How much above the advantages you name
I prize one minute's joy with you.

WILLMORE Oh, you destroy me with this endearment.

[*Impatient to be gone.*
– Death! how shall I get away [*Aside.*] – Madam, 'twill not be
fit I should be seen with you – besides, it will not be convenient
– and I've a friend – that's dangerously sick.

ANGELLICA I see you're impatient – yet you shall stay.

WILLMORE And miss my assignation with my gipsy.

[*Aside, and walks about impatiently.*

Moretta *brings* Hellena, *who addresses herself to* Angellica.

HELLENA Madam,
You'll hardly pardon my intrusion,
When you shall know my business!
And I'm too young to tell my tale with art;
But there must be a wondrous store of goodness,
Where so much beauty dwells.

ANGELLICA A pretty advocate, whoever sent thee.
 – Prithee proceed – Nay, sir, you shall not go.

[To Willmore, who is stealing off.

WILLMORE Then I shall lose my dear gipsy for ever.
 – Pox on't, she stays me out of spite.   *[Aside.*

ANGELLICA I am related to a lady, madam,
 Young, rich, and nobly born, but has the fate
 To be in love with a young English gentleman.
 Strangely she loves him, at first sight she loved him,
 But did adore him when she heard him speak;
 For he, she said, had charms in every word,
 That failed not to surprise, to wound and conquer.

WILLMORE Ha! Egad, I hope this concerns me.   *[Aside.*

ANGELLICA 'Tis my false man, he means – would he were gone.
 This praise will raise his pride, and ruin me – well
 Since you are so impatient to be gone
 I will release you, sir.   *[To Willmore.*

WILLMORE Nay, then I'm sure 'twas me he spoke of,
 this cannot be the effects of kindness in her.   *[Aside.*
 – No, madam, I've considered better on't,
 And will not give you cause of jealousy.

ANGELLICA But, sir, I've – business, that –

WILLMORE This shall not do, I know 'tis but to try me.

ANGELLICA Well, to your story, boy, – though 'twill undo me.

[Aside.

HELLENA With this addition to his other beauties,
 He won her unresisting tender heart,
 He vowed, and sighed, and swore he loved her dearly;
 And she believed the cunning flatterer,
 And thought herself the happiest maid alive,
 Today was the appointed time by both
 To consummate their bliss,
 The virgin, altar, and the priest were dressed,[101]
 And whilst she languished for th' expected bridegroom,
 She heard he paid his broken vows to you.

WILLMORE So, this is some dear rogue that's in love with me,
 And this way lets me know it; or if it be not me, she means
 someone whose place I may supply.

ANGELLICA Now I perceive
  The cause of thy impatience to be gone,
  And all the business of this glorious dress.
WILLMORE Damn the young prater,[102] I know not what he means.
HELLENA Madam,
  In your fair eyes I read too much concern,
  To tell my farther business.
ANGELLICA Prithee, sweet youth, talk on, thou mayest perhaps
  Raise here a storm that may undo my passion,
  And then I'll grant thee anything.
HELLENA Madam, 'tis to entreat you (oh unreasonable),
  You would not see this stranger;
  For if you do, she vows you are undone,
  Though Nature never made a man so excellent,
  And sure he'ad been a god, but for inconstancy.
WILLMORE Ah, rogue, how finely he's instructed!   [*Aside.*
  – 'Tis plain, some woman that has seen me *en passant*.[103]
ANGELLICA Oh, I shall burst with jealousy! do you know the man
  you speak of? –
HELLENA Yes, madam, he used to be in buff and scarlet.
ANGELLICA Thou, false as hell, what canst thou say to this?
                                                    [*To* Willmore.
WILLMORE By Heaven –
ANGELLICA Hold, do not damn thyself –
HELLENA Nor hope to be believed. –
                                        [*He walks about, they follow.*
ANGELLICA Oh perjured man!
  Is't thus you pay my generous passion back?
HELLENA Why would you, Sir, abuse my lady's faith? –
ANGELLICA And use me so inhumanely.
HELLENA A maid so young, so innocent –
WILLMORE Ah, young devil.
ANGELLICA Dost thou not know thy life is [in] my power?
HELLENA Or think my lady cannot be revenged.
WILLMORE So, so, the storm comes finely on.   [*Aside.*
ANGELLICA Now thou art silent, guilt has struck thee dumb.
  Oh, hadst thou still been so, I'd lived in safety.
                                        [*She turns away and weeps.*

WILLMORE Sweetheart, the lady's name and house, – quickly: I'm
impatient to be with her. –

[*Aside to* Hellena, *looks towards* Angellica *to watch her
turning, and as she comes towards them he meets her.*

HELLENA So, now is he for another woman. [*Aside.*

WILLMORE The impudentest young thing in nature;
I cannot persuade him out of his error, madam.

ANGELLICA I know he's in the right, – yet thou'st a tongue
That would persuade him to deny his faith.

[*In rage walks away.*

WILLMORE Her name, her name, dear boy. –

[*Said softly to* Hellena.

HELLENA Have you forgot it, sir?

WILLMORE Oh, I perceive he's not to know I am a stranger to his
lady. [*Aside.*

– Yes, yes I do know – but – I have forgot the –

[Angellica *turns.*

– By Heaven, such early confidence I never saw.

ANGELLICA Did I not charge you with this mistress, Sir?
Which you denied, though I beheld your perjury.
This little generosity of thine has rendered back my heart.

[*Walks away.*

WILLMORE So, you have made sweet work here, my little
mischief;
Look your lady be kind and good-natured now, or
I shall have but a cursed bargain on't.

[Angellica *turns towards them.*

– The rogue's bred up to mischief,
Art thou so great a fool to credit him?

ANGELLICA Yes, I do, and you in vain impose upon me.

– Come hither, boy, – is not this he you spoke of?

HELLENA I think – it is, I cannot swear, but I vow he has just
such another lying lover's look.

[Hellena *looks in his face, he gazes on her.*

WILLMORE Hah! do not I know that face –
By Heaven my little gipsy, what a dull dog was I,
Had I but looked that way I'd known her.
Are all my hopes of a new woman banished? [*Aside.*

– Egad, if I do not fit thee for this, hang me.

– Madam, I have found out the plot.   [*To* Angellica.

HELLENA Oh Lord, what does he say? am I discovered now?

WILLMORE Do you see this young spark here? –

HELLENA He'll tell her who I am.

WILLMORE – Who do you think this is?

HELLENA Ay, ay, he does know me – Nay, dear captain! I am undone if you discover me.

WILLMORE Nay, nay, no cogging,[104] she shall know what a precious mistress I have.

HELLENA Will you be such a devil?

WILLMORE Nay, nay, I'll teach you to spoil sport you will not make. – this small ambassador comes not from a person of quality as you imagine, and he says: but from a very errant gipsy, the talkingest, pratingest, cantingest little animal thou ever sawest.

ANGELLICA What news you tell me, that's the thing I mean.

HELLENA Would I were well off the place, if ever I go a captain-hunting again –   [*Aside.*

WILLMORE Mean that thing? that gipsy thing? Thou mayest as well be jealous of thy monkey or parrot, as of her, a German motion[105] were worth a dozen of her, and a dream were a better enjoyment, a creature of a constitution fitter for Heaven than man.

HELLENA Though I'm sure he lies, yet this vexes me.   [*Aside.*

ANGELLICA You are mistaken, she's a Spanish woman
Made up of no such dull materials.

WILLMORE Materials, egad an she be made of any that will either dispense or admit of love, I'll be bound to continence.

HELLENA Unreasonable man, do you think so?   [*Aside to him.*

WILLMORE You may return my little brazen head, and tell your lady that till she be handsome enough to be beloved, or I dull enough to be religious, there will be small hopes of me.[106]

ANGELLICA Did you not promise then to marry her?

WILLMORE Not I, by Heaven.

ANGELLICA You cannot undeceive my fears and torments, till you have vowed you will not marry her.

THE ROVER

HELLENA If he swears that, he'll be revenged on me indeed for all my rogueries. [*Aside.*

ANGELLICA I know what arguments you'll bring against me; fortune, and honour. –

WILLMORE Honour, I tell you, I hate it in your sex; and those that fancy themselves possessed of that foppery are the most impertinently troublesome of all womankind, and will transgress nine Commandments to keep one; and to satisfy your jealousy I swear –

HELLENA Oh, no swearing, dear captain. – [*Aside to him.*

WILLMORE If it were possible I should ever be inclined to marry, it should be some kind young sinner, one that has generosity enough to give a favour handsomely to one that can ask it discreetly, one that has wit enough to manage an intrigue of love – oh, how civil such a wench is, to a man that does her the honour to marry her.

ANGELLICA By Heaven, there's no faith in anything he says.

Enter Sebastian.

SEBASTIAN Madam, Don Antonio –

ANGELLICA Come hither.

HELLENA Ha! Antonio, he may be coming hither and he'll certainly discover me, I'll therefore retire without a ceremony.

[[*Aside;*] *Exit* Hellena.

ANGELLICA I'll see him, get my coach ready.

SEBASTIAN It waits you, madam.

WILLMORE This is lucky. [[*Aside.*]] What, Madam, now I may be gone and leave you to the enjoyment of my rival?

ANGELLICA Dull man, that canst not see how ill, how poor,
That false dissimulation looks – begone
And never let me see thy cozening face again,
Lest I relapse and kill thee.

WILLMORE Yes, you can spare me now, – farewell, till you're in better humour – I'm glad of this release –
Now for my gipsy:
For though to worse we change, yet still we find
New joys, new charms, in a new miss that's kind.

[*Exit* Willmore.

220

ANGELLICA He's gone, and in this ague of my soul
  The shivering fit returns;
  Oh with what willing haste, he took his leave,
  As if the longed-for minute were arrived
  Of some blessed assignation.
  In vain I have consulted all my charms,
  In vain this beauty prized, in vain believed
  My eyes could kindle any lasting fires;
  I had forgot my name, my infamy,
  And the reproach that honour lays on those
  That dare pretend a sober passion here.
    Nice reputation, though it leave behind
  More virtues than inhabit where that dwells;
  Yet that once gone, those virtues shine no more.
  – Then since I am not fit to be beloved,
  I am resolved to think on a revenge
  On him that soothed me thus to my undoing.   [*Exeunt.*

Scene III. *A street.*

Enter Florinda *and* Valeria *in habits different from what they have been seen in.*

FLORINDA We're happily escaped, and yet I tremble still.

VALERIA A lover and fear! why, I am but half an one, and yet I have courage for any attempt; would Hellena were here, I would fain have had her as deep in this mischief as we, she'll fare but ill else I doubt.

FLORINDA She pretended a visit to the Augustine nuns, but I believe some other design carried her out; pray Heaven we light on her. – Prithee, what didst do with Callis?

VALERIA When I saw no reason would do good on her, I followed her into the wardrobe, and as she was looking for something in a great chest, I toppled her in by the heels, snatched the key of the apartment where you were confined, locked her in, and left her bawling for help.

FLORINDA 'Tis well you resolve to follow my fortunes, for thou darest never appear at home again after such an action.

VALERIA That's according as the young stranger and I shall agree. –

But to our business – I delivered your letter, your note to Belvile, when I got out under pretence of going to mass, I found him at his lodging, and believe me it came seasonably; for never was man in so desperate a condition; I told him of your resolution of making your escape today, if your brother would be absent long enough to permit you; if not, to die rather than be Antonio's.

FLORINDA Thou shouldst have told him I was confined to my chamber upon my brother's suspicion that the business on the Molo was a plot laid between him and I.

VALERIA I said all this, and told him your brother was now gone to his devotion, and he resolves to visit every church till he find him; and not only undeceive him in that, but caress him so as shall delay his return home.

FLORINDA Oh Heavens! he's here, and Belvile with him too.

[*They put on their vizards.*

Enter Don Pedro, Belvile, Willmore. Belvile *and* Don Pedro *seeming in serious discourse.*

VALERIA Walk boldly by them, and I'll come at a distance, lest he suspect us. [*She walks by them, and looks back on them.*

WILLMORE Hah! a woman, and of an excellent mien.

PEDRO She throws a kind look back on you.

WILLMORE Death, 'tis a likely wench, and that kind look shall not be cast away – I'll follow her.

BELVILE Prithee do not.

WILLMORE Do not! By Heavens to the Antipodes, with such an invitation. [*She goes out, and* Willmore *follows her.*

BELVILE 'Tis a mad fellow for a wench.

Enter Frederick.

FREDERICK Oh colonel, such news!

BELVILE Prithee what?

FREDERICK News that will make you laugh in spite of Fortune.

BELVILE What, Blunt has had some damned trick put upon him, cheated, banged or clapped.

FREDERICK Cheated sir, rarely cheated of all but his shirt and drawers, the unconscionable whore too turned him out before consummation, so that traversing the streets at midnight, the Watch found him in this fresco,[107] and conducted him home. By Heaven 'tis such a sight, and yet I durst as well been hanged as laugh at him, or pity him; he beats all that do but ask him a question, and is in such a humour.

PEDRO Who is't has met with this ill usage, sir?

BELVILE A friend of ours whom you must see for mirth's sake. I'll employ him to give Florinda time for an escape.   [*Aside.*

PEDRO What is he?

BELVILE A young countryman of ours, one that has been educated at so plentiful a rate, he yet ne'er knew the want of money, and 'twill be a great jest to see how simply he'll look without it; for my part I'll lend him none, and the rogue know[s] not how to put on a borrowing face, and ask first; I'll let him see how good 'tis to play our parts whilst I play his – prithee Fred, do you go home and keep him in that posture till we come.   [*Exeunt.*

Enter Florinda *from the farther end of the scene, looking behind her.*

FLORINDA I am followed still – hah – my brother too advancing this way, good Heavens defend me from being seen by him.

[*She goes off.*

Enter Willmore, *and after him* Valeria *at a little distance.*

WILLMORE Ah! There she sails, she looks back as she were willing to be boarded, I'll warrant her prize.[108]

[*He goes out,* Valeria *following.*

Enter Hellena, *just as he goes out, with a page.*

HELLENA Hah, is not that my captain that has a woman in chase? – 'tis not Angellica; boy, follow those people at a distance, and bring me an account where they go in, – I'll find his haunts, and plague him everywhere, – ha – my brother –
     [*Exit Page;* Belvile, Willmore *and* Pedro *cross the stage;* Hellena *runs off.*

Scene changes to another street. Enter Florinda.

FLORINDA What shall I do, my brother now pursues me. Will no
kind Power protect me from his tyranny? – hah, here's a door
open, I'll venture in, since nothing can be worse than to fall
into his hands, my life and honour are at stake, and my
necessity has no choice. [*She goes in.*

Enter Valeria *and* Hellena's *Page, peeping after* Florinda.

PAGE Here she went in, I shall remember this house. [*Exit Boy.*
VALERIA This is Belvile's lodging; she's gone in as readily as if she
knew it, – hah – here's that mad fellow again, I dare not
venture in, – I'll watch my opportunity. [*Goes aside.*

Enter Willmore, *gazing about him.*

WILLMORE I have lost her hereabouts – pox on't, she must not
'scape me so. [*Goes out.*

[SCENE IV.] *Scene changes to* Blunt's *chamber, discovers him
sitting on a couch in his shirt and drawers, reading.*

BLUNT So, now my mind's a little at peace, since I have resolved
revenge – a pox on this tailor though, for not bringing home
the clothes I bespoke; and a pox of all poor cavaliers, a man
can never keep a spare suit for 'em; and I shall have these
rogues come in and find me naked, and then I'm undone; but
I'm resolved to arm myself – the rascals shall not insult over me
too much. [*Puts on an old rusty sword, and buff belt.*
– Now, how like a morris dancer[109] I am equipped – a fine
ladylike whore to cheat me thus, without affording me a
kindness for my money, a pox light on her, I shall never be
reconciled to the sex more,[110] she has made me as faithless as a
physician, as uncharitable as a churchman, and as ill-natured as
a poet. Oh how I'll use all womankind hereafter! What would I
give to have one of 'em within my reach now! any mortal thing
in petticoats, kind Fortune, send me! and I'll forgive thy last
night's malice – here's a cursed book too (a warning to all
young travellers) that can instruct me how to prevent such
mischiefs now 'tis too late; well, 'tis a rare convenient thing to
read a little now and then, as well as hawk and hunt.
[*Sits down again and reads.*

Enter to him Florinda.

FLORINDA This house is haunted sure, 'tis well furnished and no living thing inhabits it – hah – a man, Heavens how he's attired! sure 'tis some rope dancer, or fencing master; I tremble now for fear, and yet I must venture now to speak to him – Sir, if I may not interrupt your meditations –

[*He*[111] *starts up and gazes.*

BLUNT Hah – what's here! are my wishes granted? and is not that a she creature? adsheartlikins 'tis! What wretched thing art thou – hah!

FLORINDA Charitable sir, you've told yourself already what I am; a very wretched maid, forced by a strange unlucky accident to seek a safety here, and must be ruined, if you do not grant it.

BLUNT Ruined! Is there any ruin so inevitable as that which now threatens thee? Dost thou know, miserable woman! into what den of mischiefs thou art fallen? what abyss of confusion – hah! – dost not see something in my looks that frights thy guilty soul, and makes thee wish to change that shape of woman for any humble animal, or devil? for those were safer for thee, and less mischievous.

FLORINDA Alas, what mean you, Sir? I must confess, your looks have something in 'em makes me fear, but I beseech you, as you seem a gentleman, pity a harmless virgin, that takes your house for sanctuary.

BLUNT Talk on, talk on, and weep too, till my faith return. Do, flatter me out of my senses again – a harmless virgin with a pox, as much one as t'other, adsheartlikins. Why, what the devil can I not be safe in my house for you, not in my chamber, nay, even being naked too cannot secure me: this is an impudence greater than has invaded me yet – come, no resistance.

[*Pulls her rudely.*

FLORINDA Dare you be so cruel?

BLUNT Cruel, adsheartlikins as a galley slave, or a Spanish whore: cruel, yes, I will kiss and beat thee all over; kiss, and see thee all over; thou shalt lie with me too, not that I care for the enjoyment, but to let thee see I have ta'en deliberated malice to thee, and will be revenged on one whore for the sins of another; I will smile and deceive thee, flatter thee, and beat thee, kiss and swear, and lie to thee, embrace thee and rob thee, as she did me, fawn on thee, and strip thee stark naked, then hang thee out at my window by the heels, with a paper of scurvy verses fastened to thy breast, in praise of damnable women [112] – come, come along.

FLORINDA Alas, Sir, must I be sacrificed for the crimes of the most infamous of my sex, I never understood the sins you name.

BLUNT Do, persuade the fool you love him, or that one of you can be just or honest, tell me I was not an easy coxcomb, or any strange impossible tale: it will be believed sooner than thy false showers or protestations. A generation of damned hypocrites! to flatter my very clothes from my back! dissembling witches! are these the returns you make an honest gentleman, that trusts, believes, and loves you – but if I be not even with you – come along – or I shall –   [*Pulls her again.*

Enter Frederick.

FREDERICK Hah! what's here to do?

BLUNT Adsheartlikins, Fred, I am glad thou art come, to be a witness of my dire revenge.

FREDERICK What's this, a person of quality too, who is upon the ramble to supply the defects of some grave impotent husband?

BLUNT No, this has another pretence, some very unfortunate accident brought her hither, to save a life pursued by I know not who, or why, and forced to take sanctuary here at Fools' Haven. Adsheartlikins, to me of all mankind for protection? is the ass to be cajoled again, think ye? No, young one, no prayers or tears shall mitigate my rage; therefore prepare for both my pleasures of enjoyment and revenge, for I am resolved to make up my loss here on thy body, I'll take it out in kindness and in beating.

FREDERICK Now mistress of mine, what do you think of this?

FLORINDA I think he will not – dares not be so barbarous.

FREDERICK Have a care, Blunt, she fetched a deep sigh, she is enamoured with thy shirt and drawers, she'll strip thee even of that; there are of her calling such unconscionable baggages, and such dexterous thieves, they'll flay a man and he shall ne'er miss his skin, till he feels the cold. There was a countryman of ours robbed of a row of teeth whilst he was a sleeping, which the jilt made him buy again when he waked – you see, lady, how little reason we have to trust you.

BLUNT 'Dsheartlikins, why this is most abominable.

FLORINDA Some such devils there may be, but by all that's holy, I am none such, I entered here to save a life in danger.

BLUNT For no goodness, I'll warrant her.

FREDERICK Faith, damsel, you had e'en confessed the plain truth, for we are fellows not to be caught twice in the same trap: look on that wreck, a tight vessel when he set out of haven, well trimmed and laden, and see how a female picaroon of this island of rogues has shattered him, and canst thou hope for any mercy?

BLUNT No, no, gentlewoman, come along, adsheartlikins, we must be better acquainted – we'll both lie with her, and then let me alone to bang her.

FREDERICK I'm ready to serve you in matters of revenge, that has a double pleasure in't.

BLUNT Well said. You hear, little one, how you are condemned by public vote to the bed within, there's no resisting your destiny, sweetheart. [*Pulls her.*

FLORINDA Stay, sir, I have seen you with Belvile, an English cavalier, for his sake use me kindly; you know him, sir.

BLUNT Belvile, why yes, sweeting, we do know Belvile, and wish he were with us now, he's a cormorant[113] at whore and bacon, he'd have a limb or two of thee my virgin pullet, but 'tis no matter, we'll leave him the bones to pick.

FLORINDA Sir, if you have any esteem for that Belvile, I conjure you to treat me with more gentleness; he'll thank you for the justice.

FREDERICK Hark ye, Blunt, I doubt we are mistaken in this matter.

FLORINDA Sir, if you find me not worth Belvile's care, use me as you please, and that you may think I merit better treatment than you threaten – pray take this present –

[*Gives him a ring; he looks on it.*

BLUNT Hum – a diamond! why, 'tis a wonderful virtue now that lies in this ring, a mollifying virtue; adsheartlikins, there's more persuasive rhetoric in't than all her sex can utter.

FREDERICK I begin to suspect something; and 'twould anger us vilely to be trussed up for a rape upon a maid of quality, when we only believe we ruffle a harlot.

BLUNT Thou art a credulous fellow, but adsheartlikins I have no faith yet, why my saint prattled as parlously as this does, she gave me a bracelet too, a devil on her, but I sent my man to sell it today for necessaries, and it proved as counterfeit as her vows of love.

FREDERICK However, let it reprieve her till we see Belvile.

BLUNT That's hard, yet I will grant it.

Enter a servant.

SERVANT Oh, sir, the colonel is just come in with his new friend and a Spaniard of quality, and talks of having you to dinner with 'em.

BLUNT 'Dsheartlikins, I'm undone – I would not see 'em for the world. Hark ye, Fred, lock up the wench in your chamber.

FREDERICK Fear nothing, madam, what e'er he threatens, you are safe whilst in my hands. [*Exit Frederick and Florinda.*

BLUNT And, sirrah – upon your life, say – I am not at home, – or that I am asleep – or – or anything – away – I'll prevent their coming this way. [*Locks the door, and exeunt.*

ACT V

SCENE I. *Blunt's chamber.*

After a great knocking as at his chamber door, enter Blunt softly crossing the stage, in his shirt and drawers as before.

[VOICES] Ned, Ned Blunt, Ned Blunt. [*Call within.*

BLUNT The rogues are up in arms, 'sheartlikins, this villainous Frederick has betrayed me, they have heard of my blessed fortune.

[VOICES] Ned Blunt, Ned, Ned –   [*and knocking within.*

BELVILE Why he's dead sir, without dispute dead, he has not been seen today, let's break open the door – here – boy –

BLUNT Ha, break open the door. 'Dsheartlikins, that mad fellow will be as good as his word.

BELVILE Boy, bring something to force the door,
                  [*A great noise within, at the door again.*

BLUNT So, now must I speak, in my own defence, I'll try what rhetoric will do – hold – hold, what do you mean gentlemen, what do you mean?

BELVILE Oh, rogue, art alive? Prithee open the door and convince us.   [*Within.*

BLUNT Yes, I am alive gentlemen, – but at present a little busy.

BELVILE How, Blunt grown a man of business! Come, come, open and let's see this miracle.   [*Within.*

BLUNT No, no, no, no, gentlemen, 'tis no great business – but – I am – at – my devotion – 'dsheartlikins, will you not allow a man time to pray?

BELVILE Turned religious! a greater wonder than the first, therefore open quickly, or we shall unhinge, we shall.   [*Within.*

BLUNT This won't do – why, hark ye, colonel, to tell you the plain truth, I am about a necessary affair of life – I have a wench with me – you apprehend me? The devil's in't if they be so uncivil as to disturb me now.

WILLMORE How a wench! Nay then we must enter and partake no resistance – unless it be your lady of quality, and then we'll keep our distance.

BLUNT So, the business is out.

WILLMORE Come, come lend's more hands to the door – now heave altogether – so well done, my boys –
                    [*Breaks open the door.*

Enter Belvile [*and his Page*], Willmore, Frederick *and* Pedro.
Blunt *looks simply, they all laugh at him, he lays his hand on his sword, and comes up to* Willmore.

BLUNT Hark ye, sir, laugh out your laugh quickly, d'ye hear, and begone. I shall spoil your sport else, adsheartlikins sir, I shall – the jest has been carried on too long – a plague upon my tailor –   [*Aside.*

WILLMORE 'Sdeath, how the whore has dressed him, faith sir I'm sorry.

BLUNT Are you so sir, keep't to yourself then sir, I advise you, d'ye hear, for I can as little endure your pity as his mirth.
                                      [*Lays his hand on his sword.*

BELVILE Indeed Willmore, thou wert a little too rough with Ned Blunt's mistress, call a person of quality whore? and one so young, so handsome, and so eloquent – ha, ha, he. –

BLUNT Hark ye, sir, you know me, and know I can be angry, have a care – for adsheartlikins I can fight too – I can sir, – do you mark me – no more –

BELVILE Why so peevish, good Ned, some disappointments I'll warrant – what? did the jealous count her husband return just in the nick?

BLUNT Or the devil, sir – [*They laugh.*] d'ye laugh –
Look ye settle me a good sober countenance, and that quickly too, or you shall know Ned Blunt is not –

BELVILE Not everybody, we know that.

BLUNT Not an ass to be laughed at, sir.

WILLMORE Unconscionable sinner, to bring a lover so near his happiness, a vigorous passionate lover, and then not only cheat him of his movables, but his very desires too.

BELVILE Ah! sir, a mistress is a trifle with Blunt. He'll have a dozen the next time he looks abroad, his eyes have charms not to be resisted, there needs no more than to expose that taking person to the view of the fair, and he leads 'em all in triumph.

PEDRO Sir, though I'm a stranger to you, I am ashamed at the rudeness of my nation; and could you learn who did it, would assist you to make an example of 'em.

BLUNT Why aye, there's one speaks sense now, and handsomely; and let me tell you gentlemen, I should not have showed myself like a jack pudding,[114] thus to have made you mirth, but that I have revenge within my power, for know, I have got into my possession a female who had better have fallen under any curse than the ruin I design her: adsheartlikins, she assaulted me here in my own lodgings, and had doubtless committed a rape upon me, had not this sword defended me.

FREDERICK I know not that, but o' my conscience thou had ravished her, had she not redeemed herself with a ring – let's see't, Blunt.   [Blunt *shows the ring.*

BELVILE Hah! – the ring I gave Florinda, when we exchanged our vows – hark ye Blunt, –   [*Goes to whisper to him.*

WILLMORE No whispering, good colonel, there's a woman in the case, no whispering.

BELVILE Hark ye fool, be advised, and conceal both the ring and the story for your reputation's sake, do not let people know what despised cullies we English are; to be cheated and abused by one whore, and another rather bribe thee than be kind to thee, is an infamy to our nation.

WILLMORE Come, come, where's the wench, we'll see her, let her be what she will, we'll see her.

PEDRO Aye, aye, let us see her, I can soon discover whether she be of quality, or for your diversion.

BLUNT She's in Fred's custody.

WILLMORE Come, come, the key.

                [*To Frederick, who gives him the key; they are going.*

BELVILE Death, what shall I do – stay, gentlemen – yet if I hinder 'em I shall discover all, – hold – let's go one at once[115] – give me the key.

WILLMORE Nay, hold there colonel. I'll go first.

FREDERICK Nay, no dispute, Ned and I have the propriety of her.

WILLMORE Damn propriety – then we'll draw cuts,

                       [Belvile *goes to whisper* Willmore.

– nay no corruption, good colonel. Come, the longest sword carries her –

                [*They all draw forgetting* Don Pedro *being as a Spaniard had the longest.*

BLUNT I yield up my interest to you, gentlemen, and that will be revenge sufficient.

WILLMORE The wench is yours – [*to Pedro.*] Pox of his toledo,[116] I had forgot that.

FREDERICK Come sir, I'll conduct you to the lady.

                                      [*Exeunt* Frederick *and* Pedro.

BELVILE To hinder him will certainly discover her –   [*Aside.*
Dost know, dull beast, what mischief thou hast done.

                  [Willmore *walking up and down out of humour.*

WILLMORE Aye, aye, to trust our fortune to lots, a devil on't, 'twas madness, that's the truth on't.

BELVILE Oh intolerable sot –

    Enter Florinda *running masked,* Pedro *after her;* Willmore *gazing round her.*

FLORINDA Good Heaven defend me from discovery.   [*Aside.*

PEDRO 'Tis but in vain to fly me, you're fallen to my lot.

BELVILE Sure she's undiscovered yet, but now I fear there is no way to bring her off.

WILLMORE Why, what a pox, is not this my woman, the same I followed but now?

                [Pedro, *talking to* Florinda, *who walks up and down.*

PEDRO As if I did not know ye, and your business here.

FLORINDA Good Heaven, I fear he does indeed –   [*Aside.*

PEDRO Come, pray be kind, I know you meant to be so when you entered here, for these are proper gentlemen.

WILLMORE But sir – perhaps the lady will not be imposed upon, she'll choose her man.

PEDRO I am better bred than not to leave her choice free.

    Enter Valeria, *and is surprised at sight of* Don Pedro.

VALERIA Don Pedro here! there's no avoiding him.   [*Aside.*

FLORINDA Valeria! then I'm undone, –   [*Aside.*

VALERIA Oh! have I found you, sir –   [*To* Pedro *running to him.*
– the strangest accident – if I had breath – to tell it.

PEDRO Speak – is Florinda safe? Hellena well?

VALERIA Aye, aye, sir – Florinda – is safe – from any fears of you.

PEDRO Why where's Florinda? – speak –

VALERIA Aye, where indeed sir, I wish I could inform you, – but to hold you no longer in doubt –

FLORINDA Oh what will she say –   [*Aside.*

VALERIA – She's fled away in the habit – of one of her pages, sir
– but Callis thinks you may retrieve her yet, if you make haste
away; she'll tell you, sir, the rest – if you can find her out.

[*Aside.*

PEDRO Dishonourable girl, she has undone my aim – sir – you
see my necessity of leaving you, and hope you'll pardon it; my
sister I know will make her flight to you; and if she do, I shall
expect she should be rendered back.

BELVILE I shall consult my love and honour, sir.   [*Exit* Pedro.

FLORINDA My dear preserver, let me embrace thee.   [*To* Valeria.

WILLMORE What the devil's all this?

BLUNT Mystery, by this light.

VALERIA Come, come, make haste and get yourselves married
quickly, for your brother will return again.

BELVILE I'm so surprised with fears and joys, so amazed to find
you here in safety, I can scarce persuade my heart into a faith of
what I see –

WILLMORE Hark ye colonel, is this that mistress who has cost
you so many sighs, and me so many quarrels with you?

BELVILE It is – pray give him the honour of your hand.

[*To* Florinda.

WILLMORE Thus it must be received then.

[*Kneels and kisses her hand.*

And with it give your pardon too.

FLORINDA The friend to Belvile may command me anything.

WILLMORE Death, would I might, 'tis a surprising beauty. [*Aside.*

BELVILE Boy, run and fetch a father instantly.   [*Exit Boy.*

FREDERICK So, now do I stand like a dog, and have not a
syllable to plead my own cause with; by this hand, madam, I
was never thoroughly confounded before, nor shall I ever more
dare look up with confidence, till you are pleased to pardon
me.

FLORINDA Sir, I'll be reconciled to you on one condition, that
you'll follow the example of your friend, in marrying a maid
that does not hate you, and whose fortune (I believe) will not
be unwelcome to you.

FREDERICK Madam, had I no inclinations that way, I should
obey your kind commands.

233.

BELVILE Who, Fred marry; he has so few inclinations for woman-kind, that had he been possessed of Paradise, he might have continued there to this day, if no crime but love could have disinherited him.

FREDERICK Oh, I do not use to boast of my intrigues.

BELVILE Boast, why thou dost nothing but boast; and I dare swear, wert thou as innocent from the sin of the grape, as thou art from the apple, thou mightst yet claim that right in Eden which our first parents lost by too much loving.

FREDERICK I wish this lady would think me so modest a man.

VALERIA She would be sorry then, and not like you half so well, and I should be loth to break my word with you, which was that if your friend and mine agreed, it should be a match between you and I.   [*She gives him her hand.*

FREDERICK Bear witness, colonel, 'tis a bargain.

[*Kisses her hand.*

BLUNT I have a pardon to beg too, but adsheartlikins, I am so out of countenance that I'm a dog if I can say anything to purpose.   [*To* Florinda.

FLORINDA Sir, I heartily forgive you all.

BLUNT That's nobly said, sweet lady, – Belvile, prithee present her her ring again; for I find I have not courage to approach her myself.   [*Gives him the ring; he gives it to* Florinda.

Enter Boy.

BOY Sir, I have brought the father that you sent for.

BELVILE 'Tis well, [*Exit Boy.*] and now my dear Florinda, let's fly to complete that mighty joy we have so long wished and sighed for:

– Come Fred – you'll follow?

FREDERICK Your example, sir, 'twas ever my ambition in war, and must be so in love.

WILLMORE And must not I see this juggling knot tied?

BELVILE No, thou shalt do us better service, and be our guard, lest Don Pedro's sudden return interrupt the ceremony.

WILLMORE Content – I'll secure this pass.

[*Exeunt* Belvile, Florinda, Frederick *and* Valeria.

Enter Boy.

BOY Sir, there's a lady without would speak to you.

[*To* Willmore.

WILLMORE Conduct her in, I dare not quit my post.

BOY And sir, your tailor waits you in your chamber.

BLUNT Some comfort yet, I shall not dance naked at the wedding.

[*Exeunt* Blunt *and Boy.*

Enter again the Boy, conducting in Angellica *in a masquing habit and a vizard.* Willmore *runs to her.*

WILLMORE This can be none but my pretty gipsy – Oh, I see you can follow as well as fly – Come, confess thyself the most malicious devil in Nature, you think you have done my business with Angellica. –

ANGELLICA Stand off, base villain –

[*She draws a pistol, and holds it to his breast.*

WILLMORE Hah, 'tis not she, who art thou? and what's thy business?

ANGELLICA One thou hast injured, and who comes to kill thee for't.

WILLMORE What the devil canst thou mean?

ANGELLICA By all my hopes to kill thee –

[*Holds still the pistol to his breast,
he going back, she following still.*

WILLMORE Prithee, on what acquaintance? for I know thee not.

ANGELLICA Behold this face! – so lost to thy remembrance,
And then call thy sins about thy soul, [*Pulls off her vizard.*
And let 'em die with thee.

WILLMORE Angellica!

ANGELLICA Yes, traitor,[117]
Does not thy guilty blood run shivering through thy veins?
Hast thou no horror at this sight, that tells thee,
Thou hast not long to boast thy shameful conquest?

WILLMORE Faith, no child, my blood keeps its old ebbs and flows still, and that usual heat too, that could oblige thee with a kindness, had I but opportunity.

ANGELLICA Devil! dost wanton with my pain – have at thy heart.

WILLMORE Hold, dear virago! hold thy hand a little,

I am not now at leisure to be killed – hold and hear me –
– death, I think she's in earnest.   [*Aside.*
ANGELLICA Oh, if I take not heed,
My coward heart will leave me to his mercy.
                              [*Aside, turning from him.*
– What have you, sir, to say? – but should I hear thee,
Thoud'st talk away all that is brave about me.
                    [*Follows him with the pistol to his breast.*
And I have vowed thy death, by all that's sacred.
WILLMORE Why, then there's an end of a proper handsome
fellow,
That might have lived to have done good service yet;
– That's all I can say to't.
ANGELLICA Yet – I would give thee – time for – penitence.
                                          [*Pausingly.*
WILLMORE Faith, child, I thank God, I have ever took
Care to lead a good, sober, hopeful life, and am of a religion
That teaches me to believe I shall depart in peace.
ANGELLICA So will the devil! tell me
How many poor believing fools thou hast undone?
How many hearts thou hast betrayed to ruin?
– Yet these are little mischiefs to the ills
Thou'st taught mine to commit: thou'st taught it love.
WILLMORE Egad, 'twas shrewdly hurt the while.
ANGELLICA – Love, that has robbed it of its unconcern,
Of all that pride that taught me how to value it.
And in its room
A mean submissive passion was conveyed,
That made me humbly bow, which I ne'er did
To any thing but Heaven.
– Thou, perjured man, didst this, and with thy oaths,
Which on thy knees thou didst devoutly make,
Softened my yielding heart – And then, I was a slave –
– Yet still had been content to've worn my chains:
Worn 'em with vanity and joy for ever,
Hadst thou not broke those vows that put them on.
– 'Twas then I was undone.
            [*All this while follows him with the pistol to his breast.*

WILLMORE Broke my vows! why, where hast thou lived?
Amongst the gods? for I never heard of mortal man
That has not broke a thousand vows.

ANGELLICA Oh impudence!

WILLMORE Angellica! that beauty has been too long tempting,
Not to have made a thousand lovers languish,
Who in the amorous favour, no doubt have sworn
Like me; did they all die in that faith? still adoring?
I do not think they did.

ANGELLICA No, faithless man: had I repaid their vows, as I did
thine, I would have killed the ingrateful that had abandoned
me.

WILLMORE This old general has quite spoiled thee, nothing
makes a woman so vain, as being flattered; your old lover ever
supplies the defects of age with intolerable dotage, vast charge,
and that which you call constancy; and attributing all this to
your own merits, you domineer, and throw your favours in's
teeth, upbraiding him still with the defects of age, and cuckold
him as often as he deceives your expectations. But the gay,
young, brisk lover, that brings his equal fires, and can give you
dart for dart, he'll[118] be as nice as you sometimes.

ANGELLICA All this thou'st made me know, for which I hate thee.
Had I remained in innocent security,
I should have thought all men were born my slaves,
And worn my power like lightning in my eyes,
To have destroyed at pleasure when offended:
– But when Love held the mirror, the undeceiving glass
Reflected all the weakness of my soul, and made me know
My richest treasure being lost, my honour,
All the remaining spoil could not be worth
The conqueror's care or value.[119]
– Oh, how I fell like a long worshipped idol
Discovering all the cheat.
Would not the incense and rich sacrifice,
Which blind devotion offered at my altars,
Have fallen to thee?
Why wouldst thou then destroy my fancied power.

WILLMORE By Heaven thou'rt brave, and I admire thee strangely.

I wish I were that dull, that constant thing
Which thou wouldst have, and Nature never meant me;
I must, like cheerful birds, sing in all groves,
And perch on every bough,
Billing the next kind she that flies to meet me;
Yet after all could build my nest with thee,
Thither repairing when I'd loved my round,
And still reserve a tributary flame.
– To gain your credit, I'll pay you back your charity,
And be obliged for nothing but for love.

> [*Offers her a purse of gold.*[120]

ANGELLICA Oh that thou wert in earnest!
So mean a thought of me
Would turn my rage to scorn, and I should pity thee,
And give thee leave to live;
Which for the public safety of our sex,
And my own private injuries, I dare not do.
Prepare –   [*Follows still, as before.*
– I will no more be tempted with replies.

WILLMORE Sure –

ANGELLICA Another word will damn thee! I've heard thee talk too long.

> *She follows him with the pistol ready to shoot; he retires still amazed. Enter* Don Antonio, *his arm in a scarf, and lays hold on the pistol.*

ANTONIO Hah! Angellica!

ANGELLICA Antonio! what devil brought thee hither?

ANTONIO Love and curiosity, seeing your coach at door.
Let me disarm you of this unbecoming instrument of death
[*Takes away the pistol.*] – amongst the number of your slaves,
was there not one worthy the honour to have fought your
quarrel?
– Who are you, sir, that are so very wretched
To merit death from her?

WILLMORE One, sir, that could have made a better end of an
amorous quarrel without you, than with you.

ANTONIO Sure 'tis some rival, – hah – the very man took down

her picture yesterday – the very same that set on me last night –
blessed opportunity –   *[Offers to shoot him.*

ANGELLICA Hold, you're mistaken, sir.

ANTONIO By Heaven, the very same!
  – Sir, what pretensions have you to this lady?

WILLMORE Sir, I do not use to be examined, and am ill at all
  disputes but this –   *[Draws:* Antonio *offers to shoot.*

ANGELLICA Oh hold! you see he's armed with certain death;
                                     [To Willmore.
  – And you Antonio, I command you hold,
  By all the passion you've so lately vowed me.

        Enter Don Pedro, *sees* Antonio, *and stays.*

PEDRO Hah, Antonio! and Angellica!   *[Aside.*

ANTONIO When I refuse obedience to your will,
  May you destroy me with your mortal hate.
  By all that's holy I adore you so,
  That even my rival, who has charms enough
  To make him fall a victim to my jealousy
  Shall live, nay, and have leave to love on still.

PEDRO What's this I hear?   *[Aside.*

ANGELLICA Ah thus! 'twas thus! he talked, and I believed.
                             [Pointing to Willmore.
  – Antonio, yesterday,
  I'd not have not sold my interest in his heart,
  For all the sword has won and lost in battle.
  – But now to show my utmost of contempt,
  I give thee life – which if thou wouldst preserve,
  Live where my eyes may never see thee more,
  Live to undo someone, whose soul may prove,
  So bravely constant to revenge my love.
          [Goes out, Antonio *follows, but* Pedro *pulls him back.*

PEDRO Antonio – stay.

ANTONIO Don Pedro –

PEDRO What coward fear was that prevented thee
  From meeting me this morning on the Molo?

ANTONIO Meet thee?

PEDRO Yes me; I was the man that dared thee to't.

ANTONIO Hast thou so often seen me fight in war,
  To find no better cause to excuse my absence?
  – I sent my sword and one to do thee right,
  Finding myself uncapable to use a sword.
PEDRO But 'twas Florinda's quarrel that we fought,
  And you to show how little you esteemed her,
  Sent me your rival, giving him your interest.
  – But I have found the cause of this affront,
  And when I meet you fit for the dispute,
  – I'll tell you my resentment.
ANTONIO I shall be ready, sir, e'er long to do you reason.

[*Exit* Antonio.

PEDRO If I could find Florinda, now whilst my anger's high,
  I think I should be kind, and give her to Belvile in revenge.
WILLMORE Faith, sir, I know not what you would do, but I
  believe the priest within has been so kind.
PEDRO How! my sister married?
WILLMORE I hope by this time she is, and bedded too, or he has
  not my longings about him.
PEDRO Dares he do this! Does he not fear my power?
WILLMORE Faith, not at all, if you will go in, and thank him for
  the favour he has done your sister, so; if not, sir, my power's
  greater in this house than yours; I have a damned surly crew
  here, that will keep you till the next tide, and then clap you on
  board for prize; my ship lies but a league off the Molo, and
  we shall show your donship a damned *tramontana*[121] rover's
  trick.

Enter Belvile.

BELVILE This rogue's in some new mischief – hah, Pedro
  returned!
PEDRO Colonel Belvile, I hear you have married my sister?
BELVILE You have heard truth then, sir.
PEDRO Have I so; then, sir, I wish you joy.
BELVILE How!
PEDRO By this embrace I do, and I am glad on't.
BELVILE Are you in earnest?
PEDRO By our long friendship and my obligations to thee, I am.

The sudden change, I'll give you reasons for anon,
Come lead me to my sister,
That she may know I now approve her choice.

[*Exit* Belvile *with* Pedro.

Willmore *goes to follow them. Enter* Hellena *as before in boy's clothes, and pulls him back.*

WILLMORE Ha! my gipsy: – now a thousand blessings on thee for this kindness. Egad, child, I was e'en in despair of ever seeing thee again; my friends are all provided for within, each man his kind woman.

HELLENA Hah! I thought they had served me some such trick!

WILLMORE And I was e'en resolved to go abroad, and condemn myself to my lone cabin, and the thoughts of thee.

HELLENA And could you have left me behind, would you have been so ill-natured?

WILLMORE Why, 'twould have broke my heart, child: – but since we are met again, I defy foul weather to part us.

HELLENA And would you be a faithful friend now, if a maid should trust you?

WILLMORE For a friend I cannot promise; thou art of a form so excellent, a face and humour too good for cold dull friendship; I am parlously afraid of being in love, child, and you have not forgot how severely you have used me?

HELLENA That's all one, such usage you must still look for, to find out all your haunts, to rail at you to all that love you, till I have made you love only me in your own defence, because nobody else will love.

WILLMORE But hast thou no better quality to recommend thyself by?

HELLENA Faith none, captain: – why, 'twill be the greater charity to take me for thy mistress. I am a lone child, a kind of orphan lover, and why I should die a maid, and in a captain's hands too, I do not understand.

WILLMORE Egad, I was never clawed away with broadsides from any female before, thou hast one virtue I adore, good nature; I hate a coy, demure mistress, she's as troublesome as a colt, I'll break none; no, give me a mad mistress when mewed, and in flying, one I dare trust upon the wing, that whilst she's kind will come to the lure.[122]

HELLENA Nay, as kind as you will, good captain, whilst it lasts, but let's lose no time.

WILLMORE My time's as precious to me as thine can be, therefore dear creature, since we are so well agreed, let's retire to my chamber, and if ever thou wert treated with such savoury love! – come – my bed's prepared for such a guest, all clean and sweet as thy fair self; I love to steal a dish and a bottle with a friend, and hate long graces – come, let's retire and fall to.

HELLENA 'Tis but getting my consent, and the business is soon done; let but old Gaffer Hymen[123] and his priest say amen to't, and I dare lay my mother's daughter by as proper a fellow as your father's son, without fear or blushing.

WILLMORE Hold, hold, no bug[124] words, child, priest and Hymen, prithee add a hangman to 'em to make up the consort,[125] – no, no, we'll have no vows but love, child, nor witness but the lover; the kind deity enjoin naught but love! and enjoy! Hymen and priest wait still upon portion, and jointure; love and beauty have their own ceremonies; marriage is as certain a bane to love as lending money is to friendship: I'll neither ask nor give a vow, – though I could be content to turn gipsy, and become a left-handed bridegroom, to have the pleasure of working that great miracle of making a maid a mother, if you durst venture; 'tis upse[126] gipsy that, and if I miss, I'll lose my labour.

HELLENA And if you do not lose, what shall I get? a cradle full of noise and mischief, with a pack of repentance at my back? can you teach me to weave inkle[127] to pass my time with? 'Tis upse gipsy that too.

WILLMORE I can teach thee to weave a true love's knot better.

HELLENA So can my dog.

WILLMORE Well, I see we are both upon our guards, and I see there's no way to conquer good nature, but by yielding, – here – give me thy hand – one kiss and I am thine; –

HELLENA One kiss! how like my page he speaks; I am resolved you shall have none, for asking such a sneaking sum, – he that will be satisfied with one kiss, will never die of that longing; good friend single-kiss, is all your talking come to this? – a kiss, a caudle! [128] farewell captain, single-kiss!

            [Going out he stays her.

WILLMORE Nay, if we part so, let me die like a bird upon a bough, at the sheriff's charge, by Heaven both the Indies shall not buy thee from me. I adore thy humour and will marry thee, and we are so of one humour, it must be a bargain – give me thy hand. –   *[Kisses her hand.*
And now let the blind ones (Love and Fortune) do their worst.

HELLENA Why, God-a-mercy captain!

WILLMORE But hark ye – the bargain is now made, but is it not fit we should know each other's names? that when we have reason to curse one another hereafter (and people ask me who 'tis I give to the devil) I may at least be able to tell what family you came of.

HELLENA Good reason, captain; and where I have cause (as I doubt not but I shall have plentiful) that I may know at whom to throw my – blessings – I beseech ye your name.

WILLMORE I am called Robert the Constant.

HELLENA A very fine name; pray was it your falconer or butler that christened you? Do they not use to whistle when they call you?

WILLMORE I hope you have a better, that a man may name without crossing himself, you are so merry with mine.

HELLENA I am called Hellena the Inconstant.

   Enter Pedro, Belvile, Florinda, Frederick, Valeria.

PEDRO Hah! Hellena!

FLORINDA Hellena!

HELLENA The very same – hah, my brother! now captain, show your love and courage; stand to your arms, and defend me bravely, or I am lost for ever.

PEDRO What's this I hear! False girl, how came you hither, and what's your business? Speak.   *[Goes roughly to her.*

WILLMORE Hold off sir, you have leave to parley only.

            [Puts himself between.

HELLENA I had e'en as good tell it, as you guess it; faith, brother, my business is the same with all living creatures of my age, to love, and be beloved, and here's the man.

PEDRO Perfidious maid, hast thou deceived me too, deceived thyself and Heaven?

HELLENA 'Tis time enough to make my peace with that;
Be you but kind, let me alone with Heaven.

PEDRO Belvile, I did not expect this false play from you; was't not enough you'd gain Florinda (which I pardoned) but your lewd friends too must be enriched with the spoils of a noble family?

BELVILE Faith sir, I am as much surprised at this as you can be. Yet sir, my friends are gentlemen, and ought to be esteemed for their misfortunes, since they have the glory to suffer with the best of men and kings; 'tis true, he's a Rover of Fortune, yet a prince, aboard his little wooden world.

PEDRO What's this to the maintenance of a woman of her birth and quality?

WILLMORE Faith sir, I can boast of nothing but a sword which does me right where e'er I come, and has defended a worse cause than a woman's; and since I loved her before I either knew her birth or name, I must pursue my resolution, and marry her.

PEDRO And is all your holy intent of becoming a nun debauched into a desire of man?

HELLENA Why – I have considered the matter, brother, and find the three hundred thousand crowns my uncle left me (and you cannot keep from me) will be better laid out in love than in religion, and turn to as good an account, – let most voices carry it, for Heaven or the captain?

All cry, A captain! a captain!

HELLENA Look ye, sir, 'tis a clear case.

PEDRO Oh I am mad – if I refuse, my life's in danger –   [*Aside.*
– Come – there's one motive induces me – take her – I shall now be free from fears of her honour, guard it you now, if you can, I have been a slave to't long enough.   [*Gives her to him.*

WILLMORE Faith sir, I am of a nation that are of opinion a woman's honour is not worth guarding when she has a mind to part with it.

HELLENA Well said, captain.

PEDRO This was your plot, mistress, but I hope you have married
one that will revenge my quarrel to you –   [*To* Valeria.
VALERIA There's no altering destiny, sir.
PEDRO Sooner than a woman's will, therefore I forgive you all –
and wish you may get my father's pardon as easily; which I
fear.

> Enter Blunt *dressed in a Spanish habit, looking very ridicu-*
> *lously; his man adjusting his band.*[129]

MAN 'Tis very well, sir –
BLUNT Well, sir, 'dsheartlikins, I tell you 'tis damnable ill, sir, – a
Spanish habit, good Lord! Could the devil and my tailor devise no
other punishment for me, but the mode of a nation I abominate?
BELVILE What's the matter, Ned?
BLUNT Pray view me round, and judge –   [*Turns round.*
BELVILE I must confess thou art a kind of an odd figure.
BLUNT In a Spanish habit with a vengeance! I had rather be in the
Inquisition for Judaism than in this doublet and breeches, a
pillory were an easy collar to this, three handfuls high; and
these shoes too, are worse than the stocks, with the sole an inch
shorter than my foot. In fine, gentlemen, methinks I look
altogether like a bag of bays[130] stuffed full of fool's flesh.
BELVILE Methinks 'tis well, and makes thee look *en cavalier.*[131]
Come sir, settle your face, and salute our friends, lady –
BLUNT Hah! – say'st thou so, my little rover –   [*To* Hellena.
Lady – (if you be one) give me leave to kiss your hand, and tell
you adsheartlikins for all I look so, I am your humble servant, –
a pox of my Spanish habit.
WILLMORE Hark – what's this?   [*Music is heard to play.*

Enter Boy.

BOY Sir, as the custom is, the gay people in masquerade who
make every man's house their own, are coming up:

> Enter *several men and women in masquing habits with*
> *music, they put themselves in order and dance.*

BLUNT Adsheartlikins, would 'twere lawful to pull off their false
faces, that I might see if my doxy[132] were not amongst 'em.

BELVILE Ladies and gentlemen, since you are come so *à propos* you must take a small collation with us.　　　[*To the masquers.*

WILLMORE Whilst we'll to the good man within, who stays to give us a cast of his office.[133]　　　　　　　　　　[*To* Hellena.

– Have you no trembling at the near approach?

HELLENA No more than you have in an engagement or a tempest.

WILLMORE Egad, thou'rt a brave girl, and I admire thy love and courage.

> Lead on, no other dangers they can dread,
> Who venture in the storms o'th' marriage bed.
>
> 　　　　　　　　　　　　　　　　　[*Exeunt.*

EPILOGUE

THE banished cavaliers! a roving blade!
A popish carnival! a masquerade!
The devil's in't if this will please the nation,
In these our blessed times of reformation,
When conventicling [134] is so much in fashion.
And yet –
That mutinous tribe [135] less factions do beget,
Than your continual differing in wit;
Your judgment's (as your passion's) a disease:
Nor muse nor miss your appetite can please;
You're grown as nice as queasy consciences,
Whose each convulsion, when the spirit moves,
Damns everything, that maggot [136] disapproves.
  With canting [137] rule you would the stage refine,
And to dull method all our sense confine.
With th'insolence of commonwealths you rule,
Where each gay fop, and politic grave fool
On monarch wit impose, without control.
As for the last, who seldom sees a play,
Unless it be the old Blackfriars [138] way,
Shaking his empty noddle o'er bamboo, [139]
He cries, – good faith, these plays will never do.
– Ah, sir, in my young days, what lofty wit,
What high strained scenes of fighting there were writ:
These are slight airy toys. But tell me, pray,
What has the House of Commons done today?
Then shows his politics, to let you see,
Of state affairs he'll judge as notably,
As he can do of wit and poetry.
The younger sparks, who hither do resort,
Cry, –
Pox o' your gentle things, give us more sport;
– Damn me, I'm sure 'twill never please the court.
Such fops are never pleased, unless the play
Be stuffed with fools, as brisk and dull as they:

247

Such might the half-crown spare, and in a glass
At home, behold a more accomplished ass,
Where they may set their cravats, wigs and faces,
And practise all their buffoonry grimaces:
See how this – Huff becomes, – this Damny, – stare, –
Which they at home may act, because they dare,
But – must with prudent caution do elsewhere.
Oh that our Nokes, or Tony Lee[140] could show
A fop but half so much to th'life as you.

POSTSCRIPT

THIS play had been sooner in print, but for a report about the town (made by some either very malicious or very ignorant) that 'twas *Thomaso* altered; which made the booksellers fear some trouble from the proprietor of that admirable play, which indeed has wit enough to stock a poet, and is not to be pieced or mended by any but the excellent author himself. That I have stolen some hints from it may be a proof, that I valued it more than to pretend to alter it, had I had the dexterity of some poets, who are not more expert in stealing than in the art of concealing, and who even that way outdo the Spartan boys. I might have appropriated all to myself, but I, vainly proud of my judgment, hang out the sign of Angellica (the only stolen object)[141] to give notice where a great part of the wit dwelt; though if the play of the novella were as well worth remembering as *Thomaso*, they might (bating the name) have as well said, I took it from thence. I will only say the plot and business (not to boast on't) is my own; as for the words and characters, I leave the reader to judge and compare them with *Thomaso*, to whom I recommend the great entertainment of reading it, though had this succeeded ill, I should have had no need of imploring that justice from the critics, who are naturally so kind to any that pretend to usurp their dominion,[142] they would doubtless have given me the whole honour on't. Therefore I will only say in English what the famous Virgil[143] does in Latin; I make verses, and others have the fame.

THE WIDOW RANTER [1]

OR

THE HISTORY OF BACON
IN VIRGINIA

A TRAGICOMEDY

DRAMATIS PERSONAE

Indian King, called Cavarnio.
Bacon, General of the English.
Colonel Wellman, Deputy Governor.
Colonel Downright, a loyal, honest Colonel.
Hazard
Friendly } Two friends known to one another many years in England.
Daring
Fearless } Lieutenant-Generals to Bacon.
Dullman, a Captain.
Timorous Cornet
Whimsey
Whiff } Justices of the Peace, and very great cowards.
Boozer
Brag, a Captain.
Grubb, one complained on by Captain Whiff for calling his wife whore.
A petitioner against Brag.
Parson Dunce, formerly a farrier, fled from England, and Chaplain to the
   Governor.
[Jefery, coachman to Widow Ranter.]
[Jack, a sea-boy.]
[Cavaro.]
[Officer, Messenger, Seaman, Boy, a Highlander.]

Indian Queen, called Semernia, beloved by Bacon.
Madam Surelove, beloved by Hazard.
Mrs Chrisante, daughter to Colonel Downright.
Widow Ranter, in love with Daring.
Mrs Flirt.
Mrs Whimsey.
Mrs Whiff.
Two Maids. [Jenny, maid to Widow Ranter, and Nell, maid at the Inn.]
[Anaria, confidante of the Indian Queen.]
[Maid to Madam Surelove.]
[Singing girl.]
Priests, Indians, [Negroes,] *Soldiers, with other Attendants.*
[Bailiffs.]

Scene: Virginia, in Bacon's camp.

PROLOGUE [2]

WRITTEN BY MR DRYDEN
Spoken by a Woman

PLAYS you will have; and to supply your store,
  Our poets trade to every foreign shore:
This is the product of Virginian ground,
And to the port of Covent-Garden [3] bound.
Our cargo is, or should at least, be wit:
Bless us from you damned pirates of the pit:
And vizard-masks,[4] those dreadful apparitions;
She-privateers,[5] of venomous conditions,
That clap us oft aboard with French commissions.[6] *involuntary exile street*
You sparks,[7] we hope, will wish us happy trading;
For you have ventures in our vessel's lading;
And though you touch at this or t'other nation;
Yet sure Virginia is your dear plantation.
Expect no polished scenes of love should rise
From the rude growth of Indian colonies.
Instead of courtship, and a tedious pother,
They only tip the wink at one another;
Nay often the whole nation, pig together.
You civil beaux, when you pursue the game,[8]
With manners mince the meaning of – that same:
But every part has there its proper name.
Good Heavens defend me, who am yet unbroken
From living there, where such bug [9] words are spoken:
Yet surely, Sirs, it does good stomachs show,
To talk so savourly [10] of what they do.
But were I bound to that broad speaking land,
What e'er they said, I would not understand,
But innocently, with a lady's grace,
Would learn to whisk my fan about my face.
However, to secure you, let me swear,
That no such base mundungus [11] stuff is here.
We bring you of the best the soil affords:

Buy it for once, and take it on our words.
You would not think a country-girl the worse,
If clean and wholesome, though her linen's coarse.
Such are our scenes; and I dare boldly say,
You may laugh less at a far better play.
The story's true; the fact not long ago;
The hero of our stage was English too:
And bate him one small frailty of rebelling,
As brave as e'er was born at Iniskelling.[12]

ACT I

SCENE I. *A room with several tables.*

Enter Hazard *in a travelling habit, and a Sea-boy carrying his port-mantle.*[13]

HAZARD What town's this, boy?

BOY James-Town,[14] master.

HAZARD Take care my trunk be brought ashore tonight, and there's for your pains.

BOY God bless you, master.

HAZARD What do you call this house?

BOY Mrs Flirt's, master, the best house for commendation in all Virginia.

HAZARD That's well, has she any handsome ladies, sirrah?

BOY Oh! She's woundly[15] handsome herself, master, and the kindest gentlewoman – look, here she comes, master [[*Enter Mrs Flirt and maid,* Nell.]] – God bless you, mistress, I have brought you a young gentleman here.

FLIRT That's well, honest Jack – sir, you are most heartily welcome.

HAZARD Madam, your servant. [*Salutes her.*

FLIRT Please you to walk into a chamber, sir.

HAZARD By and by, madam, but I'll repose here a while for the coolness of the air.

FLIRT This is a public room, sir, but 'tis at your service.

HAZARD Madam, you oblige me.

FLIRT A fine-spoken person – a gentleman I'll warrant him; come, Jack, I'll give thee a cogue[16] of brandy for old acquaintance. [*Exeunt Landlady and Boy.*

Hazard *pulls out pen, ink and paper, and goes to write. Enter* Friendly.

FRIENDLY Here Nell, a tankard of cool drink quickly.

NELL You shall have it, sir. [[*Exit* Nell.]]

FRIENDLY Hah! who's that stranger? He seems to be a gentleman.

HAZARD If I should give credit to mine eyes, that should be Friendly.

FRIENDLY Sir, you seem a stranger, may I take the liberty to present my service to you?

HAZARD If I am not mistaken, sir, you are the only man in the world whom I would soonest pledge; you'll credit me if three years' absence has not made you forget Hazard.

FRIENDLY Hazard, my friend! come to my arms and heart.

HAZARD This unexpected happiness o'erjoys me. Who could have imagined to have found thee in Virginia? I thought thou hadst been in Spain with thy brother.

FRIENDLY I was so till ten months since, when my uncle Colonel Friendly dying here, left me a considerable plantation; and faith I find diversions not altogether to be despised; the god of love reigns here, with as much power as in courts or popular cities: but prithee, what chance (fortunate for me) drove thee to this part of the New World?

HAZARD Why (faith) ill company, and that common vice of the town, gaming, soon run out my younger brother's fortune, for imagining like some of the luckier gamesters to improve my stock at the Groom-Porter's,[17] ventured on and lost all – my elder brother, an errant Jew, had neither friendship, nor honour enough to support me, but at last was mollified by persuasions and the hopes of being for ever rid of me, sent me hither with a small cargo to seek my fortune –

FRIENDLY And begin the world withal.

HAZARD I thought this a better venture than to turn sharping[18] bully,[19] cully[20] in prentices and country-squires, with my pocket full of false dice, your high and low flats and bars,[21] or turn broker to young heirs; take up goods, to pay tenfold at the death of their fathers, and take fees on both sides, or set up all night at the Groom-Porter's begging his honour to go a guinea the better of the lay.[22] No, Friendly, I had rather starve abroad than live pitied and despised at home.

FRIENDLY Thou art in the right, and art come just in the nick of time to make thy fortune – wilt thou follow my advice?

HAZARD Thou art too honest to command anything that I shall refuse.

FRIENDLY You must know then, there is about a mile from James-Town a young gentlewoman – no matter for her birth, her breeding's the best this world affords, she is married to one of the richest merchants here, he is old and sick, and now gone into England for the recovery of his health, where he'll e'en give up the ghost; he has writ her word he finds no amendment, and resolves to stay another year, the letter I accidentally took up and have about me; 'tis easily counterfeited and will be of great use to us.

HAZARD Now do I fancy I conceive thee.

FRIENDLY Well, hear me first, you shall get another letter writ like this character,²³ which shall say, you are his kinsman, that is come to traffic in this country, and 'tis his will you should be received into his house as such.

HAZARD Well, and what will come of this?

FRIENDLY Why, thou art young and handsome; she young and desiring; 'twere easy to make her love thee, and if the old gentleman chance to die, you guess the rest, you are no fool.

HAZARD Aye, but if he should return –

FRIENDLY If – why, if she love you, that other will be but a slender bar to thy happiness; for if thou canst not marry her, thou mayst lie with her (and gad) a younger brother may pick out a pretty livelihood here that way, as well as in England – or if this fail, there thou wilt find a perpetual visitor, the Widow Ranter, a woman bought from the ship²⁴ by old Colonel Ranter; she served him half a year, and then he married her, and dying in a year more, left her worth fifty thousand pounds sterling, besides plate and jewels: she's a great gallant, but assuming the humour of the country gentry, her extravagancy²⁵ is very pleasant, she retains something of her primitive quality still, but is good-natured and generous.

HAZARD I like all this well.

FRIENDLY But I have a further end in this matter; you must know there is in the same house a young heiress, one Colonel Downright's daughter, whom I love, I think not in vain; her father indeed has an implacable hatred to me, for which reason I can but seldom visit her, and in this affair I have need of a friend in that house.

HAZARD Me you're sure of.

FRIENDLY And thus you'll have an opportunity to manage both our amours: here you will find occasion to show your courage as well as express your love; for at this time the Indians by our ill management of trade, whom we have armed against ourselves, very frequently make war upon us with our own weapons, though often coming by the worst are forced to make peace with us again, but so, as upon every turn they fall to massacring us wherever we lie exposed to them.

HAZARD I heard the news of this in England, which hastens the new governor's [26] arrival here, who brings you fresh supplies.

FRIENDLY Would he were landed, we hear he is a noble gentleman.

HAZARD He has all the qualities of a gallant man, besides he is nobly born.

FRIENDLY This country wants nothing but to be peopled with a well-born race to make it one of the best colonies in the world, but for want of a governor we are ruled by a council, [27] some of which have been perhaps transported criminals, [28] who having acquired great estates are now become Your Honour, and Right Worshipful, and possess all places of authority; [29] there are among them some honest gentlemen who now begin to take upon them, and manage affairs as they ought to be.

HAZARD Bacon I think was one of the council.

FRIENDLY Now you have named a man indeed above the common rank, by nature generous, brave, resolved, and daring; who studying the lives of the Romans and great men, that have raised themselves to the most elevated fortunes, fancies it easy for ambitious men to aim at any pitch of glory. I've heard him often say, 'Why cannot I conquer the universe as well as Alexander? or like another Romulus [30] form a new Rome, and make myself adored?'

HAZARD Why might he not? Great souls are born in common men, sometimes as well as princes.

FRIENDLY This thirst of glory cherished by sullen melancholy, I believe was the first motive that made him in love with the young Indian queen, fancying no hero ought to be without his princess. And this was the reason why he so earnestly pressed for a commission, to be made general against the Indians, which long was promised him, but they fearing his ambition, still put him off, till the grievances grew so high, that the whole country flocked to him, and begged he would redress them, – he took the opportunity, and led them forth to fight, and vanquishing brought the enemy to fair terms, but now instead of receiving him as a conqueror, we treat him as a traitor.

HAZARD Then it seems all the crime this brave fellow has committed, is serving his country without authority.

FRIENDLY 'Tis so, and however I admire the man, I am resolved to be of the contrary party, that I may make an interest in our new governor; thus stands affairs, so that after you have seen Madam Surelove, I'll present you to the council for a commission.

HAZARD But my kinsman's character –

FRIENDLY He was a Leicestershire younger brother, came over hither with a small fortune, which his industry has increased to a thousand pound a year, and he is now Colonel John Surelove, and one of the council.

HAZARD Enough.

FRIENDLY About it then, Madam Flirt to direct you.

HAZARD You are full of your Madams here.[31]

FRIENDLY Oh! 'tis the greatest affront imaginable, to call a woman Mistress, though but a retail brandy-monger. – Adieu! – one thing more, tomorrow is our country court, pray do not fail to be there, for the rarity of the entertainment: but I shall see you anon at Surelove's, where I'll salute thee as my first meeting, and as an old acquaintance in England – here's company, farewell.   [*Exit* Friendly.

Enter Dullman, Timorous, *and* Boozer. Hazard *sits at a table and writes.*

DULLMAN Here, Nell – Well, Lieutenant Boozer, what are you for?   [*Enter* Nell.

BOOZER I am for cooling Nants,[32] Major.

DULLMAN Here, Nell, a quart of Nants, and some pipes and smoke.[33]

TIMOROUS And do ye hear, Nell, bid your mistress come in to joke a little with us, for adzoors I was damnable drunk last night, and am better at the petticoat than the bottle today.

DULLMAN Drunk last night, and sick today, how comes that about, Mr Justice? You use to bear your brandy well enough.

TIMOROUS Aye, your sheer-brandy[34] I'll grant you, but I was drunk at Colonel Downright's with your high burgundy claret.

DULLMAN A pox of that paulter[35] liquor, your English French wine, I wonder how the gentlemen do to drink it.

TIMOROUS Aye, so do I, 'tis for want of a little Virginia breeding: how much more like a gentleman 'tis, to drink as we do, brave edifying punch and brandy, – but they say the young noblemen now and sparks in England begin to reform, and take it for their morning's draught, get drunk by noon, and despise the lousy juice of the grape.

Enter Mrs Flirt.

DULLMAN Come landlady, come, you are so taken up with Parson Dunce, that your old friends can't drink a dram with you, – what, no smutty catch now, no gibe or joke to make the punch go down merrily, and advance trading? Nay, they say, Gad forgive ye, you never miss going to church when Mr Dunce preaches – but here's to you. [*Drinks.*

FLIRT Lords, your Honours are pleased to be merry – but my service to your Honour. [*Drinks.*

HAZARD Honours, who the devil have we here? Some of the wise council at least, I'd sooner take them for hogherds.[36] [*Aside.*

FLIRT Say what you please of the doctor, but I'll swear he's a fine gentleman, he makes the prettiest sonnets, nay, and sings them himself to the rarest tunes.

TIMOROUS Nay, the man will serve for both soul and body, for they say he was a farrier[37] in England, but breaking[38] turned life-guard man,[39] and his horse dying – he counterfeited a deputation[40] from the bishop, and came over here a substantial orthodox; but come, where stands the cup? – here, my service to you, Major.

FLIRT Your Honours are pleased – but methinks Doctor Dunce is a very edifying person, and a gentleman, and I pretend to know a gentleman, – for I myself am a gentlewoman; my father was a baronet, but undone in the late rebellion – and I am fain to keep an ordinary[41] now, heaven help me.

TIMOROUS Good lack, why see how virtue may be belied – we heard your father was a tailor, but trusting for old Oliver's funeral, broke,[42] and so came hither to hide his head, – but my service to you; what, you are never the worse?

FLIRT Your Honour knows this is a scandalous place, for they say your Honour was but a broken excise-man, who spent the king's money[43] to buy your wife fine petticoats, and at last not worth a groat,[44] you came over a poor servant, though now a Justice of Peace, and of the Honourable Council.

TIMOROUS Adzoors, if I knew who 'twas said so, I'd sue him for *Scandalum Magnatum*.[45]

DULLMAN Hang 'em scoundrels, hang 'em, they live upon scandal, and we are scandal-proof. – They say, too, that I was a tinker and running the country, robbed a gentleman's house there, was put into Newgate,[46] got a reprieve after condemnation, and was transported hither – and that you, Boozer, was a common pickpocket, and being often flogged at the cart's-tale, afterwards turned evidence,[47] and when the times grew honest was fain to fly.

BOOZER Aye, aye, Major, if scandal would have broke our hearts, we had not arrived to the honour of being Privy-Counsellors – but come, Mrs Flirt, what, never a song to entertain us?

FLIRT Yes, and a singer too newly come ashore.

TIMOROUS Adzoors, let's have it then.

[*Enter girl, who sings, they bear the bob.*[48]

HAZARD Here maid, a tankard of your drink.

FLIRT Quickly, Nell, wait upon the gentleman.

DULLMAN Please you, sir, to taste of our liquor – my service to you. I see you are a stranger and alone, please you to come to our table? [*He rises and comes.*

FLIRT Come sir, pray sit down here, these are very honourable persons, I assure you, – this is Major Dullman, Major of his Excellency's own regiment, when he arrives, this Mr Timorous, Justice of the Peace in Corum.[49] This Captain Boozer, all of the Honourable Council.

HAZARD With your leave, gentlemen.   [*Sits.*

TIMOROUS My service to you, sir.   [*Drinks.*

What have you brought over any cargo, sir, I'll be your customer.

BOOZER Aye, and cheat him too, I'll warrant him.   [*Aside.*

HAZARD I was not bred to merchandizing, sir, nor do intend to follow the drudgery of trading.

DULLMAN Men of fortune seldom travel hither, sir, to see fashions.

TIMOROUS Why, brother, it may be the gentleman has a mind to be a planter, will you hire yourself to make a crop of tobacco this year?

HAZARD I was not born to work, sir.

TIMOROUS Not work, sir, 'zoors your betters have worked, sir; I have worked myself sir, both set and stripped tobacco, for all I am of the Honourable Council. Not work, quoth he – I suppose, sir, you wear your fortune upon your back, sir?

HAZARD Is it your custom here, sir, to affront strangers? I shall expect satisfaction.   [*Rises.*

TIMOROUS Why, does anybody here owe you anything?

DULLMAN No, unless he means to be paid for drinking with us – ha, ha, ha!

HAZARD No sir, I have money to pay for what I drink: here's my club[50] – my guinea. [*Flings down a guinea.*] I scorn to be obliged to such scoundrels.

BOOZER Hum – call men of honour scoundrels.   [*Rises in huff.*

TIMOROUS Let him alone, let him alone brother, how should he learn manners, he never was in Virginia before.

DULLMAN He's some Covent-Garden bully.[51]

TIMOROUS Or some broken citizen turned factor.[52]

HAZARD Sir, you lie, and you're a rascal.

[*Flings the brandy in his face.*

TIMOROUS Adzoors, he has spilled all the brandy.

Timorous *runs behind the door,* Dullman *and* Boozer *strike* Hazard.

HAZARD I understand no cudgel-play, but wear a sword to right myself.   [*Draws, they run off.*

FLIRT Good heavens, what quarrelling in my house?

HAZARD Do the persons of quality in this country treat strangers thus?

FLIRT Alas sir, 'tis a familiar way they have, sir.

HAZARD I'm glad I know it. – Pray, madam, can you inform one how I may be furnished with a horse and a guide to Madam Surelove's?

FLIRT A most accomplished lady, and my very good friend, you shall be immediately –   [*Exeunt.*

SCENE II. [[*The Council-Table.*]]

Enter Wellman, Downright, Dunce, Whimsey, Whiff, *and others.*

WELLMAN Come Mr Dunce, though you are no counsellor, yet your counsel may be good in time of necessity, as now.

DUNCE If I may be worthy advice, I do not look upon our danger to be so great from the Indians, as from young Bacon, whom the people have nicknamed Fright-all.

WHIMSEY Aye, aye, that same Bacon, I would he were well hanged, I am afraid that under pretence of killing all the Indians he means to murder us, lie with our wives, and hang up our little children, and make himself lord and king.

WHIFF Brother Whimsey, not so hot, with leave of the Honourable Board, my wife is of opinion, that Bacon came seasonably to our aid, and what he has done was for our defence; the Indians came down upon us, and ravished us all, men, women, and children.

WELLMAN If these grievances were not redressed we had our reasons for it, it was not that we were insensible, Captain Whiff, of what we suffered from the insolence of the Indians. But all knew what we must expect from Bacon if that by lawful authority he had arrived to so great a command as general, nor would we be huffed[53] out of our commissions.

DOWNRIGHT 'Tis most certain that Bacon did not demand a commission out of a design of serving us, but to satisfy his ambition and his love, it being no secret that he passionately admires the Indian queen, and under the pretext of a war, intends to kill the king her husband, establish himself in her heart, and on all occasions make[54] himself a more formidable enemy, than the Indians are.

WHIMSEY Nay, nay, I ever foresaw he would prove a villain.

WHIFF Nay, and he be thereabout, my Nancy shall have no more to do with him.

WELLMAN But, gentlemen, the people daily flock to him, so that his army is too considerable for us to oppose by anything but policy.

DOWNRIGHT We are sensible, gentlemen, that our fortunes, our honours, and our lives are at stake, and therefore you are called together to consult what's to be done in this grand affair, till our governor and forces arrive from England; the truce he made with the Indians will be out tomorrow.

WHIFF Aye, and then he intends to have another bout with the Indians. Let's have patience I say till he has thrummed[55] their jackets, and then to work with your politics as soon as you please.

DOWNRIGHT Colonel Wellman has answered that point, good Captain Whiff, 'tis the event of this battle we ought to dread, and if won or lost will be equally fatal for us, either from the Indians or from Bacon.

DUNCE With the permission of the Honourable Board I think I have hit upon an expedient that may prevent this battle; your Honours shall write a letter to Bacon, where you shall acknowledge his services, invite him kindly home, and offer him a commission for general –

WHIFF Just my Nancy's counsel – Doctor Dunce has spoken like a cherubin, he shall have my voice for general, what say you, brother Whimsey?

DUNCE I say, he is a noble fellow, and fit for a general.

DUNCE But conceive me right, gentlemen, as soon as he shall have rendered himself, seize him and strike off his head at the Fort.

WHIFF Hum! his head – brother –

WHIMSEY Aye, aye, Doctor Dunce speaks like a cherubin.

WELLMAN Mr Dunce, your counsel in extremity I confess is not amiss, but I should be loth to deal dishonourably with any man.

DOWNRIGHT His crimes deserve death, his life is forfeited by law, but shall never be taken by my consent by treachery. If by any stratagem we could take him alive, and either send him for England to receive there his punishment, or keep him prisoner here till the governor arrive, I should agree to it, but I question his coming in upon our invitation.

DUNCE Leave that to me –

WHIMSEY Come, I'll warrant him, the rogue's as stout as Hector,[56] he fears neither Heaven nor Hell.

DOWNRIGHT He's too brave and bold to refuse our summons, and I am for sending him for England and leaving him to the King's mercy.

DUNCE In that you'll find more difficulty, sir; to take him off here will be more quick and sudden: for the people worship him.

WELLMAN I'll never yield to so ungenerous an expedient. The seizing him I am content in the extremity wherein we are to follow. What say you, Colonel Downright? Shall we send him a letter now while this two days' truce lasts, between him and the Indians?

DOWNRIGHT I approve it.

ALL And I, and I, and I.

DUNCE If your Honours please to make me the messenger, I'll use some arguments of my own to prevail with him.

WELLMAN You say well, Mr Dunce, and we'll dispatch you presently.

[*Exeunt* Wellman, Downright *and all but* Whimsey, Whiff *and* Dunce.

WHIFF Ah Doctor, if you could but have persuaded Colonel Wellman and Colonel Downright to have hanged him –

WHIMSEY Why, brother Whiff, you were for making him a general but now.

WHIFF The counsels of wise statesmen, brother Whimsey, must change as causes do, d'ye see.

DUNCE Your Honours are in the right, and whatever those two leading councillors say, they would be glad if Bacon were dispatched,[57] but the punctilio of honour is such a thing.

WHIMSEY Honour, a pox on't, what is that honour that keeps such a bustle in the world, yet never did good as I heard of?

DUNCE Why, 'tis a foolish word only, taken up by great men, but rarely practised, – but if you would be great men indeed –

WHIFF If we would, Doctor, name, name the way.

DUNCE Why, you command each of you a company – when Bacon comes from the camp, as I am sure he will (and full of this silly thing called honour will come unguarded too), lay some of your men in ambush along those ditches by the sevana⁵⁸ about a mile from the town, and as he comes by, seize him, and hang him upon the next tree.

WHIFF Hum – hang him! a rare plot.

WHIMSEY Hang him – we'll do it, we'll do it sir, and I doubt not but to be made general for the action – I'll take it all upon myself. [Aside.

DUNCE If you resolve upon this, you must about it instantly – Thus I shall at once serve my country, and revenge myself on the rascal for affronting my dignity once at the council-table, by calling me farrier. [Exit Doctor.

WHIFF Do you know, brother, what we are to do?

WHIMSEY To do, yes, to hang a general, brother, that's all.

WHIFF All, but is it lawful to hang any general?

WHIMSEY Lawful, yes, 'tis lawful to hang any general that fights against law.

WHIFF But in what he has done, he has served the king and our country, and preserved all our lives and fortunes.

WHIMSEY That's all one, brother, if there be but a quirk in the law offended in this case, though he fought like Alexander, and preserved the whole world from perdition, yet if he did it against law, 'tis lawful to hang him; why what brother, is it fit that every impudent fellow that pretends to a little honour, loyalty and courage, should serve his king and country against the law? no, no, brother, these things are not to be suffered in a civil government by law established, – wherefore let's about it – [Exeunt.

SCENE III. *Surelove's house.*

Enter Ranter *and her Coachman.*

RANTER Here Jefery, ye drunken dog, set your coach and horses up, I'll not go till the cool of the evening, I love to ride in fresco.⁵⁹ [Enter a Boy.

COACHMAN Yes after hard drinking – [Aside.] It shall be done, madam.

RANTER How now, boy, is Madam Surelove at home?

BOY Yes, madam.

RANTER Go tell her I am here, sirrah.

BOY Who are you pray, forsooth?

RANTER Why, you son of baboon, don't you know me?

BOY No madam, I came over but in the last ship.

RANTER What, from Newgate or Bridewell?[60] from shoving the tumbler,[61] sirrah, lifting or filing the cly?[62]

BOY I don't understand this country-language forsooth, yet.

RANTER You rogue, 'tis what we transport from England first – go, ye dog, go tell your lady, the Widow Ranter is come to dine with her – [*Exit Boy.*] I hope I shall not find that rogue Daring here, snivelling after Mrs Chrisante: if I do, by the Lord, I'll lay him thick. Pox on him, why should I love the dog, unless it be a judgment upon me.

Enter Surelove *and* Chrisante.

– My dear jewel, how dost do? – as for you, gentlewoman, you are my rival, and I am in rancour against you till you have renounced my Daring.

CHRISANTE All the interest I have in him, madam, I resign to you.

RANTER Aye – but your house lying so near the camp, gives me mortal fears – but prithee how thrives thy amour with honest Friendly?

CHRISANTE As well as an amour can, that is absolutely forbid by a father on one side, and pursued by a good resolution on the other.

RANTER Hay gad, I'll warrant for Friendly's resolution, what, though his fortune be not answerable to yours, we are bound to help one another, – here boy – some pipes and a bowl of punch, you know my humour, madam, I must smoke and drink in a morning, or I am maukish[63] all day.

SURELOVE But will you drink punch in a morning?

RANTER Punch, 'tis my morning's draught, my table-drink, my treat, my regalio,[64] my everything; ah my dear Surelove, if thou wouldst but refresh and cheer thy heart with punch in a morning, thou wouldst not look thus cloudy all the day.

[*Enter pipes and a great bowl; she falls to smoking.*

SURELOVE I have reason, madam, to be melancholy; I have received a letter from my husband, who gives me an account that he is worse in England than when he was here, so that I fear I shall see him no more, the doctors can do no good on him.

RANTER A very good hearing. I wonder what the devil thou hast done with him so long? an old fusty weather-beaten skeleton, as dried as stock-fish,⁶⁵ and much of the hue. – Come, come, here's to the next, may he be young, heaven, I beseech thee.

[Drinks.

SURELOVE You have reason to praise an old man, who died and left you worth fifty thousand pound.

RANTER Aye gad – and what's better, sweet-heart, died in good time too, and left me young enough to spend this fifty thousand pound in better company – rest his soul for that too.

CHRISANTE I doubt 'twill be all laid out in Bacon's mad Lieutenant General Daring.

RANTER Faith I think I could lend it the rogue on good security.

CHRISANTE What's that, to be bound body for body?

RANTER Rather that he should love no body's body besides my own, but my fortune is too good to trust the rogue, my money makes me an infidel.

CHRISANTE You think they all love you for that?

RANTER For that, aye, what else? If it were not for that, I might sit still and sigh, and cry out, 'a miracle! a miracle!' at sight of a man within my doors. [Enter Maid.

MAID Madam, here's a young gentleman without would speak with you.

SURELOVE With me, sure thou'rt mistaken, is it not Friendly?

MAID No madam, 'tis a stranger.

RANTER 'Tis not Daring, that rogue, is it?

MAID No madam.

RANTER Is he handsome? Does he look like a gentleman?

MAID He's handsome and seems a gentleman.

RANTER Bring him in then, I hate a conversation without a fellow, – hah – a good handsome lad indeed. [Enter Hazard with a letter.

SURELOVE With me, sir, would you speak?

HAZARD If you are Madam Surelove.

SURELOVE So I am called.

HAZARD Madam, I am newly arrived from England, and from your husband my kinsman bring you this – 　　　*[Gives a letter.*

RANTER Please you to sit, sir.

HAZARD She's extremely handsome – 　　　*[Aside – sits down.*

RANTER Come sir, will you smoke a pipe?

HAZARD I never do madam –

RANTER Oh fie upon it, you must learn then, we all smoke here, 'tis a part of good breeding, – well, well, what cargo, what goods have ye? any points,⁶⁶ lace, rich stuffs, jewels; if you have I'll be your chafferer,⁶⁷ I live hard by, anybody will direct you to the Widow Ranter's.

HAZARD I have already heard of you, madam.

RANTER What, you are like all the young fellows, the first thing they do when they come to a strange place, is to enquire what fortunes there are.

HAZARD Madam I had no such ambition.

RANTER Gad, then you're a fool, sir, but come, my service to you; we rich widows are the best commodity this country affords, I'll tell you that.

　　　　　　　[This while she [[Surelove]] reads the letter.

SURELOVE Sir, my husband has recommended you here in a most particular manner, by which I do not only find the esteem he has for you, but the desire he has of gaining you mine, which on a double score I render you, first for his sake, next for those merits that appear in yourself.

HAZARD Madam, the endeavours of my life shall be to express my gratitude for this great bounty. 　　　*[Enter Maid.*

MAID Madam, Mr Friendly's here.

SURELOVE Bring him in.

HAZARD Friendly, – I had a dear friend of that name, who I hear is in these parts – pray heaven it may be he.

RANTER How now Charles. 　　　　　　*[Enter Friendly.*

FRIENDLY Madam, your servant – Hah! should not I know you for my dear friend Hazard. 　　　*[Embracing him.*

HAZARD Or you're to blame my Friendly.

FRIENDLY Prithee what calm brought thee ashore?

HAZARD *Fortune de la guerre*, but prithee ask me no questions in

so good company, where a minute lost from this conversation is
a misfortune not to be retrieved.

FRIENDLY Dost like her, rogue? [*Softly aside.*

HAZARD Like her! have I sight, or sense – why, I adore her.

FRIENDLY Mrs Chrisante, I heard your father would not be here
today, which made me snatch this opportunity of seeing you.

RANTER Come, come, a pox of this whining love, it spoils good
company.

FRIENDLY You know, my dear friend, these opportunities come
but seldom, and therefore I must make use of them.

RANTER Come, come, I'll give you a better opportunity at my
house tomorrow, we are to eat a buffalo there, and I'll secure
the old gentleman from coming.

FRIENDLY Then I shall see Chrisante once more before I go.

CHRISANTE Go – heavens – whither my Friendly?

FRIENDLY I have received a commission to go against the Indians,
Bacon being sent for home.

RANTER But will he come when sent for?

FRIENDLY If he refuse we are to endeavour to force him.

CHRISANTE I do not think he will be forced, not even by Friendly.

FRIENDLY And faith it goes against my conscience to lift my
sword against him, for he is truly brave, and what he has done,
a service to the country, had it but been by authority.

CHRISANTE What pity 'tis there should be such false maxims in
the world, that noble actions, however great, must be criminal
for want of a law to authorise them.

FRIENDLY Indeed 'tis pity that when laws are faulty they should
not be mended or abolished.

RANTER Hark ye, Charles, by heaven if you kill my Daring I'll
pistol you.

FRIENDLY No, Widow, I'll spare him for your sake.

[*They join with* Surelove.

HAZARD Oh she is all divine, and all the breath she utters serves
but to blow my flame. [*Enter Maid.*

MAID Madam, dinner's on the table –

SURELOVE Please you, sir, to walk in – come Mr Friendly.

[*She takes* Hazard.

RANTER Prithee, good wench, bring in the punch-bowl. [*Exeunt.*

ACT II

SCENE I.⁶⁸ *A pavilion.*

Discovers the Indian King *and* Queen *sitting in state, with guards of Indians, men and women attending; to them* Bacon *richly dressed, attended by* Daring, Fearless, *and other Officers; he bows to the* King *and* Queen, *who rise to receive him.*

KING I am sorry, sir, we meet upon these terms, we who so often have embraced as friends.

BACON How charming is the queen? [*Aside.*] War, sir, is not my business nor my pleasure. Nor was I bred in arms; my country's good has forced me to assume a soldier's life. And 'tis with much regret that I employ the first effects of it against my friends; yet whilst I may – whilst this cessation lasts, I beg we may exchange those friendships, sir, we have so often paid in happier peace.

KING For your part, sir, you've been so noble, that I repent the fatal difference that makes us meet in arms. Yet though I'm young I'm sensible of injuries; and oft have heard my grandsire say – that we were monarchs once of all this spacious world, till you an unknown people landing here, distressed and ruined by destructive storms, abusing all our charitable hospitality, usurped our right, and made your friends your slaves.

BACON I will not justify the ingratitude of my forefathers, but finding here my inheritance, I am resolved still to maintain it so; and by my sword which first cut out my portion, defend each inch of land with my last drop of blood.

QUEEN Even his threats have charms that please the heart. [*Aside.*

KING Come sir, let this ungrateful theme alone, which is better disputed in the field.

QUEEN Is it impossible there might be wrought an understanding betwixt my lord and you? 'Twas to that end I first desired this truce, myself proposing to be mediator, to which my Lord Cavarnio shall agree, could you but condescend – I know you're noble; and I have heard you say our tender sex could never plead in vain.

BACON Alas! I dare not trust your pleading, madam. A few soft words from such a charming mouth would make me lay the conqueror at your feet as a sacrifice for all the ills he has done you.

QUEEN How strangely am I pleased to hear him talk.   [*Aside.*

KING Semernia, see – the dancers do appear.

Sir, will you take your seat?   [*To* Bacon.

He leads the Queen *to a seat, they sit and talk.*

BACON Curse on his sports that interrupted me; my very soul was havering at my lip, ready to have discovered all its secrets. But oh! I dread to tell her of my pain, and when I would, an awful trembling seizes me, and she can only from my dying eyes, read all the sentiments of my captive heart.

[*Sits down; the rest wait.*

Enter Indians *that dance antics;* [69] *after the dance the* King *seems in discourse with* Bacon, *the* Queen *rises, and comes forth.*

QUEEN The more I gaze upon this English stranger, the more confusion struggles in my soul; oft I have heard of love, and oft this gallant man (when peace had made him pay his idle visits) has told a thousand tales of dying maids. And ever when he spoke, my panting heart, with a prophetic fear in sighs replied, I shall fall such a victim to his eyes.   [*Enter an Indian.*

INDIAN Sir, here's a messenger from the English council desires admittance to the general.   [*To the* King.

BACON With your permission, sir, he may advance.   [*To the* King.

Re-enter Indian with Dunce. *A letter.*

DUNCE All health and happiness attend your Honour, this from the Honourable Council.   [*Gives him a letter.*

KING I'll leave you till you have dispatched the messenger, and then expect your presence in the royal tent.

[*Exeunt* King, Queen, *and* Indians.

BACON Lieutenant, read the letter.   [*To* Daring.

DARING 'Sir, the necessity of what you have acted makes it pardonable, and we could wish we had done the country and

ourselves so much justice as to have given you that commission
you desired. – We now find it reasonable to raise more forces,
to oppose these insolences, which possibly yours may be too
weak to accomplish, to which end the council is ordered to
meet this evening, and desiring you will come and take your
place there, and be pleased to accept from us a commission to
command in chief in this war. – Therefore send those soldiers
under your command to their respective houses, and haste, sir,
to your affectionate friends –'

FEARLESS Sir, I fear the hearts and pen did not agree when this
was writ.

DARING A plague upon their shallow politics! Do they think to
play the old game twice with us?

BACON Away, you wrong the council, who of themselves are
honourable gentlemen, but the base coward fear of some
of them puts the rest on tricks that suit not with their
nature.

DUNCE Sir, 'tis for noble ends you're sent for, and for your safety
I'll engage my life.

DARING By heaven and so you shall – and pay it too with all the
rest of your wise-headed council.

BACON Your zeal is too officious now: I see no treachery, and can
fear no danger.

DUNCE Treachery! now heavens forbid, are we not Christians sir,
all friends and countrymen! Believe me sir, 'tis honour calls you
to increase your fame, and he who would dissuade you is your
enemy.

DARING Go cant, sir, to the rabble – for us – we know you.

BACON You wrong me when you but suspect for me; let him that
acts dishonourably fear. My innocence, and my good sword's
my guard.

DARING If you resolve to go, we will attend you.

BACON What go like an invader? No Daring, the invitation's
friendly, and as a friend, attended only by my menial servants,
I'll wait upon the council, that they may see that when I could
command it I came an humble suppliant for their favour – you
may return, and tell them I'll attend.

DUNCE I kiss your Honour's hands –   [*Goes out.*

DARING 'Sdeath, will you trust the faithless council, sir, who have so long held you in hand with promises, that curse of statesmen, that unlucky vice that renders even nobility despised?

BACON Perhaps the council thought me too aspiring, and would not add wings to my ambitious flight.

DARING A pox of their considering caps,⁷⁰ and now they find that you can soar alone, they send for you to knip your spreading wings. Now by my soul you shall not go alone.

BACON Forbear, lest I suspect you for a mutineer; I am resolved to go.

FEARLESS What, and send your army home? A pretty fetch.

DARING By heaven we'll not disband – not till we see how fairly you are dealt with: if you have a commission to be general, here we are ready to receive new orders; if not – we'll ring them such a thundering peal shall beat the town about their treacherous ears.

BACON I do command you not to stir a man, till you're informed how I am treated by them. – Leave me all –

[*Exeunt Officers.*

While Bacon *reads the letter again, to him the* Indian Queen, *with women waiting.*

QUEEN Now while my lord's asleep in his pavilion I'll try my power with the general, for an accommodation of a peace: the very dreams of war fright my soft slumbers that used to be employed in kinder business.

BACON Ha! – the queen – What happiness is this presents itself which all my industry could never gain?

QUEEN Sir –   [*Approaching him.*

BACON Pressed with the great extremes of joy and fear I trembling stand, unable to approach her.

QUEEN I hope you will not think it fear in me, though timorous as a dove, by nature framed; nor that my lord, whose youth's unskilled in war, can either doubt his courage, or his forces, that makes me seek a reconciliation on any honourable terms of peace.

BACON Ah madam! if you knew how absolutely you command

my fate I fear but little honour would be left me, since what-
soe'er you ask me I should grant.

QUEEN Indeed I would not ask your honour, sir, that renders you
too brave in my esteem. Nor can I think that you would part
with that. No, not to save your life.

BACON I would do more to serve your least commands than part
with trivial life.

QUEEN Bless me! sir, how came I by such a power?

BACON The gods, and Nature gave it you in your creation,
formed with all the charms that ever graced your sex.

QUEEN Is it possible? am I so beautiful?

BACON As heaven, or angels there.

QUEEN Supposing this, how can my beauty make you so obliging?

BACON Beauty has still a power over great souls, and from the
moment I beheld your eyes, my stubborn heart melted to
compliance, and from a nature rough and turbulent, grew soft
and gentle as the god of love.

QUEEN The god of love! what is the god of love?

BACON 'Tis a resistless fire, that's kindled thus – [*Takes her by
the hand and gazes on her.*] At every gaze we take from fine
eyes, from such bashful looks, and such soft touches – it makes
us sigh – and pant as I do now, and stops the breath when e'er
we speak of pain.

QUEEN Alas for me if this should be love! [*Aside.*

BACON It makes us tremble, when we touch the fair one, and
all the blood runs shivering through the veins, the heart's
surrounded with a feeble languishment, the eyes are dying,
and the cheeks are pale, the tongue is faltering, and the body
fainting.

QUEEN Then I'm undone, and all I feel is love. [*Aside.*
If love be catching, sir, by looks and touches, let us at distance
parley – or rather let me fly, for within view, is too near –

[*Aside.*

BACON Ah! she retires – displeased I fear with my presumptuous
love, – Oh pardon, fairest creature. [*Kneels.*

QUEEN I'll talk no more, our words exchange our souls, and every
look fades all my blooming honour, like sunbeams, on un-
guarded roses. – Take all our kingdoms – make our people

slaves, and let me fall beneath your conquering sword. But never let me hear you talk again or gaze upon your eyes – [*Goes out.*

BACON She loves! by heaven she loves! And has not art enough to hide her flame though she have cruel honour to suppress it. However, I'll pursue her to the banquet. [*Exit.*

SCENE II. *The Widow Ranter's Hall.*

Enter Surelove *fanned by two Negroes, followed by* Hazard.

SURELOVE This Madam Ranter is so prodigious a treater[71] – oh! I hate a room that smells of a great dinner, and what's worse a dessert of punch and tobacco – what! are you taking leave so soon, cousin?

HAZARD Yes madam, but 'tis not fit I should let you know with what regret I go, – but business will be obeyed.

SURELOVE Some letters to dispatch to English ladies you have left behind – come, cousin, confess.

HAZARD I own I much admire the English beauties, but never yet have put their fetters on –

SURELOVE Never in love – oh then you have pleasure to come.

HAZARD Rather a pain when there's no hope attends it.

SURELOVE Oh, such diseases quickly cure themselves.

HAZARD I do not wish to find it so; for even in pain I find a pleasure too.

SURELOVE You are infected then, and came abroad for cure.

HAZARD Rather to receive my wounds, madam.

SURELOVE Already sir, – whoe'er she be, she made good haste to conquer, we have few here boast that dexterity.

HAZARD What think you of Chrisante, madam?

SURELOVE I must confess your love and your despair are there placed right, of which I am not fond of being made a confidant, [*Coldly.*] since I'm assured she can love none but Friendly.

HAZARD Let her love on, as long as life shall last, let Friendly take her, and the universe, so I had my next wish – [*Sighs.*] Madam, it is yourself that I adore, – I should not be so vain to tell you this, but that I know you've found the secret out already from my sighs.

SURELOVE Forbear sir, and know me for your kinsman's wife, and no more.

HAZARD Be scornful as you please, rail at my passion, and refuse to hear it; yet I'll love on, and hope in spite of you, my flame shall be so constant and submissive, it shall compel your heart to some return.

SURELOVE You're very confident of your power, I perceive, but if you chance to find yourself mistaken, say your opinion and your affectation were misapplied, and not that I was cruel.

[*Exit* Surelove.

HAZARD Whate'er denials dwell upon your tongue, your eyes assure me that your heart is tender. [*Goes out.*

Enter the Bagpiper, playing before a great bowl of punch, carried between two Negroes, a Highlander dancing after it, the Widow Ranter *led by* Timorous, Chrisante *by* Dullman; Mrs Flirt *and* Friendly *all dancing after it; they place it on the table.*

DULLMAN This is like the noble widow all over, i'faith.

TIMOROUS Aye, aye, the widow's health in a full-ladle, Major [*Drinks.*] – but a pox on't, what made that young fellow here, that affronted us yesterday, Major? [*While they drink about.*

DULLMAN Some damned sharper[72] that would lay his knife aboard your widow, Cornet.

TIMOROUS Zoors, if I thought so I'd arrest him for salt[73] and battery, lay him in prison for a swingeing fine and take no bail.

DULLMAN Nay, had it not been, before my mistress here, Mrs Chrisante, I had swinged him for his yesterday's affront, – ah my sweet Mistress Chrisante – if you did but know what a power you have over me –

CHRISANTE Oh you're a great courtier, Major.

DULLMAN Would I were anything for your sake, madam.

RANTER Thou art anything but what thou shouldst be; prithee Major, leave off being an old buffoon, that is a lover turned to ridicule by age, consider thyself a mere rolling tun of Nants – a walking chimney, ever smoking with nasty mundungus[74] – and then thou hast a countenance like an old worm-eaten cheese.

DULLMAN Well, Widow, you will joke, ha, ha, ha –

TIMOROUS Gadzoors, she's pure company, ha, ha –

DULLMAN No matter for my countenance – Colonel Downright likes my estate and is resolved to have it a match.

FRIENDLY Dear Widow, take off your damned Major, for if he speak another word to Chrisante, I shall be put past all my patience, and fall foul upon him.

RANTER S'life, not for the world – Major, I bar love-making within my territories, 'tis inconsistent with the punch bowl, if you'll drink, do, if not be gone.

TIMOROUS Nay, gadzooks, if you enter me at the punch bowl, you enter me in politics – well, 'tis the best drink in Christendom for a statesman. *[They drink about, the bagpipe playing.*

RANTER Come, now you shall see what my Highland va[r]let can do – *[A Scots dance.*

DULLMAN So – I see, let the world go which way it will, Widow, you are resolved for mirth, – but come – to the conversation of the times.

RANTER The times, why what a devil ails the times? I see nothing in the times but a company of coxcombs that fear without a cause.

TIMOROUS But if these fears were laid and Bacon were hanged, I look upon Virginia to be the happiest part of the world, gadzoors, – why there's England – 'tis nothing to't – I was in England about six years ago, and was showed the Court of Aldermen,[75] some were nodding, some saying nothing, and others very little to purpose, but how could it be otherwise, for they had neither bowl of punch, bottles of wine or tobacco before 'em to put life and soul into 'em as we have here: then for the young gentlemen – their farthest travels is to France or Italy, they never come hither.

DULLMAN The more's the pity by my troth. *[Drinks.*

TIMOROUS Where they learn to swear mor-blew, mor-dee.[76]

FRIENDLY And tell you how much bigger the Louvre is than Whitehall;[77] buy a suit à-la-mode, get a swinging cap of some French marquis, spend all their money and return just as they went.

DULLMAN For the old fellows, their business is usury, extortion, and undermining young heirs.

TIMOROUS Then for young merchants, their Exchange is the tavern, their warehouse the playhouse, and their bills of exchange *billets-doux*,[78] where to sup with their wenches at the other end of the town, – now judge you what a condition poor England is in: for my part I look upon it as a lost nation, gadzoors.

DULLMAN I have considered it, and have found a way to save all yet.

TIMOROUS As how I pray.

DULLMAN As thus, we have men here of great experience and ability – now I would have as many sent into England as would supply all places, and offices, both civil and military, d'ye see; their young gentry should all travel hither for breeding, and to learn the mysteries of state.

FRIENDLY As for the old covetous fellows, I would have the tradesmen get in their debts, break and turn troopers.[79]

TIMOROUS And they'd be soon weary of extortion, gadzoors.

DULLMAN Then for the young merchants, there should be a law made, none should go beyond Ludgate.[80]

FRIENDLY You have found out the only way to preserve that great kingdom.   [*Drinking all this while sometimes.*

TIMOROUS Well, gadzoors, 'tis a fine thing to be a good statesman.

FRIENDLY Aye, Cornet, which you had never been had you stayed in old England.

DULLMAN Why sir, we were somebody in England.

FRIENDLY So I heard, Major.

DULLMAN You heard sir, what have you heard? He's a kidnapper[81] that says he heard anything of me – and so my service to you – I'll sue you, sir, for spoiling my marriage here, by your scandals with Mrs Chrisante, but that shan't do sir, I'll marry her for all that, and he's a rascal that denies it.

FRIENDLY S'death you lie, sir – I do.

TIMOROUS Gadzoors sir, lie to a Privy Counsellor, a Major of Horse! Brother, this is an affront to our dignities; draw and I'll side with you.   [*They both draw on* Friendly; *the ladies run off.*

FRIENDLY If I disdain to draw, 'tis not that I fear your base and cowardly force, but for the respect I bear you as magistrates, and so I leave you –

TIMOROUS An arrant coward, gadzoors.   [*Goes out.*
DULLMAN A mere poltroon,[82] and I scorn to drink in his company.
                                [*Exeunt, putting up their swords.*

SCENE III. *A sevana, or large heath.*

Enter Whimsey, Whiff *and* Boozer, *with some Soldiers, armed.*

WHIMSEY Stand – stand – and hear the word of command – do ye
see yon copse, and that ditch that runs along Major Dullman's
plantation.
BOOZER We do.
WHIMSEY Place your men there, and lie flat on your bellies, and
when Bacon comes (if alone) seize him, d'ye see.
WHIFF Observe the command now (if alone), for we are not for
bloodshed.
BOOZER I'll warrant you for our parts.
                                [*Exeunt all but* Whimsey *and* Whiff.
WHIMSEY Now we have ambushed our men, let's light our pipes
and sit down and take an encouraging dram of the bottle.
                [*Pulls a bottle of brandy out of his pocket – they sit.*
WHIFF Thou art a knave and hast emptied half the bottle in thy
leathern pockets, but come, here's young Frightall's health.
WHIMSEY What, wilt drink a man's health thou'rt going to
hang?
WHIFF 'Tis all one for that, we'll drink his health first, and hang
him afterwards, and thou shalt pledge me, d'ye see, and though
'twere under the gallows.
WHIMSEY Thou art a traitor for saying so, and I defy thee.
WHIFF Nay, since we are come out like loving brothers to hang
the general, let's not fall out among ourselves, and so here's to
you [*Drinks.*] though I have no great maw[83] to this business.
WHIMSEY Prithee brother Whiff, do not be so villainous a coward,
for I hate a coward.
WHIFF Nay, 'tis not that – but my Whiff, my Nancy dreamt
tonight she saw me hanged.
WHIMSEY 'Twas a cowardly dream, think no more on't, but as
dreams are expounded by contraries, thou shalt hang the
general.

WHIFF Aye – but he was my friend, and I owe him at this time a hundred pounds of tobacco.

WHIMSEY Nay, then I'm sure thou'dst hang him if he were thy brother.

WHIFF But hark – I think I hear the neighing of horses; where shall we hide ourselves, for if we stay here, we shall be mauled damnably.   [*Exeunt both behind a bush, peeping.*

Enter Bacon, Fearless *and three or four Footmen.*

BACON Let the groom lead the horses o'er the *sevana*. We'll walk it on foot, 'tis not a quarter of a mile to the town; and here the air is cool.

FEARLESS The breezes about this time of day begin to take wing and fan refreshment to the trees and flowers.

BACON And at these hours how fragrant are the groves.

FEARLESS The country's well, were but the people so.

BACON But come let's on –   [*They tell pass to the entrance.*

WHIMSEY There, boys – [*The Soldiers come forth and fall on* Bacon.

BACON Hah! Ambush –

[*Draws;* Fearless *and Footmen draw, the Soldiers after a while fighting take* Bacon *and* Fearless, *they having laid three or four dead.*

WHIFF So, so, he's taken. Now we may venture out.

WHIMSEY But are you sure he's taken?

WHIFF Sure, can't you believe your eyes? Come forth, I hate a coward – oh sir, have we caught your Mightiness?

BACON Are you the authors of this valiant act? None but such villainous cowards durst have attempted it.

WHIMSEY Stop his railing tongue.

WHIFF No, no, let him rail, let him rail now his hands are tied, ha, ha. Why, good General Frightall, what, was nobody able d'ye think to tame the roaring lion?

BACON You'll be hanged for this!

WHIMSEY Come, come, away with him to the next tree.

BACON What mean you villains?

WHIFF Only to hang your Honour a little, that's all. We'll teach you, sir, to serve your country against law.

As they go off, enter Daring *with Soldiers.*

DARING Hah – my general betrayed – this I suspected.

His men come in, they fall on, release Bacon *and* Fearless *and his Man, who get swords.* Whimsey's *party put* Whimsey *and* Whiff *before them, striking them as they endeavour to run on this side or that, and forcing them to bear up; they are taken after some fighting.*

FEARLESS Did not the general tell you rogues, you'd be all hanged?

WHIFF Oh Nancy, Nancy, how prophetic are thy dreams!

BACON Come, let's on –

DARING S'death, what mean you, sir?

BACON As I designed – to present myself to the council.

DARING By heavens, we'll follow then to save you from their treachery; 'twas this that has befallen you that I feared, which made me at a distance follow you.

BACON Follow me still, but still at such a distance as your aids may be assisting on all occasion – Fearless, go back and bring your regiment down, and Daring, let your sergeant with his party guard these villains to the council.

[*Exeunt* Bacon, Daring *and* Fearless.

WHIFF A pox on your Worship's plot.

WHIMSEY A pox on your forwardness to come out of the hedge.

[*Exeunt Officers with* Whimsey *and* Whiff.

SCENE IV. *The Council-Table.*

Enter Colonel Wellman, Colonel Downright, Dullman, Timorous, Brag, *and about seven or eight more seat themselves.*

WELLMAN You heard Mr Dunce's opinion, gentlemen, concerning Bacon's coming upon our invitation. He believes he will come, but I rather think, though he be himself undaunted, yet the persuasions of his two lieutenant-generals, Daring and Fearless, may prevent him, – Colonel, have you ordered our men to be in arms? [*Enter a Soldier.*

DOWNRIGHT I have, and they'll attend further order on the *sevana.*

SOLDIER May it please your Honours, Bacon is on his way, he comes unattended by any but his footmen, and Colonel Fearless.

DOWNRIGHT Who is this fellow?

WELLMAN A spy I sent to watch Bacon's motions.

SOLDIER But there is a company of soldiers in ambush on this side of the *sevana* to seize him as he passes by.

WELLMAN That's by no order of the council.

OMNES No, no, no order.

WELLMAN Nay, 'twere a good design if true.

TIMOROUS Gadzoors, would I had thought on't for my troop.

DOWNRIGHT I am for no unfair dealing in any extremity.

Enter a Messenger in haste.

MESSENGER An't please your Honours, the saddest news – an ambush being laid for Bacon, they rushed out upon him, on the *sevana*, and after some fighting took him and Fearless –

TIMOROUS Is this your sad news – zoors, would I had had a hand in't.

BRAG When on a sudden, Daring and his party fell in upon us, turned the tide – killed our men and took Captain Whimsey, and Captain Whiff prisoners, the rest run away, but Bacon fought like a fury.

TIMOROUS A bloody fellow.

DOWNRIGHT Whimsey and Whiff? They deserve death for acting without order.

TIMOROUS I'm of the colonel's opinion, they deserve to hang for't.

DULLMAN Why, brother, I thought you had wished the plot had been yours but now?

TIMOROUS Aye, but the case is altered since that, good brother.

WELLMAN Now he's exasperated past all hopes of a reconciliation.

DULLMAN You must make use of the statesman's refuge, wise dissimulation.

BRAG For all this, sir, he will not believe but that you mean honourably, and no persuasions could hinder him from coming, so he has dismissed all his soldiers, and is entering the town on foot.

WELLMAN What pity 'tis a brave man should be guilty of an ill action.

BRAG But the noise of his danger has so won the hearts of the mobile,[84] that they increase his train as he goes, and follow him in the town like a victor.

WELLMAN Go wait his coming. He grows too popular, and must be humbled.   [*Exit* Brag.

TIMOROUS I was ever of your mind, Colonel.

WELLMAN Aye, right or wrong – but what's your counsel now?

TIMOROUS E'en as it used to be, I leave it to wiser heads.

[*Enter* Brag.

BRAG Bacon, sir, is entering.

TIMOROUS Gadzoors, would I were safe in bed.

DULLMAN Colonel, keep in your heat and treat calmly with him.

WELLMAN I rather wish you would all follow me; I'd meet him at the head of all his noisy rabble, and seize him from the rout.

DOWNRIGHT What men of authority dispute with rake-hells?[85] 'Tis below us, sir.

TIMOROUS To stake our lives and fortunes against their nothing.

Enter Bacon, *after him the rabble with staves and clubs bringing in* Whimsey *and* Whiff, *bound.*

WELLMAN What means this insolence – what, Mr Bacon, do you come in arms?

BACON I'd need, sir, come in arms, when men that should be honourable can have so poor designs to take my life.

WELLMAN Thrust out his following rabble.

FIRST RABBLE We'll not stir till we have the general safe back again.

BACON Let not your loves be too officious – but retire –

FIRST RABBLE At your command we vanish –   [*The rabble retire.*

BACON I hope you'll pardon me, if in my own defence I seized on these two murderers.

DOWNRIGHT You did well, sir, 'twas by no order they acted, – stand forth and hear your sentence – in time of war we need no formal trials to hang knaves that act without order.

WHIFF Oh mercy, mercy, Colonel – 'twas Parson Dunce's plot.

DOWNRIGHT Issue out a warrant to seize Dunce immediately – you shall be carried – to the Fort to pray –

WHIMSEY Oh good your Honour I never prayed in all my life.

DOWNRIGHT From thence drawn upon a sledge to the place of execution – where you shall hang till you are dead – and then be cut down and –

WHIMSEY Oh hold – hold – we shall never be able to endure half this. [*Kneeling.*

WELLMAN I think the offence needs not so great punishment; their crime, sir, is but equal to your own, acting without commission.

BACON 'Tis very well explained, sir – had I been murdered by commission then, the deed had been approved, and now, perhaps, I am beholding to the rabble for my life: –

WELLMAN A fine pretence to hide a popular fault, but for this once we pardon them and you.

BACON Pardon, for what? By heaven I scorn your pardon, I've not offended honour nor religion.

WELLMAN You have offended both in taking arms.

BACON Should I stand by and see my country ruined, my king dishonoured, and his subjects murdered, hear the sad cries of widows and of orphans. You heard it loud, but gave no pitying care to it. And till the war and massacre was brought to my own door, my flocks and herds surprised, I bore it all with patience. Is it unlawful to defend myself against a thief that breaks into my doors?

WELLMAN And call you this defending of yourself?

BACON I call it doing of myself that right, which upon just demand the council did refuse me. If my ambition as you're pleased to call it, made me demand too much, I left myself to you.

WELLMAN Perhaps we thought it did.

BACON Sir, you affront my birth, – I am a gentleman, and yet my thoughts were humble – I would have fought under the meanest of your parasites –

TIMOROUS There's a bob [86] for us, brother. [*To* Dullman.

BACON But still you put me off with promises – And when compelled to stir in my defence I called none to my aid, and those that came, 'twas their own wrongs that urged them.

DOWNRIGHT 'Tis feared, sir, under this pretence you aim at government.

BACON I scorn to answer to so base an accusation, the height of my ambition is, to be an honest subject.

WELLMAN An honest rebel, sir –

BACON You know you wrong me, and 'tis basely urged – but this is trifling – here are my commissions.

[Throws down papers. Downright reads.

DOWNRIGHT – To be general of the forces against the Indians, and blank commissions for his friends.

WELLMAN Tear them in pieces – are we to be imposed upon? Do ye come in hostile manner to compel us?

DOWNRIGHT Be not too rough, sir, let us argue with him –

WELLMAN I am resolved I will not.

TIMOROUS Then we are all dead men, gadzoors! He will not give us time to say our prayers.

WELLMAN We every day expect fresh force from England, till then, we of ourselves shall be sufficient to make defence, against a sturdy traitor.

BACON Traitor, 'sdeath; traitor – I defy ye, but that my honour's yet above my anger, I'd make you answer me that traitor dearly.

[Rises.

WELLMAN Hah – am I threatened – guards, secure the rebel.

[Guards seize him.

BACON Is this your honourable invitation? Go – triumph in your short-lived victory, the next turn shall be mine.

[Exeunt Guards with Bacon.

A noise of fighting – enter Bacon, Wellman, *his Guards beat[en] back by the rabble,* Bacon *snatches a sword from one, and keeps back the rabble,* Timorous *gets under the table.*

DOWNRIGHT What means this insolence!

RABBLE We'll have our general, and knock that fellow's brains out, and hang up Colonel Wellman.

ALL Aye, aye, hang up Wellman.

The rabble seize Wellman, *and* Dullman, *and the rest.*

DULLMAN Hold, hold, gentlemen, I was always for the general.

RABBLE Let's barbicu [87] this fat rogue.

BACON Begone, and know your distance to the council.

> [*The rabble let them go.*

WELLMAN I'd rather perish by the meanest hand than owe my safety poorly thus to Bacon. [*In rage.*

BACON If you persist still in that mind I'll leave you, and conquering, make you happy 'gainst your will.

> [*Exeunt* Bacon *and rabble, hollowing 'A Bacon, a Bacon.'*

WELLMAN Oh villainous cowards, who will trust his honour with sycophants so base? Let us to arms – by heaven, I will not give my body rest till I've chastised the boldness of this rebel.

> [*Exeunt* Wellman, Downright *and the rest, all but* Dullman. Timorous *peeps from under the table.*

TIMOROUS What is the roistering hector [88] gone, brother?

DULLMAN Aye, aye, and the devil go with him.

> [*Looking sadly,* Timorous *comes out.*

TIMOROUS Was there ever such a bull of Bashan? [89] Why, what if he should come down upon us and kill us all for traitors?

DULLMAN I rather think the council will hang us all for cowards – ah – oh – a drum – a drum – oh – [*He goes out.*

TIMOROUS This is the misery of being great,
We're sacrificed to every turn of state.

ACT III

SCENE I. *The County Court, a great table, with papers, a Clerk writing. Enter a great many people of all sorts, then* Friendly, *after him* Dullman.

FRIENDLY How now, Major; what, they say Bacon scared you all out of the council yesterday. What say the people?

DULLMAN Say? They curse us all, and drink young Frightall's health, and swear they'll fight through fire and brimstone for him.

FRIENDLY And tomorrow will hallow him to the gallows, if it were his chance to come there.

DULLMAN 'Tis very likely; why, I am forced to be guarded to the court now, the rabble swore they would De Wit⁹⁰ me, but I shall hamper some of them. Would the governor were here to bear the brunt on't, for they call us the Evil Counsellors.

[*Enter* Hazard, *goes to* Friendly.

Here's the young rogue that drew upon us too, we have rods in piss⁹¹ for him i'faith.

[*Enter* Timorous *with Bailiffs; whispers to* Dullman, *after which to the Bailiffs.*

TIMOROUS Gadzoors that's he, do your office.

BAILIFF We arrest you, sir, in the king's name, at the suit of the Honourable Justice Timorous.

HAZARD Justice Timorous, who the devil's he?

TIMOROUS I am the man, sir, d'ye see, for want of a better; you shall repent, gadzoors, your putting of tricks upon persons of my rank and quality.

[*After he has spoken he runs back as afraid of him.*

HAZARD Your rank and quality!

TIMOROUS Aye, sir, my rank and quality; first I am one of the honourable council, next a Justice of Peace in Quorum,⁹² Cornet of a Troop of Horse d'ye see, and Churchwarden.

FRIENDLY From whence proceeds this Mr Justice, you said nothing of this at Madam Ranter's yesterday; you saw him there, then you were good friends?

TIMOROUS Aye, however I have carried my body swimmingly before my mistress, d'ye see. I had rancour in my heart, gadzoors.

FRIENDLY Why, this gentleman's a stranger, and but lately come ashore.

HAZARD At my first landing I was in company with this fellow and two or three of his cruel brethren, where I was affronted by them, some words passed and I drew –

TIMOROUS Aye, aye, sir, you shall pay for it – why – what sir, cannot a civil magistrate affront a man, but he must be drawn upon presently?

FRIENDLY Well sir, the gentleman shall answer your suit, and I hope you'll take my bail for him.

TIMOROUS 'Tis enough – I know you to be a civil person!

Timorous and Dullman take their places, on a long bench placed behind the table; to them Whimsey and Whiff, they seat themselves; then Boozer and two or three more, who seat themselves; then enter two bearing a bowl of punch, and a great ladle or two in it; the rest of the stage being filled with people.

WHIFF Brothers, it has been often moved at the Bench that a new punch bowl should be provided, and one of a larger circumference, when the Bench sits late about weighty affairs; oftentimes the bowl is emptied before we end.

WHIMSEY A good motion; Clerk, set it down.

CLERK Mr Justice Boozer, the council has ordered you a writ of ease,[93] and dismissed your Worship from the Bench.

BOOZER Me from the Bench, for what?

WHIMSEY The complaint is, brother Boozer, for drinking too much punch in the time of hearing trials.

WHIFF And that you can neither write nor read, nor say the Lord's Prayer.

TIMOROUS That your warrants are like a brewers' tally, a notch on a stick;[94] if a special warrant, then a couple. Godzoors, when his Excellency comes he will have no such justices.

BOOZER Why, brother, though I can't read myself, I have had Dalton's *Country Justice*[95] read over to me two or three times, and understand the law; this is your malice, brother Whiff, because my wife does not come to your warehouse to buy her commodities, – but no matter, to show I have no malice in my heart, I drink your health – I care not this, I can turn lawyer and plead at the Board.[96] [*Drinks; all pledge him and hum.*

DULLMAN Mr Clerk, come, to the trials on the docket.[97]

[*Clerk reads.*

CLERK The first is between his Worship Justice Whiff, and one Grubb.

DULLMAN Aye, that Grubb's a common disturber; brother, your cause is a good cause if well managed, here's to it. [*Drinks.*

WHIFF I thank you, brother Dullman, – read my petition. [*Drinks.*

CLERK 'The Petition of Captain Thomas Whiff showeth, whereas Gilbert Grubb calls his Worship's wife Ann Whiff whore, and said he would prove it; your Petitioner desires the Worshipful Bench to take it into consideration, and your Petitioner shall pray, etc.' – Here's two witnesses have made affidavit viva voce,[98] an it like your Worships.

DULLMAN Call Grubb.

CLERK Gilbert Grubb, come into the court.

GRUBB Here.

WHIMSEY Well, what can you say for yourself, Mr Grubb.

GRUBB Why an't like your Worship, my wife invited some neighbours' wives to drink a cagg[99] of cider; now your Worship's wife Madam Whiff, being there fuddled, would have thrust me out of doors, and bid me go to my old whore Madam Whimsey, meaning your Worship's wife.   [*To* Whimsey.

WHIMSEY Hah! My wife called whore; she's a jade,[100] and I'll arrest her husband here – in an action of debts.

TIMOROUS Gadzoors, she's no better than she should be, I'll warrant her.

WHIFF Look ye, brother Whimsey, be patient, you know the humour of my Nancy when she's drunk, but when she's sober, she's a civil person, and shall ask your pardon.

WHIMSEY Let this be done and I am satisfied. And so here's to you.   [*Drinks.*

DULLMAN Go on to the trial.

GRUBB I being very angry said, indeed, I would prove her a greater whore than Madam Whimsey.

CLERK An't like your Worships, he confesses the words in open court.

GRUBB Why, an't like your Worships, she has had two bastards, I'll prove it.

WHIFF Sirrah, sirrah, that was when she was a maid, not since I married her, my marrying her made her honest.

DULLMAN Let there be an order of court to sue him, for *Scandalum Magnatum.*[101]

TIMOROUS Mr Clerk, let my cause come next.

CLERK The defendant's ready, sir.   [Hazard *comes to the Board.*

TIMOROUS Brothers of the Bench take notice, that this Hector here coming into Mrs Flirt's ordinary[102] where I was, with my brother Dullman and Lieutenant Boozer, we gave him good counsel to fall to work; now my gentleman here was affronted at this forsooth, and makes no more to do but calls us scoundrels, and drew his sword on us, and had not I defended myself by running away, he had murdered me, and assassinated my two brothers.

WHIFF What witness have you, brother?

TIMOROUS Here's Mrs Flirt and her maid Nell – besides we may be witness for one another I hope, our words may be taken.

CLERK Mrs Flirt and Nell are sworn. [*They stand forth.*

WHIMSEY By the oaths that you have taken, speak nothing but the truth.

FLIRT An't please your Worships, your Honours came to my house, where you found this young gentleman; and your Honours invited him to drink with your Honours, where after some opprobrious words given him, Justice Dullman and Justice Boozer struck him over the head; and after that indeed the gentleman drew.

TIMOROUS Mark that, brother, he drew.

HAZARD If I did, it was *se defendendo*.[103]

TIMOROUS Do you hear that, brothers, he did in defiance.

HAZARD Sir, you ought not to sit judge and accuser too.

WHIFF The gentleman's i'th' right, brother, you cannot do it according to law.

TIMOROUS Gadzoors, what new tricks, new quirks?

HAZARD Gentlemen, take notice, he swears in court.

TIMOROUS Gadzoors, what's that to you sir.

HAZARD This is the second time of his swearing.

WHIMSEY What do you think we are, deaf, sir? 'Come, come proceed.

TIMOROUS I desire he may be bound to his good behaviour, fined and deliver up his sword; what say you, brother?

[*Jogs* Dullman, *who nods.*

WHIMSEY He's asleep, drink to him and waken him, – you have missed the cause by sleeping, brother. [*Drinks.*

DULLMAN Justice may nod, but never sleeps, brother – you were at – deliver his sword – a good motion, let it be done. [*Drinks.*

HAZARD No, gentlemen, I wear a sword to right myself.

TIMOROUS That's fine i'faith, gadzoors, I have worn a sword this dozen year and never could right myself.

WHIFF Aye, 'twould be a fine world if men should wear swords to right themselves, he that's bound to the peace shall wear no sword.

WHIMSEY I say he that's bound to the peace ought to wear no peruke,[104] they may change 'em for black or white, and then who can know them.

HAZARD I hope, gentlemen, I may be allowed to speak for myself.

WHIFF Aye, what can you say for yourself, did you not draw your sword, sirrah?

HAZARD I did.

TIMOROUS 'Tis sufficient he confesses the fact, and we'll hear no more.

HAZARD You will not hear the provocation given.

DULLMAN 'Tis enough, sir, you drew –

WHIMSEY Aye, aye, 'tis enough he drew – let him be fined.

FRIENDLY The gentleman should be heard, he's a kinsman too, to Colonel John Surelove.

TIMOROUS Hum – Colonel Surelove's kinsman.

WHIFF Is he so? nay, then all the reason in the world he should be heard, brothers.

WHIMSEY Come, come Cornet, you shall be friends with the gentleman, this was some drunken bout, I'll warrant you.

TIMOROUS Ha, ha, ha – so it was, gadzoors.

WHIFF Come, drink to the gentleman, and put it up.

TIMOROUS Sir, my service to you, I am heartily sorry for what's past, but it was in my drink.   [*Drinks.*

WHIMSEY You hear his acknowledgements, sir, and when he is sober he never quarrels; come sir, sit down, my service to you.

HAZARD I beg your excuse, gentlemen – I have earnest business.

DULLMAN Let us adjourn the court, and prepare to meet the regiments on the *sevana.*   [*All go but* Friendly *and* Hazard.

HAZARD Is this the best Court of Judicature your country affords?

FRIENDLY To give it its due it is not. But how does thy amour thrive?

HAZARD As well as I can wish, in so short a time.

FRIENDLY I see she regards thee with kind eyes, sighs and blushes.

HAZARD Yes, and tells me I am so like a brother she had – to excuse her kind concern, – then blush so prettily, that gad I could not forbear making a discovery of my heart.

FRIENDLY Have a care of that, come upon her by slow degrees, for I know she's virtuous; – but come, let's to the *sevana*, where I'll present you to the two colonels, Wellman and Downright, the men that manage all till the arrival of the governor.

SCENE II. *The sevana or heath.*

Enter Wellman, Downright, Boozer, *and Officers.*

WELLMAN Have you dispatched the scouts, to watch the motions of the enemies? I know that Bacon's violent and haughty, and will resent our vain attempts upon him; therefore we must be speedy in prevention.

DOWNRIGHT What forces have you raised since our last order?

BOOZER Here's a list of them. They came but slowly in, till we promised every one a bottle of brandy.

[*Enter Officer and* Dunce.

OFFICER We have brought Mr Dunce here, as your Honour commanded us; after strict search we found him this morning in bed with Madam Flirt.

DOWNRIGHT No matter, he'll exclaim no less against the vices of the flesh, the next Sunday.

DUNCE I hope, sir, you will not credit the malice of my enemies.

WELLMAN No more, you are free, and what you counselled about the ambush was both prudent and seasonable, and perhaps I now wish it had taken effect.

Enter Friendly *and* Hazard.

FRIENDLY I have brought an English gentleman to kiss your hands, sir, and offer you his service; he is young and brave, and kinsman to Colonel Surelove.

WELLMAN Sir, you are welcome, and to let you see you are so, we will give you your kinsman's command, captain of a troop of horse-guards, which I am sure will be continued to you when the governor arrives.

HAZARD I shall endeavour to deserve the honour, sir.

Enter Dullman, Timorous, Whimsey *and* Whiff, *all in buff,*[105] *scarf and feather.*

DOWNRIGHT So, gentlemen, I see you're in readiness.

TIMOROUS Readiness! What means he, I hope we are not to be drawn out to go against the enemy, Major?

DULLMAN If we are, they shall look a new major for me.

WELLMAN We were debating, gentlemen, what course were best to pursue against this powerful rebel.

FRIENDLY Why, sir, we have forces enough, let's charge him instantly, delays are dangerous.

TIMOROUS Why, what a damned fiery fellow's this?

DOWNRIGHT But if we drive him to extremities, we fear his siding with the Indians.

DULLMAN Colonel Downright has hit it; why should we endanger our men against a desperate termagant?[106] If he love wounds and scars so well, let him exercise on our enemies – but if he will needs fall upon us, 'tis then time for us enough to venture our lives and fortunes.

TIMOROUS How, we go to Bacon? Under favour I think 'tis his duty to come to us, an you go to that, gadzoors.

FRIENDLY If he do, 'twill cost you dear, I doubt, Cornet. – I find by our list, sir, we are four thousand men.

TIMOROUS Gadzoors, not enough for a breakfast for that insatiate Bacon, and his two lieutenant-generals Fearless and Daring.

[Whiff *sits on the ground with a bottle of brandy.*

WHIMSEY A morsel, a morsel.

WELLMAN I am for an attack, what say you gentlemen to an attack? – What, silent all? – What say you, Major?

DULLMAN I say, sir, I hope my courage was never in dispute. But, sir, I am going to marry Colonel Downright's daughter here – and should I be slain in this battle 'twould break her heart; – besides, sir, I should lose her fortune.   [*Speaks big.*

WELLMAN I'm sure here's a captain will never flinch.

[*To* Whimsey.

WHIMSEY Who I, an't like your Honour?

WELLMAN Aye, you.

WHIMSEY Who, I? Ha, ha, ha. Why, did your Honour think that I would fight?

WELLMAN Fight? yes. Why else do you take commissions?

WHIMSEY Commissions! O Lord, O Lord, take commissions to fight! Ha, ha, ha; that's a jest, if all that take commissions should fight –

WELLMAN Why do you bear arms then?

WHIMSEY Why, for the pay; to be called Captain, noble Captain, to show, to cock [107] and look big and bluff as I do; to be bowed to thus as we pass, to domineer, and beat our soldiers. Fight, quoth he, ha, ha, ha.

FRIENDLY But what makes you look so simply, Cornet?

TIMOROUS Why, a thing that I have quite forgot, all my accounts for England are to be made up, and I'm undone if they be neglected – else I would not flinch for the stoutest he that wears a sword –   [*Looks big.*

DOWNRIGHT What say you, Captain Whiff? [*Whiff almost drunk.*

WHIFF I am trying, Colonel, what mettle I'm made on; I think I am valiant, I suppose I have courage, but I confess 'tis a little of the d— breed, but a little inspiration from the bottle, and the leave of my Nancy, may do wonders.

Enter Seaman in haste.

SEAMAN An't please your Honours, Frightall's officers have seized all the ships in the river, and rid now round the shore, and had by this time secured the sandy beach, and landed men to fire the town, but that they are high in drink aboard the ship called the *Good Subject*; the master of her sent me to let your Honours know that a few men sent to his assistance will surprise them, and retake the ships.

WELLMAN Now, gentlemen, here's a brave occasion for emulation – why writ not the master?

DULLMAN Aye, had he writ, I had soon been amongst them, i'faith; but this is some plot to betray us.

SEAMAN Keep me here, and kill me if it be not true.

DOWNRIGHT He says well – there's a brigantine and a shallop [108] ready, I'll embark immediately.

FRIENDLY No sir, your presence is here more necessary, let me have the honour of this expedition.

HAZARD I'll go your volunteer, Charles.

WELLMAN Who else offers to go?

WHIMSEY A mere trick to kidnap us, by Bacon, – if the captain had writ –

TIMOROUS Aye, aye, if he had writ –

WELLMAN I see you're all base cowards, and here cashier ye from all commands and offices.

WHIMSEY Look ye, Colonel, you may do what you please, but you lose one of the best-dressed officers in your whole camp, sir –

TIMOROUS And in me, such a head-piece.

WHIFF I'll say nothing, but let the state want me.

DULLMAN For my part I am weary of weighty affairs.

[*In this while* Wellman, Downright, Friendly *and* Hazard *talk.*

WELLMAN Command what men you please, but expedition makes you half a conqueror.   [*Exit* Friendly *and* Hazard.

Enter another Seaman with a letter, gives it to Downright, *he and* Wellman *read it.*

DOWNRIGHT Look ye now gentleman, the master has writ.

DULLMAN Has he – he might have writ sooner, while I was in command, – if he had –

WHIMSEY Aye, Major – if he had – but let them miss us –

WELLMAN Colonel, haste with your men and reinforce the beach, while I follow with the horse; – Mr Dunce, pray let that Proclamation be read concerning Bacon, to the soldiers.

DUNCE It shall be done, sir.   [*Exit* Downright *and* Wellman.

The scene opens and discovers a body of soldiers.

Gentlemen, how simply you look now.

TIMOROUS Why, Mr Parson, I have a scruple of conscience upon me, I am considering whether it be lawful to kill, though it be in war; I have a great aversion to it, and hope it proceeds from religion.

WHIFF I remember the fit took you just so, when the Dutch besieged us, for you could not then be persuaded to strike a stroke.

TIMOROUS Aye, that was because they were Protestants as we

are, but gadzoors, had they been Dutch Papists I had mauled them; but conscience –

WHIMSEY I have been a Justice of Peace this six years and never had a conscience in my life.

TIMOROUS Nor I neither, but in this damned thing of fighting.

DUNCE Gentlemen, I am commanded to read the Declaration of the Honourable Council to you.   [*To the Soldiers.*

ALL Hum hum hum –

BOOZER Silence – silence –   [Dunce *reads.*

DUNCE 'By an Order of Council dated May the 10th 1670: To all Gentlemen Soldiers, Merchants, Planters, and whom else it may concern. Whereas Bacon, contrary to law and equity, has to satisfy his own ambition taken up arms, with a pretence to fight the Indians, but indeed to molest and enslave the whole colony, and to take away their liberties and properties; this is to declare, that whoever shall bring this traitor dead or alive to the Council shall have three hundred pounds reward. And so God save the King.'

ALL A Council, a Council! Hah –   [*Halloo. Enter a Soldier hastily.*

SOLDIER Stand to your arms, gentlemen, stand to your arms, Bacon is marching this way.

DUNCE Hah – what numbers has he?

SOLDIER About a hundred horse; in his march he has surprised Colonel Downright, and taken him prisoner.

ALL Let's fall on Bacon – let's fall on Bacon, hay –   [*Halloo.*

BOOZER We'll hear him speak first – and see what he can say for himself.

ALL Aye, aye, we'll hear Bacon speak –   [Dunce *pleads with them.*

TIMOROUS Well, Major, I have found a stratagem shall make us four the greatest men in the colony, we'll surrender ourselves to Bacon, and say we disbanded on purpose.

DULLMAN Good –

WHIFF Why, I had no other design in the world in refusing to fight.

WHIMSEY Nor I, d'ye think I would have excused it with the fear of disordering my cravat string else –

DUNCE Why, gentlemen, he designs to fire James-Town, murder you all, and then lie with your wives, and will you slip this opportunity of seizing him?

BOOZER Here's a tarmagant rogue, neighbours – we'll hang the dog.
ALL Aye, aye, hang Bacon, hang Bacon.

> *Enter* Bacon *and* Fearless, *some Soldiers leading in* Downright *bound;* Bacon *stands and stares a while on the regiments, who are silent all.*

BACON Well, gentlemen – in order to your fine Declaration you see I come to render myself –
DUNCE How came he to know of our Declaration?
WHIMSEY Rogues, rogues among ourselves – that inform.
BACON What, are ye silent all – not a man lift his hand in obedience to the council to murder this traitor, that has exposed his life so often for you? Ha, what! Not for three hundred pound, – you see I've left my troops behind, and come all wearied with the toils of war, worn out by summers' heats and winters' colds, marched tedious days and nights through bogs and fens as dangerous as your clamours, and as faithless, – what though 'twas to preserve you all in safety, no matter, you should obey the grateful council, and kill this honest man that has defended you?
ALL Hum, hum, hum.
WHIFF The general speaks like a Gorgon.[109]
TIMOROUS Like a cherubin, man.
BACON All silent yet – where's that mighty courage that cried so loud but now, 'A Council, a Council'? Where is your resolution, cannot three hundred pound excite your valour, to seize that traitor Bacon who has bled for you? –
ALL A Bacon, a Bacon, a Bacon –   [*Halloo*
DOWNRIGHT Oh villainous cowards – Oh the faithless multitude!
BACON What say you, parson – you have a forward zeal?
DUNCE I wish my coat, sir, did not hinder me from acting as becomes my zeal and duty.
WHIMSEY A plaguey rugged[110] dog – that parson –
BACON Fearless, seize me that canting knave from out the herd, and next those honourable officers.
>   [*Points to* Dullman, Whimsey, Whiff *and* Timorous.

> Fearless *seizes them, and gives them to the Soldiers, and*

takes the Proclamation from Dunce *and shows* Bacon; *they read it.*

DULLMAN Seize us, sir, you shall not need, we laid down our commissions on purpose to come over to your Honour.

WHIFF We ever loved and honoured your Honour.

TIMOROUS So entirely, sir – that I wish I were safe in James-Town for your sake, and your Honour were hanged. [*Aside.*

BACON This fine piece is of your penning, parson – though it be countenanced by the council's names – Oh ingratitude – burn – burn the treacherous town – fire it immediately –

WHIMSEY We'll obey you, sir –

WHIFF Aye, aye, we'll make a bonfire on't, and drink your Honour's health round about it. [*They offer to go.*

BACON Yet hold; my revenge shall be more merciful. I ordered that all the women of rank shall be seized and brought to my camp. I'll make their husbands pay their ransoms dearly; they'd rather have their hearts bleed than their purses.

FEARLESS Dear General, let me have the seizing of Colonel Downright's daughter; I would fain be plundering for a trifle called a maidenhead.

BACON On pain of death treat them with all respect; assure them of the safety of their honour. Now, all that will follow me, shall find a welcome, and those that will not may depart in peace.

ALL Hay, a General, a General, a General.

[*Some Soldiers go off, some go to the side of* Bacon.

Enter Daring *and Soldiers with* Chrisante, Surelove, Mrs Whimsey *and Mrs Whiff, and several other women.*

BACON Successful Daring welcome, what prizes have ye?

DARING The fairest in the world sir, I'm not for common plunder.

DOWNRIGHT Hah, my daughter and my kinswoman! –

BACON 'Tis not with women, sir, nor honest men like you that I intend to combat; not their own parents shall not be more indulgent, nor better safeguard to their honours, sir. But 'tis to save the expense of blood, I seize on their most valued prizes.

DOWNRIGHT But sir, I know your wild lieutenant-general has long loved my Chrisante, and perhaps, will take this time to force her to consent.

DARING I own I have a passion for Chrisante, yet by my general's life – or her fair self – what now I act is on the score of war, I scorn to force the maid I do adore.

BACON Believe me, ladies, you shall have honourable treatment here.

CHRISANTE We do not doubt it sir, either from you or Daring. If he love me – that will secure my honour, or if he do not, he's too brave to injure me.

DARING I thank you for your just opinion of me, madam.

CHRISANTE But sir, 'tis for my father I must plead. To see his reverend hands in servile chains – and then perhaps if stubborn to your will, his head must fall a victim to your anger.

DOWNRIGHT No, my good pious girl, I cannot fear ignoble usage from the general – and if thy beauty can preserve thy fame, I shall not mourn in my captivity.

BACON I'll never deceive your kind opinion of me – ladies, I hope you're all of that opinion too.

SURELOVE If seizing us, sir, can advance your honour, or be of any use considerable to you, I shall be proud of such a slavery.

MRS WHIMSEY I hope, sir, we shan't be ravished in your camp.

DARING Fie, Mrs Whimsey, do soldiers use to ravish?

MRS WHIFF Ravish – marry I fear 'em not, I'd have them know I scorn to be ravished by any man!

FEARLESS Aye, on my conscience, Mrs Whiff, you are too good-natured.

DARING Madam, I hope you'll give me leave to name love to you, and try by all submissive ways to win your heart?

CHRISANTE Do your worst, sir, I give you leave, if you assail me only with your tongue.

DARING That's generous and brave, and I'll requite it.

Enter Soldier in haste.

SOLDIER The truce being ended, sir, the Indians grow so insolent as to attack us even in our camp, and have killed several of our men.

BACON 'Tis time to check their boldness; Daring, haste draw up our men in order, to give 'em battle; I rather had expected their submission.

The country now may see what they're to fear,
Since we that are in arms are not secure.

> [*Exeunt leading the ladies.*

ACT IV

SCENE I.

A temple, with an Indian god placed upon it, Priests and Priestesses attending; enter Indian King on one side attended by Indian men, the Queen enters on the other side with women, all bow to the idol, and divide on each side of the stage, then the music playing louder, the Priest and Priestesses dance about the idol, with ridiculous postures and crying (as for incantations). Thrice repeated, 'Agah Yerkin, Agah Boah, Sulen Tawarapah, Sulen Tawarapah.'

After this soft music plays again, then they sing something fine, after which the Priests lead the King to the altar, and the Priestesses, the Queen; they take off little crowns from their heads, and offer them at the altar.

KING Invoke the god of our Quiocto [111] to declare what the event shall be of this our last war against the English General.

> [*Soft music ceases.*

The music changes to confused tunes, to which the Priest and Priestess dance anticly singing between, the same incantation as before, and then dance again, and so invoke again alternately; which dance ended a voice behind the altar cries, while soft music plays –

> The English general shall be,
> A captive to his enemy;
> And you from all your toils be freed,
> When by your hand the foe shall bleed;
> And ere the sun's swift course be run,
> This mighty conquest shall be won.

KING I thank the gods for taking care of us; prepare new sacrifice against the evening, when I return a conqueror, I will myself perform the office of a priest.

QUEEN Oh sir, I fear you'll fall a victim first.

KING What means Semernia, why are thy looks so pale?

QUEEN Alas, the oracles have double meanings, their sense is doubtful, and their words enigmas; I fear, sir, I could make a truer interpretation –

KING How Semernia! by all thy love I charge thee as you respect my life, to let me know your thoughts.

QUEEN Last night I dreamed a lion fell[112] with hunger, spite of your guards, slew you, and bore you hence.

KING This is thy sex's fear, and no interpretation of the oracle.

QUEEN I could convince you further.

KING Hast thou a secret thou canst keep from me? Thy soul a thought that I must be stranger to? This is not like the justice of Semernia; come, unriddle me the oracle.

QUEEN The English general shall be a captive to his enemy; he is so, sir, already to my beauty, he says he languishes for love of me.

KING Hah – the general my rival – but go on –

QUEEN And you from all your war be freed. Oh, let me not explain that fatal line, for fear it mean, you shall be freed by death.

KING What, when by my hand the foe shall bleed? – away – it cannot be –

QUEEN No doubt, my lord, you'll bravely sell your life, and deal some wounds where you'll receive so many.

KING 'Tis love, Semernia, makes thee dream; while waking I'll trust the gods, and am resolved for battle.

Enter an Indian.

INDIAN Haste, haste great sir to arms, Bacon with all his forces is prepared, and both the armies ready to engage.

KING Haste to my general, bid him charge them instantly; I'll bring up the supplies of stout Teroomians,[113] those so well skilled in the envenomed arrow. [*Exit Indian.*] – Semernia – words but poorly do express the griefs of parting lovers – 'tis with dying eyes, and a heart trembling – thus – [*Puts her hand on his heart.*] They take a heavy leave, – one parting kiss, and one love pressing sigh, and then farewell – but not a long farewell; I shall return victorious to thy arms, – commend me to the gods and still remember me. [*Exit* King.

QUEEN Alas! What pity 'tis I saw the general, before my fate had given me to the king – but now – like those that change their gods, my faithless mind 'twixt two opinions wavers; while to the gods my monarch I commend, my wandering thoughts in pity of the general makes that zeal cold, declined – ineffectual; – if for the general I implore the deities, methinks my prayers should not ascend the skies since honour tells me 'tis an impious zeal.

Which way soever my devotions move,
I am too wretched to be heard above.
[*Goes in; all exeunt.*

SCENE II.

Shows a field of tents, seen at some distance through the trees of a wood; drums, trumpets and the noise of battle with hallooing. The Indians are seen with battle-axes to retreat fighting from the English and all go off, when they re-enter immediately beating back the English, the Indian King at the head of his men, with bows and arrows; Daring being at the head of the English. They fight off; the noise continues less loud as more at distance.

Enter Bacon with his sword drawn, meets Fearless with his sword drawn.

FEARLESS Haste, haste, sir, to the entrance of the wood; Daring's engaged past hope of a retreat, venturing too far, pursuing of the foe; the king in ambush with his poisoned archers fell on and now we're dangerously distressed.

BACON Daring is brave, but he's withal too rash, come on and follow me to his assistance – [*Go out.*

A hallooing within, the fight renews; enter the Indians beaten

back by Bacon, Daring *and* Fearless; *they fight off, the noise of fighting continues a while, this still behind the wood.*
Enter Indians flying over the stage, pursued by the King.

KING Turn, turn, ye fugitive slaves, and face the enemy; Oh villains, cowards, deaf to all command, by heaven I had my rival in my view and aimed at nothing but my conquering him – now like a coward I must fly with cowards, or like a desperate madman fall, thus singly, midst the numbers.

[*Follows the Indians.*

Enter Bacon *enraged, with his sword drawn,* Fearless, *and* Daring *following him.*

BACON – Where is the king? Oh ye perfidious slaves, how have you hid [him] from my just revenge? – Search all the brakes, the furzes and the trees, and let him not escape on pain of death.

DARING We cannot do wonders, sir.

BACON But you can run away –

DARING Yes, when we see occasion – yet – should any but my general tell me so – by heaven he should find I were no starter.[114]

BACON Forgive me, I'm mad – the king's escaped, hid like a trembling slave in some close ditch, where he will sooner starve than fight it out.

Re-enter Indians running over the stage, pursued by the King *who shoots them as they fly; some few follow him.*

KING All's lost – the day is lost – and I'm betrayed – Oh slaves, that even wounds can't animate. [*In rage.*

BACON The king!

KING The general here, by all the powers betrayed by my own men.

BACON Abandoned as thou art I scorn to take thee basely; you shall have soldiers' chance, sir, for your life, since chance so luckily has brought us hither; without more aids we will dispute the day. This spot of earth bears both our armies' fates; I'll give you back the victory I have won, and thus begin anew, on equal terms.

KING That's nobly said – the powers have heard my wish! You, sir, first taught me how to use a sword, which heretofore has served me with success, but now – 'tis for Semernia that it draws, a prize more valued than my kingdom, sir –

BACON Hah, Semernia!

KING Your blushes do betray your passion for her.

DARING 'Sdeath, have we fought for this, to expose the victor to the conquered foe?

FEARLESS What, fight a single man – our prize already.

KING Not so, young man, while I command a dart.

BACON Fight him, by heaven no reason shall dissuade me, and he that interrupts me is a coward, whatever be my fate; I do command ye to let the king pass freely to his tents.

DARING The devil's in the general.

FEARLESS 'Sdeath, his romantic humour will undo us.

[*They fight and pause.*

KING You fight as if you meant to outdo me this way, as you have done in generosity.

BACON You're not behindhand with me, sir, in courtesy, come, here's to set us even – [*Fight again.*

KING You bleed apace.

BACON You've only breathed[115] a vein, and given me new health and vigour by it.

[*They fight again, wounds on both sides, the* King *staggers,* Bacon *takes him in his arms, the* King *drops his sword.*

How do you, sir?

KING Like one – that's hovering between heaven and earth, I'm – mounting – somewhere – upwards – but giddy with my flight, – I know not where.

BACON Command my surgeons – instantly – make haste. Honour returns and love all bleeding's fled. [*Exit Fearless.*

KING Oh Semernia, how much more truth had thy divinity than the predictions of the flattering oracles. Commend me to her – I know you'll – visit – your fair captive, sir, and tell her – oh – but death prevents the rest. [*Dies.*

Enter Fearless.

BACON He's gone – and now like Caesar I could weep[116] over the hero I myself destroyed.

FEARLESS I'm glad for your repose I see him there – 'twas a mad hot-brained youth and so he died.

BACON Come, bear him on your shoulders to my tent, from whence, with all the solemn state we can, we will convey him to his own pavilion.

Enter a Soldier.

SOLDIER Some of our troops pursuing of the enemy even to their temples, which they made their sanctuary, finding the queen at her devotion there with all her Indian ladies, I'd much ado to stop their violent rage from setting fire to the holy pile.

BACON Hang them immediately that durst attempt it, while I myself will fly to rescue her.

[*Goes out, they bear off the* King's *body, exeunt all.*

Enter Whimsey *pulling in* Whiff, *with a halter about his neck.*

WHIMSEY Nay, I'm resolved to keep thee here till his Honour the General comes, – what, to call him traitor, and run away after he had so generously given us our freedom, and listed us cadees [117] for the next command that fell in his army; – I'm resolved to hang thee –

WHIFF Wilt thou betray and 'peach thy friend? Thy friend that kept thee company all the while thou wert a prisoner – drinking at my own charge –

WHIMSEY No matter for that, I scorn ingratitude and therefore will hang thee – but as for thy drinking with me – I scorn to be behindhand with thee in civility and therefore here's to thee.

[*Takes a bottle of brandy out of his pocket, drinks.*

WHIFF I can't drink.

WHIMSEY A certain sign thou would be hanged.

WHIFF You used to be on my side when a justice, let the cause be how it would. [*Weeps.*

WHIMSEY Aye – when I was a justice I never minded honesty, but now I'll be true to my general, and hang thee to be a great man –

WHIFF If I might but have a fair trial for my life –

WHIMSEY A fair trial – come, I'll be thy judge – and if thou canst clear thyself by law I'll acquit thee. Sirrah, sirrah, what can'st thou say for thyself for calling his Honour rebel?

                                  [*Sits on a drumhead.*

WHIFF 'Twas when I was drunk, an't like your Honour.

WHIMSEY That's no plea, for if you kill a man when you are sober you must be hanged when you are drunk. Hast thou anything else to say for thyself why sentence may not pass upon thee?

WHIFF I desire the Benefit of the Clergy.[118]

WHIMSEY The clergy, I never knew anybody that ever did benefit by them. Why, thou canst not read a word.

WHIFF Transportation then –

WHIMSEY It shall be to England then – but hold – who's this?

                                 [Dullman *creeping from a bush.*

DULLMAN So the danger's over, I may venture out, – pox on't, I would not be in this fear again, to be Lord Chief Justice of our court.

      [*Enter* Timorous *with battle-axe, bow and arrows, and feathers on his head.*

Why, how now, Cornet – what, in dreadful equipage? Your battle-axe bloody, with bow and arrows?

TIMOROUS I'm in the posture of the times, Major – I could not be idle where so much action was; I'm going to present myself to the general with these trophies of my victory here –

DULLMAN Victory – what victory – did not [I] see thee creeping out of yonder bush, where thou wert hid all the fight – stumble on a dead Indian, and take away his arms?

TIMOROUS Why, didst thou see me?

DULLMAN See thee, aye – and what a fright thou wert in, till thou wert sure he was dead.

TIMOROUS Well, well, that's all one – gadzoors, if every man that pass[ed] for valiant in a battle were to give an account how he gained his reputation, the world would be but thinly stocked with heroes. I'll say he was a great war captain, and that I killed him hand to hand, and who can disprove me?

DULLMAN Disprove thee – why, that pale face of thine, that has so much of the coward in it.

TIMOROUS Shaw,[119] that's with loss of blood – Hah, I am overheard I doubt – who's yonder – [*Sees* Whimsey *and* Whiff.] how, brother Whiff in a hempen cravat-string? [120]

WHIMSEY He called the general traitor and was running away, and I'm resolved to 'peach.

DULLMAN Hum – and one witness will stand good in law, in case of treason –

TIMOROUS Gadzoors, in case of treason he'll be hanged if it be proved against him, were there ne'er a witness at all; but he must [be] tried by a council of war man – come, come let's disarm him –

> [*They take away his arms, and pull a bottle of brandy out of his pocket.*

WHIFF What, I hope you will not take away my brandy, gentlemen, my last comfort.

TIMOROUS Gadzoors, it's come in good time – we'll drink it off, here Major –   [*Drinks;* Whiff *takes him aside.*

WHIFF Hark ye, Cornet– you are my good friend, get this matter made up before it come to the general.

TIMOROUS But this is treason, neighbour.

WHIFF If I hang – I'll declare upon the ladder, how you killed your war captain.

TIMOROUS Come, brother Whimsey – we have been all friends and loving magistrates together, let's drink about, and think no more of this business.

DULLMAN Aye, aye, if every sober man in the nation should be called to account of the treason he speaks in his drink, the Lord have mercy upon us all – put it up – and let us like loving brothers take an honest resolution to run away together; for this same Frightall minds nothing but fighting.

WHIMSEY I'm content, provided we go all to the council and tell them (to make our peace) we went in obedience to the Proclamation to kill Bacon, but the traitor was so strongly guarded we could not effect it; but mum – who's here? –

> [*To them, enter* Ranter *and* Jenny, *as Man and Footman.*

RANTER Hah, our four Reverend Justices – I hope the blockheads will not know me – gentlemen, can you direct me to Lieutenant-General Daring's tents.

WHIFF Hum, who the devil's this – that's he that you see coming this way. 'Sdeath, yonder's Daring – Let's slip away before he advances.   [*Exeunt all but* Ranter *and* Jenny.

JENNY I am scared with those dead bodies we have passed over; for God's sake, madam, let me know your design in coming.

RANTER Why? Now I'll tell thee – my damned mad fellow Daring who has my heart and soul – loves Chrisante, has stolen her, and carried her away to his tents. She hates him, while I am dying for him.

JENNY Dying, madam! I never saw you melancholy.

RANTER Pox on it, no; why should I sigh and whine, and make myself an ass, and him conceited? No, instead of snivelling I'm resolved –

JENNY What, madam?

RANTER Gad, to beat the rascal, and bring off Chrisante.

JENNY Beat him, madam? What, a woman beat a lieutenant-general?

RANTER Hang 'em, they get a name in war from command, not courage; how know I but I may fight? Gad, I have known a fellow kicked from one end of the town to the other, believing himself a coward, at last forced to fight, found he could, got a reputation and bullied all he met with, and got a name, and a great commission.

JENNY But if he should kill you, madam?

RANTER I'll take care to make it as comical a duel as the best of them; as much in love as I am, I do not intend to die its martyr.

Enter Daring *and* Fearless.

FEARLESS Have you seen Chrisante since the fight?

DARING Yes, but she is still the same, as nice and coy as Fortune, when she's courted by the wretched; yet she denies me so obligingly she keeps my love still in its humble calm.

RANTER Can you direct me, sir, to one Daring's tent.   [*Sullenly.*

DARING One Daring – he has another epithet to his name?

RANTER What's that, rascal, or coward?

DARING Hah, which of thy stars, young man, has sent thee hither, to find that certain fate they have decreed?

RANTER I know not what my stars have decreed, but I shall be glad if they have ordained me to fight with Daring, – by thy concern thou shouldst be he?

DARING I am, prithee who art thou?

RANTER Thy rival, though newly arrived from England, and came to marry fair Chrisante, whom thou hast ravished, for whom I hear another lady dies.

DARING Dies for me?

RANTER Therefore resign her fairly – or fight me fairly –

DARING Come on, sir – but hold – before I kill thee, prithee inform me who this dying lady is?

RANTER Sir, I owe ye no courtesy, and therefore will do you none by telling you – come sir, for Chrisante – draw.

> [*They offer to fight.* Fearless *steps in.*

FEARLESS Hold – what mad frolic's this? – Sir, you fight for one you never saw [*To* Ranter.] and you for one that loves you not. [*To* Daring.

DARING Perhaps she'll love him as little.

RANTER Gad, put it to the trial, if you dare. – If thou be'st generous bring me to her, and whom she does neglect shall give the other place.

DARING That's fair, put up thy sword – I'll bring thee to her instantly. [*Exeunt.*

SCENE III. *A tent.*

Enter Chrisante *and* Surelove.

CHRISANTE I'm not so much afflicted for my confinement as I am that I cannot hear of Friendly.

SURELOVE Art not persecuted with Daring?

CHRISANTE Not at all. Though he tells me daily of his passion I rally him, and give him neither hope nor despair, – he's here.

Enter Daring, Fearless, Ranter *and* Jenny.

DARING Madam, the complaisance I show in bringing you my rival will let you see how glad I am to oblige you every way.

RANTER I hope the danger I have exposed myself to for the honour of kissing your hand, madam, will render me something acceptable – here are my credentials – [*Gives her a letter.*

CHRISANTE [*Reads.*] 'Dear Creature, I have taken this habit to free you from an impertinent lover, and to secure the damned rogue Daring to myself; receive me as sent by Colonel Surelove from England to marry you – favour me – no more – your Ranter' – Hah, Ranter? [*Aside.*] – Sir, you have too good a character from my cousin Colonel Surelove, not to receive my welcome.   [*Gives* Surelove *the letter.*

RANTER Stand by, General –
                              [*Pushes away* Daring *and looks big, and takes*
                                        Chrisante *by the hand and kisses it.*

DARING 'Sdeath, sir, there's room – enough – at first sight so kind? Oh youth – youth and impudence, what temptations are you – to villainous woman?

CHRISANTE I confess, sir, we women do not love these rough fighting fellows, they're always scaring us with one broil or other.

DARING Much good may [it] do you with your tame coxcomb.

RANTER Well, sir, then you yield the prize?

DARING Aye, gad, were she an angel, that can prefer such a callow fop as thou before a man – take her and domineer.
                                        [*They all laugh.*
– 'Sdeath, am I grown ridiculous.

FEARLESS Why hast thou not found the jest? By heaven 'tis Ranter, 'tis she that loves you. Carry on the humour. [*Aside.*] Faith, sir, if I were you I would devote myself to Madam Ranter.

CHRISANTE Aye, she's the fittest wife for you, she'll fit your humour.

DARING Ranter – gad, I'd sooner marry a she bear, unless for a penance for some horrid sin; we should be eternally challenging one another to the field, and ten to one she beats me there; or if I should escape there, she would kill me with drinking.

RANTER Here's a rogue – does your country abound with such ladies?

DARING The Lord forbid; half a dozen would ruin the land, debauch all the men, and scandalize all the women.

FEARLESS No matter, she's rich.

DARING Aye, that will make her insolent.

FEARLESS Nay, she's generous too.

DARING Yes, when she's drunk, and then she'll lavish all.

RANTER A pox on him – how he vexes me.

DARING Then such a tongue – she'll rail and smoke till she choke again, then six gallons of punch hardly recovers her, and never but then is she good-natured.

RANTER I must lay him on [121] –

DARING There's not a blockhead in the country that has not –

RANTER – What? –

DARING – Been drunk with her.

RANTER I thought you had meant something else, sir.   [*In huff.*

DARING Nay – as for that – I suppose there's no great difficulty.

RANTER 'Sdeath, sir, you lie – and you're a son of a whore.

[*Draws and fences with him, and he runs back round the stage.*

DARING Hold – hold, virago – dear Widow hold, and give me thy hand.

RANTER Widow!

DARING 'Sdeath, I knew thee by instinct Widow, though I seemed not to do so, in revenge for the trick you put on me in telling me a lady died for me.

RANTER Why, such a one there is, perhaps she may dwindle forty or fifty years – or so – but will never be her own woman again, that's certain.

SURELOVE This we are all ready to testify, we know her.

CHRISANTE Upon my life, 'tis true.

DARING Widow, I have a shrewd suspicion that you yourself may be this dying lady.

RANTER Why so, coxcomb?

DARING Because you took such pains to put yourself into my hands.

RANTER Gad, if your heart were but half so true as your guess, we should conclude a peace before Bacon and the council will – besides this thing whines for Friendly and there's no hopes.

[*To* Chrisante.

DARING Give me thy hand, Widow, I am thine – and so entirely, I will never – be drunk out of thy company – Dunce is in my tent – prithee let's in and bind the bargain.

RANTER Nay, faith, let's see the wars at an end first.

DARING Nay, prithee, take me in the humour, while thy breeches are on – for I never liked thee half so well in petticoats.

RANTER Lead on, General, you give me good encouragement to wear them.   [*Exeunt.*

ACT V

SCENE I. *The sevana in sight of the camp; the moon rises.*

Enter Friendly, Hazard *and* Boozer, *and a party of men.*

FRIENDLY We are now in the sight of the tents.

BOOZER Is not this a rash attempt, gentlemen, with so small force to set upon Bacon's whole army?

HAZARD Oh, they are drunk with victory and wine; there will be naught but revelling tonight.

FRIENDLY Would we could learn in what quarter the ladies are lodged, for we have no other business but to release them – but hark – who comes here?

BOOZER Some scouts, I fear, from the enemy.

Enter Dullman, Timorous, Whimsey *and* Whiff, *creeping as in the dark.*

FRIENDLY Let's shelter ourselves behind yonder trees – lest we be surprised.

TIMOROUS Would I were well at home – gadzoors – if e'er you catch me a-cadeeing again, I'll be content to be set in the forefront of the battle for hawks' meat.[122]

WHIMSEY Thou'rt afraid of every bush.

TIMOROUS Aye, and good reason too. Gadzoors, there may be rogues hid – prithee, Major, do thou advance.

DULLMAN No, no, go on – no matter of ceremony in these cases of running away.   [*They advance.*

FRIENDLY They approach directly to us, we cannot escape them – their numbers are not great – let us advance.

[*They come up to them.*

TIMOROUS Oh, I am annihilated.

WHIFF Some of Frightall's scouts; we are lost men.

[*They push each other foremost.*

FRIENDLY Who goes there?

WHIMSEY Oh, they'll give us no quarter; 'twas 'long of you, Cornet, that we ran away from our colours.

TIMOROUS Me – 'twas the major's ambition here – to make himself a great man with the council again.

311

DULLMAN Pox o' this ambition, it has been the ruin of many a gallant fellow.

WHIFF If I get home again, the height of mine shall be to top tobacco; would I'd some brandy.

TIMOROUS Gadzoors, would we had, 'tis the best armour against fear – hum – I hear nobody now – prithee advance a little.

WHIMSEY What, before a horse officer?

FRIENDLY Stand on your lives –

TIMOROUS Oh, 'tis impossible – I am dead already.

FRIENDLY What are ye? – speak – or I'll shoot.

WHIMSEY Friends to thee – who the devil are we friends to?

TIMOROUS E'en who you please, gadzoors.

FRIENDLY Hah – gadzoors – who's there, Timorous?

TIMOROUS Hum – I know no such scoundrel –   [Gets behind.

DULLMAN Hah – that's Friendly's voice.

FRIENDLY Right – thine's that of Dullman – who's with you?

DULLMAN Only Timorous, Whimsey and Whiff, all valiantly running away from the arch rebel that took us prisoners.

HAZARD Can you inform us where the ladies are lodged?

DULLMAN In the hither quarter in Daring's tents; you'll know them by lanthorns on every corner – there was never better time to surprise them – for this day Daring's married, and there's nothing but dancing and drinking.

HAZARD Married! To whom?

DULLMAN That I ne'er inquired.

FRIENDLY 'Tis to Chrisante, friend – and the reward of my attempt is lost. Oh, I am mad, I'll fight away my life, and my despair shall yet do greater wonders than even my love could animate me to. Let's part our men, and beset his tents on both sides.   [Friendly goes out with a party.

HAZARD Come, gentlemen, let's on –

WHIFF On, sir – we on, sir? –

HAZARD Aye, you on, sir – to redeem the ladies.

WHIFF Oh, sir, I am going home for money to redeem my Nancy.

WHIMSEY So am I, sir.

TIMOROUS I thank my stars I am a bachelor – why, what a plague is a wife!

HAZARD Will you march forward?

DULLMAN We have achieved honour enough already, in having made our campaign here –   [*Looking big.*

HAZARD 'Sdeath, but you shall go – put them in the front, and prick them on – if they offer to turn back run them through.

TIMOROUS Oh, horrid –
                    [*The Soldiers prick them on with their swords.*

WHIFF Oh, Nancy, thy dream will yet come to pass.

HAZARD Will you advance, sir?   [*Pricks Whiff.*

WHIFF Why, so we do, sir; the devil's in these fighting fellows.
                    [*Exeunt.*
                    [*An alarm at a distance.*

WITHIN To arms, to arms, the enemy's upon us.

> A noise of fighting, after which enters Friendly *with his party, retreating and fighting, from* Daring *and some Soldiers,* Ranter *fighting like a Fury by his side, he putting her back in vain; they fight out. Re-enter* Daring *with* Friendly *all bloody. Several Soldiers enter with flambeaux.*

DARING Now, sir – what injury have I ever done you, that you should use this treachery against me?

FRIENDLY To take advantage any way in war was never counted treachery – and had I murdered thee, I had not paid thee half the debt I owe thee.

DARING You bleed too much to hold too long a parley – come to my tent, I'll take a charitable care of thee.

FRIENDLY I scorn thy courtesy, who against all the laws of honour and of justice, hast ravished innocent ladies.

DARING Sir, your upbraiding of my honour shall never make me forfeit it, or esteem you less. – Is there a lady here you have a passion for?

FRIENDLY Yes, on a nobler score than thou darest own.

DARING To let you see how you're mistaken, sir, who e'er that lady be whom you affect, I will resign, and give you both your freedoms.

FRIENDLY Why, for this courtesy, which shows thee brave, in the next fight I'll save thy life, to quit the obligation.

DARING I thank you, sir – come to my tent – and when we've

dressed your wounds, and yielded up the ladies, I'll give you my passport for your safe conduct back, and tell your friends in the town we'll visit them in the morning.

FRIENDLY They'll meet you on your way, sir –

DARING Come, my young soldier, now thou'st won my soul.

An alarm beats; enter at another passage Boozer *with all the ladies; they pass over the stage, while* Hazard, Downright, *beating back a party of Soldiers.* Dullman, Timorous, Whimsey *and* Whiff, *pricked on by their party to fight, so that they lay about them like madmen.* Bacon, Fearless *and* Daring *come in, rescue their men, and fight out the other party, some falling dead.* Bacon, Fearless *and* Daring *return tired, with their swords drawn. Enter Soldier running.*

SOLDIER Return, sir, where your sword will be more useful – a party of Indians, taking advantage of the night, have set fire on your tents, and borne away the queen.

BACON Hah, the queen! By heaven, this victory shall cost them dear; come, let us fly to rescue her. [*Goes out.*

[SCENE II.]

Scene changes to Wellman's *tent. Enter* Wellman, Brag, Grubb *and Officers.*

WELLMAN I cannot sleep, my impatience is so great to engage this haughty enemy, before they have reposed their weary limbs. – Is not yon ruddy light the morning's dawn?

BRAG 'Tis, and please your Honour.

WELLMAN Is there no news of Friendly yet, and Hazard?

BRAG Not yet – 'tis thought they left the camp tonight, with some design against the enemy.

WELLMAN What men have they?

BRAG Only Boozer's party, sir.

WELLMAN I know they are brave, and mean to surprise me with some handsome action.

Enter Friendly.

FRIENDLY I ask a thousand pardons, sir, for quitting the camp without your leave.

WELLMAN Your conduct and your courage cannot err; I see thou'st been in action by thy blood.

FRIENDLY Sir, I'm ashamed to own these slender wounds, since without more my luck was to be taken, while Hazard did alone effect the business, the rescuing of the ladies.

WELLMAN How got ye liberty?

FRIENDLY By Daring's generosity, who sends you word he'll visit you this morning.

WELLMAN We are prepared to meet him.

Enter Downright, Hazard, *Ladies,* Whimsey, Whiff, Dullman, Timorous *looking big;* Wellman *embraces* Downright.

WELLMAN My worthy friend, how am I joyed to see you!

DOWNRIGHT We owe our liberties to these brave youths, who can do wonders when they fight for ladies.

TIMOROUS With our assistance, ladies.

WHIMSEY For my part I'll not take it as I have done; gad, I find when I am damnable angry I can beat both friend and foe.

WHIFF When I fight for my Nancy here – adsfish I'm a dragon.

MRS WHIFF Lord, you need not have been so hasty.

FRIENDLY Do not upbraid me with your eyes, Chrisante, but let these wounds assure you I endeavoured to serve you, though Hazard had the honour on't.

WELLMAN But, ladies, we'll not expose you in the camp – a party of our men shall see you safely conducted to Madam Surelove's; 'tis but a little mile from our camp.

FRIENDLY Let me have that honour, sir.

CHRISANTE No, I conjure you let your wounds be dressed; obey me if you love me, and Hazard shall conduct us home.

WELLMAN He had the toil, 'tis fit he have the recompense.

WHIFF He the toil, sir, what, did we stand for cyphers?

WHIMSEY The very appearance I made in the front of the battle awed the enemy.

TIMOROUS Aye, aye, let the enemy say how I mauled them – but gadzoors, I scorn to brag.

WELLMAN Since you've regained your honour so gloriously – I restore you to your commands you lost by your seeming cowardice.

DULLMAN Valour is not always in humour, sir.

WELLMAN Come, gentlemen, since they're resolved to engage us, let's set our men in order to receive 'em.

[*Exit all but the four Justices.*

TIMOROUS Our commissions again – you must be bragging, and see what comes on't; I was modest, ye see, and said nothing of my prowess.

WHIFF What a devil, does the colonel think we are made of iron, continually to be beat on the anvil?

WHIMSEY Look gentlemen, here's two evils – if we go we are dead men, if we stay we are hanged – and that will disorder my cravat-string – therefore the least evil is to go – and set a good face on the matter as I do –

[*Goes out singing.*

[SCENE III.]

Scene: a thick wood. Enter Queen *dressed like an Indian man, with a bow in her hand and quiver at her back,* Anaria *her confidante disguised so too, and about a dozen Indians led by* Cavaro.

QUEEN I tremble yet; dost think we're safe, Cavaro?

CAVARO Madam, these woods are intricate and vast, and 'twill be difficult to find us out – or if they do, this habit will secure you from the fear of being taken.

QUEEN Dost think if Bacon find us he will not know me? Alas, my fears and blushes will betray me.

ANARIA 'Tis certain, madam, if we stay we perish; for all the wood's surrounded by the conqueror.

QUEEN Alas, 'tis better we should perish here than stay to expect the violence of his passion; to which my heart's too sensibly inclined.

ANARIA Why do you not obey its dictates then, why do you fly the conqueror?

QUEEN Not fly – not fly the murderer of my lord?

ANARIA What world, what resolution can preserve you? And what he cannot gain by soft submission, force will at last o'ercome.

QUEEN I wish there were in Nature one excuse either by force or reason to compel me: – For oh, Anaria – I adore this general, – take from my soul a truth – till now concealed – at twelve years old – at the Pauwmungian [123] court I saw this conqueror. I saw him young and gay as new-born Spring, glorious and charming as the mid-day's sun, I watched his looks, and listened when he spoke, and thought him more than mortal.

ANARIA He has a graceful form.

QUEEN At last a fatal match concluded was, between my lord and me; I gave my hand, but oh how far my heart was from consenting, the angry gods are witness.

ANARIA 'Twas pity.

QUEEN Twelve tedious moons I passed in silent languishment; honour endeavouring to destroy my love, but all in vain, for still my pain returned whenever I beheld my conqueror, but now when I consider him as murderer of my lord – [*Fiercely.*] I sigh and wish – some other fatal hand had given him his death – but now there's a necessity I must be brave and overcome my heart. What if I do? ah, whither shall I fly, I have no Amazonian fire about me, all my artillery is sighs and tears, the earth my bed, and heaven my canopy. [*Weeps.*

[*After a noise of fighting.*

Hah, we are surprised, oh whither shall I fly? And yet methinks a certain trembling joy, spite of my soul, spite of my boasted honour, runs shivering round my heart. [*Enter an Indian.*

INDIAN Madam, your out guards are surprised by Bacon, who hews down all before him, and demands the queen with such a voice and eyes so fierce and angry, he kills us with his looks.

CAVARO Draw up your poisoned arrows to the head, and aim them at his heart, sure some will hit.

QUEEN Cruel Cavaro, – would 'twere fit for me to contradict thy justice. [*Aside.*

BACON [*Within.*] The queen, ye slaves, give me the queen and live!

> He enters *furiously beating back some Indians,* Cavaro's *party going to shoot; the* Queen *runs in.*

QUEEN Hold, hold, I do command ye [Bacon *flies on them as*

they shoot and miss him, and fights like a Fury, and wounds the Queen *in the disorder; beats them all out.*]

– hold thy commanding hand, and do not kill me, who would not hurt thee to regain my kingdom –

[*He snatches her in his arms; he reels.*

BACON Hah – a woman's voice – what art thou? Oh my fears!

QUEEN Thy hand has been too cruel to a heart – whose crime was only tender thoughts for thee.

BACON The queen! What is't my sacrilegious hand has done?

QUEEN The noblest office of a gallant friend, thou'st saved my honour and hast given me death.

BACON Is't possible! ye unregarding gods, is't possible?

QUEEN Now I may love you without infamy, and please my dying heart by gazing on you.

BACON Oh I am lost – for ever lost – I find my brain turn with the wild confusion.

QUEEN I faint – oh lay me gently on the earth.   [*Lays her down.*

BACON Who waits – [*Turns in rage to his men.*] make of the trophies of the war a pile, and set it all on fire, that I may leap into consuming flames – while all my tents are burning round about me. [*Wildly.*] Oh thou dear prize for which alone I toiled.

[*Weeps and lies down by her.*

Enter Fearless *with his sword drawn.*

FEARLESS Hah, on the earth – how do you, sir?

BACON What wouldst thou?

FEARLESS Wellman with all the forces he can gather attacks us even in our very camp; assist us, sir, or all is lost.

BACON Why, prithee let him make the world his prize, I have no business with the trifle now; it now contains nothing that's worth my care, since my fair queen – is dead, – and by my hand.

QUEEN So charming and obliging is thy moan that I could wish for life to recompense it; but oh, death falls – all cold – upon my heart like mildews on the blossoms.

FEARLESS By heaven, sir, this love will ruin all – rise, rise and save us yet.

BACON Leave me, what e'er becomes of me – lose not thy share of glory – prithee leave me.

QUEEN Alas, I fear thy fate is drawing on, and I shall shortly meet
thee in the clouds; till then – farewell – even death is pleasing to
me, while thus – I find it in thy arms –   [*Dies.*

BACON There ends my race of glory and of life.

                          [*An alarm at distance – continues a while.*

BACON Hah – why should I idly whine away my life, since there
are nobler ways to meet with Death? – Up, up, and face him
then – Hark – there's the soldiers' knell – and all the joys of life
– with thee I bid farewell –

                          [[Bacon *and* Fearless *go out.*]
                   The Indians bear off the body of the Queen.

    The alarm continues. Enter Downright, Wellman, *and others,
swords drawn.*

WELLMAN They fight like men possessed – I did not think to have
found them so prepared.

DOWNRIGHT They've good intelligence – but where's the rebel?

WELLMAN Sure he's not in the fight, oh that it were my happy
chance to meet him, that while our men look on, we might
dispatch the business of the war. – Come, let's fall in again now
we have taken breath.

    They go out. Enter Daring *and* Fearless *hastily, with their
swords drawn, meet* Whimsey, Whiff, *with their swords
drawn, running away.*

DARING How now, whither away?   [*In anger.*

WHIMSEY Hah, Daring here – we are pursuing of the enemy, sir,
stop us not in the pursuit of glory.   [*Offer to go.*

DARING Stay – I have not seen you in my ranks today.

WHIFF Lord, does your Honour take us for starters?

FEARLESS Yes, sirrah, and believe you are now rubbing off –
confess, or I'll run you through.

WHIFF Oh mercy, sir, mercy, we'll confess.

WHIMSEY What will you confess – we were only going behind
yon hedge to untruss a point; that's all.

WHIFF Aye, your Honours will smell out the truth if you keep us
here long.

DARING Here, carry them prisoners to my tent.

[*Exit Soldier with* Whimsey *and* Whiff.

Enter Ranter *without a hat, and sword drawn.* Daring *angrily goes the other way.* [[Dullman and Timorous *lying on the ground.*]]

RANTER A pox of all ill luck, how came I to lose Daring in the fight? Hah. – who's here? – Dullman and Timorous dead – the rogues are counterfeits – I'll see what moveables they have about them, all's lawful prize in war.

[*Takes their money, watches and rings; goes out.*

TIMOROUS What, rob the dead? – Why, what will this villainous world come to?

[*Clashing of swords just as they were going to rise.*

Enter Hazard *bringing in* Ranter.

HAZARD Thou couldst expect no other fate, young man, thy hands are yet too tender for a sword.

RANTER Thou lookst like a good-natured fellow, use me civilly, and Daring shall ransom me.

HAZARD Doubt not a generous treatment. [*Goes out.*

DULLMAN So, the coast is clear, I desire to remove my quarters to some place of more safety – [*They rise and go off.*

Enter Wellman *and Soldiers hastily.*

WELLMAN 'Twas this way Bacon fled. Five hundred pound for him who finds the rebel. [*Goes out.*

[SCENE IV.]

Scene changes to a wood. Enter Bacon *and* Fearless, *with their swords drawn, all bloody.*

BACON 'Tis just, ye gods! That when you took the prize for which I fought, Fortune and you should all abandon me.

FEARLESS Oh fly, sir, to some place of safe retreat, for there's no mercy to be hoped, if taken. What will you do? I know we are pursued, by heaven I will not die a shameful death.

BACON Oh, they'll have pity on thy youth and bravery, but I'm above their pardon. [*A noise is heard.*

WITHIN This way – this way – hay – halloo.

FEARLESS Alas, sir, we're undone – I'll see which way they take –
                                                    [*Exits.*

BACON So near! Nay then to my last shift. [*Undoes the pommel of
his sword.*] Come my good poison, like that of Hannibal,[124]
long I have borne a noble remedy for all the ills of life. [*Takes
poison.*] I have too long survived my queen and glory, those
two bright stars that influenced my life are set to all eternity.
                                                    [*Lies down.*

    Enter Fearless, *runs to* Bacon *and looks on his sword.*

FEARLESS – Hah – what have ye done?

BACON Secured myself from being a public spectacle upon the
common theatre of death.

    Enter Daring *and Soldiers.*

DARING Victory, victory, they fly, they fly, where's the victorious
general?

FEARLESS Here – taking his last adieu.

DARING Dying? Then wither all the laurels on my brows, for I
shall never triumph more in war; where are the wounds?

FEARLESS From his own hand by what he carried here, believing
we had lost the victory.

BACON And is the enemy put to flight my hero? [*Grasps his neck.*

DARING All routed horse and foot, I placed an ambush, and
while they were pursuing you, my men fell on behind and won
the day.

BACON Thou almost makes me wish to live again, if I could
live now fair Semernia's dead, – But oh – the baneful drug is
just and kind and hastens me away – now while you are
victors make a peace – with the English council – and never
let ambition – love – or interest make you forget as I have
done – your duty – and allegiance – farewell – a long
farewell –   [*Dies embracing their necks.*

DARING So fell the Roman Cassius[125] – by mistake –

    Enter Soldiers with Dunce, Timorous *and* Dullman.

SOLDIER An't please your Honour, we took these men running away.

DARING Let 'em loose – the wars are at an end, see where the general lies – that great-souled man, no private body e'er contained a nobler, and he that could have conquered all America finds only here his scanty length of earth, – go bear the body to his own pavilion – [*Soldiers go out with the body*.] Though we are conquerors we submit to treat, and yield upon conditions; you, Mr Dunce, shall bear our Articles to the Council –

DUNCE With joy I will obey you.   [*Exit* Dunce.

TIMOROUS Good General, let us be put in the agreement. [126]

DARING You come too late, gentlemen, to be put into the Articles, nor am I satisfied you're worthy of it.

DULLMAN Why, did not you, sir, see us lie dead in the field?

DARING Yes, but I see no wound about you.

TIMOROUS We were stunned with being knocked down; gadzoors, a man may be killed with the butt end of a musket as soon as with the point of a sword.   [*Enter* Dunce.

DUNCE The council, sir, wishes you health and happiness, and sends you these signed by their hands –   [*Gives papers*.

DARING [*Reads*.] 'That you shall have a general pardon for yourself and friends, that you shall have all new commissions, and Daring to command as general; that you shall have free leave to inter your dead general, in James-Town, and to ratify this – we will meet you at Madam Surelove's house which stands between the armies, attended only by our officers.' The council's noble and I'll wait upon them.   [*Exit* Dunce.

[SCENE V.]

Scene: A grove near Madam Surelove's; *enter* Surelove *weeping*, Wellman, Chrisante, Mrs Flirt, Ranter *as before*, Downright, Hazard, Friendly, Boozer, Brag.

WELLMAN How long, madam, have you heard the news of Colonel Surelove's death?

SURELOVE By a vessel last night arrived.

WELLMAN You should not grieve when men so old pay their debt

to Nature, you are too fair not to have been reserved for some
young lover's arms.

HAZARD I dare not speak – but give me leave to hope.

SURELOVE The way to oblige me to't is never more to speak to
me of love till I shall think it fit –

[Wellman *speaks to* Downright.

WELLMAN Come, you shan't grant it – 'tis a hopeful youth.

DOWNRIGHT You are too much my friend to be denied –
Chrisante, do you love Friendly? Nay, do not blush – till you
have done a fault, your loving him is none – here, take her
young man and with her all my fortune – when I am dead,
sirrah – not a groat before – unless to buy ye baby clouts.[127]

FRIENDLY He merits not this treasure, sir, can wish for more.

> *Enter* Daring, Fearless, Dunce *and Officers; they meet* Well-
> man *and* Downright *who embrace them.* Dullman *and* Timor-
> ous *stand.*

DARING Can you forgive us, sir, our disobedience?

WELLMAN Your offering peace while yet you might command it,
has made such kind impressions on us, that now you may
command your propositions; your pardons are all sealed and
new commissions.

DARING I'm not ambitious of that honour, sir, but in obedience
will accept your goodness; but sir, I hear I have a young friend
taken prisoner by Captain Hazard, whom I entreat you'll render
me.

HAZARD Sir – here I resign him to you.   [*Gives him* Ranter.

RANTER Faith, General, you left me but scurvily in battle.

DARING That was to see how well you could shift for yourself;
now I find you can bear the brunt of a campaign you are a fit
wife for a soldier.

ALL A woman – Ranter –

HAZARD Faith, madam, I should have given you kinder quarter if
I had known my happiness.

FLIRT I have a humble petition to you, sir.

SURELOVE In which we all join.

FLIRT An't please you sir, Mr Dunce has long made love to me
and on promise of marriage has –   [*Simpers.*

DOWNRIGHT What has he, Mrs Flirt?

FLIRT Only been a little familiar with my person, sir –

WELLMAN Do you hear, Parson – you must marry Mrs Flirt.

DUNCE How, sir, a man of my coat, sir, marry a brandy-monger?

WELLMAN Of your calling you mean, a farrier and no parson – [*Aside to him.*] she'll leave her trade – and spark it [128] above all the ladies at church; no more – take her and make her honest.

Enter Whimsey *and* Whiff, *stripped.*

CHRISANTE Bless me, what have we here?

WHIMSEY Why, an't like your Honours, we were taken by the enemy – hah, Daring here and Fearless?

FEARLESS How now – gentlemen, were not you two condemned to be shot for running from your colours?

DOWNRIGHT From your colours?

FEARLESS Yes sir, they were both listed in my regiment.

DOWNRIGHT Then we must hang them for deserting us.

WHIMSEY So out of the frying pan – you know where, brother –

WHIFF Aye – he that's born to be hanged – you know the rest, a pox of these proverbs.

WELLMAN I know ye well – you're all rank cowards, but once more we forgive ye; your places in the council shall be supplied by these gentlemen of sense and honour. The governor when he comes shall find the country in better hands than he expects to find it.

WHIMSEY A very fair discharge.

WHIFF I'm glad 'tis no worse, I'll home to my Nancy.

DULLMAN Have we exposed our lives and fortunes for this?

TIMOROUS Gadzoors, I never thrived since I was a statesman, left planting, and fell to promising and lying; I'll to my old trade again, bask under the shade of my own tobacco, and drink my punch in peace.

WELLMAN Come my brave youths, let all our forces meet,
　　　　To make this country happy, rich, and great;
　　　　Let scanted Europe see that we enjoy
　　　　Safer repose, and larger worlds than they.

EPILOGUE

Spoken by a Woman

BY this time you have liked, or damned our plot;
Which though I know, my Epilogue knows not:
For if it could foretell, I should not fail,
In decent wise, to thank you, or to rail.
But he who sent me here, is positive,
This farce [129] of government is sure to thrive;
Farce is a food as proper for your lips,
As for green-sickness, [130] crumped [131] tobacco pipes. [132]
Besides, the author's dead, and here you sit,
Like the infernal judges [133] of the pit:
Be merciful; for 'tis in you this day,
To save or damn her soul; and that's her play.
She who so well could love's kind passion paint,
We piously believe, must be a saint:
Men are but bunglers, when they would express
The sweets of love, the dying tenderness;
But women, by their own abundance, measure,
And when they write, have deeper sense of pleasure.
Yet though her pen did to the mark arrive,
'Twas common praise, to please you, when alive;
But of no other woman you have read,
Except this one, to please you, now she's dead.
'Tis like the fate of bees, whose golden pains,
Themselves extinguished, in their hive remains.
Or in plain terms to speak, before we go,
What you young gallants, by experience, know,
This is an orphan child; a bouncing boy,
'Tis late to lay him out, or to destroy.
Leave your dog-tricks, to lie and to forswear,
Pay you for nursing, and we'll keep him here.

POEMS

SONG
LOVE ARMED[1]

LOVE in fantastic triumph sat,[2]
Whilst bleeding hearts around him flowed,
For whom fresh pains he did create,
And strange tyrannic power he showed,
From thy bright eyes he took his fire,
Which round about, in sport he hurled;
But 'twas from mine, he took desire,
Enough to undo the amorous world.

From me he took his sighs and tears,
From thee his pride and cruelty;
From me his languishments and fears,
And every killing dart from thee;
Thus thou and I, the god have armed,
And set him up a deity;
But my poor heart alone is harmed,
Whilst thine the victor is, and free.

EPILOGUE[1]
SPOKEN BY MRS GWIN[2]

I HERE, and there, o'erheard a coxcomb cry
Ah, rot it – 'tis a woman's comedy,   [*Looking about.*
One, who because she lately chanced to please us,
With her damned stuff will never cease to tease us,
What has poor woman done that she must be,
Debarred from sense and sacred poetry?
Why in this age has Heaven allowed you more,
And women less of wit than heretofore?
We once were famed in story, and could write
Equal to men; could govern, nay could fight.

We still have passive valour, and can show
Would custom give us leave the active too,
Since we no provocations want from you.
For who but we, could your dull fopperies bear,
Your saucy love, and your brisk nonsense hear;
Endure your worse than womanish affectation,
Which renders you the nuisance of the nation;
Scorned even by all the Misses of the town,
A jest to vizard mask,[3] the pit-buffoon;
A glass by which the admiring country fool
May learn to dress himself in ridicule:
Both striving who shall most ingenious grow
In lewdness, foppery, nonsense, noise and show.
And yet to these fine things we must submit
Our reason, arms, our laurels, and our wit.
Because we do not laugh at you when lewd,
And scorn and cudgel ye when you are rude;
That we have nobler souls than you, we prove,
By how much more we're sensible of love;
Quickest in finding all the subtlest ways
To make your joys: why not to make you plays?
We best can find your foibles, know our own,
And jilts[4] and cuckolds now best please the town;
Your way of writing's out of fashion grown.
Method, and rule[5] – you only understand,
Pursue that way of fooling, and be damned.
Your learned cant of action, time, and place,
Must all give way to the unlaboured farce.
To all the men of wit we will subscribe:
But for you half wits, you unthinking tribe,
We'll let you see, what e'er besides we do,
How artfully we copy some of you:
And if you're drawn to th' life, pray tell me then
Why women should not write as well as men.

THE DISAPPOINTMENT[1]

I.

ONE day the amorous Lysander,
By an impatient passion swayed,
Surprised fair Cloris, that loved maid,
Who could defend herself no longer.[2]
All things did with his love conspire;
The gilded planet of the day,
In his gay chariot drawn by fire,
Was now descending to the sea,
And left no light to guide the world,
But what from Cloris' brighter eyes was hurled.

II.

In a lone thicket made for love,
Silent as yielding maid's consent,
She with a charming languishment,
Permits his force, yet gently strove;
Her hands his bosom softly meet,
But not to put him back designed,
Rather to draw him[3] on inclined;
Whilst he lay trembling at her feet,
Resistance 'tis in vain[4] to show;
She wants the power to say – 'Ah! What d'ye do?'

III.

Her bright eyes sweet, and yet severe,
Where love and shame confusedly strive,
Fresh vigour to Lysander give;
And breathing faintly[5] in his ear,
She cried – 'Cease, cease – your vain desire,
Or I'll call out – what would you do?[6]
My dearer honour even to you
I cannot, must not give – retire,
Or take this life, whose chiefest part
I gave you with the conquest of my heart.'

IV.

But he as much unused to fear,
As he was capable of love,
The blessed minutes to improve,
Kisses her mouth,[7] her neck, her hair;
Each touch her new desire[8] alarms,[9]
His burning trembling hand he pressed
Upon her swelling[10] snowy breast,
While she lay panting in his arms.
All her unguarded beauties lie
The spoils and trophies of the enemy.

V.

And now without respect or fear,
He seeks the object of his vows,
(His love no modesty allows)
By swift degrees advancing – where
His daring hand that altar seized,
Where gods of love do sacrifice:
That awful throne, that paradise
Where rage is calmed,[11] and anger pleased,
That fountain where delight still flows,
And gives the universal world repose.[12]

VI.

Her balmy lips encountering his,
Their bodies, as their souls, are joined;
Where both in transports unconfined
Extend themselves upon the moss.
Cloris half dead and breathless lay;
Her soft eyes cast a humid light,[13]
Such as divides the day and night;
Or falling stars, whose fires decay:
And now no signs of life she shows,
But what in short-breathed sighs returns and goes.[14]

POEMS

VII.

He saw how at her length she lay;
He saw her rising bosom bare;
Her loose thin robes, through which appear
A shape designed for love and play;
Abandoned by her pride and shame
She does her softest joys dispense,
Offering her virgin innocence
A victim to love's sacred flame;
. While [15] the o'er-ravished shepherd lies
Unable to perform the sacrifice.

VIII.

Ready to taste a thousand joys,
The too transported hapless swain
Found the vast pleasure turned to pain;
Pleasure which too much love destroys.
The willing garments [16] by he laid,
And Heaven all opened [17] to his view,
Mad to possess, himself he threw
On the defenceless lovely maid.
But oh what envious gods conspire [18]
To snatch his power, yet leave him the desire!

IX.

Nature's support (without whose aid
She can no human being give)
Itself now wants the art to live;
Faintness its slackened nerves invade;
In vain th'enraged youth essayed
To call its fleeting vigour back,
No motion 'twill from motion take;
Excess of love his love betrayed.
In vain he toils, in vain commands;
The insensible fell weeping in his hand.

333

X.

In this so amorous cruel strife,
Where love and fate were too severe,
The poor Lysander in despair
Renounced his reason with his life.
Now all the brisk and active fire
That should the nobler part inflame,
Served to increase his rage and shame,[19]
And left no spark for new desire:
Not all her naked charms could move
Or calm that rage that had debauched his love.

XI.

Cloris returning from the trance
Which love and soft desire had bred,
Her timorous hand she gently laid
(Or guided by design or chance)
Upon that fabulous Priapas,[20]
That potent god, as poets feign;
But never did young shepherdess,
Gathering of fern upon the plain,
More nimbly draw her fingers back,
Finding beneath the verdant leaves, a snake,

XII.

Then Cloris her fair hand withdrew,
Finding that god of her desires
Disarmed of all his awful fires,
And cold as flowers bathed in the morning dew.
Who can the nymph's confusion guess?
The blood forsook the hinder[21] place,
And strewed with blushes all her face,
Which both disdain and shame expressed:
And from Lysander's arms she fled,
Leaving him fainting on the gloomy bed.

XIII.

Like lightning through the grove she hies,
Or Daphne from the Delphic god,[22]
No print upon the grassy road
She leaves, t'instruct pursuing eyes.
The wind that wantoned in her hair,
And with her ruffled garments played,
Discovered in the flying maid
All that the gods e'er made, of fair.[23]
So Venus, when her love was slain,
With fear and haste flew o'er the fatal plain.[24]

XIV.

The nymph's resentments none but I
Can well imagine or[25] condole:
But none can guess Lysander's soul,
But those who swayed his destiny.
His silent griefs swell up to storms,
And not one god his fury spares;
He cursed his birth, his fate, his stars
But more the shepherdess's charms,[26]
Whose soft bewitching influence
Had damned him to the hell of impotence.

TO MR CREECH (UNDER THE NAME OF DAPHNIS) ON HIS EXCELLENT TRANSLATION OF LUCRETIUS[1]

THOU great young man! Permit amongst the crowd
Of those that sing thy mighty praises loud,
My humble Muse to bring its tribute too.
   Inspired by thy vast flight of verse,
Methinks I should some wondrous thing rehearse,
Worthy divine Lucretius, and diviner thou.
   But I of feebler seeds designed,
   Whilst[2] the slow moving atom strove
   With careless heed to form my mind:
Composed it all of softer love.

POEMS

In gentle numbers all my songs are dressed,
  And when I would thy glories sing,
What in strong manly verse I would express
Turns all to womanish tenderness within.
Whilst that which admiration does inspire,
In other souls, kindles in mine a fire.
Let them admire thee on – whilst I this newer way
  Pay thee yet more than they:
For more I owe, since thou hast taught me more,
Than all the mighty bards that went before.
Others long since have palled[3] the vast delight;
In duller Greek and Latin satisfied the appetite;
But I unlearned in schools, disdain that mine
Should treated be at any feast but thine.
Till now, I cursed my birth, my education,[4]
And more the scanted customs of the nation:
Permitting not the female sex to tread,
The mighty paths of learned heroes dead.
The god-like Virgil, and great Homer's verse,[5]
Like divine mysteries are concealed from us.
    We are forbid all grateful themes,
    No ravishing thoughts approach our ear,
    The fulsome jingle of the times,
Is all we are allowed to understand or hear.
  But as of old, when men unthinking lay,
Ere gods were worshipped, or ere laws were framed
The wiser bard that taught 'em first t' obey,
Was next to what he taught, adored and famed;
Gentler they grew, their words and manners changed,
And savage now no more the woods they ranged.
So thou by this translation dost advance
Our knowledge from the state of ignorance,
And equals us to man: Ah how can we,
Enough adore, or sacrifice enough to thee!

The mystic terms of rough philosophy,
Thou dost so plain and easily express;
Yet deck'st them in so soft and gay a dress:

336

So intelligent to each capacity,
That they at once instruct and charm the sense,
With heights of fancy, heights of eloquence;
And reason over all unfettered plays,
Wanton and undisturbed as summer's breeze;
    That gliding murmurs o'er the trees:
And no hard notion meets or stops its way.
    It pierces, conquers and compels,
Beyond poor feeble Faith's dull oracles.[6]
    Faith the despairing[7] soul's content,
Faith the last shift[8] of routed argument.

Hail sacred Wadham![9] whom the Muses grace
And from the rest of all the reverend pile
Of noble palaces, designed thy space:
    Where they in soft retreat might dwell.
They blessed thy fabric, and said – Do thou,
    Our darling sons contain;
We thee our sacred nursery ordain:
    They said and blessed, and it was so.
And if of old the fanes of silvian gods,
    Were worshipped as divine abodes;
    If Courts are held as sacred things,
    For being the awful seats of Kings.
    What veneration should be paid,
To thee that hast such wondrous poets made!
    To gods for fear, devotion was designed,
    And safety made us bow to majesty;
    Poets by nature awe and charm the mind,
Are born not made by dull[10] religion or necessity.

The learned Thirsis[11] did to thee belong,
Who Athens plague has so divinely sung.
Thirsis to wit, as sacred friendship true,
Paid mighty Cowley's memory its due.
Thirsis who whilst a greater plague did reign,
Than that which Athens did depopulate:
Scattering rebellious fury o'er the plain,

That threatened ruin to the Church and State,
Unmoved he stood, and feared no threats of Fate.
That loyal champion for the Church and Crown,
That noble ornament of the sacred gown,
Still did his sovereign's cause espouse,
And was above the thanks of the mad Senate house.
Strephon [12] the great, whom last you sent abroad,
Who writ, and loved, and looked like any god;
For whom the Muses mourn, the love-sick maids
Are languishing in melancholy shades.
   The Cupids flag [13] their wings, their bows untie,
    And useless quivers hang neglected by,
    And scattered arrows all around them lie,
By murmuring brooks the careless deities are laid,
Weeping their rifled power now noble Strephon's dead.

Ah sacred Wadham! should'st thou never own
But this delight of all mankind and thine;
For ages past of dullness, this alone,
   This charming hero would atone.
And make thee glorious to succeeding time;
But thou like Nature's self disdain'st to be,
   Stinted to singularity.
Even as fast as she thou dost produce,
And over all the sacred mystery infuse.
   No sooner was famed Strephon's glory set,
   Strephon the soft, the lovely and the [14] great;
   But Daphnis rises like the morning star,
   That guides the wandering traveller from afar.
   Daphnis whom every grace, and Muse inspires,
Scarce Strephon's ravishing poetic fires
   So kindly warm, or so divinely cheer.

Advance young Daphnis, as thou hast begun,
   So let thy mighty race be run.
   Thou in thy large poetic chase,
   Begin'st where others end the race.
If now thy grateful numbers are so strong,

If they so early can such graces show,
Like beauty so surprising, when so young,
What Daphnis will thy riper judgment do,
When thy unbounded verse in their own streams shall flow!
    What wonder will they not produce,
    When thy immortal fancy's loose;
Unfettered, unconfined by any other Muse!
  Advance young Daphnis then, and mayst thou prove
  Still sacred [15] in thy poetry and love.
  May all the groves with Daphnis' songs be blessed,
  Whilst every bark is with thy distichs dressed. [16]
  May timorous maids learn how to love from thence
  And the glad shepherd arts of eloquence.
  And when to solitudes thou would'st retreat,
  May their tuned pipes thy welcome celebrate.
  And [17] all the nymphs strow garlands at thy feet.
May all the purling streams that murmuring pass,
    The shady groves and banks of flowers,
    The kind [18] reposing beds of grass,
    Contribute to their [19] softer hours.
May'st thou thy Muse and mistress there caress,
  And may one heighten t'other's happiness.
  And whilst thou so divinely dost converse,
We are content to know and to admire thee in thy sacred [20] verse. [21]

A LETTER TO MR CREECH AT OXFORD, WRITTEN IN THE LAST GREAT FROST [1]

DAPHNIS, because I am your debtor,
  (And other causes which are better)
I send you here my debt of letter.
You should have had a scrap of nonsense,
You may remember left at Tonson's. [2]
(Though by the way that's scurvy rhyme Sir,
But yet 'twill serve to tag a line Sir.)

A *billet-doux* I had designed then,
But you may think I was in wine then;
Because it being cold, you know
We warmed it with a glass – or so,
I grant you that shie wine's[3] the Devil,
To make one's memory uncivil;
But when 'twixt every sparkling cup,
I so much brisker wit took up;
Wit, able to inspire a thinking;
And make one solemn even in drinking;
Wit that would charm and stock a poet,
Even instruct — who has no wit;
Wit that was hearty, true, and loyal,
Of wit, like Bays'[4] Sir, that's my trial;
I say 'twas most impossible,
That after that one should be dull.
Therefore because you may not blame me,
Take the whole truth as — shall sa'me.

    From White-Hall[5] Sir, as I was coming,
His sacred Majesty from dunning;
Who oft in debt is, truth to tell,
For Tory farce, or doggerel,
When every street as dangerous was,
As ever the Alpian hills to pass,
When melted snow and ice confound one,
Whether to break one's neck or drown one,
And *billet-doux* in pocket lay,
To drop as coach should jolt that way,
Near to that place of fame called Temple,[6]
(Which I shall note by sad example)
Where college dunce is cured of simple,[7]
Against that sign of whore called Scarlet,[8]
My coachman fairly laid pilgarlic.[9]

    Though scribbling fist was out of joint,
And every limb made great complaint;
Yet missing the dear assignation,
Gave me most cause of tribulation.
To honest H—le[10] I should have shown ye,

A wit that would be proud t'have known ye;
A wit uncommon, and facetious,
A great admirer of Lucretius; [11]
But transitory hopes do vary,
And high designments oft miscarry,
Ambition never climbed so lofty,
But may descend too fair and softly,
But would you'd seen how sneakingly
I looked with this catastrophe.
So saucy Whig, when Plot [12] broke out,
Dejected hung his snivelling snout;
So Oxford Member looked, when Rowley [13]
Kicked out the rebel crew so foully;
So Perkin once that God of Wapping, [15]
Whom slippery turn of State took napping,
From hopes of James the second [14] fell
In to the native scounderel.
So lover looked of joy defeated,
When too much fire his vigour cheated, [16]
Even so looked I, when bliss depriving,
Was caused by over-hasty driving,
Who saw me could not choose but think,
I looked like brawn in sousing drink.
Or Lazarello [17] who was showed
For a strange fish, to'th' gaping crowd.
    Thus you by fate (to me, sinister)
At shop of book my billet missed Sir.
And home I went as discontent,
As a new routed Parliament,
Not seeing Daphnis ere he went.
And sure his grief beyond expressing,
Of joy proposed to want the blessing;
Therefore to pardon pray incline,
Since disappointment all was mine;
Of Hell we have no other notion,
Than all the joys of Heaven's privation;
So Sir with recommendments fervent,
I rest your very humble servant.

POSTSCRIPT

On Twelfth Night Sir, by that good token,
When lamentable cake[18] was broken,
You had a friend, a man of wit,
A man whom I shall ne'er forget;
For every word he did impart,
'Twas worth the keeping in a heart:
True Tory all! and when he spoke,
A god in wit, though man in look.
– To this your friend – Daphnis address
The humblest of my services;
Tell him how much – yet do not too,
My vast esteem no words can show;
Tell him – that he is worthy – you.

SONG
ON HER LOVING TWO EQUALLY[1]

Set by Captain Pack[2]

I.

HOW strongly does my passion flow,
Divided equally 'twixt two?
Damon had ne'er subdued my heart,
Had not Alexis took his part;
Nor could Alexis powerful prove,
Without my Damon's aid, to gain my love.

II.

When my Alexis present is,
Then I for Damon sigh and mourn;
But when Alexis I do miss,
Damon gains nothing but my scorn.
But if it chance they both are by,
For both alike I languish, sigh, and die.

III.

Cure then, thou mighty winged god,
This restless fever in my blood;
One golden-pointed dart take back:
But which, O Cupid, wilt thou take?
If Damon's, all my hopes are crossed;
Or that of my Alexis, I am lost.

TO THE FAIR CLARINDA,[1] WHO MADE LOVE TO ME, IMAGINED MORE THAN WOMAN

FAIR lovely maid, or if that title be
Too weak, too feminine for nobler thee,
Permit a name that more approaches truth,
And let me call thee, lovely charming youth.
This last will justify my soft complaint,
While that may serve to lessen my constraint;
And without blushes I the youth pursue,
When so much beauteous woman is in view.
Against thy charms we struggle but in vain
With thy deluding form thou giv'st us pain,
While the bright nymph betrays us to the swain.
In pity to our sex sure thou wert sent,
That we might love, and yet be innocent:
For sure no crime with thee we can commit;
Or if we should – thy form excuses it.
For who, that gathers fairest flowers believes
A snake lies hid beneath the fragrant leaves.[2]

Thou beauteous wonder of a different kind,
Soft Cloris with the dear Alexis joined;
When e'er the manly part of thee, would plead
Thou tempts us with the image of the maid,
While we the noblest passions do extend
The love to Hermes, Aphrodite[3] the friend.

ON DESIRE[1]

A Pindaric

WHAT art thou, oh! thou new-found pain?
　　From what infection dost thou spring?
Tell me – oh! tell me, thou enchanting thing,
　　　Thy nature, and thy name;
Inform me by what subtle art,
　　　What powerful influence,
You got such vast dominion in a part
Of my unheeded, and unguarded, heart,
That fame and honour cannot drive ye thence.

Oh! mischievous usurper of my peace;
Oh! soft intruder on my solitude,
　　Charming disturber of my ease,
　　That hast my nobler fate pursued,
And all the glories of my life subdued.

　　Thou haunt'st my inconvenient hours;
The business of the day, nor silence of the night,
　　　That should to cares and sleep invite,
　　Can bid defiance to thy conquering powers.

　　Where hast thou been this live-long age
　　　That from my birth till now,
　　Thou never couldst one thought engage,
Or charm my soul with the uneasy rage
That made it all its humble feebles know?

　　Where wert thou, oh, malicious sprite,
　　When shining honour did invite?
　　When interest called, then thou wert shy,
Nor to my aid one kind propension[2] brought,
　　Nor wouldst inspire one tender thought,
　　When Princes at my feet did lie.

When thou couldst mix ambition with my joy,
Then peevish phantom thou wert nice and coy,
   Not beauty could invite thee then
   Nor all the arts of lavish men!
Not all the powerful rhetoric of the tongue
   Not sacred wit could charm thee on;
   Not the soft play that lovers make,
Nor sigh could fan thee to a fire,
Not pleading tears, nor vows could thee awake,
Or warm the unformed something – to desire.

   Oft I've conjured thee to appear
   By youth, by love, by all their powers,
   Have searched and sought thee everywhere,
In silent groves, in lonely bowers:
On flowery beds where lovers wishing lie,
   In sheltering woods where sighing maids
   To their assigning shepherds hie,
And hide their blushes in the gloom of shades.
   Yet there, even there, though youth assailed,
Where beauty prostrate lay and fortune wooed,
My heart insensible to neither bowed:
Thy lucky aid was wanting to prevail.

In courts I sought thee then, thy proper sphere
   But thou in crowds wert stifled there,
Interest did all the loving business do,
Invites the youths and wins the virgins too.
Or if by chance some heart thy empire own
(Ah power ingrate!) the slave must be undone.

Tell me, thou nimble fire, that dost dilate
   Thy mighty force through every part,
What god, or human power did thee create
   In my, till now, unfacile heart?
Art thou some welcome plague sent from above
   In this dear form, this kind disguise?
   Or the false offspring of mistaken love,

Begot by some soft thought that faintly strove,
With the bright piercing beauties of Lysander's eyes?

Yes, yes, tormenter, I have found thee now;
And found to whom thou dost thy being owe,
   'Tis thou the blushes dost impart,
   For thee this languishment I wear,
   'Tis thou that tremblest in my heart
   When the dear shepherd does appear,
   I faint, I die with pleasing pain,
   My words intruding sighing break
   When e'er I touch the charming swain
   When e'er I gaze, when e'er I speak.
Thy conscious fire is mingled with my love,
   As in the sanctified abodes
   Misguided worshippers approve
   The mixing idol with their gods.
   In vain, alas! in vain I strive
With errors, which my soul do please and vex,
   For superstition will survive,
   Purer religion to perplex.

Oh! tell me you, philosophers, in love,
That can its burning feverish fits control,
   By what strange arts you cure the soul,
   And the fierce calenture[3] remove?

Tell me, ye fair ones, that exchange desire,
   How 'tis you hid the kindling fire.
   Oh! would you but confess the truth,
It is not real virtue makes you nice:
But when you do resist the pressing youth,
'Tis want of dear desire, to thaw the virgin ice.
   And while your young adorers lie
All languishing and hopeless at your feet,
   Raising new trophies to your chastity,
   Oh tell me, how you do remain discreet?
   How you suppress the rising sighs,

And the soft yielding soul that wishes in your eyes?
  While to th' admiring crowd you nice are found;
  Some dear, some secret, youth that gives the wound
  Informs you, all your virtue's but a cheat
    And honour but a false disguise,
  Your modesty a necessary bait
  To gain the dull repute of being wise.

Deceive the foolish world – deceive it on,
  And veil your passions in your pride;
But now I've found your feebles by my own,
From me the needful fraud you cannot hide.
  Though 'tis a mighty power must move
  The soul to this degree of love,
And though with virtue I the world perplex,
Lysander finds the weakness of my sex,
So Helen while from Theseus' arms she fled,
To charming Paris yields her heart and bed.[4]

A PINDARIC POEM TO
THE REVEREND DOCTOR BURNET[1]

I.

WHEN old Rome's candidates[2] aspired to fame,
  And did the people's suffrages obtain
For some great Consul, or a Caesar's name;
  The victor was not half so pleased and vain,
As I, when given the honour of your choice,
And preference had in that one single voice;
  That voice, from whence immortal wit still flows,
Wit that at once is solemn all and sweet,
  Where noblest eloquence and judgment shows
The inspiring mind illustrious, rich, and great;
A mind that can inform your wondrous pen
  In all that's perfect and sublime:

And with an art beyond the wit of men,
  On what e'er theme, on what e'er great design,
It carries a commanding force, like that of writ divine.

II.

With powerful reasoning dressed in finest sense,
  A thousand ways my soul you can invade,
And spite of my opinion's weak defence,
  Against my will, you conquer and persuade.
Your language soft as love, betrays the heart,
And at each period fixes a resistless dart,
  While the fond listener, like a maid undone,
  Inspired with tenderness she fears to own,
In vain essays her freedom to regain:
The fine ideas in her soul remain,
And please, and charm, even while they grieve and pain.

III.

But yet how well this praise can recompense
For all the welcome wounds (before) you'd given![3]
  Scarce anything but you and Heaven
  Such grateful bounties can dispense
As that eternity of life can give;
So famed by you my verse eternally shall live:
Till now, my careless Muse no higher strove
T'enlarge her glory, and extend her wings;
    Than underneath Parnassus grove,
To sing of shepherds, and their humble love;
But never durst, like Cowley, tune her strings,
    To sing of heroes and of Kings.[4]
But since by an authority divine,
She is allowed a more exalted thought;
She will be valued now as current coin,
Whose stamp alone gives it the estimate,
Though out of an inferior metal wrought.[5]

IV.

But oh! if from your praise I feel
  A joy that has no parallel!
What must I suffer when I cannot pay
  Your goodness, your own generous way?
And make my stubborn Muse your just commands obey.
  My Muse that would endeavour fain to glide
With the fair prosperous gale, and the full driving tide.
But loyalty commands with pious force,
  That stops me in the thriving course.
The breeze that wafts the crowding nations o'er,
   Leaves me unpitied far behind
   On the forsaken barren shore,
To sigh with Echo,[6] and the murmuring wind;
While all the inviting prospect I survey,
With melancholy eyes I view the plains,
Where all I see is ravishing and gay,
And all I hear is mirth in loudest strains;
Thus while the chosen seed possess the Promised Land,
  I like the excluded prophet stand,
   The fruitful happy soil can only see,
   But am forbid by Fate's decree
To share the triumph of the joyful victory.[7]

V.

'Tis to your pen, great Sir, the nation owes
For all the good this mighty change has wrought;[8]
'Twas that the wondrous method did dispose,
E'er the vast work was to perfection brought.
Oh strange effect of a seraphic quill!
  That can by unperceptible degrees
Change every notion, every principle
  To any form, its great dictator please.
The sword a feeble power, compared to that,
  And to the nobler pen subordinate;
   And of less use in bravest turns of State:

While that to blood and slaughter has recourse,
This conquers hearts with soft prevailing force:
So when the wiser Greeks o'ercame their foes,
It was not by the barbarous force of blows.
When a long ten years' fatal war had failed,
With luckier wisdom they at last assailed,
Wisdom and counsel which alone prevailed.
Not all their numbers the famed town could win,
'Twas nobler stratagem that let the conqueror in.⁹

VI.

Tho' I the wondrous change deplore,
That makes me useless and forlorn,
Yet I the great design adore,
Though ruined in the universal turn.
Nor can my indigence and lost repose,
Those meagre Furies that surround me close,
    Convert my sense and reason more
  To this unprecedented enterprise,
  Than that a man so great, so learned, so wise,
The brave achievement owns and nobly justifies.
  'Tis you, great Sir, alone, by Heaven preserved,
  Whose conduct has so well the nation served,
  'Tis you that to posterity shall give
    This age's wonders, and its history.
And great Nassau¹⁰ shall in your annals live
    To all futurity.
  Your pen shall more immortalize his name,
Than even his own renowned and celebrated fame.

NOTES

INTRODUCTION

1. Lines 592–4 of Behn's translation of the sixth book of Abraham Cowley's *Six Books of Plants* (1689). See *The Poetry of Aphra Behn*, ed. Janet Todd (London: Pickering & Chatto, 1992).

2. From the commendatory poems in *Poems upon Several Occasions* (1684).

3. Broadside of April 1689.

4. Montague Summers, *The Works of Aphra Behn* (London: Heinemann, 1915, reprinted 1967); Virginia Woolf, *A Room of One's Own and Three Guineas* (London: Chatto & Windus, 1984), p. 61.

5. Thomas Colepeper, 'Adversaria', British Library manuscript, Harley 7588; 'Memoirs on the Life of Mrs Behn' (18 pp.), in *The Histories and Novels* (1696); 'The History of the Life and Memoirs of Mrs Behn . . .' (60 pp.), in the third edition of *All the Histories and Novels* (1698); Maureen Duffy, *The Passionate Shepherdess: Aphra Behn 1640–89* (London: Cape, 1977); Mary Ann O'Donnell, 'Tory Wit and Unconventional Woman', in *Women Writers of the Seventeenth Century*, ed. Katharina M. Wilson and Frank J. Warnke (Athens, Ga.: University of Georgia Press, 1989), pp. 341–74; Jane Jones, 'New Light on the Background and Early Life of Aphra Behn', *Notes & Queries*, September 1990, pp. 289–93. Sharon Valiant put forward the Sidney hypothesis in a paper of March 1989: 'Sidney's Sister, Pembroke's Mother . . . and Aphra Behn's Great-Grandmother?'.

6. William J. Cameron, *New Light on Aphra Behn* (Auckland: University of Auckland Press, 1961).

7. 'To the Author of the New Utopia', *The Six Days Adventure, or The New Utopia. A Comedy* (1671), reprinted in *Poems on Several Occasions* (1684).

8. 'Our Cabal', *Poems on Several Occasions* (1684); *Thomaso, or The Wanderer*, in *Comedies and Tragedies. Written by Thomas Killigrew* (1664).

9. Samuel Johnson, *The Lives of the English Poets* (1779–81).

THE FAIR JILT

1. The 1688 first edition has a dedication to the Roman Catholic Henry Nevil Payne, playwright like Behn for the Duke's Company in the 1670s

and loyal supporter and propagandist for James II. Between the dedication and the beginning of the story are two advertisements, one for a face powder and the other for Behn's *Oroonoko*. Although the title page gives the name of the story as *The Fair Jilt: or, the History of Prince Tarquin and Miranda*, the story itself begins with the title *The Fair Hypocrite: or the Amours of Prince Tarquin and Miranda*.

2. *opinionatreism*. Obstinacy in his own opinion, conceit.

3. *scrutore*. Writing-desk.

4. billets-doux. Love letters.

5. *pit and boxes*. The pit was the part of the theatre where the 'wits' sat: see Wycherley's *Love in a Wood*, 'my brisk brothers of the pit'; the boxes, which were expensive, were where ladies tended to sit.

6. Aphra Behn was a spy in Antwerp in late 1666. The *London Gazette* of 28–31 May 1666 prints the following item: 'The Prince Torquino being condemned at Antwerp to be beheaded, for endeavouring the death of his Sister in Law: Being on the Scaffold, the Executioner tied an handkerchief about his head and by great accident his blow lighted upon the knot, giving him only a slight wound. Upon which, the people being in a tumult, he was carried back to the Townhouse, and is in hopes both of his pardon and his recovery.' Another issue announces his pardon.

7. *Order of St Francis*. An austere religious order founded in 1209 by St. Francis of Assissi (1181/2–1226).

8. *Galloping Nuns*. Popular name for nuns of the Institute of the Blessed Virgin Mary (I.B.V.M.), or women who were members of a religious community, but free to come and go.

9. *Chanonesses*. Members of a Christian women's community where a rule is observed but no perpetual vows taken.

10. *Beguines*. Members of a lay sisterhood which members could leave to marry.

11. *Quests*. Members of a begging order.

12. *Swart-sisters*. Nuns dressed in black; Dominican sisters.

13. *Jesuitesses*. A name often given to members of the I.B.V.M., which was founded on Jesuit principles.

14. filles dévotes. Women consecrated by a religious vow.

15. *governante*. Woman in charge of a household or of young people.

16. *bando*. Collar.

17. *sensible*. Sensitive.

18. *Cordeliers*. Nuns of a strict Franciscan order, the members of which wear knotted cord for a belt.

19. *pistole*. A name given to certain Spanish and French gold coins.

20. beaux esprits. Wits.

21. *mal à propos*. Inappropriately.

22. *sacristy*. The room in which vestments and sacred vessels are kept.

23. *stomacher*. A panel, often richly decorated, worn by women under the lacing at the front of their bodices.

24. *sense*. Feeling, physical ardour.

25. *scapular*. 'An article of devotion composed of two small squares of woollen cloth, fastened together by strings passing over the shoulders' (*O.E.D.*). It can also mean a short cloak worn by some religious orders.

26. *provincial*. The head of the religious order in that area.

27. *gown-men*. Priests and men in religious orders.

28. *Marquis Casteil Roderigo . . . governor of flanders*. According to the *London Gazette* it was he who pardoned Prince Tarquin. Flanders was Spanish territory at the time.

29. *King Charles . . . Brussels*. Charles II was in Brussels in February and March, 1660.

30. *Tarquin . . . Rome*. Tarquin the Proud was traditionally believed to have been the last King of Rome.

31. *I have seen him*. Aphra Behn left England in July 1666 and her first letter from Antwerp was sent in August. Since the newspaper report of the failed execution is for May 1666, and the meeting with Tarquin took place about two and a half years before, there seems to be some discrepancy in dates. It is possible that she is not being accurate or that she had been to Antwerp during the previous years.

32. *laced with gold*. Decorated with gold lace.

33. *Lucretia*. The rape of Lucretia by Tarquin, son of the last King of Rome, was supposed to have precipitated the fall of the monarchy.

34. *bare*. Bare-headed (as a mark of respect to her).

35. *tuition*. Guardianship.

36. *received . . . pension*. Took him into her household.

37. *juggle*. Deception.

38. *Margrave*. Governor.

39. *mittimus*. Warrant directing a gaoler to receive and keep a prisoner until further notice.

40. *laced*. Trimmed with lace.

41. *bare*. See note 34 above.

42. *Portugal-mat*. Probably a thin rush or split-cane patterned mat from North Africa; frequently mentioned in grand settings, such as beneath state beds. See the 1683 inventory for Ham House.

43. *state-house*. Town-hall.

44. *booted . . . coach*. A coach with steps at the side for servants to sit on, or with a low compartment outside at the back or front.

45. *bruit*. News, rumour.

46. Louis d'or. A gold coin first issued in the reign of Louis XIII.

47 *holland . . . with point*. Linen cap trimmed with lace.

48. *let blood*. Opening a vein in order to let some blood, or applying leeches, was for many centuries one of the most common treatments for numerous diseases. Until comparatively recently it was used as a means of lowering blood pressure.

49. *bating*. Except for.

50. *French army . . . campaigns*. In 1667 the period of peace which had marked the beginning of Louis XIV's reign was broken; between 1668 and 1678 the King's thirst for glory, as well as political and religious considerations, led to constant military campaigns and the acquisition of a great deal of territory on the north-eastern frontiers of France.

OROONOKO

1. *Oroonoko* was first published in 1688, having been announced both in *The Fair Jilt* and in *Two Congratulatory Poems To Their Most Sacred Majesties*. It had been through several editions by 1701 and was reprinted frequently throughout the eighteenth century. It was serialized in the *Ladies Magazine*, included in revised form in Elizabeth Griffith's *Collection of Novels* in 1777, translated into French, Dutch and German, often imitated, and turned into a popular play by Thomas Southerne in 1696. *Oroonoko* was dedicated to Richard Lord Maitland, 4th Earl of Lauderdale (1653–95), a Roman Catholic and a Stuart supporter. The text here is from the copy in the Bodleian Library, Oxford. For a detailed description of the printing of the first edition, see Gerald Duchovnay, 'Aphra Behn's *Oroonoko*: A Critical Edition' (dissertation, Indiana University, 1971).

2. *. . . life*. Although it has sometimes been doubted, Aphra Behn seems to have arrived in Surinam in mid or late 1663 and left in 1664. Much of the description of the country is probably from memory, perhaps overlaid by some accounts in George Warren's short *Impartial Description of Surinam* (1667).

3. *Surinam*. The first English colonies in Surinam, later Dutch Guiana, were founded in the 1640s; in 1650 Anthony Rous and Francis, Lord Willoughby of Parham founded further settlements. After the Restoration in 1663 Charles II granted proprietary rights to most of Surinam to Willoughby. Willoughby was also governor of Barbados and he appointed William Byam as his deputy in Surinam. Byam was a powerful

figure in a colony which was more or less free of control from London in the early 1660s. Petitions to the King from some settlers suggested that Byam ruled autocratically and punished those who tried to oppose him.

4. *not natives of the place*. White Surinam planters tended to have large estates with many slaves, primarily brought from the Gold Coast. Black slaves were introduced into Surinam in 1650 by Lord Willoughby and soon outnumbered whites; there was considerable fear of an uprising among the settlers. In 1667 there were under 300 whites and over 500 black slaves. Apparently only one quarter of the slave force was labouring on the plantations.

5. *cousheries*. The local Caribee Indians spoke Galibi. Warren does not usually use Galibi terms but he does mention 'Cusharees'. Antoine Biel in *Voyage de la France équinoxiale en l'isle de Cayenne* (1654), which often gives Galibi words close to those in *Oroonoko*, calls the 'couchari' a deer (*cerf*) and the 'caïcouci' a tiger.

6. *flies*. Butterflies.

7. Indian Queen. *The Indian Queen*, written by John Dryden and Sir Robert Howard, was one of the first rhymed heroic dramas produced in London. It was first performed in January 1664 by the King's Men at the Theatre Royal in Bridges Street under the management of Thomas Killigrew. There were several revivals in the 1690s, which, together with the success of Southerne's *Oroonoko* and reprinting of Behn's story in the same years, suggests a fashion for 'Indian' subjects at this time.

8. *ell*. The English ell measured 45 inches.

9. *nice*. Reluctant.

10. *no curiosity*. This description of a natural lack of shame is a usual feature of Behn's depictions of a Golden Age world. It can be found in many pastoral writers and is a convention of the pastoral tradition expressed by Torquato Tasso in his poem '*O bella età de l'oro*', and in Behn's own adaptation, 'The Golden Age'.

11. *savannahs*. The word was also used in *The Widow Ranter* for a large heath in the Americas.

12. *Coramantien*. Cormantine, from the Dutch fort Koromantyn or Fort Amsterdam, was a settlement on the west coast of Africa, a few miles east of Cape Coast in Ghana. It was an English trading post from the 1630s and the name was used loosely for most of the area of modern Ghana. At the time it was used by the English and Dutch slave-traders as a source of supply of slaves from the Fantis, Ashantis and interior tribes.

13. *Oroonoko*. The name may be a variant of the South American river Orinoco (spelt 'Oronoque' in the contemporary *London Gazette*), or perhaps a derivative from an African word such as Oro, a Yoruba god.

Moors were commonly believed to be black or very dark, so the term was often used for Negroes as well.

14. *Civil Wars ... great monarch*. The wars of the 1640s between Royalists and Parliamentarians, culminating in the execution of Charles I in 1649.

15. *statuary*. Sculptor of statues.

16. *bating*. Excepting.

17. *politic*. Sagacious or shrewd.

18. *otan*. Perhaps for *oda*, the Turkish word for a room in a seraglio, or the Persian *otagh*, a tent or pavilion. Biel lists *outonomé* for house.

19. *governants*. Governesses.

20. *antic*. Grotesque.

21. *complaisance*. Desire to please.

22. *maugre*. In spite of.

23. The original reads 'efforts'.

24. *parole*. Word or pledge.

25. *too generous*. The 1688 edition has a comma between 'generous' and 'not' which renders the qualifying clause critical of Oroonoko but makes the whole sentence difficult to interpret.

26. *pickaninnies*. An early use of this word for black children.

27. *Trefry*. John Treffry was Lord Willoughby's agent in his plantation of Parham.

28. *backearary*. Possibly a variant of *buckra* or *bakra* (master), the word used in Surinam by the blacks for the whites. See J. A. Ramsaram, 'Oroonoko: A Study of the Factual Elements', *Notes & Queries*, 205, 1969, 142–5.

29. *osenbrigs ... holland*. Osnaburg was heavy coarse cotton or linen ('holland') fabric.

30. Caesar. It was a custom of slave-owners to give slaves Roman names.

31. *the Dutch ... in time*. The Dutch captured Surinam in February 1667; it was retaken by the English in October but was ceded to the Dutch at the Treaty of Breda in 1667. Treffry remained in Surinam and died there in 1674.

32. *Parham-House*. Parham House was part of Lord Willoughby's estate of Parham Hill.

33. *shock dog*. A poodle, or dog with long, shaggy hair. Later editions changed 'Clemene' here to 'Trefry'.

34. *allay*. Abatement, diminution.

35. *novel*. New turn in events.

36. *raced*. Slashed with something sharp.

37. *japanned*. Varnished or lacquered with a hard black gloss.

38. *high point.* A type of lace.

39. *Picts ... chronicles.* Ancient people of north Britain who were thought to paint and tattoo themselves. They are described in such contemporary chronicles as *Britannia Speculum* (1683).

40. *mutiny ... numbers.* This was a constant fear in the Caribbean and South American colonies.

41. *lives ... nuns.* This gendered reading presumably gave Plutarch's *Lives* to Oroonoko and works such as Behn's own *The History of the Nun* (1689) to Imoinda.

42. *pitching the bar.* Throwing a heavy bar was a form of athletic exercise. (D'Urfey, *Pills* III.253,4: 'I ... can ... pitch-bar, and run and wrestle too.')

43. *parted ... Dutch.* See note 30 above.

44. *Spring ... Autumn.* Cf. Warren, 'There is a constant Spring and Fall ... Some [trees] have always blossoms, and the several degrees of fruit at once' (p. 5).

45. *St John's Hill.* St John's Hill was a plantation belonging to Sir Robert Harley, probably sold to Willoughby in 1664. Harley, Chancellor of Barbados under Willoughby, corresponded with William Yearworth, possibly an agent in Surinam, who mentions 'Ladeyes' living at St John's Hill on 27 January 1664.

46. *ravishing.* The 1688 edition reads 'raving'; it was changed to 'ravishing' in the third edition. In some later editions, 'sands' became 'fancy', but this seems an unnecessary emendation.

47. *Mall.* The first two editions read 'Marl', the third emends this to 'mall', presumably a reference to the walk in St James's Park, London, where originally the game of pall-mall was played.

48. *branches.* The 1688 edition reads 'fruity bear branches meet'; the third edition emends this to 'fruit-bearing branches met'.

49. *he.* There seems some confusion over the tiger's sex. Later editions emend to 'she' and 'her' in the following lines.

50. *English ... Oliverian.* George Marten, owner of Surinam plantations, was, according to Behn, the brother of Henry Marten, one of the regicides and supporters of Oliver Cromwell.

51. *numb eel.* Electric eel. See *The Diary of John Evelyn* (18 March 1680): 'a letter from Surenam of a certaine small Eele that being taken with hook and line ... did so benumb, and stupifie the limbs of the Fisher ...'.

52. *tepeeme.* Biel claimed the Indians said *tapouimé* for 'a great number' (p. 396).

53. *numberless ... heads.* The same image occurs in Warren who, describing native arithmetic as primitive, claimed that the Indians cried '*ounsa awara*, that is, like the hair of one's head, innumerable' (p. 26).

54. *Amora tiguamy.* Biel reported that a familiar Galibi form was *acné tigami* and the second person pronoun *amoré*, so that Behn is reporting a greeting (p. 26).

55. *sarumbo . . . table-cloth.* Biel gives *chalombo* as the name of leaves of trees which he notes are used as 'serviettes' (p. 416). Cf. Warren: 'their napery is the leaves of the trees' (p. 24).

56. *prophet.* Biel describes the *piaye* as a doctor (p. 408).

57. The first edition reverses 'several other'.

58. *comitias.* Biel claimed that the Indians wore only a piece of clothing called *un camison* (p. 353). Although he notes the Spanish origin of some Galibi words, he does not connect this one with the Spanish *camisa*.

59. *. . . America.* There had been stories of a 'golden city' on the Amazon since the previous century; Sir Walter Raleigh had made two unsuccessful expeditions in search of it. His *Discovery of Guiana* (1596) includes a description of 'Eldorado' and describes the plainlands as a natural Eden. In *Paradise Lost* (published the year that Guiana was ceded to the Netherlands) Milton makes a topical reference to '. . . Guiana, whose great Citie Geryons Sons/Call El Dorado . . .' (XI.410,411). Willoughby died in a storm at sea in 1666 during the Second Dutch War. It is interesting to think of the Amazon compared with the Thames.

60. *whip and bell.* 'Something that detracts from one's comfort or pleasure' (*O.E.D.*).

61. *runagades.* Renegades; apostates and deserters.

62. *salvages.* Savages.

63. *. . . hands.* Southerne, who was impressed with Behn's dramatic presentation of *Oroonoko* and had wondered why she did not herself make the story into a play, makes Oroonoko speak in blank verse on heroic occasions such as this and differentiates him more sharply than Behn from the other blacks.

64. *cut . . . rocks.* When crossing the Alps, 'in certaine places of the highest rockes, [Hannibal] was driven to make passage through, by force of fire and vinegar' (Plutarch, *The Lives of the Noble Grecians and Romanes*, North's translation, 1579 edition).

65. *hamaca.* Hammock, from the Carib word through Spanish *hamaca*. Pepys comments on buying 'hammacoes' for the navy.

66. *Parhamites . . . Plantation.* Supporters of Lord Willoughby in the faction-ridden colony.

67. *baffled with.* Deceived and abused.

68. *cat with nine tails.* Whip with nine knotted lashes used in the British navy and army.

69. *Byam.* William Byam was the royalist governor of Surinam from *c.* 1654 and then deputy governor under Willoughby. In 1663 he became lieutenant-general, a position the narrator claims her father should have held.

70. *. . . terrible to behold.* Behn was contemptuous of turncoats, especially when they were disloyal to her respected James II, from whom support was slipping away during 1688.

71. *. . . so brave a man. The Younger Brother: or the Amorous Jilt* (1696). The Memoir of 1696 claims that Behn based the play on a true story supplied by George Marten.

72. *chirurgeon.* Surgeon.

73. *Newgate.* A London prison from which many convicts were exported to work on New World plantations. For example, in 1681 Christopher Jeaffreson bought 300 convicts from the chief gaoler of Newgate to use on his plantation in Jamaica. See also Behn, *The Widow Ranter,* p. 259.

74. nemine contradicente. Unanimously.

75. The first edition reads 'they'.

76. *mobile.* Mob, rabble.

77. *fatal stroke.* There is a parallel here with Othello, who also kills the woman he loves.

78. *gashly.* Ghastly.

79. *Banister.* Major James Bannister. In 1688, after the Treaty of Breda, he negotiated with the Dutch on behalf of the remaining English settlers and was sent as a prisoner to Holland.

80. *which they did.* See Bryan Edwards and John Stedman, *Narrative of a Five Years' Expedition Against the Revolted Negroes of Surinam* (1796) for a later description of a tortured man smoking a pipe of tobacco.

LOVE-LETTERS TO A GENTLEMAN

1. 'Love-Letters' was first published posthumously in *Histories and Novels of the Late Ingenious Mrs Behn* (1696). It was then retitled 'Love-Letters to a Gentleman' and reappeared as part of *Memoirs of Mrs Behn* by 'One of the Fair Sex' in the 1698 *Histories and Novels.* The letters are addressed to 'Lycidas' and signed 'Astrea'. It is not known when they were written, but Lycidas is probably John Hoyle, the lawyer with whom Aphra Behn's name was frequently linked. The present text is from *Histories and Novels* of 1700.

2. *complaisance*. Desire to please, or politeness.

3. *unconversable*. Unfit for social life or conversation.

4. *parole*. Word.

5. *cast*. Throw of dice.

6. *new play*. This cannot be identified with certainty, but from the remark that 'you were the man' it may be *The Rover*, Part I (1677).

7. *Philly*. Philly may be 'Philaster', to whom Behn dedicated *The Young King* in 1683. Maureen Duffy speculates that this is the Duke of Buckingham, or, as 'lover of Astrea', it might be William Scot.

8. *over the way*. Perhaps a reference to the Davenants. Sir William and later his widow were proprietor and manager of the Duke's Company of players. The household seems to have included children, stepchildren and several of the younger actresses. Aphra Behn's friend, the actress Elizabeth Barry, had been adopted by the Davenants when still a child.

9. *calentures*. A 'calenture' was either the physical condition of suffering from a very high temperature, or the psychological condition of suffering from a burning passion.

THE ROVER

1. *The Rover* is loosely based on Thomas Killigrew's *Thomaso*, Parts I and II, written in 1654 but published only in 1664, with many of its incidents based on earlier stock ones from such writers as Boccaccio and Middleton. Behn changes Killigrew's setting from Madrid to Naples and places her scene in a carnival. The theatricality, disguises and cross-dressing that this allows make comparison with the popular image of the Court of Charles II almost inevitable, although she retains the dating of the interregnum. *Thomaso* is a long, rambling but fascinating play which raises many questions about sexual relations and the nature of male and female honour. Behn's play shortens and sharpens discussion of these questions and is consequently far more dramatic and actable. Although Angellica is flanked by other prostitutes in *Thomaso* (Killigrew has a group of whores, Behn one of virgins), the main contest, as in *The Rover*, is between Angellica and a virginal young woman, Serulina in *Thomaso* and Hellena in *The Rover*. The latter is given some of the liberationist rhetoric Killigrew put into Angellica's mouth and she is more ambitious in disguise, crossing sexual as well as class boundaries. In *Thomaso*, Angellica graciously accepts her defeat at the end and Thomaso repents his libertine life. Neither of these attitudes is displayed in *The Rover*.

Both Angellica and Hellena also have something in common with Franceschina and Crispinella of *The Dutch Courtesan* by Marston, from whom Aphra Behn frequently borrowed. Many incidents like Blunt's misadventures with Lucetta are stock ones and occur in English, Spanish and French sources.

The Rover was first produced at the Duke's House, Dorset Gardens, in 1677 and was a great success. In the first recorded performance, Willmore was played by Mr Smith, Hellena by Elizabeth Barry and Angellica Bianca by 'Mrs Gwin' (Anne Quin). Unlike most of Aphra Behn's plays, *The Rover* kept its popularity on the stage in future centuries. Steele in the *Spectator*, 51, 28 April 1711, uses *The Rover* as an example of female bawdry and suggests that this reflects the character of the author: 'the men-authors draw themselves in their chief characters, and the women-writers may be allowed the same liberty'. Although Behn herself was much criticized for her bawdiness after her death, *The Rover* was produced successfully during the first half of the eighteenth century and revived in 1757. In the latter half of the century, however, her work was found immodest and a new version of the play was made to suit the times – J. P. Kemble's *Love in Many Masks* (T. and J. Egerton, 1790). In the Royal Shakespeare Company's revival of *The Rover* in 1986, John Barton substantially adapted the play by cutting, adding and rearranging it to suit assumed modern taste.

2. *The Banished Cavaliers*. The play is set during the interregnum before the restoration of Charles II in 1660. Royalists or cavaliers had joined Charles in exile. At the time, the word 'rover' could mean not only someone who wandered around the world, but also an inconstant lover or male flirt, and a sea-robber or pirate (Willmore has a ship at sea – see p. 244).

3. masqueraders ... Carnival time. The week before Lent in Italy and other Roman Catholic countries has often been spent in festivities, including dressing up in fantastic costumes and appearing incognito with a masked face. However, the masquerade had come to be a symbol of the age in England: see Wycherley, *The Gentle-man Dancing Master*, I.i, where Mrs Caution laments 'the fatal liberty of this masquerading age'.

4. *Rabel's Drops*. A patent medicine.

5. *cabal*. Faction.

6. *elves*. Malicious beings.

7. *Bating*. Except.

8. *lampoon*. Scurrilous satirical poem.

9. Behn did not claim *The Rover* until the third issue of the first edition in 1677.

10. *debauches*. Debauchees – people who give themselves up to sensual enjoyments.

11. *cits*. Ordinary citizens or shopkeepers.

12. *May-Day coaches*. On May Day it was customary to parade around Hyde Park.

13. *the Viceroy's son*. Naples was under the Spanish Crown continuously from 1503 until 1707.

14. *devote*. Nun.

15. *Siege of Pamplona*. The capital city of Navarre is in a strategic position near the Spanish border and has been besieged many times. The siege referred to probably occurred in 1653, shortly before *Thomaso* was written.

16. *jointure*. Estate settled on a wife to provide for widowhood.

17. *bags*. Wealth.

18. *Indian breeding*. American or West Indian upbringing.

19. *dog days*. The canicular or hottest days of the summer.

20. *Sancho the First*. Castile and Navarre both had kings of this name in the Middle Ages.

21. *... stretches itself ... snore or two*. The description is based on *Thomaso*, Part II, II.i, where Harrigo describes a form of matrimony to Serulina. Killigrew's description is more disgusting: '... yawns and sighs a belch or two, stales in your pot, farts as loud as a musket ...'.

22. *And this man ... lips*. *Thomaso*, Part II, II.i: his breath 'a stink compos'd of vile tobacco and dead wine, stuffed nose, rotten lungs, and hollow teeth, half whose number has been drawn with dry cheese, and tough lean beef; yet this man you must kiss; nay, you must kiss none but this, and muzzle through his beard to find his lips ...'.

23. *Hostel de Dieu*. Hospital run as a charity by a religious order.

24. *lazars*. Plague-stricken paupers.

25. *Marry ... marriage*. The servant Calis makes this speech in *Thomaso*, Part II, II.i.

26. *Don Indian ... Gambo*. Don Vincentio must have lived in an American or West Indian colony and made his money from the slave trade with Africa.

27. *grate*. Barred window of a convent.

28. *Shall I ... venture on me*. In *Thomaso*, Part II, II.i, Serulina says some words about her fitness for a convent. Instead of carnival gear she puts on Calis's old coat and veil as disguise for specific days rather than for general escape.

29. The first edition has 'whe' as an exclamation in the speech of Blunt, Frederick, Willmore and Hellena in masquerade. I have emended it to

'why' throughout, although it suggests a stronger tone than 'why' possesses.

30. *hogoes*. Strong flavours or relishes.

31. *Parliaments and Protectors ... forfeit my estate by cavaliering ... following the Court*. Royalists who fought for the king and followed the court into exile had their property confiscated by Cromwell's government.

32. *the prince*. Charles II.

33. *chapmen*. Merchants.

34. *habits*. Costume.

35. *horns*. The sign of a cuckolded husband.

36. *I like ... despised*. The play is set before the Restoration of Charles II; some of the Puritans would consider this an apt description of early post-Restoration society.

37. *bravoes*. Ruffians hired for protection or assault.

38. *Dutchman ... New Bridge*. In 1673 the Dutch lost Nieuwerbrug to the French in a humiliating defeat.

39. *cross their hands*. Pay them.

40. *parlous*. Shrewd.

41. *Jephtha's daughter*. Before sacrificing his only child in fulfilment of a vow, Jephtha allowed her two months to bewail her virginity among the mountains (Judges 11.37–39).

42. *took orders*. Entered a nunnery.

43. *Let ... that*. You can depend on her to do that.

44. *bellman*. Town crier.

45. *stock*. Money or capital.

46. *piece of eight*. Spanish dollar.

47. *honest*. Chaste.

48. *Paduana*. Woman from the Italian city of Padua.

49. *vizard*. Mask.

50. *buff*. Military coat made of strong leather. To go 'in buff' could also mean to go naked. An early eighteenth-century prompt copy (University of London) eliminates this word.

51. The first edition reads:

BELVILE What the devil's the matter with thee Ned? – Oh such a Mrs Fred! such a girl!

WILLMORE Ha! where, Fred! Ay, where! So fond, so amorous ...

52. *clap*. Gonorrhoea or syphilis.

53. *bottom*. Ship.

54. *cozened*. Cheated.

55. *errant*. Thoroughgoing.

56. *ycleped*. Called.

57. *bullies*. Ruffians.

58. *Essex calf*. Fool (particularly apt, as Blunt is from Essex).

59. *a thousand crowns a month*. In *Thomaso* the terms are more specific: the purchaser will have four days and nights a week.

60. *portion for the Infanta*. The Infanta Margarita, daughter of Philip IV of Spain, was married to the Emperor Leopold I of Austria in 1666. The *London Gazette* (21–24 May) has a report from Madrid of disputes which had occurred in the Council about such an expensive marriage. The English Ambassador, Sir Richard Fanshawe, wrote home that she had just left Madrid with 'a vast treasure in money, plate and jewels; so in that respect, will much enfeeble this summer's preparation against Portugal'. Her dowry and attendants occupied thirty galleys.

61. *anticly attired*. Dressed fantastically or grotesquely.

62. *Molo*. Mole; an extensive stone pier or breakwater.

63. *patacoon*. Spanish or Portuguese silver coin.

64. *Scene ii*. This scene follows II.iv of *Thomaso*, Part I, with much of Angellica's feminist protest at the double standard of honour omitted.

65. *Worcester*. The decisive defeat of the Royalists by Cromwell in 1651.

66. *pistole*. A name given to certain Spanish and French gold coins.

67. *black . . . sum it up*. Take your pencil and work out the calculation.

68. *the whole piece*. In *Thomaso* the maid says, 'We sell not this stuff by the yard; the whole piece, or nothing.'

69. *sell upon the Friday's Mart*. Auction at the market on Friday.

70. *Pray, tell me . . . as poor*. In *Thomaso* the emphasis at this point is not only on acquisitiveness, but also on the unjust double standard of honour which Hellena points to in *The Rover*.

71. *shameroon*. 'To sham' was late seventeenth-century slang for to cheat or deceive and '-aroon' seems to have been a derogatory colloquial suffix meaning 'fellow'.

72. *tatterdemalion*. A person wearing ragged clothes.

73. *picaroon*. A brigand or pirate.

74. *Loretto*. Shrine in the Ancona region of Italy; as a place of pilgrimage it would attract many beggars.

75. *the pip*. Applied humorously to slight diseases or depression.

76. *venture a cast*. Risk a throw of the dice.

77. *Does not . . . lovers*. *Thomaso*, Part II, III.ii: 'Do's not the little god appear upon my brow to distinguish me from the common crowd of lovers.'

78. *bona roba*. Courtesan; see *The English Rogue*, 4th Part (1671), pp. 37–9, where the terms are interchangeable.

79. *canary*. Sweet wine from the Canary Islands.

80. *hungry balderdash*. Unsatisfying and adulterated drink.

81. *All the honey . . . sting. Thomaso*, Part I, III.ii: 'All the honey of Marriage, but none of the sting.'

82. *sneak*. Skulk furtively.

83. *Capuchin*. Member of an order founded by Matteo di Bassi as an offshoot of the Franciscans; its rule was drawn up in 1529. It was called Capuchin because of the hooded habit worn.

84. *I am as . . . the inconstant*. In *Thomaso* the heroine Serulina does not mind physical inconstancy in a man, but insists 'a virgin once blown upon by the world, or touched in reputation, is for ever stained' (IV.ii).

85. *budget*. Bag.

86. *settlements*. Legal arrangements made on marriage guaranteeing a wife financial security.

87. *eighty-eight*. The great Armada of Spanish ships tried to invade England in 1588 and was defeated by the ships of Elizabeth I and by storms.

88. *shore*. Sewer.

89. *quean*. Harlot or strumpet.

90. *Prado*. A fashionable street. (Killigrew's *Thomaso* was set in Madrid.)

91. *cullies*. Dupes.

92. *disguised*. Drunk.

93. *why . . . spider*. This scene and Blunt's assault on Florinda in Act IV, scene iii are both based on Edwardo's encounter with Serulina in *Thomaso*, Part I, IV.ii: 'What do you do here alone else? in a garden at this hour, and your door set open, good spider, but to catch a passenger?' Aphra Behn has given the fool's episode to the hero.

94. *coil*. Fuss, noisy disturbance.

95. *pistole*. Edwardo offers 'a piece of eight' in *Thomaso*.

96. *chase-gun*. Gun positioned ahead or astern in a ship and used during pursuit.

97. *St Jago*. Santiago or St James, brother of St John the Evangelist; his cult was strong in Spain and Spanish colonies because of a tradition that he visited Spain.

98. *discounting*. Reducing.

99. *nicely punctual*. Scrupulously punctilious.

100. *mumping*. Sullen.

101. *dressed*. Ready.

102. *prater*. Chatterer.

103. *en passant*. The first edition reads 'e'n passant'.

104. *cogging*. Wheedling.

105. *motion*. Puppet.

106. In the first edition, this speech is given to Hellena.

107. *fresco*. In the fresh air.

108. *prize*. A ship which might be legally captured.

109. *morris dancer*. Blunt is wearing only his white linen shirt and drawers: Morris dancers throughout Europe traditionally wore white clothes.

110. *I shall . . . sex more*. A similar humiliation occurs in V.xi of *Thomaso*, Part I. The prompt copy of *The Rover* in the University of London Library marks out much of Blunt's misogyny.

111. *He*. The first edition has 'she'.

112. *damnable women*. Killigrew's Serulina in *Thomaso*, Part II, II.iv, says: 'Do not mistake me for one of those vile women.' Cf. Jonson's *Volpone*, III. vii, where the misogynist Corvino thinks up similar torment for Celia.

113. *cormorant*. A proverbially greedy bird.

114. *jack pudding*. Buffoon; cf. Wycherley, *The Gentle-man Dancing Master* (1672), 'he debases [mirth] as much as a jack pudding'.

115. *one at once*. One at a time.

116. *toledo*. Sword blade from Toledo, in Spain.

117. *traitor*. First edition reads 'taylor'.

118. *he'll*. First edition reads 'you'll'.

119. *My richest . . . value*. In *Thomaso*, Part I, II.iv, Angellica argues 'to afflict myself with the consideration of that which cannot be remedied is second folly; only (once a whore and ever) is the world adage; yet there may be degrees of all . . .'.

120. *[Offers . . . gold]*. At the end of *Thomaso*, Part II, Thomaso also resolves to return Angellica's money, but there she and another whore decide to change country, if not their lives. Thomaso concludes that there is no anger but only kindness felt for her.

121. *tramontana*. From beyond the Alps; foreign or barbarian.

122. *flying . . . lure*. One who can be trusted to remain faithful as long as she is satisfied. (In the first edition 'flying, one' reads 'flying on'.)

123. *Hymen*. God of marriage in Greek and Roman mythology.

124. *bug*. Terrifying.

125. *consort*. Company, usually of musicians.

126. *upse*. In the gipsy manner.

127. *inkle*. Linen thread and the tape made from it.

128. *caudle*. A warm drink made from gruel and wine or ale, with sugar and spices. It was given to the sick from at least the thirteenth century until the nineteenth. It was especially drunk by women after childbirth and by their visitors.

129. *band*. Collar.

130. *bag of bays*. Bag of seasoning used in cooking.

131. en cavalier. First edition reads 'e'n cavalier'.

132. *doxy*. Prostitute.

133. *a cast of his office*. An example of his work (i.e. marry them).

134. *conventicling*. A pun; a conventicle was a Dissenting meeting.

135. *That mutinous tribe*. Dissenters.

136. *maggot*. Whimsical fancy.

137. *canting*. Hypocritical use of language. 'In the seventeenth century applied in ridicule to the preaching of Presbyterians and Puritans' (*O.E.D.*).

138. *Blackfriars*. The Blackfriars Theatre was used by the King's Men from 1608 until the closing of the theatres in 1642. An enclosed or 'private' theatre, in which the audience were all seated, the prices were higher than in the open-air 'public' theatres. Scenery and music were quite elaborate.

139. *bamboo*. A cane.

140. *Nokes . . . Lee*. The best-known comedians of the day, James Nokes and Anthony Lee (or Leigh), teamed up in the 1670s and seem to have been highly skilled as a comic double act; prologues and epilogues of the period make frequent reference to or use of them. Both were with the Duke's Men and appeared in a number of Behn's plays; they acted together in *The Feign'd Curtizans*, in which the Epilogue refers to their skilful representation of 'fops of all sorts'. In *Sir Patient Fancy*, Nokes played Sir Credulous Easy and Leigh the title role. The 'Mrs Leigh' who played Moretta in *The Rover* was probably his wife. See Colley Cibber, *Apology* (1740) for accounts of both actors.

141. *stolen object*. As the many borrowings from *Thomaso* indicate, Behn is not being entirely frank here.

142. *their dominion*. In some copies of the second issue and in all subsequent editions the words 'especially of our sex' follow here, indicating a female author.

143. *the famous Virgil*. Virgil is supposed to have written some lines which were at first anonymous; when these were claimed by an inferior poet he produced some more, which included the final quotation in this postscript.

THE WIDOW RANTER

1. *The Widow Ranter* was printed posthumously and prepared for publication by G. J., who complained that in the first performance 'a

whole scene of the Virginian Court of Judicature' and 'the appearance of the ghost of the Indian King' were omitted; the latter scene is not in the text he printed, which is in a rough state with many authorial and compositorial errors, presumably because it was printed without Behn's supervision. Some of these errors were corrected in the collected edition of 1702. The editor, G. J., dedicated the play to Madam Welldon, to whom he claims Behn wanted to dedicate some of her works. In the dedication G. J. admits the play was not successfully staged: 'Had our Author been alive she would have committed to the flames rather than have suffered it to have been acted with such omissions as was made.'

The Widow Ranter was one of the few of Behn's plays not to be clearly based on a previous one, although there are echoes; for example, the Widow's house on a feast-day has something of the anarchic effect of Ursula the pig-woman's roast-pork booth in Ben Jonson's *Bartholomew Fair* (performed 1614, printed 1631), and the Widow's transvestite soldiering may be compared with that in *The Roaring Girl* by Middleton and Dekker (printed 1611) or in Shadwell's *The Woman Captain* (1680). The heroic tragedy of Bacon looks back to the plays of the late 1670s, such as Nathaniel Lee's *The Rival Queens* (1677), which seem disillusioned with the heroic politics portrayed in Restoration plays of the 1660s and early 1670s and differ greatly from the tragedies popular in the 1690s. Southerne used part of *The Widow Ranter* as the basis of his play *Oroonoko*.

The historical Nathaniel Bacon was an English settler of good family who, having lost money in England, went to Virginia in 1674 to recoup his fortune. In 1676 he rebelled against Sir William Berkeley, who had been Governor of Virginia since 1641. Although Bacon seems to have been supporting the grievances of smaller settlers against the colonial government and the cavalier monopoly of land, and although he used the Puritan rhetoric of levelling and 'the people' in his Manifesto, he had a few of the aristocratic touches Behn gives him. He called rulers of the colony 'spongers' on the public treasury and accused them of being of low extraction and vile education. In addition, he was said to be a witty and extravagant man.

Bacon believed that the Susquehanna Indians should never have been allowed to purchase firearms, and when Governor Berkeley refused to aid him in his efforts against Indian raiders he took matters into his own hands and organized a force to repel them. Having been asked to disband this force, he soon found himself at odds with the vindictive Governor, who tried to compel him to surrender. With popular support Bacon seized Jamestown and defied Berkeley, who recaptured the town only after Bacon's sudden death and with the help of forces from other states.

It is unclear where Aphra Behn obtained information on Bacon's rebellion (which, according to the 'order of Council' quoted by Parson Dunce in Act III, scene ii, she dates as 1670). Information is given in several contemporary accounts: *Strange News from Virginia: Being a full and true Account of the Life and Death of Nathaniel Bacon, Esquire . . .* and *More News from Virginia . . .*; both appeared in 1677. In 1804 the *Richmond Enquirer* published 'An account of our late troubles in Virginia; written in 1676 by Mrs An. Cotton of Q. Creeke', together with another manuscript account.

The Ranters were a sect in the interregnum described by Christopher Hill as anarchic and antinomian; they had a short prominence in 1648–50. Historians such as J. C. Davis (*Fear, Myth and History: Ranters and the Historians*, Cambridge University Press, 1986) believe they are largely a myth of later historians and not the counter-culture religious movement Hill takes them to be. Whatever the historical case, much was made in contemporary pamphlets of the Ranters' supposed sexual promiscuity and outrageous behaviour; they were also depicted as supporters of the abolished Stuart monarchy. In *A New Dictionary of the Canting Crew* (*c.* 1690) a Ranter is described as either an extravagant, unthrifty and lewd spark or a lewd woman and a whore, in addition to the definition of a member of a sect.

2. The 1690 first edition was published with a prologue by John Dryden, earlier used for Shadwell's *A True Widow*, and an epilogue previously printed in *Covent Garden Drollery* in 1672. Dryden wrote a prologue and epilogue especially for *The Widow Ranter* which were printed separately in 1689. These are reproduced here.

3. *Covent-Garden.* Though fashionable, Covent Garden and its Piazza adjoined a disreputable area and became a rendezvous for prostitutes and their clients. There was already an unlicensed market there in Aphra Behn's time.

4. *vizard-masks.* Though first worn by fashionable ladies, masks were soon adopted by prostitutes.

5. *privateers.* Armed private vessels, licensed to attack and capture ships of hostile nations.

6. *clap . . . commissions.* Reference to captured English sailors being forced to fight for the French. 'Clap' also meant gonorrhoea and syphilis.

7. *sparks.* Young men who affected elegance.

8. *the game.* Prostitutes.

9. *bug.* Terrifying.

10. *savourly.* With enjoyment.

11. *mundungus.* 'Stinking tobacco' (Johnson).

12. *Iniskelling.* In August 1689 a comparatively small number of men from Enniskillen, loyal to the regime of William and Mary, managed to defeat a Jacobite force.

13. *port-mantle.* A bag or case for travellers.

14. *James-Town.* On the James River, the town was settled in 1607 and was the capital of Virginia at the time of Bacon's revolt.

15. *woundly.* Extremely.

16. *cogue.* Small wooden cup.

17. *Groom-Porter.* Official of the royal household who regulated gaming.

18. *sharping.* Cheating.

19. *bully.* Good friend, 'mate'.

20. *cully.* Companion.

21. *flats and bars.* Kinds of dice which fall unfairly when thrown.

22. *lay.* Wager or stake.

23. *character.* Handwriting.

24. *bought from the ship.* Many immigrants had the cost of their voyage paid on arrival by someone who needed a servant, for whom they would then work without wages until they had 'paid back' this cost. The very poor and convicts were often auctioned to the highest bidder. A number of such 'indentured' servants eventually prospered.

25. *extravagancy.* Original or outrageous behaviour.

26. *new governor.* When Sir William Berkeley was recalled in 1677, the new governor, Lord Culpeper, ruled through deputies except for one brief period; he was then ordered to go back to Virginia and spent a year there before being removed from the post in 1683.

27. *ruled . . . council.* The colony of Virginia followed English models for its institutions. The executive was vested in a governor appointed by the crown and assisted by a council and an assembly of burgesses. The councillors, who held many of the most lucrative offices, were appointed by the governor; the burgesses were elected by freeholders.

28. *transported criminals.* Men and women legally condemned to exile in a colony.

29. *places of authority.* The English were outraged at the upstart nature of men who sat in the administrative bodies of Virginia (the Council and House of Burgesses) and at the colonial confounding of ranks. As early as 1618 one observer writes, 'our cowkeepers here of James citty on Sundays goes accoutered all in fresh flaming silke and a wife of one that in England had professed the black art not of a scholler but of a collier in Croyden weares her rough bever hatt with a faire perle hatband, and a silken suite . . .'.

30. *Alexander . . . Romulus.* The exploits, whether historical or mythical,

of Alexander in conquering lands from the Mediterranean to India, and of Romulus in founding Rome, were well known to seventeenth-century readers from North's translation of Plutarch's *Lives of the Noble Grecians and Romans* (1597).

31. *Madam* [Mistress, Mrs]. Used as a matter of courtesy to a woman of some social standing, whether married or not. Although Virginians traditionally see themselves as descendants of cavaliers, the bulk of the early settlers, who came in the seventeenth century, were either felons and indentured servants or from the middling and lower classes. They brought ideas of social rank from England.

32. *Nants*. Brandy from the town of Nantes.

33. *pipes and smoke*. Tobacco was introduced into England in the late sixteenth century, was used copiously from at least 1603, and was quickly associated with high living. Originally obtained through the Spanish, after 1610–11 it came primarily from Virginia where it was the major crop of the colonists.

34. *sheer*. Undiluted.

35. *paulter*. Sham.

36. *hogherds*. Swineherds, pigmen.

37. *farrier*. Someone who doctors and shoes horses.

38. *breaking*. Going bankrupt.

39. *life-guard man*. Soldier in the sovereign's bodyguard.

40. *deputation*. Document appointing him as a minister of religion.

41. *fain to keep an ordinary*. Glad to run a tavern.

42. *trusting . . . broke*. Oliver Cromwell's funeral in 1658 was magnificent, but many of the bills for it remained unpaid.

43. *excise-man . . . king's money*. Customs officer who embezzled the payments of customs duty which should have gone to the Royal Exchequer.

44. *groat*. Coin worth four pence.

45. Scandalum Magnatum. 'The utterance or publication of a malicious report against any person holding a position of dignity' (*O.E.D.*).

46. *Newgate*. The principal criminal prison in London.

47. *turned evidence*. Became an informer.

48. *bear the bob*. Sing the chorus.

49. *Justice . . . Corum* (for 'quorum'). Justice of the Peace of especial learning or ability.

50. *club*. Share.

51. *Covent-Garden bully*. See note 3 above.

52. *broken citizen turned factor*. Middle-class person who has gone bankrupt and turned to peddling the goods of others.

53. *huffed*. Bullied.

54. *make*. The first edition reads 'have'.

55. *thrummed*. Torn or cut into rags.

56. *Hector*. The heroic Trojan warrior whose exploits and tragic death had been described by Homer and Virgil was by now a familiar name to Englishmen with no classical knowledge; they associated him with strength in a fight.

57. *dispatched*. Killed.

58. *sevana* (savannah). A grassy plain; this is an example of Behn's use of words specifically associated with America. See *Oroonoko*.

59. *fresco*. The fresh air.

60. *Bridewell*. House of correction for vagabonds and prostitutes.

61. *shoving the tumbler*. Being tied to the tail of a cart and whipped.

62. *lifting or filing the cly*. Stealing or picking pockets.

63. *maukish*. Off-colour.

64. *regalio*. 'Choice or elegant repast' (*O.E.D.*).

65. *stock-fish*. Dried cod.

66. *points*. Twisted tags for fastening garments, used instead of buttons.

67. *chafferer*. Dealer.

68. In this scene, and at various other points in the play, the effect is heightened by some of the characters, particularly Bacon, speaking in language which modulates in and out of blank verse, though never set out as such. We cannot know what Aphra Behn's intentions were, as she did not live to see the play through the press. In Southerne's *Oroonoko* the hero talks in blank verse although the other characters do not.

69. *antics*. Fantastic and grotesque dances.

70. *considering caps*. 'To put on a considering cap' – to think something over.

71. *treater*. Entertainer, hostess.

72. *sharper*. Swindler.

73. *salt*. Assault, as in 'assault and battery' – an attack on somebody with blows.

74. *mundungus*. See note 11 above.

75. *Court of Aldermen*. In London this consisted of the representatives of the different wards; as in other English cities, the position of alderman has always been a prestigious one, often held by successful and established businessmen.

76. *mor-blew, mor-dee*. 'Morbleu, mordieu' – French oaths.

77. *the Louvre . . . Whitehall*. The palaces, respectively, of the French and English Kings.

78. billets-doux. Love letters.

79. *troopers.* Soldiers in a troop of cavalry.

80. *Ludgate.* A London street which was then occupied by the premises of tradesmen and merchants.

81. *kidnapper.* Kidnap – 'Originally, to steal or carry off (children or others) in order to provide servants or labourers for the American plantations' (*O.E.D.*).

82. *poltroon.* Coward or rascal.

83. *maw.* Stomach.

84. *mobile.* Mob, rabble.

85. *rake-hells.* Scoundrels.

86. *bob.* A blow or rap with the fist.

87. *barbicu.* To barbecue, or grill over a fire; a very early example of the use of this American word.

88. *roistering hector.* Blustering or boisterous 'hector', a name frequently given in the second half of the seventeenth century to 'a set of disorderly young men who infested the streets of London' (*O.E.D.*); they were rowdies who smashed windows and were quick to draw their swords in a fight.

89. *bull of Bashan.* See Psalm 22:12, 'strong bulls of Bashan have compassed me round'. Bulls of Bashan were taken as symbolic of cruelty and oppression.

90. *De Wit.* Johan de Witt (1625–72), a great Dutch statesman. Supporting a republic in opposition to the House of Orange, he raised the United Provinces to naval and commercial power and was popular with the masses until Louis XIV invaded the country, when he and his brother Cornelius were seized and torn to pieces.

91. *rods in piss.* 'Punishments in store' (*O.E.D.*).

92. *Quorum.* See note 49 above.

93. *writ of ease.* 'A certificate of discharge from employment' (*O.E.D.*).

94. *tally . . . stick.* The amount of a debt was marked by notches on a stick; the stick was then split down the middle, so that each party had legal proof of the transaction.

95. *Dalton's* Country Justice. Michael Dalton, *The Countrey Iustice, Contteyning the practise of the Iustices of the Peace out of their Sessions. Gathered for the better helpe of such Iustices of Peace as haue not beene much conuersant in the studie of the lawes of this realme* (London, 1618). New editions with additional material appeared throughout the seventeenth century. The first edition of *The Rover* contains this advertisement, among others, for 'Some books printed this year': 'The *Country Justice*, containing the practice of the Justices of the Peace, in and out of their Sessions, with an abridgement of all Statutes relating thereunto to this present year 1677. By Michael Dalton Esq.; Fol. price bound 12s.'

96. *Board.* Council-table.

97. *docket.* 'A list of causes for trial, or of names of persons having causes pending' (*O.E.D.*).

98. *affidavit viva voce.* An affidavit is a written statement, confirmed by oath, to be used as judicial proof. The witnesses have therefore made their written statements by word of mouth (*via voce*).

99. *cagg.* Keg or small barrel.

100. *jade.* First edition reads 'jude'.

101. Scandalum Magnatum. See note 45 above.

102. *ordinary.* Tavern.

103. se defendendo. In self-defence.

104. *peruke.* Wig.

105. *buff.* Military coat made of buff leather.

106. *termagant.* A violent and overbearing person (originally a supposed pagan god).

107. *to cock.* To behave in a boastful and swaggering way.

108. *brigantine . . . shallop.* Both were types of boat which could be used for passage between larger vessels and the shore.

109. *speaks like a Gorgon.* The three loathsome Gorgons of Greek mythology had no need to speak, as their piercing gaze turned anyone who looked at them to stone.

110. *rugged.* Shaggy or rough-coated. The first edition reads 'rugid'.

111. *the god of our Quiocto.* Quiocos were the second tier in a hierarchy of Indian deities; they could bring harm and had to be placated by gifts. Wooden images of them were kept in temples called 'quiocosan'.

112. *fell.* Fierce.

113. *Teroomians.* No evidence has yet been found to connect this and most of the other 'Indian' words in the play to any Amerindian language.

114. *starter.* Deserter.

115. *breathed.* Lanced, so as to let blood.

116. *like Caesar . . . weep.* According to Plutarch, when Julius Caesar was presented with the head of the defeated Pompey, he turned his head aside and wept.

117. *cadees.* Gentlemen who enlisted without a commission in order to learn the profession and earn promotion (the same word as 'cadet'; *O.E.D.* quotes this play as an example).

118. *Benefit of the Clergy.* Exemption of those in holy orders from the jurisdiction of secular courts, for many years extended to all who proved they could read, was not entirely abolished until the early nineteenth century.

119. *Shaw.* Dismissive exclamation (cf. 'pshaw').

120. *in a hempen cravat-string.* With a rope round his neck.

121. *lay him on.* Thrash him.

122. *hawks' meat.* Easy prey.

123. *Pauwmungian.* Probably a reference to the queen of the Pamunkey Indians, who ruled from 1656 for about thirty years. Their territory was the Virginia coastal plain.

124. *Hannibal.* Hannibal, the great Carthaginian general, took his own life rather than fall into the hands of the Romans.

125. *Roman Cassius.* The forces of Brutus and Cassius fought those of Mark Antony and Octavius Caesar at Philippi in 42 B.C. in the struggle for power after the assassination of Julius Caesar. Cassius killed himself during the battle, probably under the mistaken impression that they had already lost. Not only the action, but the language is here reminiscent of Shakespeare's *Julius Caesar*, Act V, Scene iii.

126. Act V has been much mutilated. There are remnants of a scene here: the 1690 text reads:

. . . in agreement.

DARING You shall be obliged – [*Exeunt* Daring, Dance, Dullman *and* Timorous, *as* Fearless *goes out, a Soldier meets him.*

SOLDIER What does your Honour intend to do with Whimsey and Whiff, who are condemned by a Council of War?

[*Enter* Daring, Dullman, Timorous, Fearless *and Officers.*

127. *clouts.* Clothes.

128. *spark it.* Show off.

129. *farce.* A pun; the word could also mean 'stuffing'.

130. *green-sickness.* An anaemic disease often believed to affect adolescent girls; chlorosis.

131. *crumped.* Curved.

132. *tobacco pipes.* Tobacco was once thought to be medicinal. (Pepys wrote in his diary for 29 June 1661, 'Mr Chetwind, by chawing of tobacco, is become very fat and lusty, whereas he was consumptive.')

133. *infernal judges.* In Greek mythology, Minos and Rhadamanthys were believed to sit in judgment over spirits entering the Underworld.

POEMS

'LOVE ARMED'

1. 'Love Armed' first appeared as 'Love in fantastic triumph sat' in *Abdelazer* (1677). It was reprinted in *Poems on Several Occasions* in 1684; the 1684 version is reprinted here.

2. *Love . . . sat.* Cf. the masque by Ben Jonson and Inigo Jones, performed in 1630: *Love's Triumph through Callipolis.*

Epilogue to *Sir Patient Fancy*

1. This formed the Epilogue to Behn's comedy *Sir Patient Fancy*, published in 1678.
2. *Mrs Gwin.* Not Nell Gwyn, who had left the stage by this time.
3. *vizard mask.* Though first worn by fashionable ladies, masks were soon adopted by prostitutes.
4. *jilts.* The first edition reads 'gilts'.
5. *Method, and rule.* The English playwrights were often contemptuous of rules in drama, which were associated with French authors.

'The Disappointment'

1. The immediate source of this poem is the French 'Sur une Impuissance' in *Recueil de diverses poesies choisies* (1661), which appeared in English translation as 'The Lost Opportunity Recovered' in *Wit and Drollery*. *Jovial Poems* (1682). The ancestor is Ovid's poem on the subject in *Amores*, Book III.7; several of Behn's contemporaries took this as their model, for example the Earl of Rochester, whose 'Imperfect Enjoyment' was published in his *Poems on Several Occasions* in 1680. Behn's poem was first printed in the same volume and was for a long time thought to be by Rochester (see David M. Vieth, *Attributions in Restoration Poetry*, Yale University Press, 1963); it was reprinted with variations in Behn's *Poems on Several Occasions* in 1684, which has provided the copy text. The poems by Ovid and Rochester and 'The Lost Opportunity Recovered' are told rather more from the male point of view than Behn's and are more comforting to the unperforming man. Ovid ends his poem with the disappointed girl pretending to maids that something has occurred between her and the man, and 'The Lost Opportunity Recovered', which is more than twice as long as Behn's poem, allows the man to succeed spectacularly on subsequent occasions. The male texts include the man's railing against his penis, which Behn omits. In *Familiar Letters of Love and Gallantry* (1718), 'The Disappointment' (here called 'An Imperfect Enjoyment') is printed with a letter allegedly by Behn to Hoyle about his 'too close familiarity' with a young man.
2. *Surprised . . . longer.* Cf. 'The Lost Opportunity Recovered':

> It chanced Lysander, that unhappy man,
> Led to it by the rashness of his love
> Assaulted the fair Cloris, who does prove
> Uneth to resist, do what she can.

NOTES TO PAGES 331–335

3. *draw him*. The 1684 version reads 'draw them'.

4. *in vain*. The 1680 version reads 'too late'.

5. *breathing faintly*. The 1680 version reads 'whispering softly'.

6. *She ... do*. Cf. 'The Lost Opportunity Recovered': 'I shall call out – don't urge me to a noise . . .'.

7. *mouth*. The 1680 version reads 'lips'.

8. *desire*. The 1680 version reads 'desires'.

9. *Each ... alarms*. Cf. 'The Lost Opportunity Recovered': 'He then a lower hidden place alarms.'

10. *swelling*. The 1680 version reads 'melting'.

11. *calmed*. The 1680 version reads 'tamed'.

12. *That fountain ... repose*. The 1680 version reads:

> That living fountain from whose trills,
> The melted soul, in liquid drops distills!

13. *Her ... light*. The 1680 version reads: 'Her eyes appeared like humid light.'

14. *Cloris ... goes*. Cf. 'The Lost Opportunity Recovered':

> Half living and half dead with the surprise,
> She suddenly did counterfeit a swoon.

15. *While*. The 1680 version reads 'Whilst'.

16. *garments*. The 1680 version reads 'garment'.

17. *opened*. The 1680 version reads 'open'.

18. *envious gods conspire*. The 1684 version reads 'envying god conspires'.

19. *Now ... shame*. Cf. Rochester's 'The Imperfect Enjoyment':

> Eager desires, confound my first intent,
> Succeeding shame, does more success prevent,
> And rage, at last, confirms me impotent.

20. *Priapas*. The god of fertility, whose symbol was the phallus.

21. *hinder*. The 1680 version reads 'kinder'.

22. *Daphne ... god*. The nymph Daphne, who (rather differently from Cloris) fled from the unwanted love of the god Apollo, and was turned into a laurel.

23. *of fair*. The 1684 version reads 'if fair'.

24. *So Venus ... plain*. Venus's beloved Adonis received a mortal wound from a wild boar when hunting; Venus rushed to his aid.

25. *or*. The 1680 version reads 'and'.

26. *shepherdess's charms*. In 'The Lost Opportunity Recovered' the lover likewise blames the lady for his initial lack of performance.

379

'To Mr Creech . . . on his Excellent Translation of Lucretius'

1. This was first published as a commendatory poem in the second edition of *T. Lucretius Caro . . . De natura rerum* (Oxford, 1683). It was dated 25 January 1682 and appeared among other commendatory poems by Waller, Evelyn, Otway, Tate and Duke. It was reprinted in *Poems on Several Occasions* in 1684, the version which is reprinted here.

Thomas Creech (1659–1700), to whom Behn also wrote 'A Letter to Mr Creech at Oxford, Written in the last great Frost', was a fellow of All Souls, Oxford in 1683, then headmaster of Sherborne School. He became so famous for his translations of Lucretius, Ovid, Plutarch and other classical writers that the author of *A Comparison between the Two Stages* (1702) could declare that Dryden was jealous of his reputation. Suffering from melancholy, and reputedly love, he hanged himself in 1700. It was said to be an act in sympathy with Lucretius, who was believed to have committed suicide.

Lucretius (c. 94–55 B.C.) was a Roman poet and philosopher conflating the philosophies of Epicurus and Empedocles and the theory of atoms from Democritus. He suggested that there was no life after death and that happiness should be gained on earth, although in *De natura rerum* he condemns atheists. The work was much criticized by Christians. Jerome claimed that Lucretius was poisoned by a love-potion, wrote the poem in lucid intervals of the resulting insanity and finally committed suicide, and this was widely believed. In fact, almost nothing is known about his life. His emphasis on the desirability of pleasure in this world came to represent the libertine philosophy of Restoration wits.

Aphra Behn seems to have provided one version of this poem for Creech and another for use in *Poems on Several Occasions*, or Creech may have changed it because of fear of its effect. In his own defensive dedication to the 1683 (second) edition in which Behn's poem first appeared, he worried about the 'venomed pill' of Lucretius and tried to separate himself from the philosophy he was translating.

2. *Whilst*. The 1682 version reads 'While'.
3. *palled*. Satiated.
4. *my birth, my education*. The 1682 version reads 'my sex and education'.
5. *verse*. The 1682 version reads 'Muse'.
6. *Beyond . . . oracles*. The 1682 version reads: 'As strong as Faith's resistless oracles.'
7. *despairing*. The 1682 version reads 'religious'.
8. *last shift*. The 1682 version reads 'secure retreat'.

9. *Wadham*. Wadham College, Oxford, from which Creech obtained his M.A. in 1683, was associated with the Royal Society whose members had met there. They included Thomas Sprat, Christopher Wren and Ralph Bathurst. The Earl of Rochester was a student from January 1660 to September 1661.

10. *by dull*. The 1682 version reads 'or by'.

11. *Thirsis*. Thomas Sprat (1635–1713), Dean of Westminster and Bishop of Rochester; he was known as a wit, preacher and man of letters. He was a student at Wadham from 1651 to 1654 and held a fellowship from 1657 to 1670. In 1667 he published his *History of the Royal Society*, of which he was a founder member. In 1659 he wrote *The Plague of Athens* in the style of the poet Abraham Cowley, an account of whose life he also composed. Chaplain to Charles II, Sprat was loyal and in December 1680 accused Parliament of being unfaithful to the King.

12. *Strephon*. John Wilmot, Earl of Rochester (1647–1680), glamorous court wit and poet, who according to Samuel Johnson 'blazed out his youth and health in lavish voluptuousness'. He went to Oxford at the age of twelve and 'grew debauched' there. He took his degree at Wadham in 1661.

13. *flag*. Droop.

14. *and the*. The 1682 version reads 'gay and'.

15. *sacred*. The 1682 version reads 'happy'.

16. *every bark ... dressed*. 'Every tree trunk is decorated with your couplets' (distichs).

17. *And*. The 1682 version reads 'Whilst'.

18. *kind*. The 1682 version reads 'low'.

19. *their*. The 1682 version reads 'thy'.

20. *sacred*. Omitted in the 1682 version.

21. As is clear from his suicide, Creech did not have the happy future Aphra Behn expected.

'A LETTER TO MR CREECH AT OXFORD'

1. The work is printed in *Miscellany* (1685) edited by Aphra Behn. In this she includes other verse letters in the Horatian mode, such as 'A Letter from one in the University to his Friend in the Country', but they are far more formal than this comic burlesque one, which resembles in style Samuel Butler's *Hudibras*, the three parts of which appeared at intervals between 1662 and 1680.

For Thomas Creech (1659–1700), see note 1 on 'To Mr Creech ... on his Excellent Translation of Lucretius'.

According to Narcissus Luttrell, the frost of 1683–4 started about 15 December and lasted until 5 February. Coaches drove on the frozen Thames, oxen were roasted and booths and printing-houses were set up.

2. *Tonson's*. The bookseller Jacob Tonson (*c.* 1656–1736), publisher of several of Behn's works, including *The Feigned Courtesans* (1679), *The Rover*, Part II (1681) and *Poems on Several Occasions* (1684). Kathleen M. Lynch, in *Jacob Tonson, Kit-Cat Publisher*, says that Tonson told his nephew that he had anonymously included in the latter a poem he had written himself, 'To the Lovely Witty Astraea, on her Excellent Poems'. He had his shop at the Judge's Head in Chancery Lane; towards the end of the century he seems to have taken over his brother's press near Gray's Inn as well. The route from Whitehall appears to be through Charing Cross to the Temple and Chancery Lane.

3. *shie wine*. Sherry.

4. *Bays*. A reference to the royalist poet John Dryden. He is satirized as 'Bayes', the laureate author of a heroic tragedy, in *The Rehearsal*, attributed to Buckingham and printed in 1672. There may also be a reference to 'A Sermon of the Poets' (*c.* 1676) attributed to Rochester and Buckingham, in which the poets, including Aphra Behn, compete in 'hopes of bays'. Behn is gently dismissed with the judgment that she should have presented herself 'a dozen years since'.

5. *White-Hall*. The palace of Whitehall, to which Aphra Behn had apparently gone to obtain money from Charles II for her propagandist services to the royalist Tory party. The palace had been built by Cardinal Wolsey and had been the principal residence of the sovereign since the time of Henry VIII. It was said in 1665 to contain over 2,000 rooms. It was mainly destroyed by fire in 1697–8.

6. *Temple*. A series of buildings on Fleet Street once owned by the Templars; they were taken over by the lawyers' societies of the Inner and Middle Temple, two of the four Inns of Court.

7. *simple*. Foolish behaviour.

8. *sign of whore called Scarlet*. The Pope's Head, a large tavern in Chancery Lane. Protestants identified the whore in Revelation 17 with the Roman Catholic Church.

9. *pilgarlic*. A bald head likened to a peeled head of garlic. In the seventeenth century the term was simply used contemptuously or in mock pity.

10. *H—le*. Probably John Hoyle, a lawyer of Gray's Inn with whom Aphra Behn was reputed to have been involved for several years and who is referred to in many of her poems of the early 1680s. (See also *Letters to a Gentleman*.)

11. For Lucretius, see note 1 on 'To Mr Creech ... on his Excellent Translation of Lucretius'.

12. *saucy Whig ... Plot.* Possibly a reference to the Whig disappointment at the discovery of the Rye-House Plot in 1683 which was supposed to have been a plan to kill Charles and James on their way from Newmarket to London.

13. *Oxford Member ... Rowley.* Sir Walter Scott recounts an anecdote which derives this nickname for Charles II from that of a pet goat kept in the Privy-garden. Rowley the goat was 'a ... lecherous devil ... good-humoured and familiar; and so they applied this name to Charles' (*Personal History of Charles II*, 1846). 'Rowley' is also said to be the name of a stallion in the royal stud. In March 1681 Charles called and dismissed a parliament at Oxford to avoid the Whig faction, strong in the City of London.

14. *Perkin ... James the second.* Perkin Warbeck had made an attempt to gain the throne in 1498, claiming that he was the younger of the two sons of Edward IV. 'Prince Perkin' was a nickname for Charles II's illegitimate son James, Duke of Monmouth, who claimed that the king had married his mother; this would have meant that Monmouth, rather than his uncle the Duke of York, would have become James II.

15. *Wapping.* This hamlet near the Tower was almost entirely inhabited by rough seamen. At the time of the Popish Plot crisis, Shaftesbury was alleged to have stirred up a rabble, including a mob of 'Wapping boys', in order to place Monmouth on the throne.

16. *his vigour cheated.* The theme of premature ejaculation is a common one in Behn; cf. 'The Disappointment' and the first part of *Love Letters between a Nobleman and his Sister*.

17. *Lazarello. The Pleasant History of Lazarillo de Tormes* (1586 and subsequent reprints): in Part II by Juan de Luna (Chapters III–V) Lazarillo recounts how, shipwrecked, he is drawn up in the nets of some fishermen along with their catch. Taking him at first for a sea-monster with commercial potential, the men realize the truth but are unwilling to forgo any profit; Lazarillo is forcibly disguised with seaweed and a tunny-fish tail, tied into a tank of water and taken around on a cart for public exhibition.

18. *Twelfth Night ... cake.* On Twelfth Night (6 January) a cake was served with a bean and a pea hidden inside. It was cut so that a man got the bean and a woman the pea and they had to be King and Queen for the evening. Pepys spent the large sum of one pound on ingredients for his Twelfth Night cake in 1668. It might have been 'lamentable' because the festival ended the time of feasting.

'ON HER LOVING TWO EQUALLY'

1. 'On her Loving Two Equally' first appeared as 'How Strangely does my Passion grow' in *The False Count* (1682). It was reprinted in *Poems on Several Occasions* in 1684, the version used here.
2. *Captain Pack.* Simon Pack (1654–1701), amateur musician and eventually a lieutenant-colonel, was well known as a composer of songs for plays. He wrote the tune for a song in Behn's *Rover* and others for plays by Dryden, D'Urfey, Otway and Southerne. See *Choice Ayres and Songs* (1679–84) and *The Theater of Music* (Books I and II, 1685).

'TO THE FAIR CLARINDA'

1. 'To the fair Clarinda' first appeared in 1688 in *A Miscellany of New Poems by Several Hands* (published with *Lycidus*).
2. *... fragrant leaves.* Cf. Stanza XI of 'The Disappointment'.
3. *Hermes, Aphrodite.* The god and goddess had a son called Hermaphroditus. When he refused to return the love of the nymph Salmacis, she prayed that they might be joined for ever and they were united in the form of a being of both sexes. The hermaphrodite was by no means always considered as a freak; it could be taken as a symbol of the creative union of opposites and was an important image in alchemy and mystical philosophies. (See also Spenser, *The Faerie Queene* (1590), III.xii.46.)

'ON DESIRE'

1. 'On Desire' was first published in the miscellany *Lycidus, or the Lover in Fashion* (1688). It was reprinted with variations, anonymously, in *Poems on Affairs of State* (1697).
2. *propension.* 'Favourable inclination' (O.E.D.).
3. *calenture.* A burning passion or a fever.
4. *So Helen ... bed.* Theseus, King of Athens, abducted the child Helen, daughter of Zeus and Leda, but she was returned unviolated to her family. She was later seduced by Paris, son of the King of Troy, when she was the wife of the Greek Menelaus.

'A PINDARIC POEM TO THE REVEREND DOCTOR BURNET'

1. 'A Pindaric Poem to the Reverend Doctor Burnet' was published in broadsheet in March 1689, the year of Behn's death.
   Gilbert Burnet (1643–1715) was a historian, clergyman and politician, familiar with Charles II and James until 1684 when he fell out of favour,

left England and became a keen supporter of William and Mary, whom he accompanied to England in 1688. He became Bishop of Salisbury in 1689. He was the author of numerous pamphlets and books including a *History of My Own Times* (1724-34) and an account of the Thirty-Nine Articles of the Church of England. Burnet appears to have invited Aphra Behn to write a poem on William of Orange despite her known loyalty to the ousted King, James II. The full title of her poem is 'A Pindaric Poem to the Reverend Doctor Burnet, on the Honour he did me of Enquiring after me and my Muse'.

2. *old Rome's candidates.* In the days of the Roman republic, candidates for consulship were proposed by the Senate and voted for by the people; in later times the Emperors chose Consuls; the Emperors (sometimes referred to as 'Caesars') were themselves theoretically chosen by senatorial votes.

3. *But yet ... given.* In a correspondence with Anne Wharton, with whom Behn had had a poetic exchange, Burnet had described Behn as an 'abominably vile' woman who mocked religion and virtue in an 'odious and obscene' manner. (See J. Granger, *Letters*, ed. Malcolm (1805).)

4. *... Kings.* Although Behn claims a low place on the poetic mount of Parnassus unlike the heroic poet Abraham Cowley, she had not only versified a long Latin poem by Cowley, but had also written many political poems on the Kings Charles and James.

5. *But since ... wrought.* Just as the sovereign's head stamped on a coin gives it value, whatever metal it is made from, so the endorsement of Burnet will now give value to Behn's writing, whatever its quality.

6. *Echo.* When her love for Narcissus was unreciprocated, the nymph Echo withdrew into a wild and rocky place where she faded away until only her voice remained. Behn's image of herself is reminiscent of several heroines in Ovid's *Heroides*; see especially the tenth letter, that of Ariadne to Theseus.

7. *joyful victory.* Moses brought the Children of Israel to the Promised Land but was forbidden to enter himself (Deuteronomy 34:1-5).

8. *'Tis to your pen ... wrought.* A perhaps bitter reference to Burnet's part in the replacement of James II with William III.

9. *So when the wiser Greeks ... conqueror in.* Following the ten years' armed struggle for Troy, the Greeks took the city by the stratagem of the Trojan horse.

10. *Nassau.* William of Orange was also Count of Nassau.

READ MORE IN PENGUIN

READ MORE IN PENGUIN

A CHOICE OF CLASSICS

Netochka Nezvanova Fyodor Dostoyevsky

Dostoyevsky's first book tells the story of 'Nameless Nobody' and introduces many of the themes and issues which dominate his great masterpieces.

Selections from the Carmina Burana
A verse translation by David Parlett

The famous songs from the *Carmina Burana* (made into an oratorio by Carl Orff) tell of lecherous monks and corrupt clerics, drinkers and gamblers, and the fleeting pleasures of youth.

Fear and Trembling Søren Kierkegaard

A profound meditation on the nature of faith and submission to God's will, which examines with startling originality the story of Abraham and Isaac.

Selected Prose Charles Lamb

Lamb's famous essays (under the strange pseudonym of Elia) on anything and everything have long been celebrated for their apparently innocent charm. This major new edition allows readers to discover the darker and more interesting aspects of Lamb.

The Picture of Dorian Gray Oscar Wilde

Wilde's superb and macabre novel, one of his supreme works, is reprinted here with a masterly Introduction and valuable Notes by Peter Ackroyd.

Frankenstein Mary Shelley

In recounting this chilling tragedy Mary Shelley demonstrates both the corruption of an innocent creature by an immoral society and the dangers of playing God with science.

READ MORE IN PENGUIN

A CHOICE OF CLASSICS

The House of Ulloa   Emilia Pardo Bazán

The finest achievement of one of European literature's most dynamic and controversial figures – ardent feminist, traveller, intellectual – and one of the great nineteenth century Spanish novels, *The House of Ulloa* traces the decline of the old aristocracy at the time of the Glorious Revolution of 1868, while exposing the moral vacuum of the new democracy.

The Republic   Plato

The best-known of Plato's dialogues, *The Republic* is also one of the supreme masterpieces of Western philosophy, whose influence cannot be overestimated.

The Duel and Other Stories   Anton Chekhov

In these stories Chekhov deals with a variety of themes – religious fanaticism and sectarianism, megalomania, and scientific controversies of the time, as well as provincial life in all its tedium and philistinism.

Metamorphoses   Ovid

A golden treasury of myths and legends, which has proved a major influence on Western literature.

A Nietzsche Reader   Friedrich Nietzsche

A superb selection from all the major works of one of the greatest thinkers and writers in world literature, translated into clear, modern English.

Madame Bovary   Gustave Flaubert

With *Madame Bovary* Flaubert established the realistic novel in France while his central character of Emma Bovary, the bored wife of a provincial doctor, remains one of the great creations of modern literature.

READ MORE IN PENGUIN

A CHOICE OF CLASSICS

St Anselm	**The Prayers and Meditations**
St Augustine	**The Confessions**
Bede	**Ecclesiastical History of the English People**
Geoffrey Chaucer	**The Canterbury Tales**
	Love Visions
	Troilus and Criseyde
Marie de France	**The Lais of Marie de France**
Jean Froissart	**The Chronicles**
Geoffrey of Monmouth	**The History of the Kings of Britain**
Gerald of Wales	**History and Topography of Ireland**
	The Journey through Wales and **The Description of Wales**
Gregory of Tours	**The History of the Franks**
Robert Henryson	**The Testament of Cresseid and Other Poems**
Walter Hilton	**The Ladder of Perfection**
Julian of Norwich	**Revelations of Divine Love**
Thomas à Kempis	**The Imitation of Christ**
William Langland	**Piers the Ploughman**
Sir John Mandeville	**The Travels of Sir John Mandeville**
Marguerite de Navarre	**The Heptameron**
Christine de Pisan	**The Treasure of the City of Ladies**
Chrétien de Troyes	**Arthurian Romances**
Marco Polo	**The Travels**
Richard Rolle	**The Fire of Love**
François Villon	**Selected Poems**

READ MORE IN PENGUIN

A CHOICE OF CLASSICS

John Aubrey	**Brief Lives**
Francis Bacon	**The Essays**
George Berkeley	**Principles of Human Knowledge** and **Three Dialogues between Hylas and Philonous**
James Boswell	**The Life of Johnson**
Sir Thomas Browne	**The Major Works**
John Bunyan	**The Pilgrim's Progress**
Edmund Burke	**Reflections on the Revolution in France**
Thomas de Quincey	**Confessions of an English Opium Eater**
	Recollections of the Lakes and the Lake Poets
Daniel Defoe	**A Journal of the Plague Year**
	Moll Flanders
	Robinson Crusoe
	Roxana
	A Tour through the Whole Island of Great Britain
Henry Fielding	**Amelia**
	Jonathan Wild
	Joseph Andrews
	Tom Jones
Oliver Goldsmith	**The Vicar of Wakefield**

READ MORE IN PENGUIN

A CHOICE OF CLASSICS